When the

GODDESS
WAKES

ALSO BY HOWARD ANDREW JONES

Upon the Flight of the Queen

For the Killing of Kings

The Bones of the Old Ones

The Waters of Eternity

The Desert of Souls

When the
GODDESS
WAKES

HOWARD ANDREW JONES

ST. MARTIN'S PRESS
NEW YORK

First published in the United States by St. Martin's Press, an imprint of St. Martin's Publishing Group.

WHEN THE GODDESS WAKES. Copyright © 2021 by Howard Andrew Jones. All rights reserved. Printed in the United States of America. For information, address St. Martin's Publishing Group, 120 Broadway, New York, NY 10271.

www.stmartins.com

Map by Darian Vincent Jones

Library of Congress Cataloging-in-Publication Data

Names: Jones, Howard A., author.
Title: When the goddess wakes : the ring-sworn trilogy / Howard Andrew Jones.
Description: First Edition. | New York : St. Martin's Press, 2021. |
Series: The ring-sworn trilogy ; book 3
Identifiers: LCCN 2021006608 | ISBN 9781250148827 (hardcover) |
ISBN 9781250148834 (ebook)
Subjects: GSAFD: Fantasy fiction.
Classification: LCC PS3610.O62535 W48 2021 | DDC 813/.6—dc23
LC record available at https://lccn.loc.gov/2021006608

Our books may be purchased in bulk for promotional, educational, or business use. Please contact your local bookseller or the Macmillan Corporate and Premium Sales Department at 1-800-221-7945, extension 5442, or by email at MacmillanSpecialMarkets@macmillan.com.

First Edition: 2021

10 9 8 7 6 5 4 3 2 1

For Shannon,
who often knows my characters better than I do,
and who loves them at least as well

PLEDGE OF THE ALTENERAI

When comes my numbered day, I will meet it smiling. For I'll have kept this oath.

I shall use my arms to shield the weak.

I shall use my lips to speak the truth, and my eyes to seek it.

I shall use my hand to mete justice to high and to low, and I will weigh all things with heart and mind.

Where I walk the laws will follow, for I am the sword of my people and the shepherd of their lands.

When I fall, I will rise through my brothers and my sisters, for I am eternal.

When the
GODDESS
WAKES

Prologue

A short wall topped with lantern-bearing pylons separated the amphitheater's descending seats from the outer grounds, and he had yet to advance past it, for the uproarious laughter of the crowd repulsed him. He leaned against the wall in the twilight, frowning at the players who walked the garishly lit stage below. It would have been gracious to excuse the people of Kanesh for failing to mark this day with proper reverence—the struggle had occurred a realm away, after all—but he was not in a forgiving mood.

Two years before, hundreds of the best and brightest of all five realms had perished snatching victory from certain annihilation. Under the leadership of Commander Renik, assisted by the tactical brilliance of N'lahr, the sorcerous might of Rialla, and the farseeing eyes of the fierce ko'aye, the Altenerai had driven back an immense Naor army that had marched into the heart of The Fragments. Yet here there were no parades featuring veterans, no banners marking gratitude, and no songs spilling out to the spirits of heroes—just an unrelated farce to divert the masses.

On stage, two men crept with exaggerated care past a sentry walking with a spear. One of the stealthy pair strove to knock the guard unconscious with a blow, missing when the sentry turned, again when he knelt to dust off a shoe, and yet again when he bent unexpectedly to sneeze. With every failure, the audience hooted in delight.

Kalandra had introduced him to this play, one of Selana's comedies. And Kalandra had insisted they attend this performance, but he found no sign of her and wasn't entirely sure he wanted to look. He longed to be away, alone with some wine, somewhere his annoyance was less magnified by the indifference around him.

"'Such a sentinel, favored by fortune, must meet a fairer snare to be undone.'"

The words were those of one of the play's intruders, pulling a wig and dress from his sack, but they were echoed by a woman behind him. He recognized Kalandra's voice, but turned to behold a stranger.

It had been a long while since he'd seen her out of uniform. A winking hairband ornamented her dark curling hair, lustrous and loose. Ordinarily she pinned it tightly back. The lantern, on the pillar behind, set her generously sleeved blouse aglow around her bared neck and shoulders. Flowing pants graced her long legs, and she had donned sandals, ornamented with delicate, sparkling filigree.

"Well, well," he said, then sketched a bow. "And until now I thought the view across the lake the finest to be had here. You've set a new standard."

"Flatterer. Sorry I'm late."

He offered only an empty hand, turned over as if it were a small matter. "No time to change?"

"The patrol ran long," he replied. The silence grew between them as he failed to admit he hadn't wanted to make the effort. She appraised him soberly while the audience clapped for the newly feminized actor sauntering seductively up to the guard, then Kalandra lightly leapt to the wall, patting the stones beside her.

He hesitated before joining her perch.

She leaned forward and spoke earnestly, in time with the distant actor/guard boasting to his "female" interest while the remaining thief slipped through the archway behind. "None dare these hallowed halls while I stand guard! No other eye is half so keen as mine!"

The crowd erupted in laughter.

Kalandra smiled at him, and her delight penetrated his gloom, softening and illuminating its source.

"You were late because you were losing time with hearthstones again." He was so sure of the answer he didn't phrase the words like a question.

She sighed at him. "Is that what you want to talk about? We're here together. Isn't this a better way to remember Rialla than sitting alone in a dark corner with a bottle and a full measure of resentment?"

The crowd was rocked with laughter in their seats.

She always saw to the heart of his thoughts, but he wasn't going to let that deter him this time. "I'm sick of those damned things. They killed Rialla. The queen and Belahn are obsessed with them, and no one can tell where Commander Renik has gone, except that he's hunting hearthstones."

"The commander always makes it back," Kalandra said confidently.

"Until now he has. Are you going to get lost, too?"

She placed a hand over his. "We need to know where they come from. What they are. How best to use them."

He swore. "So, you *are* going to keep at them."

Her voice lowered so that even he had to strain to hear. "My assignment comes straight from the queen. This is important, Kyrkenall."

"Screw the queen."

She flicked him a sly smile. "Is that who you have your eyes on next?"

Kalandra had never let him forget Queen Leonara had overtly flirted with him during a banquet a year ago. The best part had been Denaven's obvious and impotent rage while he watched farther down the table. Until that moment the reference had always amused him.

"The hearthstones may be dangerous," Kalandra conceded. "But they're a significant source of power and the queen isn't foolish to seek them. The Naor have us outnumbered ten to one, and Mazakan's still plotting our end. We need all the help we can get."

"Which is why we need all the Altenerai on the alert, not chasing pretty rocks."

She frowned. "You'd really rather argue politics than enjoy the play?"

"What I want," he said, "is for you to be safe." He realized the absurdity of that sentiment the moment he stated it, and added: "As safe as can be, given our circumstances."

"You're treading awfully close to that line we agreed not to cross, aren't you?"

"No talk of futures. Right. There's a war on, and we're in the vanguard."

"So why agonize over what we can't control? Should I rend my garments every time you scout enemy lands? We're not carefree lovers. We have jobs to do. But right now," she reminded him, "this night, we're together." She squeezed his hand. "Rialla wouldn't want us arguing. We shed enough tears the night she died."

"You're right," Kyrkenall agreed. It was that shared grief that had finally brought the two of them together, a relationship that had surprised him most of all, for he'd been fairly sure as he came up the ranks that Kalandra hated him.

"I'm usually right."

He bowed his head. "Very well. I set my worries aside. Your presence before me commands the whole of my attention. My eyes are for you. As well as my lips, and my fingertips." With slow deliberation, he lifted her hand and gently kissed it.

She repeated the gesture and he felt the light touch of her tongue against his final knuckle before she released it, even as she favored him with a lascivious side glance.

As he moved to meet her lips, the scent of honeyed blossom soaps and the softness of the fabric she wore surrounded his senses. Desire burned bright, like a sun breaking from a summer storm cloud.

She pulled away, laughing silently, and looked into his eyes. Few stared that deeply into those fully dark orbs; he knew they found them unsettling. Her regard always pleased him.

"None can compare," he announced simply.

"Not even the busty girls you were sneaking around with in Darassus in your squire days?" she teased.

As though measurements equated with beauty. He replied with formal, if slightly exaggerated, sincerity. "Milady, I am a connoisseur who has browsed amongst the lesser wines. You are the rarest vintage."

"I'd be more flattered by your analogy," she whispered, "if you weren't a fan of such syrupy sop."

He quoted Senala. "'I seek no solace in your bitterness. I'd find a sweeter wine to while the hours.'"

She laughed aloud—as did the crowd, though they were clearly attending to a different line—and he was delighted by her pleasure.

"Now hop to it, Alten," she said, and took up his hand again as she dropped from the wall. Apparently they were finished with the theater tonight. "There are moments to seize."

"Aye," he said, following. "I treasure every one that we share."

"Sometimes," she told him, "you know just what to say."

"Only sometimes?"

"Yes. Only sometimes. Now come along. It's not proper to keep a lady waiting."

1

The Crown and the Emerald

E lenai pressed her forehead to the window frame. Her fingers absently probed the sore spot on her neck where the stiff collar of her khalat had protected her from a mortal blow. With the city healers laboring long over the gravely wounded, none of their spell energy could be spared for minor injuries, much less bruises.

From her squire's quarters, she studied the jagged hole in the tiles of the stable roof as dusk claimed the sky. She deliberately avoided consideration of the crumbling height of the inner city wall beyond, and the long rows of Naor tents outlined by the fading light. Those who dwelt in the latter had destroyed the former, yet now occupied Darassan land as allies, having sworn their allegiance to her only hours before. Even having been party to the events, she had trouble believing the result wasn't a fever dream. She hadn't the mental energy to contemplate the enormity of changes to her life, and to Darassus, and so she lost herself in consideration of the dark breach. Soon the damage vanished in the deepening gray of the surrounding tiles.

She risked a look elsewhere, where the dim building edges stood out against the lighter atmosphere. A few short hours before, the dead had littered the palace grounds and draped the shattered battlements. The bodies had been carted off; twilight grayed the blood that stained the stones and obscured the trampled gardens.

Vanished, too, were the crowds who had gathered to chant her name, the councilors who hastened to grant her a seat among them, and the angry city representatives who'd cried a council seat was too paltry for the woman who had saved Darassus. The old queen, pledged to guard them, had fled. Elenai had stayed and slain the Naor leader. Who else but she, they had said, should sit the throne?

Elenai protested that she was an alten, not a ruler, an answer that satisfied none of her listeners. They continued to bicker without including her. She'd craved guidance from N'lahr or Kyrkenall, but they'd vanished after the commander had held a sobering post-battle meeting. Rylin had summarized his own terrible ordeals, then disappeared himself, leaving no one to advise her but her close friend Elik. She had finally agreed to think over the crowd's proposal, then Elik hatched their escape by pointing out Elenai needed rest.

That had been true enough. She wished dearly to lie down on her familiar bed, but neither it nor the narrow room around it belonged to her anymore. The squires had insisted her old quarters were beneath her dignity and promised to prepare a new suite. They'd carried away both her dresser drawers and the chest at the foot of the bed that had stored her possessions. She'd lost track of how long the near giddy squires had been absent since they'd begged her to stay "a few moments" in the now barren space, but she felt increasingly foolish for letting them have their way. Kyrkenall would hardly have held off sleep because he didn't want to hurt someone's feelings. She stared at the simple, yet oh-so-tempting bed a mere arm's length away and pictured what the squires might say if they found her sprawled across it.

She shook her head at herself. She was barely managing to make the most simple of decisions as an alten. How could anyone possibly think she could rule as a queen?

The rap at the door startled her and she spun, hand dropping to where her sword hilt should have been. It wasn't. What little remained of her sword had been carried off by squires.

"Elenai? Are you awake?" There was no mistaking her friend Elik's gentle baritone.

"Yes." She understood by his question he wouldn't have been insulted if she'd been sleeping. "Come in."

There was just enough space for the door to miss the footboard as it swung open. Elik halted at the threshold. He'd combed back his short, dark curling hair, and cleaned up the blood and dust and dirt. A dark abrasion stood out near the cleft of his chin. A bandage was visible beneath his right sleeve. He'd donned an older uniform coat because his new one had been cut to shreds in battle. It still bore the stitched linkage of three silver rings arranged in a chevron over two others. She realized that, as an alten, she had the authority, as well as the responsibility, to suggest him for promotion to sixth rank or higher. He'd certainly earned it.

"Your room's ready," he said with a smile. "You're going to love it. Three rooms, complete with a balcony. And it looks on an inner courtyard, so . . ." He waved at the window, indicating the battle-scarred vista. ". . . you don't have to look at that. It's Temahr's old suite," he added.

The dead alten's chambers had remained empty since the last war. Her new rooms would be in close proximity to those of N'lahr and Kyrkenall.

"You've earned this, Elenai," Elik declared with quiet conviction, as if guessing her hesitancy. His earnest declaration bore no hint of jealously. Elenai and Elik had advanced in lockstep until circumstances swept her into a promotion from fifth rank to Altenerai, an accomplishment achieved only by Alten Enada in the last fifty years.

The drum of galloping hoofbeats interrupted the twilit still, drawing their eyes to the window.

Lamplight from the sconces affixed to either side of the steps below bronzed Kyrkenall's black hair as he savagely reined in before the entrance to the Altenerai wing of the palace. It was strange to see him on a brown mare rather than his ever-faithful Lyria; the unflaggable dun had been left behind in Cerai's little realm in the shifts. Was that just earlier this afternoon?

The archer snatched his black bow from its holster, then flung himself from the wheezing mount and sprinted up the stairs.

Elenai couldn't guess which of a host of calamities would set the archer moving at such speed, but was already tense with alarm. "I think we're about to have another problem," she said.

She and Elik hurried to the main stair and started down the black granite steps. Below, Kyrkenall shouted for Thelar.

As she reached the central floor, a weary-looking third ranker stood up from the duty desk. Elenai sent him to look after Kyrkenall's horse, then followed the archer as he advanced into the central hall, still shouting for the exalt.

"Kyrkenall!" she called. "What's happened?"

The archer spun to face her and stilled, as if he needed a moment to register her or change his line of thought. Then his pupil-less black eyes fixed her with savage intensity. "I need Thelar," he said. "He may have Kalandra's gem."

Her fatigue-fogged thoughts revolved in a slow circle before she understood. Rialla had told her they might find the alten's long-lost love associated with a stone. "How do you know?" she asked.

"Rylin found her ring next to a gem on a shelf," he answered impatiently. "Do you know where Thelar is?"

Elik, at her shoulder, answered. "Exalt Thelar's in the queen's office."

Kyrkenall rushed off. Though her stride was longer than his, Elenai was hard-pressed to catch him. Elik practically ran to keep at her side. He asked softly, "What's this about?"

She couldn't answer immediately. How to explain that Kyrkenall had been absent from Darassus for seven years because he'd been obsessively searching for the missing alten Kalandra? And that they'd been told Kalandra was "in the stone on the shelf" through confusing visions from the long-dead alten Rialla? "He thinks he's found something about Alten Kalandra," she said finally. "And we know that memories can be stored in special gemstones, because we've talked with some of them."

Elik looked puzzled but held off from more detailed questions as they trailed Kyrkenall.

They advanced past the doors that led to meeting rooms and offices and on into the great hall, turning out of the Altenerai wing just past the Hall of Heroes. All but the most broken of weapons and most badly damaged armor were absent from the walls, leaving the space more blank and lonely than Elenai had ever seen it. Every one of the serviceable items had been deployed in defense of the city and none had yet been cleaned and restored to display. She hoped the treasured heirlooms had survived.

From there they turned into the central palace, and before long Kyrkenall had arrived at the entrance to the queen's private office. He threw open the door without knocking, startling one of the redheaded twin exalts—M'vai, Elenai saw, from the mole above her lip. Like Elenai, the exalt had divested herself of her khalat; she'd clothed her slim body in a white blouse and dark pants, and donned light slippers. Beside her, Thelar still wore the red-piped uniform coat of the Mage Auxiliary that had for so long siphoned resources and manpower from the Altenerai Corps. He stood entranced by a fist-sized blue stone he held in one hand and showed no reaction to their entrance.

Glass-fronted bookcases filled two of the office walls. A wide, elegant desk backed by a red-cushioned chair stood at one end of the room, fronted by twin chairs. Four more sat at a round conference table. A second doorway opened onto another room in which M'vai's twin sister, Meria, knelt on the floor beside some squires and office staff, sorting papers into piles.

In Elenai's experience, Kyrkenall was often cordial in his introductions, especially when dealing with pretty women. Tonight, though, he was gruff with M'vai. "Which gem was next to the ring?"

"The ring?" M'vai repeated in puzzlement.

"The ring." Kyrkenall raised his own alten's ring of office for extra emphasis. "Kalandra's ring."

M'vai looked blankly back.

Thelar blinked and Elenai sensed him letting go of the inner world. Dark-eyed, hook-nosed, striking in a severe way, Thelar retained an air of composure and dignity even in his obvious confusion. They had risked their lives together and overcome incredible hazards by relying upon one another, which had engendered a fondness for him no matter the brief nature of their relationship.

"Is something wrong?" Thelar asked.

"Which gemstone was next to Kalandra's ring?" Kyrkenall demanded.

"We didn't see any rings," Thelar answered. "I'm holding one of the queen's gemstones. The others are right there." He pointed to a shelf within the bookcase, and Kyrkenall stepped around him.

Elenai saw a diamond and an emerald over the archer's shoulder. His dark eyes swung back accusingly, and he pointed at the stone Thelar cupped in his left hand. "Was there anything interesting about that one?"

"It contains memories left by Kantahl." Thelar sounded as if he didn't expect to be believed.

Kyrkenall looked unimpressed, no matter that the exalt had just revealed he'd been looking upon the thoughts of a god.

"Maybe you should slow down, Kyrkenall," Elenai suggested. "We're all exhausted here."

He looked at Thelar again. "Rylin said there was a stone next to an alten's ring."

The exalt paused for a moment to reflect. "Rylin took all the rings he could find," he said. "To fight the queen. I suppose there could have been a ring next to one of these stones."

Kyrkenall frowned and he paced a couple of turns before grabbing the emerald and lifting it. "This one. Kalandra used an emerald to record her thoughts back in the shifts. Remember?" He looked to Elenai.

She nodded.

He held it out to her. "Open it."

But she didn't take it. Tired as she was, she didn't dare attempt anything magical. "I'm spent, Kyrkenall."

The archer's attention shifted to Thelar. Kyrkenall thrust the gem toward him, but the exalt made no move to accept it.

"That one has wards on it, Alten," he explained.

"Wards?"

"It's going to be tricky to open," M'vai explained. "I can see the threads that close it off, like knots. And we're a little tired tonight, as Elenai said. We shouldn't take any chances until we're better rested."

Kyrkenall's expression clouded. Elenai recognized something she'd rarely seen from him: he was actually fighting to master his anger.

"Why are you so interested in it?" Thelar asked.

"There's a chance Kalandra's trapped inside."

Thelar's thick eyebrows rose; he exhaled sharply and pushed back dark hair, already mussed. "You mean a memory she left?"

"I mean *her*." Kyrkenall seemed to understand further explanation was necessary, adding: "That's what we've been told." His tone sharpened, "But I won't know until someone opens it."

Thelar's gaze shifted to the gem, the other seeming forgotten in his grasp.

Kyrkenall spoke with biting rancor: "There's no rush. It's not like she's been missing for seven years, or might have insight into the hearthstones and the queen."

Elenai winced at his sarcasm in front of their newly acquired allies. "Never rush a mage, Kyrkenall. Thelar and M'vai are just as tired as I am."

His gaze, and his ire, shifted to her. Out of long practice, she ignored it and interrupted before he could start something more unpleasant. "Mistakes happen when mages are tired," she said. "And magical mistakes are dangerous. It will be safer for all of us—and Kalandra, if she's really in there—if we wait until tomorrow."

Kyrkenall's lips twitched; he said nothing, but his hand clenched around the gem so tightly the dusky skin of his knuckles whitened.

"I'll take a look," Thelar said.

"Are you sure that's wise?" Elenai asked.

"I'll just make a quick try of it." Thelar extended his hand

Kyrkenall transferred the emerald into the exalt's outstretched fingers with an impatient delicacy. Thelar passed the blue stone to M'vai.

Candlelight flared in the emerald's facets as Thelar turned it.

"Where did you hear about Kalandra being in the stone?" Elik spoke at her shoulder. Though his voice was soft, the question might as well have been shouted, so quiet were those in the office.

"From Rialla," Elenai said. "I know it sounds impossible, but she's been conveying key information to me for weeks."

Elik made an astute guess. "Through a hearthstone?"

"I think so."

Thelar looked up from his examination. "Alten Rialla, who's been dead for a decade?"

"Yes." Kyrkenall answered with barely contained exasperation. "We've both seen her, and she's the one who got us back to Darassus in time for the battle. She also gave advice that saved my life. And no, I don't know how she's doing it, but she's been right every time." He paused before barreling on. "She said Kalandra was in a stone on a shelf. And here are these gems, on the shelf, and one was next to an Altenerai ring."

Thelar checked with Elenai, as if attempting to gauge the truth of these outrageous claims. She offered an affirming nod.

"I shouldn't be surprised, I suppose," Thelar said. The lines in his face were deep with fatigue. "Though I've been in this room, and I don't ever remember seeing a ring."

"This isn't a risk you need to take now," Elenai cautioned. She looked over to Kyrkenall as she was speaking. "No matter how much pressure you feel."

"I'll use a hearthstone shard to bolster my energies," he assured her. "And I'll just look lightly."

Elenai knew he studied the stone through the inner world. She felt a wave of energy the moment he activated his shard. She'd grown as sensitive to hearthstones as she was to the change in atmosphere before an oncoming storm. Instantly she knew the shard rested in a leather pouch on the table near the bookcases.

Thelar's face was lit eerily from below as the emerald brightened from within. Elik tensed beside her, and Kyrkenall's lips opened in anticipation.

A slash of green lightning burst from the gem. Thelar fell backward, his limbs rigid. The glowing emerald popped from his hand, bounced off a table leg, and tumbled into a corner.

Kyrkenall scrambled after it. Elenai and M'vai crouched by Thelar, who writhed on the floor, his eyes rolled back into his head. Only the whites showed.

"Thelar!" M'vai seized his shoulders. The exalt continued to shake.

Elenai opened her sight to the inner world and threw threads toward Thelar's shard, trying not to be excited to access its power. The artifact's sharp kick of energy was entirely different from the spikelike whip of power that held Thelar's aura to the outer facets of the emerald. "Get that damned thing as far away from him as you can," Elenai ordered M'vai. "Don't touch it magically!"

M'vai's reluctance to leave her friend was evident on her face, but she snatched the emerald from Kyrkenall and hurried into the hall.

Elenai had once assisted her aunts untangling trailing ends of yarn that had come off their spindles, and this process was somewhat similar, except that each contact with the glowing green spellthreads delivered another charge. She gritted her teeth and ignored the stinging pain. Each time she managed to get a line free of Thelar the intrusive thread snapped back into the retreating gem. His single touch had completely ensnared him.

At first the emerald's distance seemed to make no difference, but as M'vai drew farther and farther off the threads grew less substantial and Elenai found each stung a little less as she touched it. More importantly, Thelar's convulsions lessened.

She grew conscious that someone else had entered the room but she dared not divert her attention to learn their identity. She winced at another jolt, and continued work.

Finally, as she undid a particularly troublesome knot, the attack against Thelar subsided. He stopped shaking, and breathed normally, if rapidly. She turned to where Elik had been and found him vanished, along with Kyrkenall. N'lahr and Rylin stood in their place. The commander's gaunt features were strained and tired, and a day's growth of dark stubble stood out on his long, sharp-planed face. Dark circles showed beneath his deep-set eyes. Rylin looked more like his usual handsome self, now that he'd shaved, although there was a serious look in his eyes where there used to be a merry spark. Elenai wondered if that was a permanent change, and whether her own manner communicated the same sober sense of loss.

"Rylin," she said, "Find M'vai. Ask her if the gem's energy's off yet."

Rylin hurried after the exalt. N'lahr bent beside Thelar.

He blinked up at them.

"How do you feel?" Elenai asked.

"Better." Thelar's voice was weak. "I'm not sure how much more of that I could have taken." She put fingers to his neck, staying him with a hand as he made to rise. His heart sped as though he'd been running laps.

"What do you think?" he asked.

She smiled. "I think you'll live."

His dark eyes met her own, and he spoke with soft sincerity. "Thank you."

"We've gotten into the habit of helping each other." She offered him a hand and he sat up. Elenai studied him for a moment more, making sure he was steady.

"Is everything under control here?" N'lahr asked.

"I think so," Elenai replied. "Where did Elik go?"

"I had a job for him."

"Tell me that the emerald's open, at least," Thelar said.

Elenai shook her head. "Not that I could tell." With her aid, Thelar climbed dizzily to his feet and promptly sank into the nearest chair.

N'lahr stood. "How is he?"

"I don't think there's permanent damage." With an inward sigh, Elenai released her magical hold of the hearthstone shard.

"Were you trying to access a memory stone?" N'lahr asked.

"There's no way to know what the emerald is," Thelar answered. "We couldn't get it open."

"I had to send it out of the room," Elenai explained. "To lessen the effect of its protective ward."

Kyrkenall returned, a few steps in front of Rylin and M'vai, who started to come to attention at sight of the commander.

"Belay that," N'lahr said.

"What's happened?" Elenai asked M'vai.

"The stone's stopped glowing." M'vai couldn't seem to decide if she should speak to Elenai or N'lahr, and kept looking from one to the other. "But I don't think it's drained. I think it would react the same way if we poked at it again."

"Where is it?" Elenai asked.

"I've got it." Kyrkenall spoke as Rylin pointed at him.

"You brought it back here? Near Thelar?" Elenai asked in disbelief.

"I couldn't very well just leave it in the hallway. How's Thelar doing?"

"I *think* he'll be fine," Elenai said.

Kyrkenall spoke softly to Thelar. "Sorry about that."

"You couldn't have known what would happen," the exalt replied weakly.

"Do you think you'll be able to get it open later?" Kyrkenall asked.

"No," N'lahr said firmly. "We're not going to risk opening it again until it's studied carefully."

"Well, yes, of course," Kyrkenall said.

N'lahr looked away from him and off to the open doorway, where Meria watched in pained interest. Elenai wondered how long she'd been standing there.

"Exalts," N'lahr said, "have you learned where the queen went?"

"No," Thelar answered.

"We're still sorting the queen's papers, sir," Meria said from the doorway. "There are some interesting things here, but there's no large scale transport spell. We don't know how she vanished herself, dozens of others, and a huge statue from the arena, much less where they went."

"Show me what you've found," N'lahr said. Meria stepped out of the doorway so he could stride through. Elenai, Rylin, and M'vai followed. Kyrkenall crouched down beside Thelar.

All the furniture in the large sitting room beyond had been pushed to the edges, leaving space for papers to be arranged across the surface of the parquet floor. They'd been sorted into a variety of stacks, each one beside a paper upon which someone had scrawled a label in large, square handwriting. The first Elenai saw read: "speech." Another said: "prayers."

Meria walked past these piles, her booted stride quick and crisp, and turned up the nearest wall lantern so that its glow blazed bright. "The queen was making notes about the realms and the relative strengths of their borders and magical resonances and other things I don't really follow."

N'lahr paced with her past five more piles, stopping beside one where a sketch of what looked like a mountain range lay. "What's this?"

Meria looked back from where she was adjusting the nearest lantern. "Things we can't identify. A lot of them are maps, but most are fanciful."

"What do you mean?" N'lahr asked.

"They're full of features that don't tend to occur together. Like lakes atop mountains." She pointed to one he was holding. "Waterfalls amid sand dunes. Or huge crystal formations in forested areas. Some of them look like the queen's sketched the same place, but . . . they're like something a child would design, just a lot more complicated and skillfully drawn."

N'lahr took a knee and searched through the papers.

As the commander shuffled through them, Elenai caught glimpses of the artwork. Some parchments held a few lines of writing or a handful of images, often scribbled over, and others were decorated with full-page sketches. Some depicted plants she'd never seen, but most were weird landscapes. None of the pictures struck a familiar chord.

N'lahr stopped at last at a detailed rendering that ran to the edges of the paper. He'd picked a topological, colored map of a land ringed by hills on nearly every side. Orchards and streams ran abundantly through it in symmetrical patterns, and it was favored by small lakes in each quadrant, as well as low tree-topped hills. The rendering was more crude than many of the others.

"It's larger than a Fragment," N'lahr murmured.

Rylin had drawn up beside the commander and looked over his

shoulder. "It's hard to tell the scale," he said. "But if those are individual hills, this looks roughly the size of Ekhem."

"It was near the bottom of the stack of papers on the queen's desk," Meria said. "I think that means she drew it when she was at her most frantic."

"Frantic?" Elenai asked.

"I guess that's the best way to describe it," Meria answered thoughtfully. "A few weeks back she started working day and night."

"It was right after the keystone disappeared," M'vai added. "She was trying to remember what she'd seen on it, and used spells to aid her recollection."

"Then she was trying to remember a place that doesn't exist," Rylin said. "There's no land like this, anywhere. Some of the Naor realms are just as large, but none have so many rivers, or any gardens."

"This is where she's taken the hearthstones," N'lahr said, and rose.

Kyrkenall, now in the doorway, scoffed. "What makes you say that?"

"This is Paradise, Kyrkenall. The first realm. That's what the queen has sketched here. Flowing rivers. Vast orchards. Abundant fields. Lakes. 'A land of plenty, where soft rains fall and trees are ever heavy with the sweetest fruit.'"

Elenai had never heard the commander quote anything before, much less a sacred text.

Kyrkenall swore in astonishment, which sounded even more coarse than usual, following scripture as it did. "Figures I never found it."

As Kyrkenall walked into the room, N'lahr passed the paper to him, then turned to Rylin. "Varama discussed the keystone in passing. Did you look into it?"

"No, sir."

"Doesn't she have it?" Meria asked. "You two took it. I don't mean to be accusatory, but—"

"We took it," Rylin said. "But Cerai stole it. That stone was more important to her than Alantris. What did the queen want with it?"

"We don't really know," Meria said. Elenai was learning she was the more talkative of the two sisters. Meria continued: "She was furious when it disappeared. She said she had to have it to fulfill the vision of the Goddess."

"I believe that it had a record of the realms, in their perfect, original state," Thelar suggested from behind.

Elenai turned to find him leaning heavily against the doorframe.

"Do you know anything about this map, or where the realm lies in relation to the others?" N'lahr asked.

"I'm sorry, Commander. No."

"We must talk with Varama, then," N'lahr said. "As soon as possible. The queen will want to finish her work undisturbed, where no one can reach her. This is the place."

"And you think Varama will know where that is?" Kyrkenall asked.

"You've known her longer than I have," Rylin said. "You know if she saw it in the keystone, she can remember it."

"Sure," Kyrkenall said, "but will she know where this lost land is in relation to anything else? I've been nearly everywhere in the realms and have never caught wind of it. Maybe we should talk to Cerai. She actually has the keystone."

"You think Cerai's going to help us?" The challenge in Rylin's voice startled Elenai. "She's a traitor," he continued. "She abandoned Alantris to the Naor. She's a murderer a thousand times over."

"That's a bit dramatic, isn't it?" Kyrkenall asked, which under any other circumstance would have struck Elenai as ironically amusing. If there was one alten known for drama, it was he.

"Dramatic?" Rylin repeated.

"Enough." N'lahr's soft command finished the debate. "Unless there's been some development I haven't heard, we don't have a way to contact Cerai."

No one answered.

"Kyrkenall?" N'lahr prompted.

"No. I don't know a way."

Thelar volunteered, "We could attempt a hearthstone sending. I'm certain Cerai has some."

Elenai had grown familiar with the concept of a sending, but didn't know how easily it could be done.

"She's a long way into the shifts," M'vai objected. "That would be courting disaster."

N'lahr looked to Thelar for confirmation.

"She's right," he said. "The farther apart the sender and receiver are, the greater the danger something will break the sender's spirit from his body. Or consume it. Hearthstone-enhanced sending is more powerful, and protective of the sender, but would Alten Cerai welcome the connection, or use it to attack?"

N'lahr decided. "We'll consult with Varama first. If she has the answers, we won't risk contacting Cerai."

The last Elenai had heard, the greatest intellect of the Altenerai remained days from Darassus, riding back from Alantris.

"It'll be a long time before we can talk to Varama," Kyrkenall said. "Even if we rode out to meet her."

"Varama retains a hearthstone and she's much closer than Cerai," N'lahr said. "Thelar can attempt a sending to her." His gaze turned to the exalt. "But in the morning. Rest is needed now."

"I should help," Rylin asserted. "Varama doesn't know what's happened here, or that Thelar's allied with us. If he reaches out to her she may think it's an attack."

"Very well," N'lahr said. "Rylin, Thelar, that's your first priority come the dawn. Now everyone get out of here and find your beds. We've much to do tomorrow. Elenai, let's talk in the office."

As Elenai nodded, the commander added: "Rylin, take Thelar up to the healers and have them look him over before he turns in."

After the others blew out the lanterns in the sitting room and departed, Kyrkenall lingered by the door, Kalandra's emerald in his hand. "What do you think we should do with this, for now?" he asked.

"That's Kalandra's stone?" N'lahr asked.

"Yes."

"Keep it someplace safe."

"I don't like to keep my lady waiting," Kyrkenall said, as though to himself, then spoke to them once more: "You need anything?" He hesitated with his hand on the door latch.

"Tomorrow, yes," N'lahr answered. "Kyrkenall . . . I know Cerai sponsored you to the ring. But she's not one of us anymore."

"The hearthstones twisted her," Elenai said.

"Probably," Kyrkenall agreed. "But I think she still holds to the oath, as she sees it. Belahn was altered, but we tried to save him, didn't we?"

"Belahn's actions hadn't killed thousands," Elenai interjected.

"They might have killed hundreds," Kyrkenall countered. "He trapped everyone in his village in an unbreakable magic suspension, remember?"

"Their motives are entirely different," Elenai said. "Belahn was trying to protect people he loved. If you're going to compare Cerai to anyone, it should be the queen. Or Denaven. Their level of conceit is about the same."

"Rialla showed Cerai how to use the transport magics that sent us here," Kyrkenall said. "Why would she do that unless she knew Cerai was going to help us at some point?"

Elenai hadn't thought of that. "Rialla did show Cerai how to open a portal," she admitted. "But she sure didn't look happy about it. I bet she knows Cerai's untrustworthy."

"But she's still a possible ally," Kyrkenall said. "And we might need every one of them we can get."

N'lahr spoke at last. "The point's moot, Kyrkenall. Cerai is out of play for now."

Kyrkenall nodded. "I'll see you two in the morning." He left, closing the door after. They heard his footsteps recede.

N'lahr sat down on the edge of the desk and massaged his forehead.

"Why is he so attached to Cerai?" Elenai asked. "Is it because she's beautiful?"

"I think it's because *he's* beautiful."

At her confused look, he continued. "She was the only upper ranker who consistently favored him, even before he'd begun to distinguish himself. Her attention seemed more focused on his superficial attributes than his potential, at least initially, but his admiration of her daring, her lone treks into the wilds, probably furthered her interest. There's no other alten she ever stood for the ring. Kyrkenall has had few enough supporters. He values them the more."

Kyrkenall had told her that Cerai had sponsored him, but until now she hadn't understood the context. Before Elenai could follow up with more questions, the commander changed the subject. "I want to talk to you about the throne."

"You mean this notion of me being queen?"

"It's more than a notion. You have an instinct for finding your way to the right course."

She laughed. "I'm not sure that's true. And in any case, my instinct is to run as far as I can from talk of crowns."

"That's wisdom. But then didn't some playwright say to never trust a woman who longs for the throne?"

"Several playwrights say something like that," Elenai said, and as she searched her memory to quote one, N'lahr held up a hand.

"If I'd wanted a recitation I'd have asked Kyrkenall to stay. The people trust your judgment. So do I."

Elenai swallowed hard, hoping her cheeks weren't reddening. "I'm honored you would say that. But you know as well as I do that a lot of my 'decisions' might have been Rialla's more than mine."

Apparently he didn't know, because he frowned thoughtfully. "What do you mean?"

"My glimpses of the future didn't happen until after I started using Rialla's hearthstone. I don't think I'm as much of an oddsbreaker as you believe I am." It pained her to admit she didn't live up to his appraisal, but better he knew now than think her more capable than she was.

"Hearthstones awaken and enhance magical gifts."

It seemed as though he was being unduly thick. But then, she supposed, he was at least as weary as she was. She tried again. "When Kyrkenall and I met Rialla, at Cerai's fortress, Rialla made clear she was manipulating events to get the outcome she most desired. I think all along she's been pushing me to deliver what she needed at key moments."

His tired eyes were bright with amusement. "I see. Did she tell you how to open my hearthstone prison?"

"I think she might have," she admitted. "I felt called to do so. And I glimpsed possible outcomes when Denaven and the Altenerai closed on us that time we were riding through The Fragments."

"Did she tell you how to guide us through the shifts?"

"No."

"Did she tell you how to marshal the eshlack?" N'lahr asked. "Did she hold up your sword during the battle with Mazakan's honor guard? Did she negotiate with the ko'aye?"

"No . . ." Elenai had picked up on his intent to disprove her fears but didn't object as he continued.

"Did she master a dragon and fly it through the air?"

"Now there I think she may have helped. I saw how to free the dragon from its encasement far more easily than I had any right. But I seemed to have a natural knack for making the dragon move," she admitted.

"You're right to give credit where it's due. But you don't give yourself the credit you're owed. It wasn't Rialla who defeated Denaven, and it wasn't Rialla who outfought Chargan and then swayed the Naor to our side."

"I understand what you're saying, but—"

"Do you?" His voice had taken an edge. "Because it sounds like you're suggesting you're not qualified to be a queen or an alten."

"I'm definitely not qualified to be a queen." Elenai hesitated before explaining further. "And I worry Rialla's hearthstone made you think me worthy of being an alten."

"You don't need a hearthstone to be an alten. Your use of one was always temporary. It had to be. You've seen what they do to those who depend on them."

"I keep telling myself I'm lucky mine is gone. But I think that severs me from the powers that made me . . . great."

"Your actions saved the city when those powers were gone, not before," N'lahr said. "You earned the fealty of your foes and the gratitude of your people."

"What is it you want of me?" she asked.

He placed a hand to the smooth wood of the desk and felt it for a time. When he spoke, his usual cool reserve cracked wide open. "Oh, Elenai. I want you content and fulfilled. Finding happiness. You've earned it. But I don't always get what I wish."

"You think I should take the throne?"

"You will serve your people in whatever you decide. But you must be at peace with whatever is lost on the path not taken."

Not so long ago, he'd spent a long morning coaxing the governor of Arappa into consideration of the throne. Surely he hadn't forgotten that. "I thought you were pointing Verena to the crown."

"She would make a fair queen, but she's not here. And you'll recall I needed her resources at the time. With some, you have to remind them of their desires before they do the right thing. I don't think I ever need to remind you."

She had come to understand, finally, why Kyrkenall both loved and cursed him. "Damnit, N'lahr, you've steered me here."

"No. I could not have predicted the events that would lead the people of Darassus to shout your name. But I saw what had to happen the moment you won the allegiance of the Naor. You want my opinion? You *must* take the throne, at least until the crisis is passed, and you surely know why."

She let out a slow breath and reasoned it out in the seconds before her answer. "Because we can't be slowed down by the council. They won't know how to deal with the Naor. Or the queen's betrayal. Even if they arrive at the right solutions, they won't know how to manage things quickly enough."

He nodded. "Yes. We can't afford delay, or lengthy debate."

Another course occurred to her. "You could be king. You're the wisest man I know and a miraculous savior back from the dead."

A thin smile ghosted over his features. "Darassus has had no king in generations. And they will not have one now. The people have already chosen you."

She sighed. "Assuming we survive, I guess I can always step aside later."

"Given that the world we know will cease unless we stop Leonara, we needn't worry much past the immediate future."

"I seem to recall that one of the queen's worst crimes was taking action without consulting the council. You're suggesting we fix her mistakes by doing the same."

"Tyrants can rise when shortcuts are taken, but you will not be a tyrant, and under your stewardship a better government can rise. New safeguards must be enacted to ensure that the queen's power will be checked should another madwoman ascend the throne. But for now . . ."

"For now I have to be queen," she finished slowly.

"Yes."

2

The Missing Mage

As Vannek advanced into the wide central lane that bifurcated the Naor camp, distant sounds of singing drifted out from their hosts' damaged city, a quarter mile to his rear. There was sorrow and loss in the melody, and the threnody put him in mind of the man he might have loved.

Vannek scowled at himself, for such sentimental drivel led to despair, which had utterly neutered him in the preceding days.

Two nights ago he'd seen his brother was mad, and hadn't moved against him. The shame of his failure in Alantris and pain at the death of Syrik had so devastated him that he found life too much trouble to engage with. He'd allowed himself to be carried along on currents of others' design. Only as he plummeted from the sky with a dragon who died beneath him had he realized how fiercely he still wished to live. In the hours since, he'd sworn he would never again permit himself to descend into fatalism.

Now, alerted by a messenger, he walked toward the first test of his new resolve. Challenges to his authority always differed in the particulars but were broadly, monotonously similar. To beat back a fleeting desire for return to a state beyond care, he reimagined his father's admonition against weakness: *find your steel*.

His brother's few surviving officers sat in a circle on low stools in front of a tent so stiff and clean and white it must have been unused before today. As Vannek diverted to approach from the left, two looked up, eyes shifting to the lone bodyguard accompanying him, the only one of Chargan's personal guard left alive and unmaimed. Zinar, the youngest of the three officers, climbed respectfully to his feet, the left side of his bearded face purple and swollen. A moment later, the graybeard next to him rose with an awkward head bob.

Vannek came to a halt behind the only chieftain in the group. Anzat had to turn on his stool to face him, then apparently decided to stand. He threw back his shoulders and looked down on Vannek from a towering six and a half feet. A massive man in the prime of life, he offered no welcome.

Vannek wasted no time with greetings as he addressed them bluntly. "A war council should always include the leader."

"Chargan is dead," Anzat growled. "And great Mazakan is dead. We need a new leader."

This again. He meant himself, of course. "We already have a leader," Vannek said.

A smooth voice cut in from their left, "We certainly do, Lord General Vannek." A man of middle years garbed in simple traveling clothes had stopped just beyond their little circle. Vannek shifted his footing so he might observe the interloper without losing sight of Anzat.

It took a moment for Vannek to recognize one of his grandfather's advisors, Muragan, without the man's vibrant red robes of office. At first glance he was utterly unremarkable; a man of middle age with a receding hairline, of average height, and average breadth, though he had grown stout. Like many well-to-do older Naor, his beard was neatly trimmed, reddish brown like his hair. Ordinary, except that his blue eyes were bright with intelligence, and he carried himself in the presence of high-ranked officers with profound self-assurance no normal man would have dared.

All of Mazakan's advisors were said to have perished with him. Yet here was one of his most valuable mages, strolling into their closely guarded encampment many days journey from where he should have fallen in company with the god-king.

"Another mage." Anzat's voice was heavy with disgust. Apparently the chief recognized Muragan but lacked any curiosity at his unexpected appearance.

"I served as Mazakan willed." The man's voice was not especially loud, but it possessed a vibrant, compelling quality. "And now you will serve the third and wisest son of Mazakan's favored heir."

"Who are you to say whom I serve?" Anzat said with a growl. "Where were you in the battle for Darassus, when it mattered? Why should we heed you now?"

Muragan's left hand rose, fingers splayed. On the instant, Anzat sucked in a sharp breath. His face reddened and thin lines of blood trickled from his nostrils. The towering officer put a hand to his hilt and managed two steps forward before sinking to one knee and pulling at his collar with both hands. The other leaders watched with poorly masked horror.

Vannek had anticipated killing Anzat to prove his rule by arms, but this . . . Well, trust a mage to misunderstand the wielding of power. He snapped a command. "Stop the spell."

Anzat dropped to his belly, his fingers scrabbling in the grass as though a close grip of the slender green blades would help him cling to life. Muragan's eyes narrowed in concentration.

"Stop it!" Vannek roared.

Muragan dropped his arm with reluctance. Blood dripped from his clenched fist. He must have deliberately cut it to use its energy in his spell. On the ground Anzat shuddered convulsively and fumbled at his belt, dragging his knife free.

Vannek kicked the hand that held the weapon, which went sliding under the folds of a nearby tent.

"Fool!" Vannek glared at Anzat, then the other officers, then turned to take in a ring of Naor warriors who'd gathered to watch. Many wore bandages and bore obvious injuries. "I'm surrounded by fools," he growled to them. "There are so few of us left, but still you'd cull our numbers in petty dispute. This is why the Dendressi best us! They stand together instead of snarling over scraps."

Anzat glowered as he struggled to his knees, wiping red spittle from his lips.

Vannek continued: "Only an idiot would let blood when he's already weak. It's a time to bind our wounds and hone our blades." He turned to Anzat: "I give you your life this night."

The chieftain's newly harshened voice could barely be heard over the murmur from those surrounding. "I want no favors from a woman."

Vannek's face flushed, but he kept his voice level as he moved within whispering distance. "I don't need gratitude. I need officers. Find your sense, and then we can talk." Seeing Anzat's burning gaze fix upon the mage, he added: "He is not for you to deal with."

Vannek addressed the group at large. "I expect your evening reports in my tent the next hour. This talk of succession is concluded." He turned sharply, offering his back to Anzat, both as insult, and to demonstrate his fearlessness to the onlookers, who parted before him. Vannek heard his bodyguard fall in behind, and from a second set of footfalls knew Muragan came after.

He didn't acknowledge the mage's presence, in part because he wanted to demonstrate his confidence, and in part because he was uncertain what Muragan was after. Vannek held little actual power, and his grasp upon it was tenuous. Surely the mage understood that. So, how could his grandfather's advisor stand to benefit from backing him here?

Once returned to the tent that had belonged to his brother Chargan, Vannek found his men-at-arms setting out the evening meal. As the two bowed near the fold-away camp table, Vannek idly wondered what had happened to the Dendressi woman his brother had slept with, the one who'd laid food for him on this very table two days previous, before the battle that killed her captor.

"Food's been readied for you from the remaining stores, Lord General," the shorter of the servants said. "But your cook's dead, so we had to make do, sir," he finished quickly.

"I need no fineries." As Vannek sat on one of Chargan's stools he realized it was cushioned, making mockery of his declaration. He decided to divest himself of the soft furniture later, rather than call further attention to the incongruity. The tall bodyguard, stationed now to one side of the tent opening, eyed the mage with suspicion as Muragan entered and bowed.

Vannek raised a staying hand to the bodyguard, then motioned Muragan forward. The men-at-arms deposited a final platter of salted meat along with some soft cheese and dried fruits upon the table, then poured wine into a goblet.

"What's this?" Vannek demanded. "Don't we have any ale?"

The men-at-arms exchanged a look. "Your pardon, Lord General," the elder of them said. "We assumed you'd want Chargan's—"

"Just ale tonight."

"Yes, Lord General. Forgive me." One set the bottle and goblet aside while the other fumbled in the little cabinet and pulled out a rams-head stoppered jug decorated with silver filigree. From it he poured liquid into a bowl, which he then set beside the meat. Clearly his brother's containers would have to be replaced along with the furnishings. He waved the servants away. They bowed themselves out.

Vannek hadn't noticed how hungry he was until the scent of the cheeses struck him. He'd thought he was only tired, and pained, both from the injury to his ear and the bumping he'd taken from the dragon's bad landing. He understood now he was ravenous.

He didn't let this weakness show. Instead, he unsheathed his knife and turned it. He wondered how long the mage would keep silent. Not much longer, as it turned out.

"This isn't what I expected to find," Muragan said.

"Oh?" Vannek said casually. "What did you expect?"

"Chargan promised the end to Darassan power. But I hear every man in the army has pledged themselves to a Dendressi doxy instead."

How tiresome. "That 'doxy' bested Chargan and both his wizards in single combat, then sucked down his magic and swept us from the walls. This earns Elenai Halfsword an insulting name?"

He grunted noncommittally. "You sound as though you admire her."

"I thought I made clear I'm done with idiots, Muragan." The mage nodded as if with approval, which soured Vannek's mood further. "Have I passed some test of yours?"

The mage stepped to within four paces and dropped his voice. "What do you plan?"

Vannek set the blade down beside the food and answered in a level, careless voice. "Why should I tell you?"

"I was one of your grandfather's chief advisors."

"And what are you now? Why are you here?"

"When Mazakan fell, I rode as swiftly as I could to join Chargan. I mean to serve Mazakan's successor."

Vannek waited and ignored his grumbling stomach. "Chargan told me some of our kings survived the battle. Why didn't you ride off with them?"

"They've no doubt returned to their own lands to wrestle for power. It's as you said just now. Our alliance will crumble without Mazakan to hold it together. Unless . . ." He let his voice trail off and stared pointedly at Vannek.

"I've no interest in marching into each of our realms to beat the tribes into submission. You can tell the kings that."

"I don't serve the kings."

"Oh?" A spy for any one of them would certainly say the same thing.

The wizard's chin rose proudly. "I serve your family alone."

"Why?" Vannek asked. He indicated the tent flap beyond the motionless bodyguard. "Why not ride away? Go serve the strongest king. I've pledged to fight for Elenai Halfsword."

"And she's promised to lead you to victories?"

"She has. As I'm sure you know."

"The Altenerai hold to their pledges," Muragan said, as though they should be pitied for it. "What will you earn for your service?"

Vannek didn't answer that. "You're wearying me, and I'm hungry. I still haven't heard how you can be of use to me."

"Very well," Muragan said. "Your grandfather knew when it was time to be blunt, too. And he led me well. You may not know that I've traveled Dendressi lands for years, learning their secrets. Cultivating useful connections." He shifted into a convincing Dendressi manner of speech. "There are things you may not know. Have you heard the fae lost their queen this day?"

"I have."

"Did you know one of their altens, called Rylin of the Thousand, attacked that queen, landing a mortal wound, but she did not die? Though he single-handedly slew her most powerful sorceress acolyte and half a dozen of her followers, she fled through mysterious magics with many more."

Vannek pretended to show no reaction to this news. "You may cease with the accent. These accounts are true?"

His voice returned to its normal inflection and timbre. "Verified through numerous reliable sources. The Dendressi are not so frivolous as our tales hold, and their Altenerai, though strange, are more deadly than any single man among us. But more importantly, their old queen lives to wield a power beyond any we've known. She abandoned this place rather than turn her great powers against Chargan, taking all the hearthstones she's been hoarding. Do you know what those are?"

"Trinkets mages use for power. What does she intend?" Vannek no longer pretended disinterest.

"They're more than trinkets, but that's a tale for another time. No one knows what the old queen intends, or at least, no one here."

Vannek had wanted the answer and was disappointed that the mage lacked it. He waited for the man to continue.

"You said the Dendressi are strong because they never war among themselves, and that was true for centuries. But they have split into two groups. The queen and her side imprisoned N'lahr and claimed he was dead. Now N'lahr's faction, led by Elenai, has captured Darassus. If you wonder where she means to lead you, I think you can guess."

"Against the old Dendressi queen, the one named Leonara," Vannek said. "How soon?"

"That I do not know. But I can learn," he added.

"Interesting," Vannek said. "All right, Muragan. What is it you want from me? A mage who served my grandfather would be welcomed by any of the Naor kings. And you may be the last one of any real skill."

"I'm done with Naor lands," Muragan said. "I don't want to slink back to the cold and dark to prop up kings while they fight for bones. It's as you said. There's more to be gained here."

"In that we concur."

"You have a plan, I know it." His eyes begged for further information.

"I do," Vannek said.

"But you won't share it, even with a friend?"

"No. Not yet. And I have no friends, Muragan." He eyed him to emphasize the difference in their station.

The mage bowed in acknowledgment.

"I welcome an advisor who will help me protect my people and see them prosper."

Muragan grunted. "You must keep Elenai from throwing the lives of your people away in her fight."

"You state the obvious."

"And you don't truly control a people. You have only warriors. There are no homes, or craftsmen, or farms to feed them. You need them to grow a kingdom. And there are no women."

Vannek braced himself to hear an insult about his gender, but none came. "I'm aware of all this." He glanced at his meal. "I will have you," he said finally. "I want to know more from you. But now I'm going to eat. Find my servants and have them assign you lodgings, and food. We'll talk again when you're settled."

Muragan bowed his head and started to turn away.

"Oh," Vannek said, as though it were an afterthought. "You must be swifter to obey, in the future. If you'd slain Anzat, I would have killed you."

"I meant to demonstrate my loyalty."

"And your power. To impress me with theatrics. I'm not so simple. My position . . ." Vannek thought to elaborate and then decided against further explanation. "I must rule through my own strength. Is that clear?"

"I understand, Lord General." Muragan bowed his head.

"See that you do."

3

Breakfast with the Queen

No matter the clean, crisply turned linens and inviting fluffy pillows, the chambers of Elenai's new Altenerai suite seemed more museum than home, from the cavernous rooms and the heavy old-fashioned furniture with their detailed carven flourishes, to the wide empty bed. The dark wood paneling that lined the walls drank in the light.

She wondered about the long generations of men and women who'd called these rooms their own, and she decided against looking at it through the inner world lest she encounter some haunting remnant of the previous occupants. Besides, she was exhausted. Somehow, after everything else, she and N'lahr had managed to draft a letter to the Naor leader suggesting they conference in the morning, though honing its phrasing had briefly appeared one mountain too many.

She dropped into a bedside chair to remove her boots just before a glowing woman shimmered into existence on her left. Elenai's heart leapt, and she leaned away even as she recognized the transparent intruder for Rialla, a short, wide-hipped woman with a high forehead, wearing a khalat hooked all the way to her collar. The apparition's brows were creased with worry.

"He has to jump left," Rialla said. Her voice possessed an odd, hollow quality, less substantial than at their last encounter.

"What?" Elenai could scarce believe Rialla had reappeared only to repeat herself.

"Kyrkenall has to jump left," Rialla insisted.

"He has to jump again?" Elenai asked.

"I don't understand you."

"He already jumped left," Elenai explained. "Off the Naor dragon. That's what you're talking about, isn't it?"

Rialla's puzzled expression hadn't cleared. Elenai struggled to clarify with more information. "We already had that conversation, in a dream. I got him to jump left. Is there anything else you can tell me?"

"In a dream?" Rialla sounded thoughtful.

The alarm of Rialla's appearance had been eclipsed by growing frustration. How could she have forgotten how difficult Rialla could be? "Look, there's so much you can tell us. Do you know where the queen is? How to stop her?"

"I am with the queen," Rialla said.

Elenai felt a chill down her spine. Did Rialla mean she was in league with Leonara, or that she expected Elenai to be queen? She swallowed. "I'm trying to find Queen Leonara. Do you know where she is?"

"We'll talk again," Rialla said, and winked away just as suddenly as she'd appeared.

Elenai swore, using words that would have shocked her only weeks before. Then she put a hand to her temple and spoke Kyrkenall's name like it, too, was a foul word, for repeatedly exposing her to so many of them.

Finally, she gathered her energy reserves and opened herself to the inner world, then stared around the room with trepidation.

Naturally, she found no sign of Rialla. Nor did she perceive vaporous forms of any of her predecessors, khalat wearing or otherwise. Frowning, she looked away from the inner world and finished readying for bed.

It wasn't until she was in the sheets that an important observation occurred to her. Heavy as her eyelids were, she lay staring into the dark in consternation. She'd assumed Rialla was centered upon her because she was using the alten's favorite hearthstone. Yet Rialla had found her, even with the artifact shattered. Did that mean her possession of the hearthstone hadn't contributed one way or the other to the ability to communicate with the long dead alten? What did any of this mean as far as Elenai's own glimpses of the future? Were those, then, as N'lahr believed, something innate her exposure to the hearthstone had unlocked?

She could think of no way to know for certain, not without asking Rialla, who only ever seemed to have time for her own concerns, primarily involving Kyrkenall's continued existence. She had once voiced alarm about the end of the world, but that might simply be because Kyrkenall required a world to live in.

Elenai tired of mysteries and left them behind as she drifted at last to sleep.

Morning dawned sooner than she would have liked. She woke to a steady rapping, and groaned. She forced herself up, groaning again as she registered pains she'd ignored last night. Maybe this is what it feels like to be old, she thought, and to the insistent knocking on the outer door she shouted she was coming even as she threw on a shirt and pulled on uniform pants. She pushed hair back from her face and stumbled to the door, only to find a nervous first ranker, his face swollen around a gash sewn closed above his right eye.

At the sight of him, Elenai's ill humor vanished, and even as she returned his crisp salute she pointed to his face. "That looks like it hurt."

"It was a glancing blow from a Naor arrow, Alten," the squire said. "I scarcely noticed it at the time." He gingerly touched the edge of the wound and withdrew his fingers. "I'm sorry to disturb you." He adopted a more formal tone as if reciting lines. "Councilor Brevahn wishes to join your meeting with the Naor general this morning, and asked your indulgence for a preparatory conference at eight bells."

Could he do that? she wondered. And then realized yes, of course he could, because the three surviving councilors were the highest-ranking leaders left in the city. Probably she or N'lahr should have thought of that last night. This was the beginning of a new life she didn't want. "Eight bells," she remembered aloud. "What time is it now?"

"Half past six."

She hadn't heard any bells whatsoever and rather thought she might have slept into the afternoon. The gods knew her body needed it. But then she thought of Thelar, likely already up and working to find the queen through contact with Varama. Her hours of sleep had been a tremendous gift.

"Is there anything I can assist you with? Do you want breakfast?"

She started to demur, for she wasn't awake enough to be hungry. But she knew she would be, soon. "That would be wonderful, thank you. Are any of the other Altenerai awake?"

"Commander N'lahr is. I haven't seen Alten Rylin or Alten Kyrkenall."

"How about the exalts?"

"I'm not sure, Alten. I haven't seen any of them this morning."

The last had been a stupid question. If this squire were posted to the Altenerai wing of the palace he'd be unlikely to see any exalts. She wondered why N'lahr had let her sleep, then realized it wasn't his job to get her up. That was something she should have planned for. She had much to learn.

"Alten, can I ask you something?" The squire struggled to hide his nervousness.

"Of course."

"Is it really true about the queen? That she's got some ancient magic artifacts that are very dangerous?"

The squire, naturally, had never heard of a hearthstone. Just as Elenai hadn't known what they were only a few weeks ago. She could see no benefit in concealing the information, and was drawn to speak the truth in any case. "Yes, she does. They're called hearthstones."

"What does she want with them?"

"She's convinced herself she can use them to awaken an old goddess. And she managed to convince some other people to support her new religion even though it endangers the realms." Seeing that this information did nothing to reassure the squire, she added: "We're going to find her, and we're going to stop her."

That seemed to lift his spirits, for the young man smiled as he saluted. He bade her farewell and left.

Elenai had just shut the door and turned away when she heard another knock. She assumed her messenger had forgotten to tell her something, so was surprised when she opened it again to discover Kyrkenall with a wicker basket of food. The crisp loaf of bread poking up along one side was so fresh it still produced curling steam.

Kyrkenall's magnetic black eyes were marred by dark circles. But he appeared to be in high spirits, for he grinned, then presented the basket as if certain he deserved praise.

"I brought us some breakfast. It's good to see you already up."

She mumbled a welcome and motioned him in. He took in the outer chamber with a sweeping glance to left and right. He paused in consideration of the walls, barren of any tapestries, painting, or other decor.

"I like what you've done with the place," he said, then hooked a chair with a foot, pulled it out, set down the basket, and produced a plate. He must have anticipated the cabinets were entirely empty because he pulled cutlery from a belt pouch, then plopped down in the chair and continued unpacking.

He was pulling out some cheese when Elenai walked over to look at him. "Make yourself comfortable."

He disregarded her sarcasm. "I'll feel more comfortable with some food in me. Hey, you should open the curtains. Get us some more light."

Elenai wondered why she was doing that even as she wandered over to follow his suggestion.

As promised, the view showed her no signs of the siege, looking as it did on a well-tended inner courtyard. Kyrkenall poured something into a goblet and pushed it toward her.

She took it and drank. It proved a young wine stored in some cool place. Despite the sweetness, she enjoyed the wonderful wet on her throat. And yet, she was irritated as she lowered the goblet. She could guess why Kyrkenall was here.

"You look like you're in a bad mood," he said. "We just beat the Naor, remember?"

"I need more sleep. It looks like you do, too."

"Usually. But we've a lot to discuss, don't we?"

She didn't really want to talk about Kalandra, or how to contact her through the emerald. She needed some breathing room. "I'm going to freshen up." She retreated to the bedroom, where she poured water into a ludicrously beautiful porcelain washbasin.

"Hey," Kyrkenall said through the door, "remember when you used to finish every sentence you said to me with the word 'alten'? Who'd have guessed how soon you'd be turning your back on me and stomping into the next room."

She decided against telling him she hadn't stomped. The frown he inspired looked back at her beneath tired eyes in the highly polished bronze mirror above the washbasin.

She splashed water over her face, gargled, and slowly combed out her hair. Long days in the sun had brightened the ruddier shades in her auburn locks.

As she finished her preparations, she decided upon morning prayers, reasoning that even if the Gods had been mere ancestors, as their recent travels had suggested, they still deserved respect. Or maybe she just wanted a few more minutes alone. Once she rose, she obstinately decided against donning the khalat.

When she rejoined Kyrkenall, he was crunching into a slice of buttered bread. Cherry pits and crumbs littered his plate.

He pointed to the scrambled eggs, as well as some sausages, well seared, and a wheaty-looking loaf, already sliced.

She sat down across from him, used a spoon to serve up the lukewarm eggs, and helped herself to some of the bread he'd brought. She ate.

"Oh, thank you, Kyrkenall." The archer spoke in a terrible falsetto. "You're so thoughtful and kind to bring me food. I shall be forever grateful." He dropped the impression. "I wanted to welcome you here officially, with a proper breakfast, because I remember how damned lonely these old suites are."

"Thank you," she said gruffly.

"Is there anything wrong with that? I seem to recall saving your life a few times yesterday. Are we no longer friends?"

"Of course we're friends. But I wish you'd just get to your point." She helped herself to more wine and discarded the temptation to thank him for it.

Kyrkenall reached into a belt pouch, removed a shimmering silk bag, and from it produced a fist-sized emerald. He set it on the table.

"I'm not going to try to open that this morning."

He held up a placating hand. "I saw what it did to Thelar."

"It almost killed him. Opening that stone can't be attempted unless there's a host of mages ready to help. And right now we can't risk any."

"You want to find the queen, right? Well, here's this stone." Kyrkenall rapped the table next to it. "It's obviously important, because it was in her chambers. It's obviously really important, because she protected it."

He had a point. "Do you think the queen was afraid someone would try to learn something secret?"

"Maybe," Kyrkenall said. "But it was secured in her office, and she surrounded herself with sycophants who wouldn't dare cross her. Do you really think this spell's there to keep people *away* from the stone?"

Elenai found herself taking him seriously about this subject for the first time. "Why do you think the ward is there?"

"It's not to keep people out. It's to keep something in."

She chewed some of the sausage as she decided how to broach her worry delicately. She swallowed. "Kyrkenall, you should know that this is probably another memory stone. Maybe it's a more sophisticated one, but we have no evidence there's anything to keep in. And I know you'll tell me that N'lahr was preserved, but he was imprisoned as a side effect of hearthstone damage. Full-sized. It was a freak accident and I doubt the queen could even fully explain it, much less duplicate it."

"Maybe that's all true," Kyrkenall conceded. "But then why did Rialla say Kalandra was 'in' the gem?"

"Rialla's vague, Kyrkenall. Maybe she meant all that's left of Kalandra is in a 'stone on the shelf.' We're not even sure this emerald is what she was talking about."

"You're not listening. Again, if it's a memory stone, why is it locked off, like there's something inside the queen was afraid could get out? The other two stones in the queen's office weren't protected that way. And one of the others contained the memories of a god."

He'd latched onto this singular idea, like a climber scrabbling desperately for purchase lest he slip to his doom.

"Let's say Kalandra's not even involved. Let's just consider the scene and wonder which of the three stones left in Leonara's office is likely to hold the most important information. Maybe the stone that no one can open?"

Elenai set down her goblet. "You're right. We should prioritize trying to open it. When we can muster the resources."

"Yes." He tried not to sound eager. "But right now you can scout it out—just to look at it, not open it. To see if you can tell more about how it's closed."

"Without getting blasted," she suggested.

"Of course! Can you just look at it without activating anything?"

"You mean just view it through the inner world? I saw it last night."

"Sure. But did you really look at it?"

"Kyrkenall, no."

"I'm not asking you to touch it, just to look at it. That's not going to set anything off."

"What is it you want me to look for?"

He held off answering, abruptly embarrassed, then worked past the feeling. "Could you sense any life inside?"

A flood of sympathy swept her irritation away. "Oh, Kyrkenall."

"I don't need pity. Rialla said Kalandra was in there. Maybe you can confirm it."

"No, I'm afraid I can't. Certainly not without activating its protection. You shouldn't get your hopes this high."

"We've seen a lot of strange things," Kyrkenall continued. "Things that should have been impossible."

"That's absolutely true. And you're absolutely right. That gem may hold important information. But I'm not looking now. And I don't want you asking anyone else, either."

"Is that an order, Your Majesty?"

"Stop that."

She hadn't meant to put quite as much snap into her voice. She saw him bristle, and then he looked away.

"Sorry," he said softly. "I . . . sorry."

"It's fine. I know how important this is to you."

"She's been gone a long time," he said quietly.

At the ringing of temple bells proclaiming the hour, she was reminded of her schedule. "N'lahr and I are meeting the Naor general next hour. Along with one of the Erymyran councilors."

Kyrkenall gently retrieved the emerald and returned it to the bag, and then his belt pouch. "Which one?"

"Councilman Brevahn."

"Him?"

"Do you know him?" She hadn't paid enough attention to Darassan politics to recognize any councilors by name. From Rylin she'd learned he was one of the only councilors to survive an attack by the queen, by virtue of being absent when she had killed everyone in the council chamber yesterday. Apparently their crumbling crystalline bodies still stood like statues within the hallowed hall, along with that of poor Alten Lasren, who'd died trying to shield them.

"Sure, I know him. Brevahn's been leading the call for criminal charges against me."

"Oh," she said, knowing another wave of foolishness for not wondering more about who wanted to speak with her.

"You're a power now. He's going to want to see how malleable you are."

"I am not 'malleable.'"

He grinned. "Don't I know it." He added: "As long as we're on the subject of councilors and thrones, and all that, there's something I think I should say."

"Oh?" Elenai mentally braced herself.

He laughed at her.

"What?" she asked.

"You look as though I announced I was going to hit you. I just have some advice."

"What is it?"

He fell silent for a long while. Elenai grew more and more curious as his expressions shifted between concern and worry and then on to wistful reverie. Finally, those eerie, pupilless eyes focused upon her. "Do you remember when I faced the kobalin at the bridge?"

"I'll never forget it, or his name. Vorn."

"Aye. Well, it doesn't always play out like that. I often win by walking in as if I'm already victorious. I don't have to fight; my foes will lay down their weapons before we start. It's like what you did last night, at the end of the battle."

"You mean when I bluffed about being able to destroy the Naor?"

"That was a bluff?" Kyrkenall laughed. "Maybe you don't need my advice."

"No, go on," she said, intrigued. "What are you saying?"

"I'm saying you've earned a reputation. And a lot of fights are won with how you present yourself."

"So, you pretend confidence even when you don't have it."

"Oh, I always have confidence. And at this point so should you. Don't let anyone push you around. Kobalin, Naor, councilor, you name it."

"That sounds like arrogance."

"There's a fine line," Kyrkenall admitted. "And maybe I err on the wrong side sometimes. But what I don't want to see is you erring too much the other way. Yes, keep the whole judging with heart and mind thing close to your, uh, heart, but act as the ruler we all know you to be."

She so regularly thought of Kyrkenall distracted by his own needs, that she sometimes forgot he possessed keen emotional insight. His concern for her, and faith in her character, touched her, and she felt a surge of warmth for him. "Sometimes," she said, "you know just what to say."

He gave her an oddly piercing look. She was about to ask him what that was about when a loud rap on the door startled them both. Kyrkenall immediately turned in his chair.

"Kyrkenall, Elenai, are you in there?" N'lahr asked, his voice taut.

"We're here," Kyrkenall said, rising. "I thought that was your knock."

The commander opened the door without invitation and stepped inside, his expression grave. "Throw on your khalat," he ordered Elenai, then shifted to Kyrkenall. "Grab Arzhun. We have a problem."

4

A Long Strange Road

Roused by the morning horn call, Rylin didn't truly feel awake until he splashed water over his face. He would have given a lot for some of Varama's fortifying juices and smiled to think he could tell her so soon.

He eyed himself in the bronze mirror and rubbed his chin stubble. He'd never gotten used to the beard and he didn't want it to return, so after throwing on fresh undergarments, he lathered on soap and readied his razor blade on the hanging strop.

He'd just finished when he grew aware of a light rapping on the outer door.

The last person who'd interrupted his morning routine had been Varama. He knew it couldn't be her, but felt a burst of excitement as he rinsed his face and threw on a shirt. He hooked it closed as he advanced across the floor, paused to tuck the garment into his uniform pants, then opened the door.

He tried to disguise his disappointment at the sight of Thelar, whose own clothes looked clean and pressed even if he himself appeared exhausted.

"Good morning," the exalt said stiffly.

Rylin returned the greeting and ushered the man into his suite.

"You look well rested," Thelar observed.

Rylin laughed. "I wish I felt it. Hey, are you hungry? I . . ." Rylin's voice trailed off.

"Is something wrong?"

Rylin shook his head, his good mood dissipated. "I'd hired a cook. And she kept the larder full. But after I . . . had to flee, I don't guess she had any reason to be here." He met the exalt's dark eyes. "And I just realized I've no idea what happened to her. Maybe she's fine." He showed an empty hand. "Anyway—there's probably nothing to eat here, or drink."

"I've already broken fast," Thelar said.

"Of course," Rylin said, feeling awkward. "I'll be back in a moment. Make yourself comfortable."

He left Thelar wandering toward the balcony while he stepped away to finish dressing.

When he returned, Thelar was seated at the small dining table, where he'd placed a slim shining shard of a light blue hearthstone before him.

"Was the healer right?" Rylin asked. "You're feeling fit for magics this morning?"

"Fit enough."

"It looked like you and he knew each other," Rylin continued, having seen the warm glances that had passed between Thelar and the lean, freckled man last night. "And here I thought you had something going on with one of those twins. Or maybe both."

Thelar frowned and Rylin remembered too late how new and fragile their good fellowship was. "No offense meant. I just thought . . ." He cleared his throat and took his seat before starting over. "It's good to see you have somebody."

A flash of perturbation crossed his face, but Thelar appeared to have decided against taking insult. "Do you have someone?" he asked politely.

"Me?" Rylin started to smile and then felt it slide away. It was his fault for bringing up the subject. "There was someone who liked me, back in Alantris," he answered slowly. "She was brave, and skilled, and probably too young. And now she's dead."

Thelar watched, apparently uncertain what to say.

Rylin filled the awkward silence. "Maybe there's Tesra, but she's with the queen, isn't she? I swear I saw her hesitate right on the edge of the queen's portal, as though she might have thought about staying. But she went through."

Thelar eyed him dubiously. "Tesra. Really. She knows you tricked her."

"I can't imagine I'm high on her favorite people list."

"No."

"In my defense, I had to find out what you exalts were up to."

"I suppose," Thelar said doubtfully, and Rylin understood that it was more the method he'd used than the information he sought which troubled the exalt. Rylin repressed a surge of defensive anger as he sought a response, but then Thelar cleared his throat and continued. "I could have been a better friend to her." Rylin wondered if the disapproval he'd heard in the man's voice only a moment before had been aimed more at himself. "She'd grown suspicious of Synahla and the queen before I did," Thelar finished.

"Then why didn't she side with us?"

"I don't know." Thelar shifted, as though the wooden chair were uncomfortable. "I was too angry for letting you fool her, so I didn't enjoy her confidence from then on."

Rylin remembered the events of that day: his lies to Tesra about leaving the Altenerai to join the Exalts, his "friendly bout" with M'vai and Meria, during which Thelar had cheated, the tryst with Tesra that she had instigated, but which would never have happened if he hadn't misled her. At the time he'd been pleased to have gained so much information about the enemy, but he had since grown uncomfortable with his actions, because the line between playing a convincing role and taking advantage of the situation had been muddled.

Thelar continued: "If I hadn't borne that grudge, if I'd been a better friend, Tesra might have turned to me instead of losing herself with them."

Rylin's first impulse was to remark that Thelar had always been a champion grudge bearer, but he held off. Even after they'd stood side by side in battle some old prejudices flared up too easily. Much as he had come to respect and depend upon Thelar, he wondered if past history might preclude the development of a real friendship.

Realizing such pessimistic musings wouldn't make their work this morning any easier, Rylin decided to focus on next steps. "All we can do," he said, not unsympathetically, "is acknowledge our errors and move forward, together."

"You're right."

Rylin gestured to the shard. "What do we do first?"

"If you'd like me to attempt the sending, you can monitor. I've much more experience with hearthstones." He sounded like his old pompous self until he added quickly, "Unless you'd rather try."

Rylin understood then that Thelar, too, recognized the fragility of their newfound alliance. "I'm sure you're right about experience, but I know Varama. And knowing her will make her easier to find, won't it?"

"It's the hearthstone she's using that will make it possible to find her. But the point you made last night is compelling. She's far more likely to greet you warmly."

"I'm not sure she greets anyone warmly," Rylin said, and then at Thelar's questioning look explained further. "She keeps her feelings pretty well hidden. Anyway. What's the process?"

"Once I activate the shard, root yourself to it as deeply as possible. I can help with that. I also can feed energies into the connection to strengthen it. Then you need to ignore nearly every tenet you've ever heard about spell casting. Extend yourself and reach toward your intended target."

Rylin nodded as though he weren't the least bit troubled. He knew many stories illustrating what could happen if a spell caster sent his spirit too far from his body. The least of these dangers was confusion, moving on to dissolution, or the consumption by entities hungry for life energy. In some reports, the souls of sorcerers watched helplessly as strange beings used their abandoned bodies to commit atrocious deeds. He pretended ease. "How far and how fast can I reach?"

Thelar spoke with the enthusiasm of a scholar talking of his area of interest. "Theoretically you move at the speed of your own imagination. In real life it would take days to reach Erymyr's border even traveling at a good clip. But if you remember key details and landmarks you might manage it in an eyeblink. Stretch for one remembered point, then the next, then on for the border itself."

Rylin remembered the wayposts where he and Elik and the governor of The Fragments, as well as poor Lasren, had exchanged horses. "And what about reaching across the Shifting Lands? There are no landmarks there."

"That's when you think about the other side of the border."

"And then I just kind of . . . search along the road until I find Varama?"

"Yes. That's what I'd do. If you weren't sure which way they were coming, I'd say you were in for a huge challenge."

They'd been told Varama and much of the relief force sent to Alantris were riding to Darassus via the Alantran Way. It was the most logical path in any case.

"She won't be traveling with the hearthstone active," Rylin said. "How will I find it?"

"You might be able to sense it even when it's off, if you're close. Varama will likely travel at the head of troops. She shouldn't be that hard to find. The challenge will be getting her to see you if she's not already using her magical sight."

"Her ring," Rylin said. "If I come close enough, my presence should activate her ring."

"Of course," Thelar acknowledged with chagrin.

Rylin thought again about those vast, hungry entities he'd encountered the last time he crossed the border. "What do I do if I'm attacked in the shifts?"

Thelar lifted the shard. "Just picture this stone in this room, clearly, and you should snap back here."

"You make it sound easy."

"In some ways it is. You're moving at the speed of your own thought. I'll monitor the threads attaching you to the stone. If something starts to go wrong, I'll sense it and warn you. You can do this," Thelar assured him. It was strange to hear him speak so earnestly.

Rylin smiled as though he were not remotely terrified of hungry beings of unstoppable force lurking ahead of him. Last time he'd met them they'd been distracted by eating a horse, and he'd had rings to enhance the integrity of his existence. And he'd been in his body. He'd have none of those advantages for this journey.

He examined his surroundings in detail. He'd lived in this apartment for years, but it had been a while since he truly paid attention to it. He did so now, seeing the way the morning light brought out the lightest patches on the smooth old floorboards, rubbing his hands against the wooden table to feel its grain, and noting the dust motes settled over surfaces. He thought about his location within the palace, its proximity to the stairs, and the windows that overlooked the courtyard. He couldn't recall exactly how many steps one climbed to reach the second floor, which was funny, given how many times he'd walked or ran up them. He supposed Varama would know. But probably the exact number wasn't important.

He set his right hand to the irregular shard, which was cool beneath his fingers. He felt the shard's rough, faintly iridescent edges. If this truly was a broken piece of some frozen aspect of the Goddess, touching it was like putting his hand on her bones. It troubled him he wasn't more repulsed. Another worry struck him. "Is there a chance I'll alert the queen when I use this?"

"We're far from the other stones. I think. Probably the queen's exalts are busy enough and can't be bothered to monitor us."

"You're sure?"

"No. I'm only guessing, Rylin."

He recognized he was delaying the inevitable. It was time to act. "I'm ready if you are," he said.

"I'm ready."

Rylin tightened his hand around the shard and thought briefly of Elenai. Maybe a lot of spell casters had gone mad using the things, but she seemed to have come through intact. He hoped he'd be able to say the same.

The shard opened easily to him. He thought he'd been prepared, but the rush of energy was so pleasant it still made him gasp.

Each of the stones he'd wielded had evoked a different emotion. This one filled him with confidence. It wasn't just that he had energy to spare, he had utter faith he would succeed in whatever he set forth to do. As he grinned at Thelar he saw his companion relax and smile with uncharacteristic ease, for he, too, was sorcerously linked to the stone. We're happy as fools, he thought, knowing it was the stone, and telling himself he'd have to be careful. In this state he might well overestimate his capabilities.

Rylin pushed deep into the shard, glorying in access to its power. Thelar was there with him, ushering him forward. The exalt, like himself, strove not to come into especially close contact, wishing to avoid the accidental sharing of surface thoughts, let alone anything deeper.

Rylin threaded his spirit through the stone and then back through his own body before launching from it. In a heartbeat he'd passed through the door and into the hallway, then down the stairs and out to the stables. A moment later he floated beyond the gates of the inner city, contemplating the hole in the skyline where Darassa's statue had stood for millennia. He had been partly responsible for her destruction, and felt a pang of guilt, knowing she still lay, prone and battered, across the avenue.

He shifted his concentration for a brief moment to ensure his body still touched the hearthstone, then resumed the view from his spirit and thought about the broken wall near the city gate. In an instant he floated there, and while he knew anger to see the crumbled stones, he felt assured by his unnatural confidence that repairs would be simple. He looked out to the ribbon of masonry marking the Darassan Way and pushed along it, passing a trio of horse troopers completely oblivious to his invisible presence, then launched toward a hill.

In moments he had flown vast distances with disturbing ease. He knew he should feel worry as he left his body farther and farther behind, but rising joy superseded all else.

His view of the inner world was overlaid across existing landscapes, and sometimes revealed startling differences from previous mundane travel. An entire village, complete with temple, could be seen superimposed on a set of old stone walls. He passed a mysterious glowing tower a half mile beyond the road that had no presence at all in the physical world, and over one stretch of ground he glimpsed vaporous marching figures—some ancient host had left an echo of their travel.

As much as he realized that he moved impossibly fast, Rylin had the faintest worry that he still took too long, and reminded himself that the longer he was away from his body the greater was his danger. He decided to accelerate his progress rather than to savor these strange experiences. He pictured the hostel on the Erymyran side of the Shifting Lands, at the closest point to The Fragments. He recalled that the sign hanging in front of it had a large crack running through its silver raven's beak.

He had only to wish he might look upon that sign, and he appeared beside it. He heard horses neighing in the stalls, and the chatter of voices and the rattle of utensils from inside the stone building.

He laughed in delight at his accomplishment, reminded himself, again, that this was no pleasure trip, and looked behind him. A silvery thread stretched from the sole of his right foot into the distance. That slim line was the link to his own body, the energy that, if severed, would make return nearly impossible. He touched his hand to it and felt the life force surging there, bolstered by the hearthstone shard.

He considered the landscape that stretched ahead. The Shifting Lands appeared calm. Through the inner world, the terrain beyond the border was insubstantial, little more than a dream of landscape. But no storms churned in the sky, and he sensed none of those powerful presences that had chased him during his last crossing. The shifts seemed as safe as it was possible for them to be.

Even with his bolstered confidence Rylin understood that this crossing was the most dangerous moment before him. Appearances were deceptive in the shifts and Rylin could think of no reason the insubstantial tract should be unprowled. Once he ventured into the home of energy-hungry spirits, he might as well be a fishing lure tossed into a lake, an irresistible morsel of life delightfully seasoned with magic.

But what more could he do? He knew of no protective measures save to get done and get back, fast. He'd best be on with it.

He called to mind the little way station on The Fragments side of the border, where he'd spoken with Governor Feolia and Lasren prior to their terrible crossing. In moments he was there in the daylight beside the stable fence, looking back down the line of his energy that stretched across the border. He wondered how much warning he'd have if one of the hungry spirits wandered upon his thread, and if he'd be able to get back if they tried to break it.

He decided not to think about it, and pushed himself down the road. He didn't want to advance too quickly through remembered places, worried he might skip past the people he sought. After a short while, he increased his speed, advancing only to landmarks he perceived ahead of him.

His sense of time was distorted, but he guessed it really wasn't very long before he spotted a dust cloud that had to be the main body of an army. Soon he saw the vanguard of cavalry, and riding even in advance of those warriors was a pair of riders in Altenerai khalats. He closed in, joyous with anticipation.

But he discovered Varama was neither of the two. One was Tretton, dark-skinned, his beard hair gray-flecked. The other was Gyldara Dragonsbane, her gold-blond hair pulled tightly back from her exquisitely fine features.

Surely Varama was somewhere nearby, for she would be just as eager as they to reach Darassus. He was starting to glide past when the rings of both Altenerai lit. The two reined in. While Gyldara scanned the surrounding terrain, Tretton's eyes shifted. So far as Rylin knew, Tretton had no weaver's sight, yet the alten looked toward him as he put hand to his sword belt.

"Who's there?" Tretton demanded, his graying mustache rising as his lip curled. Rylin had never examined Tretton's aura before. Naturally the older man's ring glowed with magic, but so too did his knife and sword, and a necklace pendant. The famously formal veteran had more surprises than Rylin had guessed.

Rylin remained above the grass blades only a few feet in front of the veteran. "Hail, Altenerai. It's me, Rylin."

Tretton heard him, for he saw the alten's eyes twitch. Rylin's respect for the man rose a notch. Some non-mages were sensitive to the inner world, but he'd never heard that Tretton was one of them, and he wondered if one of the magical tools he wore enhanced his perception.

"Hail, Alten," Tretton said, his hand still upon his sword. "Are you a spirit, or is this a spell?"

"I live, but this is a long send. It will be more secure if I can link to Varama's hearthstone. Where is she?"

Gyldara cut in. "Who is it? What's this about?"

"It's Rylin. He's trying to find Varama. She's not here, Rylin. What's happened? Was Darassus truly attacked?"

"Attacked and preserved. The Naor were defeated. We need your troops to hold the surviving prisoners in check; although I suppose they're technically allies, now." He swiftly changed the subject. "I'll explain later. I need to find Varama."

"She left in the middle of the night," Tretton said. "On a ko'aye."

"Varama?" Rylin could scarce believe the news. She hated heights, and had steadfastly refused to fly with even the friendliest of ko'aye, Lelanc. "You're sure?"

Tretton chuckled. "I'm sure. She was even paler than usual when she strapped herself in, but she was determined to get to Darassus."

"Well then," Rylin said. "I guess I'm here for nothing."

Gyldara peered in his direction. "Ask him if there were casualties."

"He can hear you," Tretton said. "You just can't hear him."

"Too many," Rylin answered with a pang. "Lasren. Dozens of citizens. Lots of squires. And we lost an exalt and some aspirants; a few of them switched sides to defend the city. The queen fled Darassus with the hearthstones and the remains of her auxiliary rather than aid in its defense."

Tretton's mouth thinned as he relayed this information to Gyldara, whose eyes rounded in disbelief.

Gyldara was asking Tretton for details when Rylin felt a tug on his shoulder. An actual, physical pull. His vision wavered.

Tretton's brows drew taut. "Rylin? Is something wrong?"

"I must go," he said, even as he felt another forceful squeeze. He thought of the details of the shard before him and the feeling of the wood beneath one hand and the cool stone in the other. . . .

The miles between his spirit and his body passed in a dizzying whir of blue sky and sloping green hills and suddenly he sat breathless in his chair. He had to blink to register the room and verify it wasn't moving toward him. He steadied against the table to prevent a crash with the dark paneled wall on his right.

Thelar was no longer across from him, but bent beside him, and he was talking as he released Rylin's shoulder. "There's an emergency."

5

Internal Division

Still dazed from his trip through the inner world, Rylin had trouble latching onto the significance of what the exalt had told him until he saw Elenai waiting impatiently near the door. He was once again struck by the change in her. Elenai was tall and slim, with striking gray eyes and fine auburn hair. She'd always possessed an appealing determination and energy. Now that was coupled with confidence and certitude that was almost regal. Rightly so, he thought with a smile. "What's happened?" he asked.

"The commander needs Thelar's help," Elenai answered. "We might need yours, too."

Rylin didn't notice Elenai was extending his sword belt to him until he stood. He reached for it, then grabbed his khalat, which someone had draped over a nearby chair.

He shrugged into his uniform. "What's wrong?"

"Early this morning an exalt broke into the infirmary upstairs," Elenai said.

Rylin's eyes shifted to Thelar, who appeared just as dismayed as Rylin felt. "Which one? Why?" Surely it wasn't Meria or M'vai.

"Someone named Nerissa," Elenai answered.

Rylin recognized the name, recalling why as he finished hooking his uniform clasps. She'd stopped him, Lasren, Feolia, and Elik on the border only a few days ago.

"She tried to free the exalts and aspirants under guard in the infirmary," Elenai continued. "Because we don't have enough guards to go around, N'lahr ordered the prisoners sedated last night, then placed the only antidote elsewhere in the complex. But Nerissa must not have known about that."

He wondered how the exalt had gotten past the security cordon outside the infirmary. Probably because squires had trusted their fellow rankers. As he buckled on his sword belt he noticed no weapon hung from Thelar's waist.

The exalt saw his inquiring look. "I didn't think I'd need a sword in the palace."

How times change, Rylin thought. He addressed Elenai's back as she headed out the door. "So what's Nerissa doing now, and what are we going to do?"

She turned her head but didn't stop walking. "She brought four squires and an aspirant with her, from their patrol. One of her squires was killed in their ambush on the guards. Another began to question Nerissa's skewed version of events when he saw the captured exalts and aspirants were well tended; he alerted us when Nerissa sent him to get the antidote. As for us, we're going to stop her."

Elenai turned down the hallway toward the servants' stair. A second ranker—the one Elenai had commended for his efforts on the wall yesterday—walked behind them, along with two older women who'd donned leather surcoats from the squire armory. He recognized them as healers. Many of the best medical practitioners were aged, for long years of study were required for mastery of their art.

Rylin returned his attention to Elenai. "Is there anything else we should know?"

"They're holding at least one guard, a healer, and a nurse hostage. Two of the watch are dead and another's wounded. We're not sure about the fourth."

"They've killed people? How are we going in?"

Thelar answered: "The commander wants me to try to talk with Nerissa, through the door."

N'lahr waited for them at the top the third-floor servants' stair, with a squire Rylin vaguely recognized from his encounter with Nerissa's group at the border—a dark first year with tight braids and light brown eyes.

"Did you make contact with Varama?" N'lahr asked.

"Not exactly," Rylin said. "But she'll be here soon."

N'lahr nodded curtly. "Details later, then. Squire Pelin here has briefed me while we got our approach ready. Nerissa possesses a hearthstone."

"Will the other squires fight with Nerissa?" Rylin asked.

"That depends on how convincing we can be." N'lahr looked significantly at Squire Pelin. "They've been serving with her for the last eight days, on patrol. One is a cousin. The other was an intimate of the squire killed." His attention shifted to Thelar. "You have your shard with you?"

"Yes, sir."

"I want you to focus on talking. Loan the shard to Elenai."

As the exalt reached into his belt pouch, N'lahr faced Elenai, lean and attentive as a hound waiting in its traces for the command to hunt.

"How long will it take you to access Thelar's shard?" N'lahr asked.

"Only an instant," Elenai answered.

"Good. Don't trigger it until I give the word. We don't want to alarm the exalt or her aspirant."

"What should I do?" Rylin asked.

"Stand ready in case Nerissa finds some magical means to wake the prisoners."

That would mean four more allies on Nerissa's side. Owing to the tremendous skill of the palace healers, all but one of the underlings Rylin had fought on the stairs yesterday had lived through the encounter, including the woman who'd taken a terrible sword wound to the face.

The infirmary and its associated offices occupied a substantial portion of the third floor's west wing. Rarely a bustling center of activity even on an ordinary day, this morning the hallway brooded with shadows. No one moved along the carpet stretching down its center and the doors to smaller wards, offices, and labs were closed. Down the hall to the right, at the head of the main stairs, three squires waited alertly in the furnished lounge. They returned N'lahr's "hold position" signal.

To the left, the hallway extended past only a few more closed office doors before terminating at the entrance to the infirmary itself. Conspicuously absent from the chairs just outside it were the guards he and Thelar had encountered last night.

N'lahr pointed Elenai's second ranker to a closed door near the infirmary. The squire opened the door, then scanned the room before waving the healers inside. Apparently N'lahr was staging them out of harm's way as battle medics.

The commander advanced to the chairs outside the infirmary, and spared a moment to consider something on the floor, a sticky splotch of blood staining the carpet. The light-eyed squire looked away in shame.

N'lahr checked to ensure Elenai held Thelar's shard, then nodded his head to the exalt, who stepped to the door and rapped it twice before speaking. "Nerissa, this is Thelar. I want you to remain calm, because no one else has to be hurt."

The silence was so pronounced Rylin feared Nerissa and her occupiers had already fled. And then a woman's voice, thick with anger, answered.

"Well, they will be hurt, unless I'm allowed to leave with my people. They should be *your* people. Why have you joined *them*? You were the one who always complained about their corruption! That they weren't living their oaths."

It wasn't so difficult to imagine Thelar once having said such things. During their squire days, Rylin's chief impression of his new friend had been of a bristly, humorless malcontent. When Rylin had been promoted to fifth rank in advance of him, Thelar had accused the higher-ups of playing favorites, and resigned to accept a post in the newly created Mage Auxiliary.

"There was corruption in the Altenerai Corps," Thelar said. "But I was blind to the corruption in ours. An exalt and an alten murdered Master Asrahn. Do you know why?" He waited a suitable interval, and, hearing no reply, answered the question himself. "To protect their secrets. We were lied to. Commander N'lahr wasn't dead. They'd imprisoned him, and they killed Asrahn to cover it up. Denaven knew. Synahla knew. And so did some of the exalts."

"Altenerai killed Synahla!" Nerissa's voice shook with rage. "And you're with them?"

Thelar checked with N'lahr, who motioned for him to continue.

"Did you hear me, Nerissa? Corrupt elements of both the auxiliary and the Altenerai led to a whole host of unjust deaths."

In Thelar's voice Rylin heard the threat of rage he remembered coming so easily to him. Too easily. This time, though, he understood it, and shared his feelings.

The exalt continued. "Synahla was a champion liar. She could be very convincing. I think she used hearthstone magic to change thoughts. She might have cast magic to change yours, which is why you have to reason this out, Nerissa. You admired Asrahn as much as I did. And he's dead because of Synahla and the queen."

"You're wasting your breath, traitor," Nerissa said. "I have a knife to the throat of this healer and my companions have the guard and the orderly. If you and the Altenerai try to get through, we're going to open their necks. You won't have time to stop us before they die. Is that clear?"

Thelar sucked in a long, slow breath, and his hands tightened into fists. After he exhaled, his voice was calm. "It's clear. But you need to listen."

"No, *you* listen. If I so much as feel the beat of a hearthstone from you I'm going to kill them."

Thelar looked helplessly back at the commander, who walked up beside him. "I don't know exactly what you've been told, Exalt Nerissa," the commander said to the door. "But Thelar has told you nothing but the truth. This is Commander N'lahr. I would be happy to sit down with you, unarmed, to explain. We don't want you harmed or imprisoned. We need you in the larger fight to preserve our realms."

Did he mean that? Even after Nerissa had killed innocent squires?

Elenai apparently wondered the same thing, for she met Rylin's eyes with a questioning look before glancing two doors down, where the second-rank squire lingered in the doorway. The young man's head was turned away from them, his attention rooted to something inside. Rylin's wariness eased when he realized the squire was monitoring an object or person within, probably under orders from N'lahr.

"I don't know who you are," Nerissa's voice came back dully. "But I know some of my best friends were wounded by yours, and I mean to leave this palace with them."

"Where would you like to go?" N'lahr asked.

There was a pause, then Nerissa answered, "Away."

"Maybe we should let them go," Rylin whispered to Thelar, hoping the commander could hear. "Follow them to the queen."

Thelar shook his head and replied, his voice low. "Nerissa wouldn't know where the queen's taken the other exalts. She's never been part of the inner circle. That's why she was given border duty."

The second ranker in the doorway down the hall looked their way, raised a hand and lowered it. N'lahr noted it with a nod. A moment later the squire lifted his hand and waggled it, whatever that meant. N'lahr motioned for the nervous first-rank squire, Pelin, to move farther off.

"There's a lot of dangerous territory between here and 'away,'" N'lahr said. "We need to discuss arrangements to get you to that goal."

"Is there any chance we can talk about this face-to-face?" Thelar suggested.

The squire in the doorway raised one finger, and stood waiting, as if for a response. N'lahr raised a hand indicating him to hold.

Nerissa screeched her reply. "You think that will make any difference, Thelar?! I can barely stomach hearing your voice! You betrayed the queen! You betrayed the Goddess!"

"Exalt Nerissa," N'lahr said sternly, "the five realms need you. And they need the lives of your hostages. We've lost too many people already. Let's talk about what we can do to get you out of here."

"Enough talk! You're only trying to confuse me. You think I didn't plan very well. You think you can trick me!"

N'lahr, with a sad sigh that was more physical than audible, slowly drew Irion until the long straight blade was ready in his hands. He motioned Thelar back and faced Elenai. He mouthed the words "ready" then looked to Rylin.

He drew his own sword, wishing he could think of something inspired to say or do.

"There's still time to settle this peacefully," N'lahr pleaded. "What's the first step you'd like us to take?" His free hand was raised in a conciliation Nerissa couldn't see.

"I'd like you to take me seriously! Maybe this will help." A strangled cry rose from within the infirmary, followed by a scream.

N'lahr swept his hand down. The second ranker whirled and mimicked the gesture. From within the infirmary came a crash of glass, and on that instant Rylin felt Thelar's shard flare to life. Threads pulsed out from it and blew the door open.

N'lahr charged through.

He pushed past a dresser that had apparently been blocking the door before Elenai's blast had toppled it. Rylin vaulted after him into the wide, sunny room. One squire stood indecisively at the duty desk in the infirmary's center, sword raised over a wounded guard. The other had been posted near the storage room door holding an orderly, and now backed away, wild-eyed. Nerissa, a slender, dark-skinned woman in an exalt's khalat, lay twitching on the floor, in line with a wide window bearing a smashed square, an arrow buried in the back of her head. Before her a kneeling healer was grasping at his throat, blood pouring from between his fingers.

Rylin sent a blast of wind against the man crouched beside the desk. He blew him backward. Elenai, just behind Rylin, brought one hand down like a knife blade. Energy rushed past Rylin, and each of the enemy squires slumped limply to the floor. It was an impressive display.

Thelar rushed in to the pale healer and activated Nerissa's hearthstone to slow the man's bleeding. The gash in his throat was still giving up alarming quantities of red, and the gurgling sounds from his attempts to draw breath did not bode well. The armored healers rushed in with the remaining squires and bent to attend him.

Rylin reviewed the rows of beds beneath the windows where the men and women he'd injured yesterday still lay unconscious. On the floor a few feet away from the storeroom lay the bodies of three first rankers—two guards and one clearly just in from patrol. He didn't know his hands had tightened into fists until his fingers dug into the skin of his palms.

Elenai stepped to the window, her hand raised in the sign to stand down. Kyrkenall must have found a vantage point, and the second ranker had been notifying N'lahr when he was in position.

Rylin pushed a table away from one of the storage rooms, and opened the door. A nervous young woman emerged, from her green sleeve band one of the attendant nurses.

Thelar stepped back from the knot of healing professionals crouched beside Nerissa's victim. He nodded tightly to Rylin, then returned his attention to their efforts. Whether their patient was his lover, friend, or relative, he didn't know. Also unknown, the numbers of other loved ones who would be grieving today for the dead squires who'd survived a Naor attack only to be slain by their allies. He couldn't help wondering how the realms could stand against outsiders when they couldn't stand together.

6

A Land of Plenty

As the evening rays of the great golden sun poured down, Tesra eyed the lush blueberry bushes flourishing upon a ridge. Plump berries weighed down their branches, yet she could have sworn they had been picked clean just this morning.

Probably they had been. The queen had delivered them unto paradise, where life was easy. Any resource they required was ready to hand.

She started down the moss path. An hour of daylight remained, which meant most of the others would continue working. Only an hour after that, a huge silver moon would rise and set the nightflowers and all their grasses glowing in strange splendor, and by their light the most dedicated of the exalts and aspirants would continue their examination of the hearthstones.

She felt a fresh wave of guilt that she'd lost interest in their labors and wished Synahla were here. In recent weeks the exalt commander had proven indispensable whenever Tesra felt doubt. Talks with her inevitably stiffened Tesra's resolve and redirected her energy so that she no longer felt lost or uncertain.

She didn't dare to tell anyone else of her misgivings. So far no one really seemed to have noticed her frequent breaks. The queen herself sat in a trance before the statue of the Goddess so much of the time that leadership had devolved to others, and a solid core of seven remained absolutely dedicated to assembling the statue of the Goddess by night and day with only short breaks. The rest spent much of their time exploring the impossibly beautiful land.

As she wandered on, she nibbled from a bunch of deliciously sweet red grapes. In the near distance a mountain soared, ringed with greenery and capped by snow. A stunning waterfall dropped from its height, plunging thousands of feet.

It was serenely beautiful, yes, but Tesra felt more and more out of place, oddly repulsed by the ardent fervor of her fellows. Not for the first time she wondered what might have happened if she hadn't walked through the portal. She kept hearing Rylin's voice as he declared the queen had no right to wake the Goddess without consent of the people. And he had acted to save the people of Darassus rather than the Goddess in her hearthstones. Couldn't the queen have repelled the Naor and then resumed their devotions? Surely many Darassans had died in the attack. Would the Goddess truly restore them all?

She knew from personal experience Rylin was a liar. Yet he had apparently convinced Thelar, who had never been easy to deceive, and who had no good reason to side with his hated rival.

A conversation about her misgivings with anyone here would elicit the usual explanations: evil was insidious, even attractive, and she'd allowed herself to be led astray before. The others would surely tell her she must repent and redouble her efforts on behalf of the Goddess. Tesra couldn't bear the pitying recriminations to which she'd be subjected. Only Synahla had seemed to accept her doubts and ease them. She missed the peace that flowed from unswerving connection to a greater, glorious whole. To know where the answers lay.

Tesra rounded a hill as she reluctantly walked back toward the statue, passing through vibrant grasses. She paused to drink in the meadow where the rainbow-hued statue of the Goddess towered, one hand outthrust, still supported by scaffolding. The assault by the Naor dragon had blown hundreds of hearthstones free, but the statue remained exquisite, and her immortal beauty grew more and more certain as the exalts and aspirants restored the pieces.

They crouched at the statue's feet amid neat piles of shards and hearthstones. Their work was challenging without the reference books left behind in Darassus. Every stone had to be tried in all possible configurations.

Supports had been crafted from trees so perfect it felt criminal to fell them. They had no tools, but with magical energy so abundant they'd easily shaped additional scaffolding and ladders. Men and women perched upon the rungs and platforms, puzzling over the fit of each piece. Progress was frustratingly slow, yet the mood remained upbeat.

Watching their patient zeal brought no accord, and so Tesra turned to contemplate the line of smaller statues erected across an ancient reflecting pool. Seven stood at its far end, each formed of some seamless, gleaming metal, and while they were dwarfed by the hearthstone Goddess, the images of smiling young men and women still towered like giants.

Six were the false Gods she'd been taught to worship from childhood, five of whom had betrayed the Goddess. It was easy enough to guess the identity of half-feral Kantahl even if most of the other Gods didn't look the way they were depicted across the realms. Darassa could be identified from her sword and curling hair. And Syrah, youngest of them all and the last in line, was obvious, a crown of flowers in her long straight locks.

But who was the first one, androgynous, somewhat morose? He/she was the same size as the others, though stood apart.

The queen spoke from just behind her right shoulder. "This land is a wonder."

Tesra forced herself into calm as she turned.

Queen Leonara's expression was vague. She had grown even more otherworldly and strange since their arrival.

"Yes, my queen," Tesra agreed belatedly, then added: "It's wonderful here. Thank you for bringing us."

Not so long ago, the queen had smiled to receive such praise, inviting it as her due. Now her response was distracted, as if she listened less to what had been said and more to the tune of her inner thoughts. "Soon all the realms will resemble this one. It is a time of miracles."

The queen pressed her hand to her heart. Tesra vividly recalled that there had recently been a wound just under that point on her shimmering green dress. She had witnessed Rylin's attack, and known it for a fatal blow. But not a mark was left upon the queen. The injury had healed instantly. Leonara had told her worried followers she had felt little pain. She'd repaired the rent garment just as easily.

The queen uncharacteristically noted the direction of her gaze. "I see that you contemplate my mortality. I am beyond such concerns, as you will be soon. With our hearts totally devoted to the Goddess, we are perfected, holy and immutable."

"I'm sure you're right," Tesra said, discomfited rather than inspired. "You're very wise."

"We are close," the queen declared. "So very close now. Only days separate us from the return of our Goddess."

Tesra had been certain the queen would complain she wasn't working hard enough, but the ruler of the five realms simply stood there, vacantly contemplating the horizon.

Tesra cleared her throat and dared a question. "Are you worried that the Altenerai will find us?"

The queen answered without looking at her. "My child, this realm is impossible for them to find. We are safe. I wish only that I had been pure enough for its existence to be revealed sooner."

Pure. Holy. Leonara had used those words liberally since their arrival. Tesra wondered why her own faith had weakened so. Even confidence in her leaders had faltered. She began to feel less as though she missed Synahla, and more as though she resented her, though she couldn't identify the reason.

"Besides," the queen continued breezily, "should the traitors somehow find their way here, we will deal with them. You need not fear when you are with me and the Goddess." She favored Tesra with an icy smile, then wandered off toward the towering, inhumanly perfect statue without farewell.

With abrupt, searing certainty Tesra understood that proximity to the queen and her statue was the most frightening place of all.

7

———≈———

The Throne of the Queen

Elenai would vastly have preferred a long quiet jog around the city walls, or a ride through the countryside. Instead, a meeting with the councilor and Vannek loomed, and she couldn't feel less ready. She excused herself to wash up while she sorted through the jarring events of the last hour.

Foremost in her mind was Nerissa's blindness to reason. Even if she wasn't aware of the lies and murders the queen had suborned, how could the exalt have thought it a moral choice to kill noncombatants? Had she been born that twisted, or had something warped her so that she believed all who lacked her perspective deserving of death? What could be done with those who shared that viewpoint? Would the imprisoned exalts and aspirants be just as intransigent, just as recklessly destructive?

When she finished washing, she stared hard into the mirror. These were among the many impossible problems that others would look to her to solve, and she wondered that anyone thought her suited to sit the throne when someone nearby was clearly better. N'lahr time and again set everything on the right course. He knew not only what steps to take, but the precise moment to act. She doubted she would ever hone her instincts so finely, no matter how much experience she gained. Just as she would never match Kyrkenall's deadly proficiency, shooting a moving target through a pane of glass at an angle from at least a hundred paces out. It was practically unbelievable. Because of those two, they'd lost only one misguided exalt, beyond the three squires perished at Nerissa's hand.

When she emerged from her quarters N'lahr was waiting for her.

"I understand Councilor Brevahn will be joining our meeting," he said.

The commander seemed to learn everything. "Yes."

"Brevahn has asked for a moment alone before the general turns up, but I hope you won't mind me accompanying you."

"I welcome it."

"Good," he said. She fell in step with him and they moved toward the main stairs. "I had hoped we could begin our relationship with the Naor general on a simpler footing," he continued. "General Vannek will be wanting reassurance and you must not let Brevahn interfere."

Reassurance? "We gave our word," she said.

"They're Naor," the commander reminded her. "Oaths for them can only be relied upon to the extent they can be enforced or incentivized."

"What makes you think Councilor Brevahn will interfere?"

"He'll be focused on controlling the Naor as a threat, not on nurturing an alliance against a greater threat."

Of course. The council had plentiful reasons to support the choice of a new queen, but only a few Altenerai knew the true danger Leonara still posed.

They passed the duty desk, returning the salute from third-ranker Welahn as he stood at attention. Like so many, he'd fought with distinction and was deserving of commendation and possibly promotion. Elenai glanced at N'lahr as they moved on. "I've been meaning to ask, sir," she said, surprised at how in her nervousness she was switching to more formal address.

N'lahr looked at her sidelong, arching an eyebrow.

"I'd like to recommend Elik for a promotion. As well as Derahd."

"I already promoted Elik to the sixth rank," N'lahr said.

"Oh. Where did you send him last night?"

"To organize the dispatch of mounts along the Darassan Way."

N'lahr didn't explain the obvious—much of the Darassan army had been dispatched to Alantris. He wanted its cavalry returned as soon as possible to monitor their Naor allies, and to speed their progress had put someone competent in charge of arranging fresher horses along their route.

N'lahr returned to the central topic. "Submit the names of others you wish to recommend for promotion or commendation to Squire Welahn. I've made him secretary for now. We'll be pressed for time. You may want to dictate letters."

Elenai was flabbergasted by the realization that as an alten she could, indeed, dictate to a squire rather than struggle with ink stains on her fingers and drips on her parchment.

"You're so good at this." She sighed. "How do you always know the right path?"

N'lahr favored her with a brief smile. "I had wise counsel. I will do my best to provide the same to you."

She nodded her thanks, deciding against reiterating he would be better with the crown. "There's one other thing I've been curious about," she said, as they headed deeper into the palace. She wanted to ask how he was feeling, whether he'd had any more ill effects of his years of hearthstone imprisonment.

"What's that?"

She decided not to pry about that subject, and turned to another. "Where are the other three sixth rankers?"

"Oradai remains in command in Ekhem. Enada left the other two to safeguard Kanesh when she rode for Alantris with most of the realm's cavalry."

Those choices made sense. The Naor frequently probed the border of Kanesh. She imagined all three of the officers would forever regret not participating in the recent battles, just as sure as she knew any veterans would tell them they should count themselves fortunate.

Brevahn sat in the morning room, aptly named for the wide windows looking east over a garden resplendent with bright rows of yellow and red tulips. He rose from his amber-shaded chair and bowed. Elenai opted on a formal inclination of her head, as she'd seen queens in stage plays do.

Brevahn wore loose dark pants tucked into buffed black boots, and a long-sleeved beige shirt. He'd carefully brushed his dark, gray-streaked hair, trimmed to the nape of his neck. Though his light brown eyes were bagged from lack of sleep or an excess of worry, they were piercingly alert.

"Ah, Alten Elenai," he said. "Thank you for agreeing to see me."

"I'm sorry to have kept you waiting." Elenai wasn't sure how to explain the averted hostage crisis upstairs.

"I'm sure there are many pressing concerns." Brevahn gave his attention to N'lahr, apparently untroubled by his presence. "Commander, let me commend you upon engineering our victory yesterday. I shall never forget your arrival, a miracle from beyond the grave. Your orders were clear, clever, and certain. You saved the city. You saved our people."

N'lahr accepted the praise with a grave nod. "That is kind. The day was won through a thousand different decisions and sacrifices made by its defenders."

"Of course. But you would be blamed if the defense had failed and you should accept credit for its success."

"I will allow some." N'lahr smoothly changed subjects. "You posted charges against Alten Kyrkenall, and I'm aware of pending charges against both Alten Rylin and Alten Varama. I hope the council will see fit to dropping those immediately."

"Ah. Yes. We received the letters of testimony you sealed with Governor Verena in Arappa. Very compelling. A floor discussion was scheduled for later this week, but as the charges were approved in their current state by a full quorum of the city council, we really need a majority of twelve to rescind them." He turned up his hands. "We only have three surviving members."

He continued in a more conciliatory tone. "I'm confident my remaining colleagues will agree to withdrawal, and that a new council could be seated in a matter of weeks with a queen's support." He checked Elenai for reaction, then, finding none, he smoothly proceeded. "But there's really no danger. No one would dare enforce any order against heroes of the realms in this climate."

"I understand," N'lahr said, "but I'd like you to prioritize an announcement of intent today."

Brevahn chuckled. "I think in this instance the government can be counted upon to act immediately. Now if you don't mind discussion of the Naor problem before us, I've arranged for Alten Elenai to meet the general in the Receiving Room. But I rather thought she'd be wearing something regal."

She hadn't considered dressing differently for this occasion. "They surrendered to her in this uniform," N'lahr said before Elenai could register much embarrassment.

Brevahn considered that for a long moment. "I see your point. They might expect a martial look for our new ruler."

"I'm not the queen." Elenai wondered why she should have to make this clear. "And I don't think I should be representing myself as such under current circumstances."

"The swearing-in is another formality that we must discuss," Brevahn said. "A pity events necessitate a more hastily arranged affair, but—"

"Being sworn in is more than formality," Elenai said, surprised by her own ire. "There's a reason it's considered a sacred ceremony. The throne's a tremendous responsibility lent to the ruler by the people. Assuming it cannot be rushed."

Brevahn smiled. "Your reasoning speaks well of your understanding of the responsibility. But we need an appropriate show of strength and stability before these barbarians."

"This isn't a time for subtlety, Alten Elenai," N'lahr said. "The Naor swore allegiance to you. They need to see that you hold power."

Elenai managed not to sigh. "Very well." She didn't care to be maneuvered against her instincts, but Kyrkenall had advised her to act as a ruler, and she was fairly certain she could depend upon N'lahr's counsel. Brevahn was another matter.

"For how much longer do you intend to remain in the Altenerai ranks?" The councilor asked politely.

She'd been dreading that question, and her response was sharper than she intended. "I've no intention of leaving until the current crisis is resolved. Perhaps not even then."

"I'm not sure that's appropriate," the councilor said.

"That's a discussion for another time," Elenai insisted, firmly polite.

Brevahn inclined his head ever so slightly, then ably shifted to a different topic. "As to these Naor, they need to be escorted from our land as quickly as possible. I understand that they're under watch, but even if the bulk remain in their camp, a few could slip into Darassus some nightfall and do any number of terrible things. We must keep the people safe. So, how can we organize their exodus?"

Elenai looked to N'lahr for guidance. He nodded once, imperceptibly, as if she knew how to answer.

After a brief hesitation, she supposed that she did. "We can't risk a confrontation with the Naor before our army returns from Alantris, and that's several days from now. We have to keep the Naor close, because we may need their help against the queen."

Brevahn's brows rose. "You're joking." He looked to N'lahr. "She's joking, isn't she?"

"Not in the least," N'lahr replied.

"You'd send Naor against our own queen? That smacks of . . . well, it doesn't seem appropriate. Can't the Altenerai simply arrest her?"

"That's what we'd prefer, but it won't be easy," Elenai said. "The queen has most of the hearthstones." Belatedly Elenai realized he might not have been briefed on the artifacts. "You're aware of those?"

"I've been informed. They're a kind of magical energy source." Again he looked to N'lahr.

"There's more to it than that," Elenai continued. "Those hearthstones the queen took had been stabilizing our realms and without them the storms are stronger and the lands are weakening. She plans to assemble the hearthstones in a certain order, then activate them; the queen and her followers believe that will summon an old goddess to remake the realms in a perfected state, but we think she's going to trigger a huge magical backlash—one so powerful it will destroy the realms."

"You're serious?" Brevahn's voice rose in consternation. "I knew the queen was slipping into some sort of nonconventional religious zealotry, but you're suggesting she's completely lost her mind."

"She *has* lost her mind," Elenai said.

Brevahn's poise had been shattered. His intent shifted, finally, from the Naor. "What are you doing to stop this madness?"

"We're trying to learn where she's gone," Elenai answered. "As soon as we know, we'll stop her."

Brevahn stared a moment longer. "This explains why you're less focused on containing the Naor."

"We can provide more details to you and the other councilors later today," Elenai suggested.

"That would be wise," Brevahn agreed. "If the Naor must remain, then surely there are some steps you mean to take to protect our people from them."

"Until the army returns, careful diplomacy is the best way to keep them in line," Elenai said.

"You're going to count upon the Naor to protect us from themselves?" Brevahn sounded as though Elenai had gone as mad as the queen.

"Essentially, yes."

Brevahn again checked with N'lahr. He indicated Elenai with a shift of his hand.

"Councilor, we're not going to take anything for granted," she explained. "We'll watch them carefully. But we believe the Naor leader will have every reason to stay in our good graces."

"And why would that be?"

Elenai had doubts of her own about that, but answered him confidently. "The Naor have sworn allegiance. They will be loyal so long as we lead them to victories."

"Alten Elenai will reinforce that they must follow our laws to follow her," N'lahr added.

Brevahn pressed his lips into a thin line. "This is a dangerous experiment, for dangerous times. I will not oppose your efforts, at least for now. But I won't be the only one losing sleep with those murderers at our gates, and it's only a matter of time before some incident shatters what little peace is left."

"We will act with care, but with speed," Elenai assured him. She gestured toward the door. "Shall we be on with it?"

Brevahn did not move. "We've yet to discuss when you'll be sworn in." He held up a hand as she started to object. "I realize that many matters demand attention, but that is precisely why I feel your coronation should be sooner rather than later. We need the succession settled."

Elenai wasn't sure how to answer, so prevaricated. "Perhaps when the matter with the queen is resolved." That, at least, would buy her time to act as queen until the danger was over, and then step aside.

"That leaves too nebulous a time course," Brevahn objected. "What if the efforts against Queen Leonara stretch on for longer than you anticipate? The government cannot long function without properly appointed officeholders."

Much as she disliked his reasoning, Elenai understood that Brevahn was fundamentally correct. She wasn't sure how to answer. Fortunately, N'lahr stepped in.

"Wisely said," the commander replied. "And something to discuss, soon. But not at this juncture."

"Let us make plans later today. But for now, you're right—we should see to the Naor." The councilor motioned her to precede him.

She entered the receiving room through a door hidden behind a curtain slightly ahead of the raised dais holding a single chair of dark wood. Two attendants were unrolling a blue carpet from the foot of the dais to the double doors sixty feet on. Blue curtains slashed with gold hung along either side of the narrow room.

N'lahr had briefly excused himself, but the councilor remained beside her as she contemplated her future. Elenai had seen the chamber, and this chair, but never supposed she'd sit in it. Its back was straight, with embroidered azure cushions and golden arms that flared as they swept forward.

She walked to its side. This, she thought, has come too easily, and I've accepted it with too little question. How soon did she want to step down from the Altenerai? Never? Altenara had led her warriors and remained queen, so there was some precedent. But then, lacking a hearthstone, perhaps it would be better to allow some more competent candidate to take her place as one of the Altenerai. She shook her head at herself. And do more of this? Already she disliked the thought of meetings with dignitaries and difficult choices like passing judgment upon aspirants and exalts.

She would have to worry about that later. Now the Naor had to see a ruler on the throne. She reminded herself of Asrahn's constant advice to focus on the moment. Regardless of what she planned for the future, she had to project dignity and power to maintain the strange alliance. And while she had no experience being a ruler, long familiarity with the stage would serve her well. She had witnessed her father guide actors through the portrayal of queens, kings, and governors, coaching them to sit with dignity, listen attentively, and weigh the words of those speaking as if they didn't know their coming lines. Think before you speak, he'd said, even if you already know the answer.

The palace servants finished unrolling the rug and presented themselves with formal curtseys. They were calm, middle-aged women in blue gowns. One stepped forward and asked if she required anything.

"Not just now," Elenai answered. Feeling like a child playing dress-up, she lowered herself into the chair and bent to adjust a pant leg. She was undoing the lower hooks of her khalat so it would hang better when N'lahr returned, presenting himself with a formal bow. Kyrkenall would have somehow managed sarcasm in the action. N'lahr was deadly serious, which, for some reason, annoyed her.

"Stop that," she said.

"You look as though you belong there," he said.

"So might anyone, seated here."

"No," N'lahr said. "I don't think so."

"Nor do I." Brevahn bowed with an arm flourish. "Did you know it is customary for the Altenerai commander to be the first to bow to a new queen?"

She remembered now, and she bowed her head in return, startled that she should play a part in reenacting the famed moment when Meraht bowed to Queen Altenara.

"For now, during this audience, I will refer to you as Your Majesty," Brevahn said. "Our visitor won't understand the finer points of our politics."

"Understood."

"There's one last thing," N'lahr said. "We have two visitors, not one. The general's brought an advisor: the sorcerer we fought at the Battle of Vedessus."

Elenai's eyebrows rose, for she remembered that mage's power, and how certain she'd been that one more attack from him would have finished her.

"Do you think we are in any danger from his magics?" the councilor asked.

Elenai didn't think that had been N'lahr's point at all. He had merely meant to prepare her for surprises.

"No."

She settled into the chair and placed her hands upon its arms. "Let's get this meeting under way."

N'lahr signaled to the servants, who'd taken positions by the distant doors. They took hold of the polished handles rising vertically along the dark wood, then pulled upon them, their timing so exquisite that both moved at the same rate of speed at the same moment.

A third attendant opened her hands to the waiting Naor. "Welcome, visitors. Please follow me." She then pivoted with precision that would have earned a grunt of appreciation from Asrahn himself, and started down the blue carpet for the throne.

Trailing her were two figures. Vannek, in brown leggings and black lacquered armor. Her—no, his, she needed to remember that—waist and hips and chest were well-concealed by his thick garments. His right ear was bandaged. Straight brown hair framed his beardless, comely features.

The other person, two steps behind and on Vannek's right, was the man she'd last seen staring at her in the moments after N'lahr had slain Mazakan. He was blue-eyed, bearded, with receding brown hair with a hint of red. He wore a red robe, belted in black.

The palace servant halted eight paces out from the dais, lowering her left hand, gently emphasizing that was where visitors should stop. She glided to the right, where she stood motionless beside one of the curtains.

While the mage bowed from the waist and opened his scarred palms, the general met Elenai's gaze with cool appraisal before turning in open curiosity to N'lahr.

The mage addressed Elenai as he straightened. "We bid you greeting, Majesty," he said, his tone warmly formal. "And you as well, Commander N'lahr. You Altenerai are a constant source of surprise."

"We could say the same of the Naor," Elenai replied. "We welcome you to these halls. How are you called?"

"I am Coadjuter Muragan, of the Red Horn Mountains. And this is Lord General Vannek, grandson of Great Mazakan."

At mention of that name, Elenai struggled to maintain a neutral expression. Mazakan was responsible for untold thousands of murders, rapes, kidnappings, thefts, and destruction of property, along with countless other crimes.

Confronting his descendant now, the strength of her hatred for the Naor burned like a living fire in the depths of her heart. A steely tone she hadn't intended entered her voice. "You know Commander N'lahr and myself. With us is Councilor Brevahn. We want to make sure that you understood our missive last night. You must swear that you and your people will obey our laws, or there can be no peace."

The general bowed his head, as if expecting this. Muragan answered in his place. "The Lord General has read carefully, including your outline of major laws, and affirms his understanding. His wish is for peace between our people, and for stability and security for his followers as well as yours."

"What does the general himself say?" Elenai asked.

Muragan looked to his leader, who remained silent for a moment, then raised a hand to the mage. His voice proved gruff, his manner blunt. "My people need to know they have not been tricked. That they are not prisoners."

"They are not prisoners," Elenai said. "They're allies."

"We are watched," Vannek said. "We are guarded. You and I, we know trust will take time. But my soldiers are unsettled."

"They need to see some other gesture," Muragan said.

"A gesture," Elenai repeated. "Your soldiers invaded our land and killed our people. And they want a gesture?"

"This was a contest." Vannek sounded confused. "Both of us strove our utmost, and your side won."

"It was a contest we didn't ask for. And if we won a contest, what are our spoils?"

"Your spoils are our warriors," Vannek said, dismay at something so obvious clear in his voice. "They are ready to fight for you. Come, tell them what you plan for them."

Elenai tried to decide what someone wise might answer, and noticed the sharp look N'lahr gave her. He was trying to warn her. He'd said the Naor general might be worried about the security of his command, and she'd lost sight of that. She wondered how to shift to a more reassuring tone.

Then Muragan provided an opening. "The Lord General intends to aid your fight against the old queen."

She should not have been startled the Naor knew that.

Vannek wasted no time expanding on that idea. "You wish a swift strike? Your soldiers and mine can mount the land treaders and take the battle to her. And there is more. Muragan is restoring one of the dragons you downed in the battle over the plains. It will be yours to command."

Elenai had wondered what other surprises she'd learn about.

N'lahr spoke. "When do you expect your dragon to recover?"

The general looked to his mage, who answered. "It's hard to know, Commander. It may require some days yet."

"When will you launch your attack?" Vannek pressed.

Elenai had no intention of revealing that the Altenerai had no schedule because they hadn't learned how to reach the queen. "We're finalizing our plans." She regarded Vannek, standing proud and impatient. Much as she disliked the idea of treating with the blood of Mazakan, it would be far easier to work with these new allies if they were held in check by a leader with whom she could actually maintain a dialogue. "Are you prepared to receive Alten Rylin today so he can accustom your men to our horn calls and maneuvers?"

"His instruction is welcome," Vannek said. "We're allies now and must move together."

"Our allies do not use blood magic," Elenai said. "How was your dragon saved?"

After a short pause, Vannek inclined his head. "I see your concern. Muragan had already begun the process before we received your note. But no man, woman, or child was injured in his sorcery."

"You used blood from the conjured beasts, then," N'lahr speculated.

The mage answered. "And another dragon, dying. Yes."

"Your Majesty, black magic should not be permissible in the five realms," Brevahn said with disdain.

Elenai lifted the fingers of her hand on the chair arm, and that small, controlled gesture stilled everyone. The reaction surprised and pleased her. "Will more blood magic be required to finish its healing?"

"Yes," Muragan answered.

"I will permit it," Elenai said, wondering if she had agreed too quickly. "In the future, take no magical actions, especially involving blood magic, without prior consent."

"If that is your wish," Vannek said with obvious reluctance.

"It is. Now if you think it will be good for morale, notify your troops I will speak with them this afternoon."

"Good," Vannek said, and then, as if aware that he had not sounded the least bit deferential, bowed his head. "Troops should know their ruler."

"I agree." Elenai was acutely conscious of Brevahn at her shoulder and guessed that he would want her to talk about the Naor presence over the long term. Now might not be the time for specifics, but surely she should introduce the topic. "Over the next days we'll have to discuss your plans for the future."

"I tire of Naor realms," Vannek said. "Your people have resources mine do not. It seems to me you might share some of your land with allies."

"Out of the question," Brevahn said quietly, but not so quietly it could not be heard throughout the room.

Elenai felt a similar sentiment. N'lahr stirred beside her, but she guessed what he would advise. "We might welcome allies in our homelands," she said, then paused for a moment while she organized her thoughts. "But only if they can truly follow our customs. I would want it clear that you and your people understand them." How to explain culture to a Naor? "For example, women have an equal place in any society that exists within our realms, and the vulnerable are protected."

"I'm certain we can have many thought-provoking discussions on the subject," Muragan said. "But the customs of our people will be unlikely to shift quickly."

"I mean to shift them," Vannek said doggedly. "But Muragan is right. It will not be a simple matter."

Elenai appreciated the honest answers. On reflection, she saw that both had been forthright with all of their requests as well as their intentions. Just as her chamber had been illuminated this morning when she parted a curtain, she understood with incredible clarity that ensuring Vannek's command over his people wasn't just preferred, it was crucial. The Naor general was uniquely suited to bring their people together, and despite herself, she sensed a growing rapport. Until that moment she had thought of the Naor as an irritating necessity. Now she perceived a whole range of possibilities that had never before existed.

Placed along the border, Vannek's tribe could be an excellent buffer against foreign raiding that would almost certainly resume. And a Naor settlement that prospered without slaves and without the strong preying upon the weak might inspire changes among the external Naor, maybe even lessening their incentives for conquest.

"We have much more to discuss over the coming days," Elenai said. Waxing optimistic, she decided to put words to her hope. "Though centuries of distrust lie between us, let the two of us pledge to work for a future that will better both of our peoples."

Vannek's expression softened ever so slightly. "If you promise to treat my soldiers with the care you treat your own, then I will swear this with you."

"I swear it," Elenai said. "By my ring." She raised her left hand, showing her knuckles to the general, and set her sapphire glowing.

Vannek lifted his own hand, then smote his breastplate above his heart. "Then I swear it by my blood."

"So be it. I'll visit this afternoon, on the third bell."

Vannek looked as though he planned to say more, then stopped, and Elenai realized that a squire had entered from the side door and waited with a note. It was Derahd, the second ranker she'd stood the wall with yesterday. He started to smile at her, then the apparent gravity of the moment struck and he grew rigidly serious, aware he was a lowly soldier in the presence of the mighty.

While she would never encourage fraternization among the ranks, Elenai resolved then and there she would never permit full formality between herself and those who'd defended Darassus with her yesterday, and returned a slight, answering smile. He brightened, and she returned her attention to the Naor.

"We will receive you with honor," Vannek said, then offered a short bow.

Elenai responded with what she hoped was a regal nod.

An uncomfortable moment followed while she and the general looked back and forth at one other. Elenai wasn't certain how to conclude the meeting.

N'lahr signaled to the lead servant, who bowed with great formality to Elenai, then walked to the Naor and gestured toward the door.

Muragan presented a formal bow, and then both the general and the mage followed the servant for the double doors opening before them.

"Your pardon," N'lahr said, and stepped over to Derahd, who saluted and then spoke softly to the commander.

Elenai waited until the door shut behind the Naor before climbing to her feet and stretching sore shoulders, watching N'lahr's face as he listened to the report. The commander's head rose, his expression clearing, by which she understood the news had been good. Derahd's delight was easier to read, though he quickly subdued his own grin. He then saluted N'lahr and bowed formally to Elenai.

Brevahn spoke to her as the squire departed. "You aren't really going to give the Naor any of our lands, are you?"

"If we're going to civilize them, we need to keep them close to our civilization, don't we?" While Brevahn stared fish-mouthed at her, N'lahr rejoined her and spoke before the councilor could object further.

"Varama has arrived. She thinks she knows how to reach the queen."

8

Chamber of the Ring

Y ou must forgive us," Elenai said to a discomfited Councilor Brevahn. "I'll send word to you after the meeting."

"Please do," he said. "We have much more to discuss before you address the Naor general and her troops."

"His," N'lahr corrected on his way out the door.

Elenai realized it would take some effort on her own part to get that gender tag right. At sight of Brevahn's furrowing brow she decided to make clear she wanted his advice. "Give the wording I need to use some thought. I'll welcome your ideas."

"I appreciate that. And we've still to discuss a timetable for your swearing in and formal coronation."

She nodded once as though the thought of that conversation wasn't cringe inducing, then raised a hand in farewell and followed the commander.

She caught up to N'lahr in the hallway, matching his long strides as they passed paintings and banners from the history of the five realms.

"Nicely handled," the commander said. "With both the Naor and the councilor. You should be wary of both, though."

"I don't think I fully reassured either."

"Command is a challenging path."

They arrived at the statue of a stern bronze woman in armor guarding dark paneled double doors. N'lahr paused to return the statue's salute and Elenai repeated the gesture, temporarily overwhelmed. It had been a long morning, and now, like all Altenerai who'd come after Altenara's death, she was saluting the queen's life-size image. While Elenai was fully a member of the corps the long-dead queen had founded, she had never participated in this particular ritual.

She studied the monarch's somber features. Here, from across the centuries, she beheld her predecessor, both queen and alten. She felt an intense and unexpected kinship for the young-looking woman, and worried that she might be her mirror image. Rather than a queen who became alten, launched the corps, and founded the realms, she might be the alten who became queen, and oversaw the final days not only of the corps, but the kingdom itself.

No. She had learned about the foundations Altenara had laid, and the trials she had endured to strengthen her fragile alliance, and came more fully to attention. "I will not let you down," she vowed, as much to herself as her corps' namesake. Then she followed N'lahr through the double doors.

She had wrangled permission to be part of the chamber's cleanup crew when she was a second ranker, so the six-sided room with its wood-paneled walls and high stained glass wasn't a novelty to her. That didn't change the honor she felt to be entering as a member for the first time.

Light streamed through multihued windows below the ceiling dome, five of them illuminating beautifully wrought landscapes from each of the realms, the remaining window of opaque beveled panes decorated with a shining sapphire beneath a slender silver crown, symbolizing the Altenerai Corps and the authority of the queen.

Below those windows sat a hexagonal table, three chairs on each side for each of the five realms, and another trio reserved at the head for the Master of Squires, the Altenerai commander, and the queen. Seventeen seats meant for Altenerai in all. She wondered how long it had been since that many were seated here. Not since the early days of Renik's command, probably.

On the left, Kyrkenall hunched forward in his chair, speaking earnestly with Varama. Elenai couldn't recall the last time she'd seen the tall, spare alten in uniform. Though it was easy to remember Varama's skin held a bluish tint, upon seeing her, that tone was always more subtle than she recalled. The older woman had pushed back her unruly curling hair so that her high forehead was even more prominent. Her face was lined with worry and fatigue.

N'lahr spoke with two squires by a side door. One was the third ranker Welahn, holding a sheaf of papers, pen, and ink bottle. The other carried a portable desk and chair. After a moment the squires saluted and set up to the right of the central door.

Elenai was of Arappa, so it only made sense she occupy one of the three seats at that side of table. She approached a chair one section over from where Rylin and Thelar were completing a tense exchange under the stained glass of Erymyr. Thelar nodded gravely to her and stepped away. Rylin smiled with a trace of his old charm. "Hail."

"Hail, Alten Rylin."

As N'lahr lowered himself into the commander's chair, the others shuffled into their seats.

"'Well met is well meant, for good is the order.'" N'lahr used a well-known quote from an Altenerai legend. The answering tones of "Hail, Altenerai" rang through the hall, with particular gusto from Kyrkenall.

"This is all of us in Darassus," N'lahr said. "Tretton and Gyldara are en route. Enada commands the recovery forces in Alantris. And Cerai has left us, in word and deed. I've invited Exalt Thelar to join us, as he'll figure prominently in the plans we make. Varama has vital information in forming those plans, but we have a few important details to manage first."

He paused, and the moment stretched on longer than was comfortable. Elenai wondered if he was having another spell where time had slowed for him. Just as she was readying to ask, he continued. "I'm told my predecessor dispensed with note-taking. So I've no idea how many meetings have been called during my absence. I propose this be counted as Meeting One of our new era, in the name not of the queen who abandoned us, but for memory of Queen Altenara. What say you?"

A chorus of ayes answered as the squire in the corner scribbled furiously.

"Next," N'lahr continued, "we must welcome Alten Elenai Dartaan to the table. She has never sat in this company before."

She felt herself blush as she was greeted officially by her assembled comrades.

As N'lahr readied to resume, Thelar cleared his throat. "Commander, if I may." The exalt rose from a chair he'd taken beneath the stained glass of The Fragments, lovely green mountains cut by a shining blue river.

N'lahr arched an eyebrow at the interruption.

"Please forgive me," the exalt said with formal dignity. He placed a hand on the table, then lifted it to reveal a sapphire ring. "Alten Rylin presented this ring to me prior to our confrontation with the queen, so that I might be better protected against her. I wish to return it so it may be passed on to a worthy candidate."

Rylin watched glumly.

"You are Commander of our Mage Auxiliary, Thelar," N'lahr said. "If Rylin trusts you enough to provide such a tool, I will not gainsay him. He granted it to you during a time of crisis. That time is hardly over."

The exalt bowed his head solemnly and Elenai understood he had been deeply moved. He closed his hand over the ring and returned it to a belt pouch.

N'lahr then praised the fallen squires and Altenerai. Surprisingly, he mentioned Denaven as well. "It's fitting we honor him, not for who he had become, but because he risked his life untold times for the safety of the realms in the last war."

Elenai expected a sly word from Kyrkenall, but the archer remained silent.

"Finally, the fate of one of our missing was ascertained by Altens Kyrkenall and Elenai." N'lahr looked across the table to his best friend.

"Aye," Kyrkenall said with a solemnity uncharacteristic of him. "Elenai and I came to a place the kobalin had declared holy because they worship a war god who fell there." He set a sapphire ring on the table before him. "They were paying homage to Commander Renik. He fell in battle against more than sixty kobalin, most of them lords, and he's lain there ever since."

There was no missing the sharp intake of breath from one side of the room. It had come from the famously emotionless Varama. Her change in affect was subtle, but for her such demonstrative emotion was tantamount to wailing with hands pressed to eyes.

"We recovered his ring," Kyrkenall continued, "but we couldn't retrieve his remains."

"It must be done," Varama said. Elenai had forgotten how high and remote her voice was.

"Yes," Kyrkenall agreed. Once more he offered an empty hand. "We've a long to-do list."

"We will make time to properly honor all the dead," N'lahr said. "And we will take time to honor the survivors, and rebuild the corps. But now we must focus on proximal threats. Yesterday, Leonara fled with close to thirty followers and an immense supply of hearthstones. Exalt Thelar predicts she will be capable of opening them within the next four days. If she does, the result will almost certainly be catastrophic. She has to be found, and she has to be stopped. Rylin, have you had a chance to brief Varama?"

"Yes, in the essentials."

"I was able to examine the keystone for a short time before it was stolen by Cerai," Varama said. Elenai wondered if she always sounded slightly sad like this, and if she'd somehow missed it before. "I therefore know how to reach the Lost Realm, and I agree that it is Leonara's likely location." The lanky alten rested a hand on the table, and Elenai noticed that the tip of one of her long fingers was missing. "The journey will require many days travel below the realm of Erymyr."

"Below?" Thelar asked curiously.

"It's possible to travel 'sideways' through the shifts," Varama explained, unperturbed. "The trick is knowing the precise character of your destination."

"And do you?" N'lahr asked.

"I don't have to. It should be possible to detect even inactive hearthstones in the immense mass that Leonara has conveniently gathered, providing we know which general direction to search in."

"You mean extending our spirits all the way to this Lost Realm?" Rylin asked.

"Exactly." Varama looked as though she were about to speak further, but fell silent and stared at a space below Ekhem's window.

Elenai's arm hairs pricked up, along with those on the back of her neck. Her ring flared blue, as did those of all the Altenerai at the table.

Rialla appeared beside Kyrkenall, her image washed out, as though she stood in bright sunlight.

Kyrkenall shoved his chair away from the table and regarded the ghostly figure beside him with wide eyes.

Rialla's voice echoed around the hall. It seemed to originate from somewhere other than her moving lips. "N'lahr, is this when you're trying to find Queen Leonara?"

N'lahr stared in level regard before answering. "It is."

"The queen's readying to unbind them all, near the pool of seven statues. It's on the map. Strike tonight and you will fail. Delay for three noons, and you arrive when the Goddess wakes. That is too late."

N'lahr opened his mouth as if to make inquiry, but Rialla continued before he could.

"You find them in three groups upon the hills beyond the statues, where they have built the Goddess. Striking it will complicate their efforts. If your attack is a surprise the queen will be delayed. I open the way outside Darassus's central gates at second dawn. Then you appear in a field beyond the hills, so your horses can build speed. Deploy a small force as only sixty-six can be moved. Spread out so she cannot catch all in a single blow. Bring mages to shut the hearthstones as they brighten."

"I understand," N'lahr said.

Elenai was glad someone did.

"How many times have you done this?" Varama asked her.

"What about Kalandra?" Kyrkenall asked at the same time.

But Rialla had already vanished as abruptly as she'd appeared. Elenai wasn't surprised to hear Kyrkenall swear.

"She's never good about answering questions," Elenai said in the confused silence.

"That was Rialla?" Thelar asked. "I know what you said last night, but she's been dead for more than ten years."

"What I don't understand is why sometimes she appears in my dreams, and sometimes in person," Elenai said.

Varama fixed her with that penetrating gaze. "When's the most recent time you spoke with her?"

"She appeared late last night. In person again, and didn't seem familiar with the idea of talking to me in dreams. She tried to warn me Kyrkenall needed to jump left. But he'd already done that. She doesn't seem to be able to keep track of when she's spoken with me and what she's said."

"Interesting," Varama said.

"Something?" N'lahr extended his hand to her.

As Varama pursed her lips, Kyrkenall scooted his chair back to the table. "If you've got some kind of explanation, I'd love to hear it."

"I don't like to speculate," Varama said.

"Is it possible she's not dead?" Kyrkenall's voice held a hopeful note, much as it had this morning. "That she's trapped somewhere like N'lahr was, and that she's projecting herself?"

Varama answered carefully. "I think something else more likely."

Kyrkenall frowned. "You're deliberately drawing this out."

"No; I wish to be certain none of you take my explanation for flawless deduction. I have been wrong in the past because I lacked information. For instance, while I correctly deduced you were innocent of Asrahn's murder, I incorrectly predicted you would ride for Alantris because I did not know you would find N'lahr alive, or that you would chance upon a Naor invasion, then ride off to fight for Arappa."

Kyrkenall spun his hand in the air to suggest accelerating her narrative.

"Very well. I will first lay out facts for those not present for the events. Rialla was attacked during the first battle of Alantris and thought to have been mortally wounded when assaulted by the projected spirits of multiple Naor mages. Her body lived without her spirit for just over six hours, which exceeds by two hours more the length of time any other known person has managed to survive after a similar accident. Kalandra monitored her, and confided to me that she was certain Rialla tried to return no less than three times. Though her body should simply have lain comatose until overtaken by death, she did not remain completely still."

"I was there, too," Kyrkenall asserted. "I saw the same thing."

Varama continued: "Kalandra was a keen observer, a shrewd woman, and a reliable witness. If we assume her observations were accurate, Rialla was, in fact, still connected to her body. Either she was unable to take possession of it, owing to damage wrought to her connection by the attack of the Naor mages, or she chose not to repossess it for some reason."

"Why would she do that?" Kyrkenall asked.

"Let her finish," N'lahr suggested.

Kyrkenall sighed dramatically.

Varama resumed. "Rialla did remain connected to the hearthstone, and Kalandra likewise reported she felt certain Rialla drew energy from it even though her spirit was absent."

"Do you think she was coming back for spell energy?" Rylin asked.

Thelar nodded. "Could she have been creating some kind of powerful magical duplicate of herself? One that's been activated somehow?"

Elenai hadn't conceived of that and looked to Varama for an answer. She recalled that Rialla had sometimes squired with Alten Varama.

"Those are interesting ideas," Varama said. "While Rialla was certainly working spells it is doubtful she created a duplicate. Illusory magic was never her forte. I believe we have just encountered exactly what she was doing. What she *is* doing."

"What was that?" Kyrkenall demanded, impatient.

"For those six hours, she was throwing herself forward and trying to preserve her friends and the five realms."

For a long moment, everyone was silent. Elenai struggled and failed to understand how a spell like that might work, even as she admitted to herself Varama's explanation fitted much of what she'd seen from Rialla.

"You're saying she's jumping in time?" Kyrkenall asked finally.

"Yes."

He scoffed. "If she can do that, why can't she just go back and, I don't know, kill the queen or Mazakan or something."

Varama shook her head. "She seems only capable of limited insight into the future, or she'd be more precise. Hence her difficulties in communication with Elenai. To us, it might seem as though she has all the intervening years to play with. But she doesn't. She only has those six hours of life, which are advancing for her spirit regardless of her location in time."

Kyrkenall let out a low oath.

Thelar broke the ensuing silence. "That's an interesting theory. But it does seem there are more effective things she could have done."

"She had only six hours," Varama repeated. "To look at every moment that matters up until the world ended which, I imagine, is what she saw first. Or perhaps she glimpsed the many ways Kyrkenall might die. Either way, she has been working backward from those moments, trying to nudge us into a future that doesn't end in disaster, or the death of her closest friend."

Elenai saw at last what Rialla must have been working for, again and again. Having occasionally seen branching realities when she herself glimpsed flashes of the future, she could imagine Rialla walking countless labyrinths of possibility to see how a dire moment might be undone. And if she really had only six hours as she lay dying a decade ago, her hurried manner made much more sense.

In sorrowful awe, Elenai understood who and what she'd been dealing with for the last few months. Rialla was no terrifying entity from beyond the grave, or an all-knowing oracle. She possessed astounding abilities, it was true, but at heart she was only a frightened young woman, awarded the ring earlier in the day before frantically struggling to preserve her people through vague glimpses of terrible futures.

"Damn." Kyrkenall said softly. "So Rialla really is dead."

"Long ago," Varama agreed, "but not yet. She saw the queen's intent and spent the rest of her hours attempting to unravel it. She sacrificed herself to save us. And the realms, and the outer lands. Everything."

"Is there anything we can do to help her?" Elenai asked.

"If I can communicate with her even for a few moments to gain additional information, we may be able to improve the odds that her great sacrifice will not have been in vain."

"So why does she appear in waking hours sometimes and in dreams at others?" Elenai asked.

"She may be saving her greatest energy for when she's needed most. Or perhaps you're seeing her visits out of your chronological order, before it occurred to her she might save energy by speaking to you in dreams. I can't say with certainty."

N'lahr rapped the table. "I'm loathe to trust our victory to someone who can't explain her methods, but . . . if Varama's right, Rialla has already gone so far above and beyond her duty I have no right to question her process." He looked at his charges. "We will select our troops and be prepared for battle two mornings hence."

"That means Tretton and Gyldara can't get here in time," Rylin said.

Not to mention the Erymyran army and Kaneshi cavalry they led. Elenai hadn't realized how far out they still were. She looked to N'lahr.

"That's why it's good that we have some help from the Naor," the commander said. Naturally he'd already noticed the problem, for he sounded unperturbed. "For now, let's adjourn to the map room and discuss tactics. I think I know the depiction Rialla referenced."

Thelar raised his hand. "Commander, if we attack the statue of the Goddess there will be another discharge, like the one that brought down the Naor dragon in the arena."

Elenai was impressed the exalt had managed to fix on that problem during the flow of information.

"I have the answer for that," N'lahr said. "With Rialla acting as our scout, we now have a leg up. Let's plan a victory."

9

The Third Matter

Vannek passed a goblet to Rylin, standing near the tent's central fire, then eyed his own as if seeing the gaudy jewels decorating the silver cup for the first time.

The Naor leader looked up at him after a moment, full lips almost prim with distaste. Still he didn't speak for a time, and Rylin took in the whole of the tent, its fire beneath the circular hole in the roof, its small but well-carved wooden cabinet, the rug, and two canvas partitions.

"All of this was my brother's," Vannek said, as if in apology. He then pointed to the entrance with his free hand and Rylin turned to see the guard bow and depart into the twilight, the canvas flap falling behind him.

"Chargan?" Rylin asked.

"Yes, Chargan." Vannek drank again. "My younger brother, Koregan, wouldn't have cared for any of this. Do you have brothers?"

"I have one."

"Is he a squire?"

Rylin laughed. "No, my brother builds boats. So does my sister."

Vannek tried and failed to disguise his curiosity, and studied Rylin as though he sought hidden meaning. He had pretty eyes; no matter the broken nose and ill-fitting garb, Rylin found him attractive.

Vannek drank deep. "Your evenings are hot here."

This one was, particularly. But then they'd spent all afternoon in the sun as Rylin introduced the Naor troops to Altenerai signaling methods. The wine was fruity and crisp, and Rylin drank almost all of it down, saving only a little for a later sip. He didn't want to relax too much. "Summer's nearly here," he said.

"When you say that they build boats, you mean that your family pays people to build them, don't you?"

"No, they build them. They pay some employees to help. Why are you so interested?"

"I want to know about your people. So how did your family benefit from your change in status?"

He puzzled over the question. "You mean when I became an alten? They get no special favors."

"What if you had children? Would it be easier for them to become squires?"

"Everyone has to earn their place. The corps takes only the best. That's why we keep kicking your ass."

Vannek's laugh was short and unguarded. Still showing the trace of a smile, the general put his wine on the cabinet and sat down on the camp stool near the fire, pointing to the one nearby.

Rylin took the seat. The flames burned low, and the smoke drifted up through the circular opening at the roof's peak. The fire appeared to have been set solely for a light source.

Vannek planted a hand on his knee and leaned forward. "So then, what's it like to be Altenerai?"

He'd been asked that before, but never by a Naor. His life had been full of firsts lately. How best to explain it? "Have you ever fought and worked for something, then realized when you got there it was different from what you expected?"

"Yes," Vannek answered. "What was different for you?"

"I grew up listening to tales about Kyrkenall and Queen Altenera and Decrin of the Shining Shield. They all sounded carefree, as though they traveled from place to place having adventures and saving people. Their lives were full of excitement."

"Surely you've seen your share of battles and excitement."

"More than I need. It turns out that it's not that much fun to have people depending on you all the time. If you fail, some or all of them could die."

Vannek sat, somber and mysterious, as if processing this information.

"What about you?" Rylin asked. "What did you want from your path?"

He gave Rylin a penetrating stare before speaking. "Do you know, only my father has ever asked me what I wanted. Everyone else just assigned me to some role, either because they had no vision, or because it would further their plans. Marry me to some chieftain, or king. Father was the only one willing to let me choose my own way."

Rylin wondered why he had such a difficult time imagining a Naor parent caring about his child, and recognized some of the barriers that still lay between them. "Your father was Mazakan's son?" he said, regretting how appalled he sounded.

Vannek laughed once. "His favorite son! You'd think Grandfather would like all the ruthless asses who cozied up to him, but Father charted his own way and stood up to Grandfather from the start. Instead of cutting him down to size, Grandfather favored him above all others. If your Temahr hadn't killed my father, things might have been very different."

That killing had brought Temahr's own death; Mazakan himself had slain the alten and worn half his mummified sword hand about his neck for long years. That image stilled an instinctive burst of sympathetic feeling and rendered Rylin mute.

"Is your father a warrior?"

Rylin smiled to hear the suggestion. "My father is a sailmaker. My mother heads our family's shipwright business."

"So ships are in your blood." Vannek eyed him as though he were a puzzle. "Why aren't you a boat builder?"

"My mother saw I had some talent, and encouraged me. When she was younger, she reached the second rank."

"So she was a warrior?"

"Yes." He shrugged. "I was encouraged. I worked hard. And here I am."

"Here you are. Drinking with the grandchild of your greatest enemy."

"These are strange times." Rylin finished his goblet at last, then shook his head when Vannek pointed to the decanter. "I never thought a Naor would be taking notes from me on culture. Or maybe plying me to search for weaknesses."

"A leader always looks for weakness," Vannek admitted. "Given our history, I'd be foolish not to. But I find you Dendressi interesting. A Naor man would be bragging to the moon if his father had once held rank in an elite force like your Altenerai squires. Yet you tell me first about the boats your family builds. Your people have more space in their lives for things other than war. You're not as soft as you're made out to be, but your people aren't as tough as ours overall."

"That depends on how you define 'tough,'" Rylin said.

"Take my warriors as an example. They know their work, don't they?"

"I think they'll do."

"Hah! That almost sounds like a compliment."

"I'll compliment them if they win."

Vannek laughed. Rylin was starting to sense the Naor general liked him in spite of his own instincts. There was still an amused glint in his eye as he pointed at Rylin. "Are the other Altenerai like you?"

"We're all different."

"But could I sit down with them? Like you and I are doing?"

"Some of them," Rylin admitted, thinking of Kyrkenall and Elenai and possibly Enada, whom he knew mostly by reputation.

Vannek quaffed another drink. "I liked your queen's speech to my people yesterday. I like her fire. She looks young and simple, but she's clever, isn't she?"

Rylin had never thought of Elenai as scheming, which is what he thought Vannek implied. "She's kind," Rylin said. "That might come off as young, or naïve, but she wants the best for the people she works with."

"So she's a leader."

"Without question." Rylin smiled, remembering how Elenai had so often given time to work with less seasoned squires.

"Has she always been a powerful mage?"

"I usually heard more about her sword work, until recently."

"I've seen her practice both arts, and she's formidable. Did she learn from N'lahr?"

"She didn't meet Commander N'lahr until she'd been honing her craft for years. She studied under the great Asrahn, just like the commander. And me."

"Asrahn Sword-Father was a legend among our people. He trained two or three generations of your most dangerous warriors. Did your queen really have him killed?"

Rylin hated to answer that. "Yes."

"Why would she do that?"

It took a moment to condense his knowledge into a simple explanation. "It was more important to her to keep secrets than to protect her people. She was a lousy queen."

"And she locked up N'lahr to keep these secrets," Vannek said. He was certainly well informed.

"She did," Rylin confirmed.

"I hear you tried to kill her."

"I felt my blade touch her heart, but she didn't die."

The general's eyes bored into his own, and then he sat back, impressed. "You speak the truth."

"I'm sworn to do that."

"I know about your oaths. In times of war, you're free to lie."

He spoke carefully, meeting Vannek's eyes the while. "To the enemy. You're our ally now, and you ought to know the strengths and weaknesses of our common foe."

"You should have taken her head."

That would have seemed even more brutal than his reluctant attack, but the general did have a point. "I will, next chance I get."

"I believe you mean that," Vannek said with approval. He glanced at the decanter, as if debating whether or not he wanted more, then must have decided against it, for he returned his attention to Rylin. "Tell me about N'lahr."

"What do you want to know?"

"What pushes him? Fame? Power?" Vannek paused. "Love?" he added skeptically.

"He's not that mysterious. He means what he says. He does what he thinks is best for the people he commands, and the people he's protecting. I'm not sure if he thinks about anything except that. It's simple, really."

"Not so simple," Vannek said. "You admire him."

"Yes. And I think you do, too."

"A lot of us have admired him for a long time. That may sound strange."

"He's the best at what he does, but that's really about *all* he does. If you were hoping for some dark secret or weakness, I don't know that there is one."

"What about Varama?"

"That's different."

"She's different. Why is she blue?"

Rylin smiled thinly. Her skin hue was the least important of all her characteristics. "The Gods slept with mortals in the old days, and sometimes that blood turns up in their descendants."

"She beat my brother. Do you know that she shot one of her own rather than let her be taken prisoner?"

Rylin knew that all too well. "Yes."

"You Altenerai *are* tougher than you look. I can see it in your eyes, when you say certain things. Did you really sneak into a meeting with my brother?"

"I did."

"That was bold. Was I there?"

"You were."

Vannek smiled slowly. "You're more cunning than you seem. Elenai's the same way. You are open, but wily at the same time. Is that something else you learned from Asrahn?"

It would take days to impress upon the general all that they had learned from Asrahn, and even then he wasn't sure he could do the man justice. "He taught us to shoot straight and speak the truth."

"I like that."

"It's an old saying."

"Let me ask you about another saying. What's a hastig?"

"Where did you hear that word?"

"It's been shouted by your people when you fight."

Rylin was surprised the general hadn't ever had it explained before. "A hastig is someone who doesn't know their birth mother."

"And that's an insult for your people?"

"Well, yes."

"Because the lineage of both parents is important to you," Vannek reasoned out. "That makes sense."

"You shouldn't be surprised."

"Is there anything that surprises you about us?"

"In a good way?" Rylin asked with a smile.

Vannek laughed.

"I'm surprised you're taking Anzat with you. It's obvious he wants your command and will undercut your efforts wherever he can."

"He's not subtle, is he? He was readying to challenge me only a few nights ago. I spared him."

"Why?"

"He got lucky."

"Why are you taking him with you?"

"If I leave him here, he'll be alone with the troops while we're away, stabilizing his position. If I take him with me, I can keep an eye on him."

"Suppose he distinguishes himself," Rylin asked.

"It could happen. He's reputedly a bold warrior. But I'll be in the front. The troops will see me in command, leading the charge. It will make it harder for him to challenge me."

"Do you mean to convert him into an loyal retainer?"

Vannek snorted. "It's possible. But I don't expect him to change. He'll never accept someone he sees as weak in command."

"He's blind if he sees you as weak."

Vannek looked at him in a different way, as though he were uncertain of a comment that pleased him. "He doesn't see that strength is more than size. He's smart enough to think it through, but I don't know that he ever will."

"People can change."

"Only a very few, in my experience," Vannek said. "Most perform to type. Tell me. Is there anything else that surprises you about us?"

"I never thought I'd enjoy talking with a Naor general."

Vannek's smile was thin but approving. "Nicely turned. You've been good company. We shall have to do this again." With that, he stood. "I'm sure you have arrangements of your own to make."

Rylin climbed to his feet. "Much like you. I thank you for your hospitality, General. With your leave, I'll run your men through more drills in the morning."

"And then comes the day of battle."

"Yes."

"Good," Vannek said, with surprising vehemence. Over the space of a few moments he had transformed from someone open and thoughtful into a certain warrior, eager for the kill. Seeing Rylin's reaction, a smile spread slowly over the general's face. "I surprised you again, didn't I?"

"Not all surprises are bad ones," he said.

For a brief, unguarded moment he saw something warm flash in the general's eye, and then Vannek laughed, either at himself, or at the both of them. "Until the morning, then."

He left the general in the tent, climbed into his saddle, and turned his mount toward the city, smiling wryly at the complexities of this new world. Asrahn had long ago instructed all of his squires to know the ground where they would fight. This time they had a landform map drawn by their enemy, and a scouting report delivered by a ghost. Strange times, indeed.

He arrived at the city gates and returned the salute of its guards, watching from on high. Only nominally damaged during the attack, the gates would be sealed every evening as they had since time immemorial, although the routine was almost comical, for great gaps loomed in the walls. Masons had labored through the day to repair the largest of them—new bricks could be seen rimming an immense opening to the left—but their work was not even a quarter complete. Had Rylin wished, he could easily have leapt the barrier.

The debris and bodies had been cleared from the long avenue into Darassus, but the paving itself remained in terrible condition. Many bricks were misplaced or crumbling, and even large areas were sunken in. The weight of the enormous Naor land treaders had wreaked havoc even upon this well-packed thoroughfare.

And so, too, had the fall of the statue of Darassa. The crown of her head shone amidst the rubble of road and market as Rylin rode forward, and he frowned at the thought of his involvement in the statue's destruction. The great ruin divided the town square and nearly filled the main avenue for several blocks, so Rylin had to maneuver his horse along the building walkways to bypass. Some doubted it would even be possible to restore her, which made him heartsick, for the statue had loomed over the city since the time of the Grandmothers.

Darassans filled the streets, walking for the homes of friends and families, or returning from shops and wells. Children chased and called to one another.

Nearly all of them paused at Rylin's passage. His uniform accorded him a measure of respect, but until recently, most had barely known his name. They might have stared or greeted him formally. Now, the children of Darassus paused in their play to regard him with shining eyes. Adults stopped in the midst of errands to raise hands in solemn salute.

He returned their greetings. He tried not to meet their eyes, where admiration and hope were paired. They believed without question that he would protect them, and didn't seem to understand he might fail. It was strange that the better he knew himself, the less he felt others saw who he really was.

With relief he finally arrived at the wall to the inner city. Here he traded salutes with fellow veterans; here he rode toward the palace without scrutiny.

He had missed the evening meal by almost an hour, which suited him, for he'd thought he wanted no company. Yet when he found himself alone in the cavernous dining hall, its emptiness was a ponderous weight to dull the flavor of his lentils and fish. He finished his meal and returned to the duty desk to inquire about Varama's whereabouts. The irony that she would once have been the last person he wished to see didn't escape him.

He found her in the office of the Altenerai commander. She studied a weathered parchment spread on the desk before her. To one side sat an open wooden box Rylin knew well, for it contained the spare sapphires and Altenerai rings he had borrowed and returned. To the other sat a sheaf of paper, and an inkwell and stylus.

Varama looked up at him and blinked, as if it were work to change focus. Rylin noted an ink smudge along her forehead.

"I thought I'd find you in the workshops," he said.

She frowned. "My workshops are a shambles."

"I didn't think the Naor made it that far." He paused to honor Asrahn's bust, beside the door, then dropped into one of the two seats across from the desk.

"The exalts tore it to pieces after we left. My people and our exalts are searching the auxiliary hall, but Synahla hid my notes and journals well."

"Gods. I'm sorry."

"I doubt they would have destroyed any of it. But I cannot currently waste mental energy in a search."

"How are you?"

"Not very different since the last time you asked."

Rylin realized he'd have to be more specific. "I don't believe you're actually feeling well."

Varama pushed back from the desk. "I am well enough to function, and to aid our efforts. I suppose my emotional state might be better."

"I'm worried about you," he said. "I have been for some time."

"You were right to fear for me. These are terrible times for many of us. I feared for you and it was good to find you whole."

"Is there something I can do to help with whatever you're doing here?"

"Not at this juncture."

"What is it, exactly, that you're working on?"

"Your description of linking the rings was inspiring. I'm searching through some of Herahn's old texts for information on their construction to see if I can improve the protective radius they may offer to all ring-sworn on a battlefield. If I am successful, the whole of our troops might receive the same kind of benefit you and your exalt friend did while standing close together."

It wouldn't have occurred to him to extend the idea, primarily because he wouldn't have known how to attempt it. "That sounds challenging."

"It is. Especially since Herahn was smarter than I am."

"That's difficult to believe."

An amused smile crossed her face. "I appreciate your high regard. Perhaps I should say that in addition to brilliance, Herahn possessed great power as a mage. His calculations and notes assume an easy familiarity with concepts that I must plod to follow because I have never practiced the sort of magic he wielded with ease. Herahn was a savant, and I suspect that he had access to the original hearthstone discovered by our queen. Leonara, I mean."

"I knew who you meant." It disappointed him that she had to confirm his comprehension of even simple topics sometimes.

She waved a hand at the piles of parchment on the desk. "My researches are made more difficult because I must refer to original documentation."

"Aren't the originals better?"

"No. Foreseeing the utility of reference to his notebooks in years to come, later in life Herahn oversaw their copying into more legible script, to which he occasionally added explanatory notes. Unfortunately, Denaven allowed Synahla to borrow these books. Your friend Thelar believes she did so in an ultimately failed effort to improve the functionality of the ruby rings worn by the exalt auxiliary. But Herahn's books have not yet been found. Thus I must work with the originals, absent his additional notes, and compounded by his cramped handwriting upon fragile pages."

Rylin shared her indignation. "That's frustrating."

"It is beyond that," Varama said sharply. "It is the height of arrogance to sweep into power and blithely disregard centuries of tradition because you're too ignorant to understand why it's there. I'm all for cutting to the chase when results are needed quickly, but when you risk the loss or destruction of items that helped build the state and safeguard its future because you can't be bothered to keep records of where you took them . . ." Her voice trailed off.

Rylin wasn't sure he'd ever seen Varama so angry.

She sighed. "I have digressed."

He turned up his hands to show her it meant nothing. "Sometimes you have to let anger roll off of you. Not just to get a point across to other people, but to spill out the bad air. When you keep it in, it's like staying inside a sickroom. You need to throw open the windows."

"That is an apt analogy. I would do well to pay better heed to such advice. Sansyra tried to tell me as much." Varama abruptly fell silent.

"She thought the world of you," Rylin said gently. "I was sorry to learn that she'd died, and still haven't heard the details."

The answer came slowly. "I had ordered her to hold the gate. But she left it in the hands of Iressa and rode off to battle. To her death."

"She probably thought she was needed elsewhere."

"I told her what she must do," Varama said truculently. "Why won't people listen to me? She could be here, now. She would be wearing the khalat and . . ." The words had grown slower and slower, as though Varama were a clockwork toy that needed winding.

"It's hard to know how to decide things in the heat of battle," Rylin said. "She must have seen something else that needed to be accomplished."

She met his eyes, and he felt that gaze like the blaze of the summer sun. "So many died on my watch, Rylin."

"You can't blame yourself for that."

"I do blame myself, wondering what more I might have done. If there were mistakes I might have foreseen. A word of advice I might have offered that would have saved just one more."

"Even if so, you would still mourn for the rest of those lost."

"Of course! It's not logical. I know that. But I will mourn them for the rest of my days."

He hesitated, then broached a subject he would never have known was delicate before a few days ago. "I should like to extend my condolences to you for Renik. I hadn't realized that the two of you were close." At her pained expression, he regretted saying anything at all. "Forgive me," he added.

"You are kind, Rylin," Varama said. "I'm not angry with you. It is foolish of me, but after N'lahr was found alive, I began to hope that Renik might live as well."

Just as Kyrkenall hoped still for Kalandra, he thought. He wondered if there had been something more between Varama and Renik. If so, he'd never heard rumors about it, and the squires were always eager for gossip about the Altenerai. Thus most had heard about the prolonged, sweet courtship between the stern Master of Squires and his husband, and Denaven's affair with the queen.

But then Rylin had since learned of other relationships that had somehow remained secret, like Denaven's long infatuation with Rialla, or the famously amorous Kyrkenall's abiding love for Kalandra. Might Varama's regard for Renik be another tale of doomed love? Or was he merely reading more into it than had existed?

"I've read the histories," Rylin said. "We know how much all of you who knew him revere him. Renik must really have been something."

She stared off into the distance, as she so often did. This time, though, her pale blue eyes held a lost and wistful quality. She did not speak for a long while, and he held off saying more, for he could tell she gathered her thoughts.

"Imagine N'lahr without the somber demeanor," she said finally. "Someone who knows exactly what to say, and to do, but who bears that weight casually. I do not mean to belittle N'lahr. He's excellent at what he does, and accommodates himself to others because he has to to achieve his goals. He's far better with people than I've ever been—he certainly inspires greater loyalty. However, he keeps who he is pretty tightly hidden, as do I, and I think only those who know him best truly love him."

She smiled sadly. "Renik wasn't like that. Everything came easily to him. Athletics. Magic. Friends. Some people born with such gifts lord it over others and foster jealousy. But Renik led. He gave of himself. Generously. Maybe he wasn't the very best swordsman the Altenerai ever fielded, but he was certainly close. And maybe he wasn't the very best mage, but he was surely in the top ranks. N'lahr is a better general. No one, I think, has ever approached N'lahr in that arena. But Renik was born to command. He inspired all of us. He never stopped working. Until the queen's hearthstone obsession, all his labors seemed easily borne. You would have liked him. He would have liked you."

"I wish I could have met him."

"In a better world, you would have." He had never heard Varama sound so bitter. "It was the queen who killed him, with her selfish and relentless search for hearthstones. It is her I blame, even more than the Naor, for Alantris, and for Sansyra, and for Darassus, and for Asrahn and Kalandra. And for Renik. I wish that those of us who were close had not looked the other way so easily. We, too, must shoulder blame. Decrin and Asrahn and Tretton were too loyal to the laws, living by their wording instead of their intent. I was too absorbed with my own studies, walled off from the rot around me. Belahn and Cerai were corrupted and Kyrkenall lost with his own woes and Enada with her own joys. Remember that, Rylin. That we must do more than serve. We must stand sentinel not just for outward threats, but for those insidious inward hazards as well."

"I'll remember."

"I think you will." She shifted closer to the desk. "Now I have enjoyed your visit, but I must return to work."

He climbed to his feet. "Do you want me to send in some food?"

"Thank you, no. I do not want to risk damaging these documents."

He reached for the door and then turned, his hand on the latch. "Do you know, there's something I've always wondered."

"Yes?" she answered, with an ease unfamiliar to him.

"I once asked why you chose me to help you, instead of the other junior Altenerai." He smiled, thinking how he had once bristled to be described as junior, then continued. "You said there were three reasons. That I needed more to do, that I had a connection to Tesra, and then you said there was a third thing you'd keep to yourself."

"Yes," she answered, and said nothing more.

He looked hopefully at her.

She chuckled. "And you wonder about the third? Oh, Rylin. Lasren would have required vastly more work than you, and Gyldara was grieving and unlikely to be swayed by logic. You were the only choice. You did need something to do, so you didn't end up like the worst of us, and you had connection to someone within the exalt auxiliary. It was a series of circumstances that proved fortuitous."

He nodded to himself. "So there wasn't a third reason?"

"Of course there was. You remind me of Renik."

He hesitated before answering, lest his chest swell with pride. "That's high praise."

"Yes. You are different, of course, and you haven't his inborn magical endurance, but there are clearly similarities."

"Well. That's unexpected. Thank you for that."

"I couldn't have told you then, of course. You were fairly insufferable already."

"I guess I was."

"Go. I'll send for you if I need you."

He put his hand to the latch, then turned a last time as he opened it. "You can always send for me, Varama, and I will come."

She bowed her head solemnly to that. "I know. Thank you."

10

The Sorceress in the Dawn

As a young squire Elenai hadn't understood how the veterans could center themselves upon the moment rather than worrying about the future. She no longer felt that a mystery, for as she finished fastening her khalat, noon today seemed as distant as the stars themselves, a remote possibility well beyond her reach. With even the dawn still hours off, her gear was packed and ready, complete with a well-balanced, razor-keen new sword that the master-of-arms Sharn had presented her the evening before.

A squire lingered outside the door to her suite, in case Elenai should call for his aid. She did not. Her morning prayers were complete, and she had twice reinspected her equipment. Fully dressed, helm under her arm and satchel over shoulder, she left her rooms. As she neared the stair Rylin stepped into the dimly lit hall. The two exchanged greetings then started down the steps together.

In the rooms below they joined N'lahr, Kyrkenall, and Varama, along with Thelar, M'vai, and Meria. The three exalts now served in the role that Denaven had always pledged, falsely, that he intended them for, as a Mage Auxiliary of the Altenerai Corps. A fourth faithful exalt with healing talents had survived the battle of Darassus, but formally resigned, declaring he would prefer to serve the realms by continuing to treat the many still recovering from their wounds. None of the hospitalized exalts or aspirants could yet be trusted, but squire Pelin was working with them.

By unspoken agreement, everyone at the tables kept the conversation superficial, speaking only of the quality of the food and other light matters. Even Kyrkenall kept his sardonic comments to himself this morning. The sun was still anticipated rather than evident when they left the hall. Stars sparkled in the cool air. Torches flared in their wall niches, setting the well-brushed flanks of waiting mounts aglow as they approached the stables.

Tending those horses were squires, both the two dozen assigned to ride with them and those few stationed to remain in Darassus. Some held the reins of the animals and the rest came to attention at Elik's sharp command. Near the front, Elenai spotted four former aspirants; the skinny man and the trio of young women were now indistinguishable from the surrounding squires, for they were garbed in leather and ringmail armor, breveted to second rank.

N'lahr halted before Elik, at attention at the formation's front. "How stand your soldiers, Squire?"

Elenai's old friend saluted. On his sleeve shown the diamond of an alten of the sixth circle. "Accounted and ready, Commander."

N'lahr's eyes roved over the group, some forty strong. "You seem to have more warriors here than I mean to deploy."

Elenai knew the commander well enough to detect a lightness in his tone.

"Yes, sir," Elik said. "The corps is here to send us off. They wouldn't take no for an answer."

"Well then," N'lahr said. "There's only one thing to do with that." He put a parade snap in his voice. "Altenerai, exalts, stand as one!"

Elenai and her companions smartly formed a line facing the squires.

"Squires, attention!" Elik barked. As one, the men and women in tabards behind him brought heels together, even those beside mounts. As they saluted, N'lahr and the Altenerai and exalts returned the gesture.

"We thank you for this honor, squires," N'lahr said.

They were simple words, delivered with gruff feeling. An outsider might not have understood the significance of the gesture both the squires and the Altenerai had formally traded with one another, but Elenai teared up.

The commander ended the moment as simply as it had begun. "At ease." He paused as the squires and their officers relaxed, then spoke in a softer tone. "Find your mounts."

Kyrkenall was first to lightly swing onto a small bay.

Elik led Elenai to a horse farther down the line. "I was sorry to hear about Aron," he told her. "I think you'll find Gemon here dependable; he has a similar temperament."

Gemon proved a piebald with black cheeks. Elenai was certain Elik had already triple-checked the tightness of the girth and the fit of the bit, but she checked them herself anyway.

As soon as all the appointed warriors had mounted, the remaining squires came once more to attention while a bugler sounded a fanfare. At that same moment, a pair of squires opened the gates leading out of the inner city and N'lahr ordered his troops forward.

While Varama had been named second-in-command and would normally have ridden at N'lahr's side, the commander had pointed Elenai there instead. She hadn't asked about the positioning, and assumed it related to her status as almost-queen.

Elenai had promised Brevahn she would finally attend a formal swearing in ceremony upon her return from this battle and he had grudgingly assented, saying that would suit, since elections for new councilors were going to be held over the next week. After the battle—and she hoped her survival was not an arrogant assumption—she would have seen Darassus through its most dangerous period, and could turn the crown over to someone better suited for it, like Governor Verena.

On the surface, this idea sounded like the perfect solution to her problem, so during the rare idle moments of the preceding days she had wondered why she sometimes felt such reluctance at the thought of stepping away from the throne.

Beyond the gate to the inner wall, she discovered another honor. No matter the early hour, the people of Darassus lined the streets, solemn and bleary-eyed under the boulevard lanterns.

A lump rose in Elenai's throat, along with an immense sense of affection and pride for the adults and children who had turned out to watch their departure.

By the time they had neared the immense sandaled bronze feet of fallen Darassa, Elenai felt a change in the air, an expectation she knew meant the approach of dawn. There was as yet no glow of it upon the horizon, but the world tensed for its coming.

Beside the city gate waited members of the assembly, Governor Feolia, Brevahn and the surviving councilors, and other dignitaries, along with the officers and soldiers of the city guard, even the injured ones in their bandages and casts. They saluted, hand to heart.

N'lahr ordered his command to return the salute, then activated his ring and lifted it, sapphire outward. The Altenerai with him repeated the gesture. So, too, did the exalts, each of whom now wore sapphires themselves, along with the aspirants and a scattering of higher-ranked squires.

Over the history of the corps, rings occasionally had been loaned to worthy warriors, a few of whom had later risen to the seventh circle. But never before had rings been granted to so many. Every spare sapphire had been fitted into a housing. N'lahr had ordered it done, confiding later that the queen's attack against Elik and Lasren had proven those who didn't wear the rings, or remain near those who did, were in mortal danger from Leonara.

A few hundred yards beyond the city gate, thirty of the allied Naor waited beside one of their immense, shaggy land treaders, a behemoth that was a dark mound against the horizon. As they neared it, two horse-mounted warriors in the small Naor host started forward.

N'lahr ordered his own warriors to halt, then bade Elenai to ride with him. The two met Vannek and Muragan between their forces.

The Naor general raised his hand in greeting.

Elenai returned the gesture, momentarily distracted by a flutter of wings to her left. A quick glance clarified: a flight of ko'aye circled the air, and two were descending.

Drusa and Lelanc, almost surely. Though the situation had been explained to the feathered lizards, neither had been entirely certain they wished to fly through a portal—apparently Lelanc had conveyed her dislike of the experience to Drusa—or fight on a side with Naor. Now Elenai saw the distinctive outlines of saddles upon their backs and smiled, knowing how they had decided.

"Hail, General," N'lahr said to Vannek.

"Hail, Commander and future Queen," Vannek said. His voice was hoarse this morning.

"Good morning, General, Coadjuter," Elenai said. This had to be the reason N'lahr had placed her beside him.

Muragan formally bowed his helmeted head. He had traded out his robes for simpler garb, covered over with sturdy ringmail.

"Varama has finished a special protective measure." From a pouch, N'lahr removed an amulet upon a necklace. Elenai heard the rattle of its robust chain as he gathered it and extended it toward the Naor leader.

Vannek looked down at the stone in the circular housing. In the darkness, it was not clearly identifiable by color, but the general must have recognized the cut. "This is an Altenerai sapphire," he said doubtfully.

"It is," N'lahr confirmed.

Vannek's voice was sharp with challenge. "You expect me to wear it? A symbol of your people?"

"It is an honor," Elenai began, but N'lahr raised a hand to her.

"I loan this gem so that you might live."

Vannek's reply was cool. "I can live without it."

"Unlikely," N'lahr said curtly. "Heed me well, General. The queen can slay with a single spell. Even Alten Lasren, wearing a sapphire, was not shielded from her. But Alten Varama has modified every single stone in our arsenal so that all are linked. So long as you are within the radius of an active sapphire, a zone that extends out to a spear's length from your body, you are shielded by the power of every sapphire upon the battlefield."

Vannek still did not take the offered necklace. "What of the rest of my people? Is there nothing for them?"

"Had I the means, I would protect us all," N'lahr said. "But I lack a treasury of sapphires. They are apportioned to those I expect to find closest to the old queen. And I loan this to you, not only because I expect to see you there, but because our alliance is nothing without you."

"You should take it," Muragan advised.

"I will take your sapphire." Vannek thrust forth his hand, and N'lahr placed the jewelry in his palm. "I thank you. How does it work?"

"Its protections activate when magics are used against you."

Vannek peered at the gem as if it would reveal secrets, even in the gloom. He removed his helmet to place it around his neck, and Elenai glanced down at her side to make sure her own helm was still ready on the saddlebag strap.

The general adjusted the necklace so that it lay beneath his armor, speaking as he did so. "If it takes only a minor adjustment to make your sapphires more powerful, why wasn't this done before?"

"This is more than just a minor adjustment," Elenai replied. "It required a substantial application of effort and ingenuity." She decided against revealing that the sapphires would likely be drained by this action. Under normal use their powers regenerated, but Varama hadn't been able to guarantee they would recover from this strain, and had no idea whether she could restore them if they faded completely. The loss of the sacred rings, along with so much else, was a worry for another time.

Vannek finished adjusting the pendant chain when it was completely tucked beneath his garments and turned to his sorcerer. "I advise you to ride close, Muragan."

"I'll do my best."

"Your men are ready?" N'lahr asked.

"They are ready, and eager. When will your sorceress open her portal?"

Almost as though she had been listening, Rialla appeared a dozen paces to Elenai's right. She was far brighter than any other figure on the battlefield, as if she stood in a beam of light.

From the Naor came unmistakable gasps. Vannek straightened in his saddle and passed his hand through the air in a swift gesture Elenai couldn't follow.

The murmuring among the Naor continued for a moment before a harsh voice from their ranks silenced them.

As Rialla beckoned, Elenai perceived a lightening of the horizon. The sun was on its way. She turned her mount toward Rialla, and Gemon responded easily, even though approaching the strangest figure he was likely ever to have sensed. N'lahr rode with her, and the two Naor leaders came after. From the three dozen members of the Altenerai force, Varama and Kyrkenall cantered forward.

N'lahr swung down before the short figure and Elenai dropped beside him. Vannek and Muragan moved closer but remained seated on their restive horses, while Elenai's and N'lahr's exhaled loudly, seemingly to express distaste at their larger cousin's ill manners.

Rialla returned their salute. "Hail, Altenerai." Her voice, while synchronized with the movement of her lips, didn't seem to emanate from her, but rather echoed in Elenai's mind.

Elenai and N'lahr answered as one. "Hail."

Rialla's gaze passed over the pair of Naor, watching with wary awe. "Greetings, Naor."

Vannek only stared; Muragan bowed his head with great formality.

Varama and Kyrkenall reined in, the archer dropping from his saddle before his horse came to a full stop.

Rialla didn't acknowledge them. Her high brow was furrowed as she scanned the distant group. "Where is Lasren?"

"He was killed by the queen," N'lahr answered.

Rialla sounded troubled. "He was here the last two times."

"Two times?" Elenai asked. Did she mean that this had happened twice before, and she didn't have a memory of it?

"Was he necessary for victory?" Varama asked.

Rialla ignored Elenai's question and replied to Varama. "We've yet to succeed, so I cannot say. But none of my adjustments should have impacted his actions. This worries me."

Varama agreed. "It suggests the existence of a greater degree of random result even when the same individuals are presented with nearly the same options."

"I'm afraid so, Alten."

Though the women looked very different, they communicated in a similar, clipped manner.

Rialla held a hand to Varama. "Four times," she said. "You usually ask. And, yes, you can watch, but I do not have time to teach you. I taught Cerai because I was trying to drain power from the battlefield, but that didn't work." Turning to N'lahr, she said, "The disposition of the queen's forces has always been the same."

"It seems you can anticipate our questions well," N'lahr said as Elenai was trying to work out what that middle part meant. It had been about portals, she guessed.

"You've asked them before. Kyrkenall, I will do what I can for Kalandra if we get through the battle."

Though this statement confused Elenai it must have made eminent sense to Kyrkenall, who raised a hand in acknowledgment.

"I must reserve some energy should things go poorly again," Rialla said. "N'lahr, let Vannek spur forward when the queen flies up." Before he could answer, she went on, "I will speak to the others, and then we must start." She winked out of sight.

"Does this make sense to you, Commander N'lahr?" Vannek asked.

"Yes. This is just information on the finer details."

"Where did she even go?" the Naor general demanded in frustration.

Kyrkenall pointed back the way they'd come. "Over there."

Sure enough, the shining figure had appeared in front of the exalts and squires and was raising one arm to gesture their direction. Elenai noticed someone was now standing with the ko'aye. Rylin, probably.

"Does she always drop in and out like that?" Vannek asked. "And is she a spirit, or some new kind of witch?"

"It's complicated," N'lahr said.

Vannek looked even less satisfied by that answer than he had been a moment before.

Kyrkenall spoke up. "There'll be time to explain if we win this. And not much point if we don't."

Vannek took a breath as if to say more, then closed his mouth. "Enough talk then. Let's get to the battle."

11

The Blood of Paradise

The portal swirled into existence at ground level thirty feet below, just to the right of the ghostly alten. Rylin kept his eyes upon it even as Lelanc turned in the air beneath him, the russet-colored feathers of her tapering wings smoothed flat by the wind.

The hole broadened swiftly from a strange violet disk to a pulsating circular gateway wide almost as the entry to Darassus. Disturbingly, as they continued in their circle, Rylin saw the portal seemed not to exist when viewed from the rear.

"It has a wind that is strange," Lelanc called to him. "I do not like the magic of these tunnels."

Rylin patted her back, meaning to reassure. "We'll travel this road together," he vowed, voice raised to counter the air rushing past them.

The small invasion force had lined up behind the hairy Naor land treader in their forefront. At N'lahr's shouted command, it lumbered toward the magical gateway, lowing in dismay. Rylin spared a glance for the drover and Meria and M'vai, seated just behind him on benches built into a platform erected on the creature's back. As the drover shook the reins, the beast put down its head and broke into a charge that kicked up a plume of dust.

Kyrkenall circled with Drusa in the lightening sky overhead. Rylin glanced up at them, the weight of his own helmet almost unfamiliar after so many battles without it. In the early morning, Drusa's blue feathers looked almost black, and her white underside nearly gray. Her deep ebon beak, though, gleamed like bronze.

As Lelanc continued her turn, Rylin saw ranks of Darassan men and women standing on the city walls, outlined by that bright line of gleaming gold on the eastern horizon, heralding the sunrise.

The huge Naor beast vanished within the portal. Vannek and his blood mage galloped on their heels. Immediately after came N'lahr and the Altenerai forces, all thirty of them on horseback, disappearing in groups of two. After them ran the Naor infantry.

In a few moments only three figures remained: ghostly Rialla, Varama, and a squire holding two horses, one for himself and one for Varama, who would be passing through as soon as she finished observing Rialla's spell.

"Follow me!" Kyrkenall roared. Drusa let out a caw and dove for the glowing portal.

Lelanc followed. As his ko'aye friend shifted in the air, Rylin held tight to the saddle horn, his stomach lurching in a familiar and not unwelcome rush of excitement.

Kyrkenall and Drusa dove into the upper third of the large opening, lit by its violet glow. The moment they passed within, their forms snapped forward so that both appeared to have moved a quarter mile in a single breath.

Lelanc dropped lower, and lower yet, until they were only a spearlength above the ground. She flapped once to correct herself, seeming nervous about centering on the tunnel. Rylin raised his shining ring in salute as they neared Rialla and Varama, and then they had swooped inside.

He'd been told what to expect, but he still hadn't fully imagined what the portal would be like. He took in a nervous breath and discovered the tunnel's air was thin and cool. Cliffs and plains flashed by to left and right, now dark, now light, as if they looked upon the Shifting Lands through a moving window. Kyrkenall, on Drusa's back, looked impossibly far ahead. The archer was a black blot perched upon a line that was Drusa's extended wings.

Sound was muted. Lelanc shrilled another cry, and the strange conditions magnified and distorted the noise so that it left Rylin crinkling his face in discomfort.

He was about to ask her to quiet down when they soared out into an idyllic twilight land where the rim of the sun sank beyond a line of hills. Once again they were near Drusa and Kyrkenall, rising swiftly above the long grasses. Lelanc fell silent at last and beat her wings with great force so they climbed after.

Ahead of them the great Naor beast thundered straight for a giant wooden scaffolding. The head of the immense crystalline statue it supported caught the failing light and sprayed rainbow shadows across the hills.

Their little army raced toward their appointed targets, the mounted troops making for the farther twin hills to the left while the foot soldiers rushed the nearer hill to the right.

The Naor beast roared and hit the immense statue.

Just before the moment of impact, Meria and M'vai dropped from the animal, and Rylin didn't have to be watching through the inner world to see that they used magic to slow their descent, the drover borne between them. As the twins touched gently down with the Naor warrior, the land treader slammed its head into the huge crystalline icon.

The hearthstone Goddess rocked backward into the scaffolding and then fell with it and struck the earth with a thunderous crash. Its arm and head broke free and one leg cracked in half. Hundreds of hearthstone shards caught the light as they flew in from every direction. The scaffolding toppled with the statue and broken lengths of wood tumbled through the air.

The magical backlash swept up from the fallen stones and splashed against the poor land treader like a silver wave. In a heartbeat the great beast's forward quarter was encased in a crystalline prison. Rylin knew a stab of pity as its back legs scrabbled for purchase before they stilled, overrun with crystal, encasing it like melted wax. Even anticipated, the creature's fate was ghastly to witness.

The enemy exalts and aspirants struck from the three nearest hillsides. Two of the queen's people sent blue fire lancing from extended hands, blasting onrushing squires from their saddles. Other magic proved less visible, for charging Naor troops dropped yards from gesturing exalts, no outward sign of damage upon them.

Elenai led a charge up one of the two hills assigned to cavalry, sword high, shouting the old cry: "Strike as one!"

Only then did Rylin recall that he had once wished to serve under a vigorous warrior queen like the great Altenara, and smiled, for his dream had come true without him realizing it. Elenai bore down upon a pair of exalts, guiding her mount with legs alone. She turned a sword blow from one, then deflected a crackling red-white energy spike with her off hand.

Lelanc turned and he could no longer watch. The ko'aye flew out of the setting sun, shrunk to a mere sliver, her goal a band of exalts on the closer hill. Rylin's first spear toss caught the foremost spell caster, a pale man who hadn't bothered to pull on his khalat. It was his last mistake, for the spear went straight through him. His spell sparked uselessly in his fingers as he writhed out his life in the grass.

Lelanc soared on. Rylin's ring lit, and he felt dim impulses to flee or surrender. Multiple exalts had targeted him, their assault backed by hearthstones, opening brightly in the grasses to his right, but their power was countered by that of the Altenerai sapphires, working in concert.

"Did you feel that?" Lelanc called back to him. "It was like the mind stealing Cerai did to me!"

Pained fury rang in her voice. He touched her side. "Your mind is safe with me," he shouted. His ring would protect Lelanc almost as well as himself.

They passed over a beautiful reflecting pond lined with statues. On the southern hill, N'lahr rode through a knot of defenders, effortlessly driving them back with his flashing, deadly blade. Muragan and Vannek were only a half horselength behind. Kyrkenall flew past to shoot two exalts who'd thrown fire.

Thelar slowed his horse at the side of Meria and M'vai, already advancing into the field of hearthstones and the immense sections of the fallen Goddess statue. They were pointing the aspirants to work as Varama and a single squire galloped up from the rear.

Lelanc banked, cawing in confidence. So far it looked like a rout. Careful planning, guided by Rialla's scouting, seemed to have worked for them. The hearthstone statue was shattered and the queen's followers were either surrendering or dying, overmatched and outnumbered. But where was the queen?

So far Rylin hadn't seen Rialla, either. Or Tesra, but he was glad for that. He wasn't sure he could attack her, nor did he want to see her fall. N'lahr had told them that they should spare lives when possible, but not to risk themselves to do it, for these people would be trying to kill them.

The queen was his true target. N'lahr had appointed him and Kyrkenall to neutralize enemy mages until they saw her rise into the air.

The mages on their side were advancing through the hearthstones, shutting them down. Elenai cantered down from a hilltop to join them.

Something popped up on the edge of his field of vision. He turned to find the queen suspended in the air. She opened her arms, and a hundred more of the hearthstones brightened.

"There she is," Rylin cried.

"I see!" Lelanc called.

Rylin didn't need to tell the ko'aye what to do. Already she was banking, moving so the dying sun would be at their back.

He should have known Kyrkenall would reach Leonara first. Drusa flew in from the side with her head low, and Kyrkenall launched arrow after arrow.

Not a one of them struck the queen, whose wind gusts sent the shafts spinning uselessly. Drusa flapped, struggling to climb past the buffeting currents.

Leonara raised her hands as if she intended further mischief, but before she could act, Rialla appeared beside the scattered hearthstones. Rylin didn't have to see through the inner world to know the lost alten pulled on the queen's spellthreads, for Leonara dropped like a kite yanked to earth by its master.

Lelanc finished her turn and dove toward their enemy.

Leonara flailed as she was dragged toward the ground, finally halting only five feet above it. She drew silvery threads from one of the hearthstones and whipped them at Rialla.

Their ghostly ally, rooted to the same energies used by the queen, spun up a translucent shield that wavered under the attack. It shuddered like heat haze. Varama and Elenai stood to either side, feeding energy into Rialla's spell.

Lelanc's body rumbled with a repressed urge to cry, but the ko'aye remained silent as they closed on the queen. Rylin tossed his spear and it drove deep into the queen's side. Success!

Rialla poured energy at Leonara, who crashed to earth only a few yards from M'vai and Meria.

Leonara climbed to her feet, shouting in fury. The spear dropped away. No blood flowed; no wound shone. She lifted hands overhead as if she hefted an invisible boulder, and silver lightning gathered above her. Before she could release it, dark-feathered Drusa swept in and Kyrkenall launched another set of arrows. Fierce gusts tore two away, but a third struck above the queen's collarbone. It drew no more blood than Rylin's spear, or his blade a few days previous, but the attack spoiled her spell, and the energies were swept away.

N'lahr and Vannek spurred in from the right, the Naor general leaning out from his mount, sword blade low.

The queen lashed at them with an expanding scythe of white energy. Their horses dropped on the moment, squealing in pain and fear. N'lahr and Vannek tumbled clear, the commander rolling immediately to his feet. Rylin's own ring flared, dimmed, then stuttered on and off.

Elenai shouted in alarm and whipped a loop of blue burning energy at the queen. Leonara raised a hand, and the attack dissolved into blue mist. She returned to her silvery attack upon the commander, and Rylin's ring blinked once more as N'lahr bore the brunt of her fury. Rylin's heart thudded in fear for him, now on one knee and struggling to rise, moving like a man bearing a weight through water.

Lelanc, banking tightly, cawed in fierce joy, for they neared the queen. Rylin threw another javelin. The queen's shielding wind sent this one spinning. The ko'aye beneath him banked once more and flapped to take them high.

At a dual onslaught of energies from both Varama and Elenai, the queen turned from N'lahr to rain crystalline energy at them. Rialla's shield held the attack, then burst into pieces as the spell broke with it.

Thelar and the twins hurried forward to assist, but Rialla screamed at them to keep shutting down the hearthstones. They backed reluctantly off.

Drusa had fought the winds to dare her closest pass yet, and when Kyrkenall threw his own spear it drove through Leonara's chest.

The queen staggered and her hands dropped. Her spells unraveled.

It was then Vannek reached her, sword upraised.

Now facing forward as Lelanc lined up for another pass, Rylin witnessed the Naor general's strike. It was an ideal blow, wielded against an armorless target. The sword sliced just above the arrow shaft protruding from Leonara's collarbone and sent the head hurtling away. The queen's body dropped. Little blood fountained from the stump.

The head struck the ground beside a shining purple hearthstone and then rolled into the grass.

Lelanc opened her beak and released a cry of delight. Her whole chest shook with it and Rylin joined her in a delighted roar. So great was his exultation that a long moment passed before he noted the incongruity that he celebrated the death of a queen at the hands of a Naor general, and then he laughed, thinking how Vannek would likely lord that over him for the rest of his days.

Lelanc soared out toward the statues near the reflecting pool and then circled back so Rylin could see the whole of the battlefield. Most of the enemy were down; a handful of the surrendered walked with hands raised, surrounded by squires escorting them toward the reflecting pool. Their own dead were few: There was the beast, encased in crystal. Two squires who lay unmoving. A handful of Naor sprawled and broken at the foot of the hill.

A shout erupted from a band of Naor above them. "The queen is dead," one of them called. "All hail Lord General Vannek!" While they began to chant and shake their weapons at the sky, their general stared down at the queen's body, as if in disbelief.

Drusa landed beside N'lahr, who'd made it to his feet, and Kyrkenall threw himself out of the saddle with a whoop of joy.

Rylin smiled to see all this, but his mood ebbed when he saw Varama and the rest of their spell casters working among the hearthstones. He heard Rialla shouting and couldn't make out her words but the tone was frantic.

All of the hearthstones lit at once. Those scattered in the grass burned like colored lanterns, those in larger clumps and grouped in recognizable body parts grew into a blinding blaze. Worse, threads of energy swirled up from them in a great spout, as if some invisible force was pulling on all the threads at once and draining them into the sky.

Rylin's elation had been entirely eclipsed by alarm verging on terror. "Get me down by the mages!" he shouted to Lelanc. "Hurry!" He was fighting to unbuckle even before the ko'aye reached the earth, so that he was out of the saddle the moment his friend had finished her landing run. In real time, the descent must only have taken three or four bell tolls, but it felt an eternity, especially because the winds swirled more and more forcefully, tearing at his khalat. Rylin shouted for Lelanc to get out and clear.

Rialla still called for everyone to hurry, and Rylin joined their efforts, shutting down a glittering red stone near his feet. Elenai and Varama worked with three of the aspirants on one large, brilliant hunk of what had been the statue's left calf. He joined Thelar, only to see the nearest stones fade to gray before the entire leg disintegrated into black powder.

Elenai had always struck Rylin as demure and poised, but at sight of this she swore colorfully.

He knew how she felt. He scanned the rest of the grounds and saw the remains of the statue crumbling even as its energies streamed into the sky, shaping a great dark female form. Like the queen had been, she was suspended above the earth, limbs hanging slack, eyes closed. A gossamer ebon gown billowed in the air, which churned more and more swiftly. The queen's winds were as nothing to the hurricane that gathered around this behemoth. The dust from the hearthstones swirled, half obscuring their surroundings, and nearby trees shed their leaves in the lashing. With the sun almost down and the hearthstones dimmed, the darkness summoned with the winds was near complete.

A bank of Naor spearmen charged in to hurl their weapons, but the javelins fell into white ash a few paces out from the whirling energies, and swept up and away.

"Fall back!" Rialla wailed. "Retreat!"

She herself, though, advanced, yanking an immense band of energies away from the motionless figure in the sky. Meria reached forward to assist as Rialla directed the threads ground-ward.

The giant woman, eyes still closed, lifted one hand and tugged on the energies, pulling them back toward her. With the other she made a brushing motion toward Meria and Rialla.

Meria disintegrated into white flakes; Rialla blinked out of existence.

Vannek turned to flee and was blown from his feet as the wind rose into a full-throated storm. Rylin saw him slam into the ground, leg bent at a terrible angle. He did not rise; he did not move. The wind swirled up in an obscuring shroud and Vannek was lost to sight.

"Retreat!" N'lahr shouted. There was a desperate urgency in his voice. "Pull back!"

Above them, the dark figure opened enormous black eyes, and gazed down upon them.

The Goddess had awakened.

Beyond the Walls

Elenai did not heed Rialla's call to retreat, racing instead to assist her, Thelar and Rylin at her side. But then Rialla vanished and Meria died in front of her. Elenai stumbled to a horrified halt, her feet kicking up the ashes of crumbled hearthstones. N'lahr called to retreat and she backed away.

A portal winked into existence a hundred feet to their left, where Kyrkenall supported N'lahr. Of course; Rialla had disappeared to arrange their retreat. So long as she still existed, they had a chance.

"Fall back!" Kyrkenall shouted, and waved for them. "Over here!"

The Goddess descended toward the earth and great blasts of wind sent dust and dirt spinning. Elenai lost sight of everyone but those closest to her.

Too overwhelmed to think of much else, she ran for the shimmering violet portal, Kyrkenall and N'lahr before her and a trio of squires after. She couldn't see Thelar and Rylin. Someone screamed in defiance, and she thought it might have been M'vai.

Supported by Kyrkenall, N'lahr reached the portal and as Elenai hesitated, looking back at the shifting curtain of dust that had spun up behind them, the commander pointed her through. His arm trembled as if with palsy. "Go!" he cried.

Rather than remaining fixed, the mouth of this portal pulsated between oval and circle. Belatedly she searched to right and left for her horse, but could not spot him. As Elenai raced inside, the walls contracted and expanded around her at uneven intervals. She feared it was about to collapse, and had no idea what would happen to anyone inside if the magic failed. Elenai ran for the light at the far end, impossibly distant until it raced toward her and she pitched clear outside the high wall of Cerai's fortress, upon a grassy sward in afternoon light.

Cerai stood to one side of the portal, warded by a quartet of muscular spear-bearing men in leather breastplates. The sorceress wore her Altenerai khalat. Her beautifully coiffed dark head was bent, her arms outthrust toward the portal, her brow creased.

Elenai had assumed too quickly that her hopes were real. Cerai had opened this portal, not Rialla. So where had Rialla gone? Could the Goddess have truly annihilated her? Or had her spirit gone somewhere else?

She searched the grounds, finding three wide-eyed squires who'd retreated behind her. Cerai's soldiers waited both upon the walls and in three separate ranks of ten nearby. Beyond the fortress and the portal the ground sloped down toward the orderly rows of identical single-story, thatched roof homes and tilled fields.

Struggling to catch her breath, Elenai turned back toward the portal just as Drusa soared out, legs close to her chest so they wouldn't strike the ground. Elenai threw herself flat and felt the brush of air from the close passage. She looked up as Lelanc emerged and followed the same path, beating her wings furiously to climb above the fortress wall. She cawed in rage and despair.

After them a pair of squires ran through, one after the other, and then Thelar, and Kyrkenall, supporting N'lahr by the arm. The commander appeared to have trouble moving his legs, and Elenai searched him for sign of a wound, finding nothing.

A small band of Naor emerged next, led by Anzat, Vannek's burly second-in-command. He searched to right and left. "Where are we?" he roared at the commander.

But N'lahr, still held steady by Kyrkenall, didn't answer, and the archer, peering at his friend, didn't pay the Naor any heed.

So many had yet to evacuate. The mouth of the tunnel whirled, violet light fluctuating along its edges. All four aspirants ran free, followed a moment later by Rylin, shepherding a small band of frightened squires. Elenai still hadn't seen Elik, Varama, M'vai, Vannek, or Muragan, let alone a dozen or more squires, foot soldiers, prisoners, and horses.

"Have you seen M'vai?" Thelar called.

"I couldn't find anyone else," Rylin answered. "Varama's holding the portal on the far end—it's starting to collapse!"

The tunnel mouth narrowed. Cerai gritted perfect white teeth, her arms shaking. It didn't look as though she'd be able to hold it much longer.

Elenai cursed. Though she mentally recoiled at the thought, she hurried to Cerai's assistance. Better an uncertain fate in the lands of a smooth-tongued traitor than certain death at the foot of the hearthstone Goddess.

Two of the renegade alten's blank-faced, smooth-skinned warriors blocked her progress with leveled spears.

"I'm here to help," she told them, but they would not stand down.

She was being stupid. Proximity didn't matter. Elenai opened herself to the inner world. She'd already sensed the hearthstone energy pouring through Cerai; now she perceived that it blazed from the wooden chest near the woman's feet, tracing through her and wrapping vine-like about the portal, as though the colorful tendrils pulled open the hole in reality. Excess energy streamed from the opening into the soil itself.

Cerai's spell work was far less refined and more energy consumptive than Rialla's portals, fueled less by finesse than brute force.

Elenai reached for the stones with her own threads and funneled power toward Cerai, whose head rose as though the aid had allowed her a deeper breath.

A blast of gold light flared from within the tunnel and a dozen squires straggled out in the brilliant blaze, Elik at their rear. He was a welcome sight. With him came a dark-haired female exalt Elenai didn't recognize, one of the queen's people. A moment later M'vai wandered clear, her face pale and bloodless, helmet missing, red hair hanging wild. Her bright green eyes roved over her surroundings without seeming to see them.

Cerai shouted to Elenai: "She's fighting me!"

The portal narrowed even farther, some of its energy flowing into the ground nearby. She wondered if Cerai was fighting not to keep it open, but to close it.

Twenty or so Naor warriors fell through at almost the same time, stumbling over one another. Their eyes were wide in fear and they stared over their shoulders.

The opening swelled both in size and brightness. Elenai sensed something of immense power latch hold of it. She paled in fear, knowing with certainty that the Goddess was widening the way.

Cerai fought the transformation, blue-white energy glowing all along her arms and out in streamers toward the portal. Elenai yanked more threads from the stones and fed them to her. The renegade alten wove them with her work, and twisted, tugged, and pulled until, with a final wrench, the portal snapped closed.

Nothing of it remained, and the air above the courtyard grasses looked completely ordinary.

Cerai leaned heavily against one of her soldiers.

"Varama's still back there!" Rylin cried. "Open the portal!"

Elenai found him at her side, his eyes fierce slits. His bared sword was leveled at Cerai. Her ring of guards lowered their spears at him.

Elenai interposed herself, one palm toward Rylin, one toward the guards.

"Varama's still back there!" Rylin repeated, as though he hadn't been heard the first time.

Cerai pulled herself fully erect. She said nothing as she pushed coal-black hair from her damp forehead. Even disheveled the woman was supremely, almost impossibly beautiful, slim, tall, her long-lashed blue eyes bright with arrogant intellect. If not for a handful of facial lines, her age would have been impossible to guess. Elenai knew she had sorcerously modified herself, and supposed Cerai had retained some signs to physically communicate wisdom.

Cerai smiled sadly at Rylin, but it was hard to tell if she empathized or merely pitied his stupidity. "She's dead, Rylin. I felt her ring wink out just before the Goddess got hold of the tunnel."

At some level, Elenai had feared that, but hadn't permitted herself to draw the conclusion. She shook her head impotently.

Cerai raised her voice to address them all. "Anyone back there is gone," she said. "The Goddess is reducing them and the land they occupied to component parts."

Gasps and shocked cries followed this blunt announcement. Rylin turned away, sucking in a huge breath as he did. He sheathed his sword, looking at his hands as if he wasn't sure what to do with them.

He wasn't the only one mourning. M'vai stood with balled fists, face tear-streaked while Thelar spoke gently to her ear, hand on her shoulder.

Elenai looked numbly over their assembly, confirming that neither Vannek nor the blood mage had gotten free, either. So much for the future of the Naor alliance.

The two ko'aye called back and forth as they circled overhead. They spoke in their own birdlike language, and though Elenai didn't know a word of it, Lelanc's agitation was obvious. Probably she had no wish to be here again, in the clutches of Cerai. Elenai didn't blame her.

At least N'lahr looked better. He stood unsupported, if unsteadily, wiping his bloody blade on a scrap of cloth while Kyrkenall watched.

Elik arranged the squires in a wedge around the commander, weapons sheathed but ready for action. Anzat, the Naor officer, had loosely organized his own force. More than thirty of Cerai's identical soldiers calmly leveled spears at both groups.

Cerai took in the situation with amused indifference. "Well. We're all on the same side here. There's no need for unpleasantness. N'lahr, tell your squires and those Naor to stand down before someone gets hurt, and then we must chat. We've much to do, and little time."

"We thank you for your assistance," N'lahr said levelly. "My troops need shelter. And some require medical aid."

"That can be provided." Cerai turned her head to her troops. "Sorak?"

The blank-faced assistant who had waited on them during the previous visit stepped out from the ranks of soldiers.

"Yes, Goddess?" he asked.

Elenai groaned inwardly to hear that manner of address again.

Cerai waved vaguely at the squires and Naor troops. "Arrange quarters for these guests. See that they're given anything they require. Have the men relax."

"As you command," Sorak said with a head bow. He barked at Cerai's soldiers to lower their weapons, and they quickly obeyed.

"Elik," N'lahr said, "Anzat, see that your soldiers are cared for and I'll be by for your report within the hour."

Elik saluted and turned to the squires. Anzat looked confused and mutinous. Elenai expected him to object, but when Cerai strode off, calling for N'lahr to follow, the bearded man frowned irresolutely and remained with his men. Elenai hoped he'd be smart enough to do as N'lahr bade. She looked to the cloudless sky, but the ko'aye had flown out of sight.

It was a small band who trailed after the renegade alten. N'lahr, Kyrkenall, still at his friend's elbow, Rylin, torn somewhere between fury and grief, Thelar, and M'vai, clearly given over to the latter, hands to her face, though she fought to control herself. The dark-haired exalt from Leonara's side had an arm about her and spoke soothingly as they walked.

This time Elenai noted the seamless stone walls without wonder as they passed through the immense black iron gates. She was too heartsick to be impressed again.

In moments they had left the vast, parklike courtyard beyond the gates and passed into the cool depths of the fortress.

They eventually reached a silk-lined chamber with a long, elegant rectangular table. A throne-like chair with flared arms sat at its far end, and benches flanked it. Light filtered in through wide windows overlooking a small inner courtyard in which tiny yellow songbirds flitted. Their cheerful chirps seemed an unwelcome and discordant intrusion.

Cerai reached the head of the table but did not yet seat herself, gesturing magnanimously for her guests to take their places. When they had done so, Cerai assumed the chair with such easy grace Elenai was envious.

"Welcome," Cerai said. "I didn't expect to get quite so many, and the Naor were, shall I say, an unexpected bonus?" She smiled as if the matter were a trifle. "But any who wish to aid are welcome in this time of trouble. We'll only get through this if we work together."

Rylin's voice was caustic. "You didn't want to work together before. Why now?"

"This isn't the time to waste on recriminations, or emotional outbursts. That thing the queen released will be hammering at these gates soon enough. She surely sensed my hearthstones, as their energy powered my magics with the portal. And she'll want every part of her that's missing."

Her statement didn't cow Rylin. "If you knew where we were, you could have helped sooner."

It was an excellent point.

Cerai sighed lightly. "I'm not omnipotent, dear Rylin. I do keep an eye on the hearthstones, but I wasn't alerted to your battle until I sensed all of them activate. You really ought to be more grateful."

Rylin looked as though he might spring up and throttle her.

N'lahr had taken the position on Cerai's right, with Kyrkenall beside him. Elenai noted that the height of the benches put even the commander's head below that of the realm's ruler. He addressed their host. "How long before she arrives?"

"It depends on how she prioritizes remaking the world versus completing her own rebirth."

"Has anyone seen Rialla?" Kyrkenall asked.

"She disappeared before my eyes," Elenai answered. "Either the Goddess destroyed her, or she blinked away; I don't know how to tell."

Kyrkenall was uncharacteristically speechless.

"That's unfortunate," Cerai said calmly. "Do you have any way to contact her?"

"No," Elenai answered bitterly. Why hadn't she thought to ask for a way to do so before the battle?

"That's too bad then," Cerai said, sounding no more troubled than a dinner guest informed dessert wouldn't immediately follow the main course. "Although there are any number of issues we could discuss, why don't we get to the problem at hand. Namely, that Leonara's ridiculous plan actually worked, and now her 'goddess' is alive and coming to destroy everything."

An unfamiliar voice spoke from Elenai's side of the table. After Thelar, on Elenai's left, was M'vai, and then the dark-haired exalt, whose voice was soft, deferential. "We don't know that last for certain."

Kyrkenall spoke sharply. "Who the *fuck* are you?"

"This is Tesra." Thelar swept a hand toward her. "She wasn't trying to fight us."

The archer's mouth twisted in disgust. "So that gets her a say? She was working with the queen."

N'lahr held up a hand. "Let her speak."

Tesra hesitated, as if uncertain the rest of them would really obey. Elenai saw her meet Rylin's eyes across the table, though she didn't fully understand the look that passed between them. Finally, she spoke. "Queen Leonara said that the Goddess would restore the realms. We don't know that she's going to destroy anything."

Thelar's mouth opened in disbelief. "Tesra, that Goddess' first act was to sweep our friends, her so-called followers, into *nothing*." His voice was more strained than Elenai had ever heard, even during a battle. He turned from Tesra to address the rest of them. "I saw a group of the queen's exalts running toward the Goddess while attacking squires with spells. She waved a hand and they all just . . . disintegrated."

Elenai was glad she hadn't seen that. She'd have enough mental scars from Meria's death.

M'vai choked back a sob and Thelar put a hand to her shoulder.

Tesra continued. "Maybe she'll restore them when she restores the realms. That's what the queen said would happen to the people in Darassus."

"What lovely hearsay." Kyrkenall spoke with barbed emphasis, and Cerai grinned. "I guess we should bear witness to more of the rantings of a deluded despot who caused the deaths of thousands? Thank you, no. I've heard enough religious crap to last me a lifetime."

But Tesra wouldn't relent. "The Goddess might have hurt them because she thought she was being attacked. What if she was defending herself?"

"Would you *please* shut up?" Kyrkenall asked.

N'lahr raised both hands in a calming gesture before anyone else could speak. Elenai couldn't help noticing that the left hand trembled. The commander stared at it without comment, then lowered his hands to the table. "This isn't helpful." He returned his attention to Cerai. "As to the Goddess. Our Gods killed her once. She was at full strength then. I don't think she is now. Can we find the power to fight her?"

Cerai eyed him for a moment, as if uncertain how she should respond. A pair of servants arrived with platters of wine decanters and goblets, and she watched in silence as they set everything down on the table before them. She shooed the servants away, then addressed her guests. "Please. Help yourselves. Food should be here shortly. N'lahr, you've beaten me to the thrust. I don't know how I could have forgotten how quickly you pinpoint the weak spot."

Seeing the hesitance with which everyone considered the goblets, Cerai reached out and poured a drink for herself. She then set the decanter in front of the commander.

While everyone sparingly served themselves, Cerai swirled the wine in her goblet and conspicuously consumed half its contents. She lowered it. "I've built my realm to not only withstand hearthstone magics, but to absorb them. I was expecting to deal with the energy of a realms-ending explosion, mind you, not a concentrated attack from a living deity, but my realm is far more resistant to the entity's magics than any other."

Elenai sipped and discovered not wine, but chilled sunberry juice.

"So you're suggesting we make a stand here," N'lahr guessed.

"You are correct again. I need the help of skilled mages to bolster my defenses. And the keen eye of a tactician wouldn't hurt, either." She inclined her head to N'lahr. "With the right preparations, I think we can succeed in destroying this goddess when she gets here. Furthermore, I know where to find the device originally used to fracture her consciousness."

"A weapon was used?" Elenai asked. She had assumed that their Gods had used their inborn abilities to kill the Goddess. Only a few days before, Cerai had told them how the Gods of the realms had banded together to kill their own mother, the Creator Goddess, when she had decided to destroy the realms to fashion something more to her liking.

N'lahr spoke a single word, sharply. "Explain."

"The people we used to call Gods crafted a weapon specifically designed to rip apart one of the most powerful beings that has ever existed."

"How do you know?" Rylin asked. Elenai thought it an excellent question.

"I've had access to almost all the memory stones ultimately surrendered to Leonara, and one or two I reserved for my own use. It's a shame I didn't get the keystone before she did. But no matter." Cerai paused to sip from her goblet.

Why hadn't she mentioned this when she and Kyrkenall were here the last time? Elenai had a hard time holding her tongue, as she guessed N'lahr would advise.

"You said you knew where to find it," Kyrkenall said.

Cerai smiled at him. "The Gods hid it, of course, like the frightened children they were. You can't really destroy a being of this magnitude, you see. The energy's still there, just in a different form, and they were afraid she might come back together. So they wanted the weapon usable if they had to wield it again. Yet it was too dangerous to simply leave lying around."

Cerai all too obviously enjoyed drawing out the anticipation of her audience.

Kyrkenall hadn't the patience. "So where is it?"

"Safe within 'a place of order, hidden by chaos.'" Cerai finished as if her statement had rendered everything perfectly clear. She appeared to be quoting something and Elenai decided not to ask, anticipating it would just lead Cerai to toy with them longer.

"Why don't we get past the riddles, and get down to business, Cerai," Kyrkenall suggested.

"I doubt it's just randomly lying around in the Shifting Lands," Cerai said. "A lot of the fragments didn't even exist when the Gods fought. I think the people we thought were Gods would have wanted to hide the weapon some place more permanent, a place they already knew. I think it's hidden in one of the five realms they themselves created."

"That's lot of territory," Kyrkenall said.

"Yes. I was flummoxed for a long while."

For the first time in days, Elenai experienced a faint light-headedness and a spiraling of her vision. And then multiple futures stretched before her: she and Kyrkenall gliding over a field of brown dunes on the back of ko'aye, she and Kyrkenall easing across desert flats upon a huge land treader, she and Kyrkenall leading flagging horses through a canyon. None of these, though, were right, and the threads pulled onward and past a blur of other possibilities and permutations until she experienced one of herself beside Kyrkenall, upon his faithful Lyria, riding past high mounded sand dunes, then standing upon a rocky upthrust of ground. A ruddy mountain with a cracked peak rose in the distance, above the surrounding desert. Closer at hand a floppy-eared kobalin jumped joyously up and down while shaking a longish object.

Before she could scrutinize what he held, she was sitting once more at the table; the moment passed as though it had been a dream. She blinked and steadied herself by gripping the edge. She'd never been to that place, but she had studied the geography of the five realms and knew what region she had glimpsed.

Cerai was talking: ". . . a safe, orderly place, with a hiding screen of chaos. Do you see? And then I got a look at all the maps the Gods left on the keystone. Do you know what's not in the keystone?"

"The wastelands of Kanesh," Elenai said.

It pleased her to see the utter bafflement upon Cerai's face. Those finely sculpted eyebrows twitched as the renegade alten strove to master a display of curiosity. "What an astute guess," she said. "How did you come to make it?"

Elenai wished she knew the answer. A few weeks ago she had thought these glimpses of future were due to her attunement with Rialla's old hearthstone. More recently she had begun to think Rialla herself had been sending her nudges toward the best path, via that same hearthstone. But the stone was shattered and drained and Rialla vanished, likely dead for good now. "I'm an intuitive guesser," Elenai said, and was further pleased by Cerai's frown.

"Well, you're right," Cerai said. "The wastelands aren't part of the map on the keystone. I think they were added to the realm afterward, as a place to hide the weapon."

"That doesn't narrow a search area by much," Thelar said. "The wastelands themselves are immense. And difficult to travel. Do you have an idea in what section it might be hidden?"

Almost, Elenai volunteered that she knew, but she felt she had drawn too much attention to herself already.

"I think a mage familiar with hearthstones might be able to sense the weapon, though the search will have its challenges. The weapon's going to feel almost like the absence of a hearthstone. If you know what to look for, it could stand out. It also will require a good bit of luck to find it quickly." Her gaze shifted to Kyrkenall. "You have a marked ability for achieving the impossible. I thought I might send you and a dozen of my best men. They're all sensitive to magic. You can take one of your mages with you, if you like, but I'll need the bulk of them to further fortify the magics here."

"I volunteer," Elenai said, not to Cerai, but N'lahr.

He saw her steadfast look and surely knew that there was more to it. He nodded once.

"You want to search hundreds of miles of wasteland with only a dozen men and a single mage?" Rylin asked, sounding insulted by the obvious absurdity.

"You clearly understand why I haven't attempted the search before," Cerai said. "But then, I didn't have Kyrkenall."

It occurred to Elenai that Cerai might have expended energy on a portal solely to scoop up her favorite alten so he could go fetch for her. But hadn't Rialla said something about using the portal to siphon energy, as well?

N'lahr closed his hand, no longer shaking, around the stem of the goblet. He looked across the table to Elenai. "Do you think Drusa and Lelanc will want to accompany you?"

She shook her head. "No. We'll have to ride. The question is how we'll get there. I assume you mean to send us through a portal, Cerai?" Strange, she thought, to call her so casually by her first name when they weren't friends. She no longer thought of the woman as an alten, though, and she'd be damned before she referred to her as "goddess."

Cerai took no umbrage and answered easily. "That was my thought."

"How will we get back?" Elenai asked.

"Contact me with a hearthstone. I'll have to loan you one of mine. And you'll need supplies."

N'lahr answered for them. "Yes."

Kyrkenall looked first to Elenai, then to N'lahr, opening his mouth as if to ask a question. Then he wisely shut it.

"I just don't understand," M'vai blurted out. As the entire table shifted their attention to her, she pushed back her hair, not as someone aware of a poor state of grooming, but as though she pressed in upon her head to keep something terrible at bay. "The plan worked. We got to the queen before she started opening the hearthstones. When we killed her there were only forty or fifty of them still open. A bunch of them weren't even connected, and the body of the Goddess was shattered into pieces. It shouldn't have worked!"

"It doesn't make sense," Tesra agreed. "The queen was certain we needed almost every piece of her in the proper order for the Goddess to return."

"Well," Cerai said, and cleared her throat. She waited until that had drawn all of the attention to her end of the table. "It wouldn't have mattered if Leonara had put them together as a likeness or arranged them like a giant hat. Once she had enough in one place and started opening them, the end result was going to be the same; they'd start feeding on each other. You might have been able to stop the process if you'd closed them faster, but it was probably a foregone conclusion."

"You knew that?" Tesra asked. "Why didn't you say something to us about it? We wasted years!"

"That was rather the point," Cerai said. "Leonara just wasn't very bright, and I needed to buy some time."

Kyrkenall snorted, then let out a hearty laugh. "You suggested arranging them in a statue to her, didn't you?"

"I may have," Cerai admitted with a sly smile, and Kyrkenall laughed once more, not looking remotely awkward despite the fact no one else but Cerai appeared the least bit amused. Rylin and N'lahr sat stone-faced. The three exalts stared at Cerai in a mix of disgust and astonishment.

"Perhaps you should further explain what you've learned of hearthstone magics to our spell casters so they can assist your defensive improvements," N'lahr said. "I need to get these two ready for their journey." He indicated Kyrkenall and Elenai.

Cerai hesitated, then seemed to decide she was getting what she wished. "I'll have the servants ready travel supplies, and horses."

While she reached behind her to pull a black bell cord, N'lahr looked across the table. "Tesra, I hope you're with us in this. If not, you will not be harmed, but you'll have to surrender until this conflict is at an end."

The dark-haired woman licked her lips and lowered her head.

"She'll come around," Cerai said as she faced forward once more. "It's a difficult adjustment, but she can see where her future lies. Can't you, Tesra?" Cerai favored her with a smile that didn't touch her eyes.

The exalt nodded without looking up and Elenai felt a twinge of pity for her.

"Kyrkenall, why don't you three do your scheming in my reception hall?" Cerai asked. "The one with the fish. I'll get the rest of what you need together and meet you in the stables. I'm sure you'll want to be off as soon as possible."

N'lahr gave her a polite head bow as he climbed to his feet. Against her own inclination, Elenai did the same. Only Kyrkenall traded salutes. To Thelar's troubled glance Elenai gave a tight smile she hoped was reassuring, and then she was following the commander and Kyrkenall from the room.

N'lahr strode right past the reception hall and exited the building. He paused in the sunlight and looked out across the courtyard with its scattered shade trees. The slope-roofed stable was built against the wall opposite them. The commander stood in contemplation of it and then walked across a flagstone path that led to a large well and a small, single-story thatched-roof building beside it.

Kyrkenall spoke quietly as they left the fortress. "You had another vision?" he asked Elenai.

"I did."

"And you didn't want to meet in her reception hall because you thought her people might be listening?" Kyrkenall asked of N'lahr.

"And because I want to keep her off step." N'lahr stopped at the side of the well and looked up at the battlements, where Cerai's nearly identical and nearly shirtless men patrolled.

N'lahr tried the door on the little outbuilding. It opened to him, and Elenai looked past to find an orderly hut with table and chairs. The walls were built of removable panels to convert the structure into a shaded outdoor eating area. It smelled faintly of newly stained wood and candle wax.

N'lahr motioned them in after him, then closed the door. Sunlight strayed only feebly between the wood slats.

Elenai didn't feel like sitting. Kyrkenall lowered himself onto the edge of the table and faced his friend.

"How are you feeling?" Elenai asked.

"Not entirely well," N'lahr admitted. "But I'm right enough for the moment, and my condition's not something you can do anything about."

"You want to be more specific?" Kyrkenall asked.

"I'm feeling some hearthstone effects."

"I should look at you," Elenai said. "You took the full brunt of the queen's attack."

"Yes. And I'm sure I'd be dead twice over if Varama hadn't linked the rings, even with Irion in my hands."

"It may have accelerated your condition," Elenai said. "I should really—"

He cut her off with a chopping motion of his hand. "Save your strength. Thelar or Rylin will help. Now tell me what you saw, and quickly."

Understanding N'lahr's haste, she recounted her vision.

"I'm not entirely sure how I feel about having you rely on what I saw," she said afterward, "but it seems like the other visions have led me true, regardless of where they came from."

"You haven't steered us wrong yet," Kyrkenall said.

"I know," Elenai agreed. "I just wish I knew where these glimpses of the future were coming from. It can't be Rialla though, right? If she were still alive, she'd make herself known like she did before, wouldn't she?"

"If she were alive she'd simply be resetting the game board," N'lahr said. "We have to assume she's gone. I trusted her too far."

"You don't think you can trust her?" Kyrkenall sounded shocked.

"I took her at her word, like she was a seasoned scout. Like she was a seasoned alten. But she wasn't. She was still the same person we knew all those years ago." He paused, as if to decide how to explain. "When Rialla was faced with a problem, she planted herself solidly and hammered at it. She was never flexible under stress. You heard her. She told Varama she'd waged the battle with the queen four times. We have no memory of her doing that. Do you know what that must mean?"

Elenai had found little time to consider any of Rialla's recent statements.

Kyrkenall summarized: "She's erasing potential futures so they never happened. Like wiping down a chalkboard."

"Exactly," N'lahr said. "The clues were there, before Varama even explained it. But it didn't occur to me to rethink the situation until Rialla spoke to us at the portal. I worried about the wrong things."

Kyrkenall was gently mocking. "You mean like planning the tactics that would have won the battle against anything but a god?"

"I missed something crucial, but there's a chance you two can make it right. If Rialla is still alive in her time and she returns to speak with you, you have to convince her to speak to us years earlier. She could have popped in as a spirit that night she lay dying, and warned Kyrkenall about everything."

"You don't know she can do that," Elenai said.

"I don't know that she can't," N'lahr said with uncharacteristic venom, and Elenai saw it was self-directed. "I didn't ask. Varama said Rialla had just over six hours. If she spent all of it trying to stop Kyrkenall from falling off a dragon, then running the battle with the queen over and over, I doubt she took a lot of time to reflect upon other possibilities. But we must. I should have seen it."

He was being too hard on himself. "You did the best you could, with the information you had," she said. "You can't—"

He talked over her. "I don't want your absolution. I want you to learn." He paused and locked eyes with her, ascertaining he truly had her attention. In all the days she'd known him, no matter the challenges of the situation, he'd never been so forceful. "A leader always has to think, deeply, before acting. I didn't do that. I focused on my specialties. My preferences. A good leader can't afford to be so limited. You can't necessarily choose the ground where you'll fight, but you can understand the ground that you have to use." N'lahr paused to put the right words together. "If all of your advisors keep handing you rope, you might forget you can build a ladder. Or invent a better way to climb. You have to keep thinking."

"How hurt are you, really?" Elenai asked. Beside her, Kyrkenall said nothing, though he had been watching his friend carefully.

"You shouldn't give up on me yet," N'lahr said. "And Cerai would do better to not underestimate those she's taken in. But your focus is to find that weapon and learn how to use it yourselves, so we put an end to her scheming. Clear?"

"Yes, sir," Elenai said.

"If Rialla warns us back then," Kyrkenall said slowly, "nearly everything changes."

"Yes," N'lahr said.

The archer spoke as if in reverie. "Kalandra wouldn't be lost. Asrahn would be alive. You'd never have been trapped, and you wouldn't be in danger now." He paused, then swore almost reverently. "Damn. Decrin and Commander Renik wouldn't be dead, either. We could even warn Temahr so he wouldn't ride into that ambush."

"There're many that could be saved," N'lahr said. "Most importantly, we could have stopped the queen before any of this came close to happening. And that has to be weighed against the good moments we would lose." He looked to Elenai, and his gaze, even in that dim space felt pointed.

Only then did she realize that if Rialla changed the flow of time earlier, neither of these living legends would know her, much less be her friends. Gone as well would be the close bond she'd formed with Gyldara during the battle against Mazakan, and the similar connections forged with Thelar and M'vai and others, not to mention her ascension to the ring.

Her heart ached at the thought even as she knew that those moments were nothing when measured against the betrayals, disappearances, murders, and thousands of needless deaths.

"I understand," she said.

He offered a glum smile, then worked to dismiss the weighty idea with the suggestion of concrete action. "Now let's get you two on your way."

No fool, Kyrkenall must have reached the same conclusions, for he clapped the back of her shoulder and left his hand there as they followed the commander to the stable.

The archer smiled broadly when he saw Lyria, his responsive dun, in the nearest stall. The horse whickered in recognition and stepped to the gate.

While Kyrkenall cooed and stroked the side of Lyria's head, Elenai stopped to visit with Steadyfoot, Ortok's former mount, and let the large, calm horse eat grain from her palm while she thought of her kobalin friend and wondered as to his fate. If they were meeting with one kobalin out in the wastes, might they meet with Ortok as well? She hoped so.

Cerai arrived only a few moments later, trailed by a band of soldiers and servants who saddled the animals.

The realm's ruler said nothing about their presence here rather than within the suggested room. She simply greeted them and showed Elenai a small green hearthstone. "This one's easy to use. Have you ever searched for hearthstones before?"

"No."

Cerai smiled thinly. "Kyrkenall and N'lahr think well of you, and you've obviously got some talent. You can sense the hearthstones at a distance when they're in use?"

"Yes. Recently I've been able to do so even if I'm not in the inner world." Elenai wished she hadn't added the last, though it earned a nod of approval.

"You know what it's like to search for life through an Altenerai ring. What you must do now is search for normal matrices inherent in the world around you. Every region has a slightly different feel. Once you get to the wastes, familiarize yourself, fast, with what the place is like, so you can sense things that don't belong. Do you understand?"

"I do." She supposed this tutorial might be important, even if her vision had showed her a kobalin finding the weapon.

"So," Kyrkenall said, "Elenai's looking for something that doesn't have any kind of matrix?"

"Not really. Magically it's not just going to have an absence of the matrix—it's going to register like the opposite of the organized power of the hearthstone. Do you understand?"

"I believe I do," Elenai replied.

"I hope so, for our sakes." Cerai extended her hand and Elenai carefully picked up the hearthstone, wishing she didn't constantly feel inferior to the woman who thought her so. Cerai was the one who'd abandoned Alantris, she reminded herself. She was the one who had played along with the queen for her own advantage, rather than alerting everyone when Leonara could still be stopped.

"As far as contacting me, here's a pebble I pulled from the garden. That should help you fix directions. Then you're going to have to anchor yourself to the hearthstone and send your spirit here until you reach me." She dropped a slim gray rock into Elenai's outstretched hand.

Elenai ran a thumb over its smooth surface. "How do I signal you?"

"Oh, I'll know you're here when you send. You've reached out with a hearthstone or shard before, haven't you?"

She had reached out to N'lahr with the shard she'd left in Darassus. "Yes," she answered distractedly, for at the thought of it she wished she'd brought it with her. It had seemed appropriate to leave it behind, for its proximity to N'lahr appeared to worsen his symptoms.

"You'll have twelve of my most magically sensitive soldiers," Cerai said. "They've hunted hearthstones in all kinds of places." She looked past Elenai once more and spoke to Kyrkenall. "You've always been lucky, Kyrkenall. Here's hoping that helps."

One of the servants presented Elenai with the reins of a beautiful black horse. It turned out that she and Cerai's guards had each been equipped with what appeared to be identical copies of the same animal. As the soldiers lifted supply packs upon the others Elenai suppressed a shudder. She remembered the orchards and fields the alten Belahn had shaped, every branch and leaf exactly the same. Was that the kind of world Cerai envisioned?

Before too long, Elenai, Kyrkenall, and the guards—almost as similar in their own way as the horses—were in the courtyard with the realm's ruler and N'lahr.

When Elenai and Kyrkenall stopped before him, N'lahr saluted with his ring, then looked down at the feeble light shining from his sapphire.

"Mine's like that, too," Kyrkenall said as he returned the salute.

Elenai studied hers, aghast that its energies had dwindled almost to nothing.

"Your rings look like they're almost completely drained," Cerai said. "I didn't know that could happen. Did the Goddess do it?"

"Varama linked all the rings so we were protected by their combined power," Elenai explained. "Defending against one of the attacks almost drained them."

Cerai's eyebrows rose. "Well, well. Trust Varama to keep coming up with clever new ideas. Right up until the end. She was quirky but useful."

Quirky but useful, Elenai thought, disgusted by the cavalier dismissal of one of the most brilliant people she'd ever met. She wondered how Rylin would have reacted to that sentiment.

N'lahr stepped closer to Kyrkenall and they clasped arms just below the elbow. They held that pose for a moment while Elenai wondered what both were thinking.

They were so very different in temperament. It sometimes struck her that their friendship made little sense. Either functioned perfectly well without his friend, yet both drew strength from the other. Kyrkenall was more settled around N'lahr, as if living were easier with him in charge.

And the commander, always troubled, was lighter—more hopeful—in the presence of his lively brother-in-arms. Seeing their silent regard, she envied them that closeness, wondering if she would ever know such companionship, and she worried that this might be their final moment together.

Both men broke the clasp at the same moment. N'lahr stepped away, then presented himself to Elenai, formally offering his hand.

"Ride well, Alten." His grip was firm. "You would rise to the ring in any circumstance," he promised.

"That's not the important part," she said.

At that he smiled. "Spoken like a true champion. Good luck. I'm sure I'll meet you, one way or another."

As they broke the grip, Cerai looked bemused, though she chose not to seek explanation. "I'll wish both of you good fortune as well," she said, then turned to her soldiers. "Men, you have your orders."

At her signal, they climbed into their saddles. Kyrkenall swung into his, and Elenai's black horse stood rock steady as she put her foot into the stirrup and threw her leg over the saddle. She felt a pang of regret that she had lost her new horse, Gemon, and wondered what this one was named.

Cerai already manipulated sorcerous threads within the courtyard.

Elenai watched through the inner world, thinking she might learn the secrets of the portal spell, but Cerai's movements were so intricate she scarcely registered more than a few basic concepts.

Lyria snorted in alarm at the shining violet circle swirling into existence before them, and laid back her ears. Kyrkenall soothed her with a quick pat on the neck. Elenai's horse, as well as those of the men behind her, reacted hardly at all, and she guessed they had been designed to be pliable. She couldn't help wondering if Cerai fashioned her soldiers the same way.

Kyrkenall looked over his shoulder to see N'lahr raise his hand, returned the gesture, then sent Lyria galloping forward. Elenai waved goodbye, then followed the archer. Close behind she heard the hoofbeats of the other mounts.

Before very long at all, they were on the other side, where a hot wind blew under pale blue skies, and a white-yellow sun glowed low on the horizon. They had turned up in the early evening. Beneath the burning orb lay a sharp, distant mountain range, and closer, on their right, a low run of brown hills sparsely covered with scrub brush. Elenai saw no sign of the particular mountain from her vision, much less a friendly kobalin.

Everything between them and those distant peaks was sand, though she did not spot dunes until she stared into the horizon. Somewhere in that vast expanse lay a small, rocky plateau with an artifact that was their last chance against a malevolent goddess.

Kyrkenall took a long look at the scenery. "Are we close to where we need to be?"

"It doesn't look like it," Elenai said. "This may be a little more challenging than I thought."

He didn't seem troubled by that. "It always is. We never get the easy jobs."

13

A Meeting of Minds

Rylin didn't know why the commander, Kyrkenall, and Elenai had so quickly agreed to a search with such long odds, and assumed the three possessed information he lacked.

With them gone, he listened dispiritedly as Cerai described the physical and arcane features of her land while pointing to them on a large map a servant had brought in.

More of the muscular attendants arrived with platters of bread and fruit, boiled vegetables, and some kind of roasted bird meat. The four aspirants turned up, still in their squire armor and looking lost and bewildered. Cerai bade them join the meeting. Apparently, they'd been sent for during some command Rylin had missed.

The food lacked seasoning, but Rylin doubted he would have enjoyed it regardless, for he had no appetite. As Cerai caught the aspirants up on what she'd said so far, it came to him that he was failing strictures Asrahn had ground into all his squires. The instructor had promised their very survival might one day depend upon their ability to recall vital details acquired under distracting circumstances. That's why mental clarity exercises and memorization techniques were taught to every squire from almost the first day of their training. A good soldier had to make quick evaluations of terrain and enemy holdings so they could be accurately reported and acted upon. Improperly remembered details could result in the death of allies and innocents, and end in defeat.

Over the last few weeks, he thought he'd understood and applied those exercises better than ever. And yet, their defeat and Varama's death had staggered him so deeply he was hard pressed to follow anything Cerai said. He noticed with gratitude that Thelar soaked up the information and asked smart questions. Rylin couldn't help admiring the man's composure, especially given that Thelar knew Cerai had abandoned Alantris, where Thelar's family lived.

M'vai was mostly silent, her expression glazed and empty. Tesra had composed herself. He'd met her eyes several times but wasn't sure what he saw there. It was almost as though she sought connection at the same time she felt a contrary impulse to despise him. Maybe he deserved that.

Once Cerai finished explaining the more obvious features of her realm, she discussed the magical threads underpinning it. She had designed the realm so that energy directed at it from afar would be funneled to key points constructed for their resiliency.

"I thought that would be useful when Leonara unleashed a cataclysm," Cerai said. "These points also act like deep reservoirs of magic, from which I can draw later."

He wondered if that was why she'd been pulling energy out of the portal when she should have been strengthening it to secure everyone's escape. Had she taken advantage of the moment to increase her own supply? A fresh wave of fury deafened him to what was being discussed.

When he focused again, Tesra was saying something about the design being impressive, and Cerai pretended it was a simple matter when one had access to hearthstones.

"How many do you have?" Rylin asked. It was the first question he'd voiced in some time, and it stopped the conversation short.

"Over two hundred." A smile crooked briefly on Cerai's face. "It wasn't easy parting with those Leonara craved when I still needed her support, but I found ways of retaining the most intriguing, and my collection grew faster as she lapsed into her zealous stupor."

The other exalts and aspirants looked uncomfortable, but Thelar spoke without rancor. "You have more than I would have guessed. This is certainly the largest collection left."

"I'm sure it is," Cerai agreed. "Some weavers certainly have kept one or two, and there are probably a few odd ones scattered here and there across the cosmos, but if this entity makes hearthstone recovery a priority, my little kingdom's going to be her first stop."

"What are we going to do?" M'vai's green eyes were large with alarm. "There's no telling how long it will take Kyrkenall and Elenai to find that weapon."

Rylin studied M'vai with fresh eyes and was struck by her youth. Likely she was no more than twenty. Almost everyone at the table had been taking hard emotional blows over the last weeks, but what must it be like for her, to side against the majority of her friends, to hazard her life in multiple battles, and then to witness not only the deaths of those friends, but her twin sibling? She and Meria seemed to have moved almost as one through all the times he'd seen them.

It was no wonder she sounded close to breaking.

Tesra reached out to squeeze her hand.

"You're right to be concerned," Cerai said. "But we're not defenseless. And this might work to our advantage."

At a loud thud from the far end of the table, Rylin whirled in his chair, hand to his knife.

"Sorry." It was a young woman's voice, and Rylin saw the smallest of the aspirants, a woman even younger than M'vai, looking shamefacedly at the rest of them. "I was just . . . taking off my armor," she said. "It slipped."

The other three aspirants looked almost as embarrassed as she did.

"No apology necessary," Rylin told her. "It's not your fault we're all on edge, and you acquitted yourself bravely during the battle." Their expressions eased. The young woman looked especially grateful for the kind word, even as she adjusted the ringmail on the floor behind her.

He'd spent time thinking about the feelings of the loyal exalts, but he'd spared none for these four, who had likewise turned their backs on the queen and their friends and fought to save Darassus from the Naor invasion. While he'd heard their names, he didn't recall a one of them. He decided to remedy that.

"As long as we're on the subject of armor," Cerai said, as if irritated attention was distracted from her, "what I'm after is an armoring of the realm. You can help me to finish strengthening it so that it's more resilient to directed attacks."

"A warrior needs a sword as well as armor," Thelar pointed out.

Rylin thought that sounded like something N'lahr might have said, or perhaps Asrahn.

"But of course," Cerai said. "As it happens, I developed a countermeasure should any curious mages ever get too close to my realm. It might slow down the entity as well, but I doubt it'll be as effective as the weapon that originally stopped her."

"What mages were you expecting?" Thelar asked, as if he feared the answer.

"Well." Cerai's look was almost apologetic. "Exalts, really. I thought

Leonara would find out about my realm at some point, and come for my hearthstones."

Rylin saw that she'd startled the other exalts again, probably for her own amusement. He decided to put a stop to it. "You should tell us about the countermeasure," he suggested.

"I'm getting there, my dear. I have spirits of chaos." This time there was no missing the pride in her voice. "I've captured several of the larger ones."

"Spirits of chaos," Rylin repeated, reasoning it out as he spoke. He couldn't help sounding astonished. "You mean the hungry entities from the deep shifts?"

"Yes, that's exactly what I mean."

The last time he'd passed through the shifts during a storm, he'd done so in the company of Lasren, Elik, and the governor of Alantris. The chaos spirits had hunted them, and he would never forget the chill certainty that death had missed them only because it had stopped to consume two of their horses. "How did you manage that?" Rylin asked.

"Why would you even try?" M'vai asked.

"If you've ever dealt with them, you know how fearful and dangerous they are. I thought they'd be of use against my enemies. As to how I did it, well . . ." She paused as if torn between bragging and revealing too much. Clearly the need to impress won out, for she continued, "They can't stand to be surrounded by solid order. They can't cross the larger borders because, while they're attracted to life energy and magic, too much order is overwhelming; it's too great a hindrance to them. Once I understood *that*, the matter seemed obvious. I lured them close and then completely encased them within an orderly prison."

That didn't seem at all obvious to Rylin.

"If they're repelled by order how will you react if you set them loose against the Goddess?" Thelar asked. "Isn't she nothing but order?"

"She's also nothing but magic," Cerai said. "The most powerful of all magic sources. And the chaos spirits love magic. I think they'll head straight for her. I can guess what will happen when they reach her; it should be most diverting."

"But you can't be sure," Thelar said doubtfully.

"No. Don't look so surprised. I didn't capture the spirits to fight the original manifestation of order in the universe. I never expected to have to do that."

"You talk about using order to trap the chaos energy," Thelar said. "Can we use their chaotic energy to trap her order?"

Cerai nodded. "That's essentially what I'm hoping will happen if we unleash the chaos spirits. Although chaos, by nature, can't wall her in, not like order can wall in chaos. It's too unstable to form a true barrier."

"What if we drained away her energy?" Thelar suggested. "She's an energy source, isn't she? We could try pulling some of it away."

Though he understood the fundamentals of the magical discussion, Rylin's attention wandered again. He tried to ask himself what Varama would be doing, were she here. Probably she'd be ten steps ahead of them in this magical theory. He could never manage *that,* but he could anticipate what she would have suggested *he* do. "This technical talk is beyond me." He put his hands to the table. "If you don't mind, while the rest of you are working all of this out, I'd like to look at the keystone."

Cerai's slim brows arched. "That's a waste of time. There's nothing on it that can help."

"Maybe there's something you missed," he said, working to sound less challenging.

"There isn't."

He continued with cool calm: "The queen was desperate for it. You left a battle for it, even though I know you're no coward. There must be something important there, and I'd like to make sure you haven't missed it."

"There was no point in trying to defend Alantris when it was going to fall, or putting myself at risk when I'm the only one who can rebuild," Cerai said. "And there's no point in your looking at the keystone. Not now. It's my rebuilding plan, that's all."

"I hear what you're saying," Rylin said. "But I owe a debt, and I mean to pay it. If Varama had lived, she would want to look at the keystone. And since she can't . . ." He let the thought trail off rather than be overcome with emotion.

Thelar finished for him. "I know it was important to the queen, Alten Cerai. Maybe there's additional information on it. Something Rylin might notice, with fresh eyes."

Cerai's lashes fluttered. "Very well. I suppose you're not very useful here anyway, Rylin." She waited, as if she expected him to protest. When he didn't, she called for one of her servants to lead him to a private room where he could look at the stone. As if to indicate her utter lack of interest in his involvement in her more important efforts, she told him to take as much time as he wished.

Rylin thanked her, raised a hand in farewell to the others, and followed one of her guards from the chamber.

Shortly thereafter, he was seated at a table in a small room on the third floor. A single arched window looked down upon the empty courtyard.

A round opalescent stone larger than his fist sat upon a blue pillow in a wooden box that the servant had brought. It certainly looked like the keystone he'd seen in Varama's possession.

He eyed the orb before touching it. He remembered Varama saying it wasn't a true hearthstone, but a repository for maps, and once again wished that she were here, with him. He knew all too well that he was no replacement for her even on his brightest day. He pushed back a wave of sorrow. Now wasn't the time for feelings; it was time to emulate her methods. She'd had only a brief opportunity to study it. What secrets might it still hold, and how could he apply himself to discovering them?

He located the weak spot within the keystone's sorcerous energy matrix and it opened to him. He didn't find himself awash with energy, as he would have the moment he made contact with a hearthstone, but it did at least sustain rather than tire him.

The stone proved both like and unlike what he had pictured from Varama's description. He looked upon images fashioned as though someone had gazed upon landforms from above and painted them with lifelike detail. He saw streams and mountains, plains and forests. What he did not observe were any settlements or roads, even in the places where he knew them to be. He was certain of the location of his birth town, along the shores of Lake Dahrial, in Erymyr, and he well knew the point below the mountains where Darassus lay. The settlements simply weren't there.

He reminded himself that the images within the stone must be ancient, created before the realms had human buildings.

As he peered with great interest at the border of Erymyr, the image increased in size and detail, as though he were plunging out of the air and down toward the trees. Momentarily alarmed by the simulated fall, he pulled away, discovering that intense scrutiny increased the size of each image so that, on closer inspection, finer detail became apparent, even down to individual leaves. The foliage looked so astonishingly realistic he might as well have been holding it in his hand.

Fascinating though this exercise proved, he began to suspect Cerai was right, and that there was nothing immediately useful stored upon the stone.

He pulled back from small scale contemplation and sorted through the contents, discovering renditions of all the realms, as Varama had described. He paused while examining the map of the Lost Realm, central yet apart, where they'd faced the queen, then moved on to other images.

He'd thought at first he was looking at the dark and wintry Naor realms and kobalin shards, but most of the remaining images turned out to resemble half-finished sketches abandoned by their artists. They were alive with soaring mountains and deep ravines and other oddities. It struck him that the keystone contained blueprints, not just maps. Just as a builder of a temple or fortress would draw their plans before construction commenced, the Gods apparently had made record of their intentions, even experimenting with other ideas before choosing the ones they liked best.

As his examination continued, Rylin came upon more and more unfinished areas. He found a small realm all of water with tiny round islands; an immense, snow-capped mountain with sheer sides rising alone from a vast evergreen forest; a dark realm where glowing scarlet-leaved trees leaned down from serrated ridges; and other, stranger places. The most interesting of these incomplete ideas was a less-detailed map off to the side where each of the known realms was separated without the usual gaps of Shifting Lands and laid out upon an immense globe. Completely new landforms and large bodies of water were stitched between and beyond them.

Each of the sketches was unique and curious, but none seemed remotely useful in their current predicament.

When at last he ceased his study, he grew aware he'd left himself completely unprotected. Anyone might have crept up behind him while his attention was so diverted.

But the room sat empty. The outside light possessed an aged quality, as of the late afternoon. He had wasted hours, and was frustrated and angry: first, because Cerai was right that he'd found nothing of use; and second, because he was certain Varama would have discovered something important; and third, that she was not here. They needed her mind, not his.

He left the keystone in its box and then found a servant to ask where the commander had gone.

He was led to another third-floor room, where he found M'vai sitting alone on a couch. The servant looked confused. "Where is the N'lahr commander?" he asked M'vai.

"Through the next door," she answered. "Talking with your goddess and the Naor leader."

The servant turned to Rylin. "He is talking with the goddess in her office." He pointed toward the door at the room's far end.

"I'll wait here," Rylin said. And then, when the fellow stared at him, gave him permission to leave.

"They're so strange," M'vai said softly after the man had departed.

"That they are," Rylin replied.

He and M'vai were in a rectangular room divided in half by a grouping of chairs and couches. The side with the door to the office was, apart from being well-ordered, reminiscent of Varama's laboratories. Glass jars and vials filled with numerous dried ingredients sat upon shelving units along one wall above a row of closed white cabinets. Two tables supported larger glass containers as well as scales and other measuring tools.

The couches and chairs dividing the room faced a desk and cushioned chair in front of yet another cabinet. The young exalt sat upon a couch against the wall, in line with another of the arched windows. She had taken off her khalat, laid it on the couch beside her, and rolled up the sleeves of her white blouse past her elbows, showing freckled arms.

"How are you holding up?" Rylin sat on the desk edge, facing her. She looked exhausted or sick.

"I'm working hard to not lose my mind. How are you?"

"Not much better. I'm sorry about your sister."

"Yes." Her voice sounded tired and small as she turned away. "I'm sorry about a lot of things."

"What are they doing in there?"

"Anzat wanted to talk with Cerai, and the commander wanted to hear. And I'm keeping an eye on him, so here I am."

"Why are you keeping an eye on him?" Rylin asked.

"Haven't you looked at the commander lately? Through the inner world?"

"No."

"The queen's attack did something to him. His energy matrix is all overgrown."

Rylin remembered how the commander's hands had shaken several times during the early part of the meeting, and chastised himself for not paying more attention. "What's it doing to him?"

"He's starting to have trouble moving," she said. M'vai didn't ask if he'd noticed that, but it was apparent in her critical look.

He reminded himself that given her current circumstance, her mood wasn't likely to be at its best. "I saw that," he said. "There have been a lot of things to worry about."

She sniffed and wiped at her eyes. "You're right. I just can't help wondering how things might have been different if I'd listened to Meria sooner. She knew there was something wrong with the way Commander Synahla and the queen were acting. I knew it, too." Her eyes glistened, and Rylin hopped down from the desk to offer a cloth from his utility belt.

"Thank you." M'vai blotted at her eyes as Rylin retreated to the desk. "I told Meria they were just under stress, and that she was being flighty again. She never wanted to stay the course. She's the one who talked me into joining the exalt auxiliary, and then there she was wanting to leave it!" She let out a shuddering sigh and wiped her eyes again.

"How long ago was this?" Rylin asked.

"For the last few months." M'vai's voice dropped. "I used to admire Cerai, but I know what Meria would say now. The woman can't be trusted."

Rylin nodded in agreement.

"If anyone is going to see us through this, it's the commander," M'vai continued. "We have to make sure he recovers."

"Can you do that?"

"I'm certainly going to try." She looked as though she meant to say more, but the far door swung open and she turned to watch as N'lahr emerged, followed by Anzat, then Cerai.

"Well, well," Cerai said to Rylin. "Did you find any surprises?"

"I wish I had."

M'vai climbed to her feet and bent down to shoulder into her uniform coat.

"I told you so. I'm going to inspect Anzat's troops, and then I'm going to start working with the mages. M'vai, why don't you round all of them up. The healers, too. We'll let Rylin shepherd Commander N'lahr for a while."

M'vai looked doubtful, but Rylin gave her a comforting nod. "All right," she said, though the look in her eyes was a plain, almost desperate message: keep N'lahr safe.

Anzat watched with frank appraisal as M'vai walked toward him, and then all three left.

"Cerai knows we're going to talk, and doesn't care," Rylin said in disgust after the door had closed behind them.

"She knows we'll talk, here or somewhere else," N'lahr said. "Letting you know that is a power play. She's grown in arrogance since last I knew her."

"What did Anzat want?" Rylin asked.

"He was trying to get the lay of the land. And I'm afraid he has it."

"Anzat's going to back Cerai, isn't he?"

"He's clever, in his way. She does hold the high ground."

"I thought he'd hate following a woman."

"He said something to the effect of how he approved of following a woman who actually had power, and wasn't pretending to be a man."

Rylin winced. He was going to miss Vannek. "He just wants power himself."

"Yes. And Cerai is curious to see the capability of his troops. Aside from sheer numbers, her own men may not be as effective as warriors."

"What's wrong with them, anyway?" Rylin asked.

"Kyrkenall says that they used to be kobalin and that Cerai 'rewarded' them with human bodies."

The enormity of Cerai's power alarmed him. "I suppose that explains some of it," he said. "As for Anzat, he doesn't have to lead the Naor. We could find someone else."

"Even if we could remove him without making the rest of the Naor suspicious or resentful, whichever one of them commands is liable to follow the strongest leader."

"And right now that looks like Cerai."

"Right now that *is* Cerai."

That N'lahr acknowledged the problem so bluntly troubled Rylin. "So what are we going to do? Have Elenai and Kyrkenall already left?"

"They have. But we won't be idle. Did you learn anything useful?"

"From the keystone? No. Maybe Varama would have seen something, but . . ."

Of all the times to finally lose composure, it was then, as he was presenting information to the man he most admired. He turned away to gather his breath. "Pardon me."

N'lahr said nothing, and Rylin felt rising shame until the commander stepped closer. His voice was low. "Don't give up on Varama."

The advice surprised him. "You think Cerai's lying about her?"

"She might have sensed Varama's ring go out because it absorbed another attack."

"An attack from the Goddess would have killed her," Rylin said.

"Almost certainly. If Varama stood still for it."

Rylin started to object that she had been standing still, since she'd been holding the portal open. And yet, it was surely possible Cerai had misjudged information. The commander was trying to communicate something more than he was saying aloud.

N'lahr mouthed two words. "She lives."

14

A Field of Stars

From the foot of the hill where he lay, Vannek watched the gigantic demon drift into the distance. Her ebon hair and flowing garment were so black they seemed to repel even the darkness, so that she was visible for leagues as she retreated into the night. Vannek's hate followed like a well-honed spearpoint, raised for casting.

But the demon being was long out of range, and a spear against her would have been useless. Hating her had no more effect than wishing.

Vannek smelled blood, and wondered whether it was his own. And then came clarity, and the awareness that while some of the blood might have been his, Muragan had worked a spell, for as he shifted to look at the bloodmage he found him sweating. The source of the stench grew readily apparent: under the bright full moon and the shining stars he perceived a pair of the vaunted Altenerai horses lying dead in a steaming pool of blood only a sword's length away.

Vannek reached up to probe a sore spot on the back of his head.

"The wind threw you into the hill pretty hard," Muragan said wearily. Vannek guessed that he'd been winded by magic work. "Your leg got the worst of it. How does your head feel?"

"I'll live." According to legend, blood mages had first discovered their calling upon the battlefield, and ever since, their greatest practitioners were employed, like lowly but necessary nurses, to heal the most important of the wounded warriors. Muragan had once knit a gaping spear wound in Mazakan's side, and the old monarch had kept him near, like a lucky charm, ever after.

As Vannek gathered his wits, he recalled that his right calf had been alive with agony when the Goddess' storm had slammed him here. Unconsciousness had descended mercifully. He flexed his knee, then his ankle. It felt bruised, but neither sprained nor broken.

He took stock of his immediate surroundings. He saw only a scattering of motionless bodies in the moonlight. A large, roughly oblong block of crystal that encased the land treader sat near the smashed wreckage of the huge wooden scaffolding. A long straight pathway began nearby and stretched off into the darkness. That was new.

"Where is everyone?" Vannek realized his throat was dry even as Muragan handed him a wineskin. He took it without comment as he sat up.

"A storm came in," Muragan said. "When it was gone, most of the survivors were gone with it. Through a portal."

The sweet Dendressi wine was a welcome pleasure he didn't have the mental strength to trouble over. He took a long drink, handed the skin back, and experimentally climbed to his knees. They seemed steady, so he pushed up with the aid of his right hand, ignoring Muragan's offered arm. On the left lay the headless body of the Dendressi queen. He knew he should have felt pride and wondered why he experienced not the faintest trace of it. He did not see her head, and wondered if it, too, had been caught in the wind.

Muragan saw the direction of his gaze.

"Dead, by your hand." He sounded as though the idea was hard to credit.

Vannek understood that. He would never have dreamed he would kill the Dendressi queen, much less that he would do so at the side of the Altenerai. He tried to imagine what his family would have said, had they been alive, and he felt so removed from them and their concerns he abandoned the idea.

He recalled that his own followers had rejoiced. "Did my men get away?"

"The Dendressi who fled took most of them. Along with Anzat."

"Why didn't they take us? Was that deliberate?"

"I don't think so. It was hard to see during the great storm. I heard them calling for all to follow."

"And you didn't go with them."

"Not until I knew whether you were dead."

Again he wondered at Muragan's strange loyalty. He searched for explanation and still couldn't read whatever lay hidden behind his eyes. "I thank you," Vannek said, and wondered why the gratitude came so hard. Probably because he had yet to divine what Muragan really wished from him.

"Where do you think the fae death goddess was going?" Muragan asked.

Vannek's gaze tracked toward the direction she had drifted, and the long road she had left in her wake. "Who can say? Maybe she's off to destroy all our lands, like the Dendressi claimed."

"If that were her aim, I don't know why she wouldn't have finished this place, with us as well."

This was the first thing he'd said that really grabbed Vannek's attention, because the mage's point was valid.

"And she could have killed them, too." Muragan pointed off to the right, and the side of a low hill.

Vannek looked past the finger to a group of figures circled about something lying on the ground. They wore khalats, but even from a distance he sensed they were not the Altenerai. These, then, were the enemy exalts, and they argued amongst themselves. One swept a hand at whatever lay there.

Vannek bent, lips compressed, and reached for the sword that lay beside him. It had been cleaned of blood; Muragan, then, had also worked to make sure he had a weapon handy. He was well-schooled in a ruler's needs. Vannek started forward.

"What are you doing?"

"Something's upsetting them," Vannek said. "Maybe it's something we need."

Muragan fell in step, and they moved down past the stupidly happy statues casting long moon shadows across the inky black pool of water.

Vannek's first steps were uneven, but soon his stride felt comfortable enough. He looked to his companion, realizing that his thoughts were growing less muddled. An obvious question came to him. "Why didn't you retreat with the rest?"

"I was looking for you," Muragan answered. "I told you that. Remember?" His brows furrowed in worry, and Vannek gave him a hard look.

"I remember. But I don't understand. There's nothing more I can do. I've no army, or if I still do, there's no way to get to them before the demon goddess does."

"There's a power in you," Muragan said, "and it grows with every trial."

Vannek laughed.

The blood mage spoke sharply, as if to cut him off. "What other Naor leader slew a Dendressi queen?"

Vannek ceased his laughter partly because the statement's truth reached him and partly because he recognized madness in the sound and didn't like it.

As he and Muragan drew closer the exalts ceased their debate and watched them. They stood around a recumbent person, a figure either unconscious or dead.

All four looked to be in their midtwenties, two women and two men. One man's uniform was splattered with dark stains that had to be blood, though it didn't seem to be his. None carried weapons, and as Vannek stopped a few paces out, bared sword in his hand, he wondered if they'd try spell work.

They studied him less with fear than distaste, as though he were an unexpected guest turning up from a disfavored clan. Vannek wondered why they weren't more angry at the sight of him. In the chaos of the fight they might not have seen him take the queen's head.

The figure at their feet moved, sluggishly, then sat upright. She raised one hand to her head.

It was Varama, hair wild, helmet vanished. Vannek had hoped it was Rylin, or N'lahr. Any of the others, really, even Elenai.

But it was Varama, the blue-skinned one with the long chin and the odd curling hair. Varama, who had harassed them from the hidden recesses of Alantris and engineered the death of his younger brother and so many strong officers. Varama, who had burned Alantris rather than let Vannek rule. If not for her tenacious resistance, Syrik might yet live, and that thought, at last, roused an emotion that wrested a sudden breath from his lungs. He stood staring, without comment.

"What do you want, Naor?" the man in the bloodstained uniform asked Vannek.

"She's seen the Goddess in her glory," a short woman beside him said. "They've come to surrender to us."

"No," Vannek said flatly.

The exalts shifted uncomfortably.

"Don't fight them now." Varama's high-pitched voice was gruff with fatigue and seemed aimed at him, rather than her countrymen. She pushed to her feet and stepped apart from the exalts, who gave her a wide berth. Varama bent to the ground and rose with a long, straight, and bloodied blade. It shook for a moment before the alten's hand steadied. "The battle's over." Varama's voice was high and clear, and rang like hard steel struck with a hammer. She retreated to Vannek's side. She addressed him, though her eyes did not leave the exalts. "Is there anyone else?"

"No one alive," Muragan said. "Why didn't you escape with the others?"

"The portal was being closed from the other end. I had to hold it open."

"Your ghost friend couldn't keep it open?" Vannek asked.

Varama's answer was clipped. "My 'ghost friend' wasn't involved."

"I saw the Goddess chase after some as they went for the portal," Muragan said. "If you were holding it, how did you survive?"

"Apparently the portal was of far greater interest than I." The alten didn't bother elaborating.

"But if she didn't hurt you," Muragan persisted, "why were you lying on the ground?"

"I've never held open a portal," Varama said. "I found it taxing."

Muragan looked as if he planned to ask more questions, but Vannek interrupted. "Do you know where the Goddess is going?"

"Not with any degree of certainty, no."

The bloodstained man spoke up with breathless fervor, sounding very much like a priest. "She's gone forth to begin the cleansing, and to rework the realms so that all of them are paradises. Soon she will return, and lead us there. If you open your souls and swear allegiance, she may yet spare you."

"Your reasoning is flawed," Varama replied.

"What are you planning?" Vannek asked her, ignoring the fools.

Varama removed a rag from a waist pouch and carefully wiped down the steel. "I'm going to leave. I may need your assistance." She turned to face the exalts, watching warily. She sheathed her weapon, then spoke to them as though they were reasonable. "While the Goddess has been restored, she is manifestly not the beneficent deity that you seem to have anticipated, as is readily apparent from her actions. She has slain my people as well as yours, indiscriminately."

The deep-voiced man replied. "Not all can achieve a perfect faith, yet we live. She favors us. She will return and restore the others."

The alten pushed unruly hair back from her high forehead and tried again. "You have misplaced your trust. If the Goddess does return, she's unlikely to display any greater degree of interest in your well-being that she already has."

This time the other man spoke. "My faith is certain. The Goddess will return, and all truths shall be revealed. She will soothe our pains, vanquish our enemies, and make all lands into paradise."

"We know that she will reward us," the small woman declared. Her companion nodded beside her.

"Then I wash my hands of you," Varama said. "You're of no use to the realms. Or to anyone at all." She turned to Vannek. "I'm going to leave. If you wish to accompany me, we need to gather supplies."

"Where are you going?" Vannek asked.

"I'll explain that later." Varama moved off.

After searching the eyes of the exalts, Vannek determined they were unlikely to attack, and followed the alten, Muragan with him. He found himself staring at the back of the alten's neck with the same intensity he had stared at the retreating demon and sneered, both at her, and at himself. Now was not the time for vengeance.

Muragan glanced over his shoulder at the exalts before speaking. "I think they're too full of faith to challenge us."

"They're too full of fear," Vannek said.

"I don't think they're afraid of us."

"No, they're afraid of acting without permission. They've been followers too long."

Varama arrived at a pillared temple built into the hillside behind the statues.

She spoke to them. "Gather the supplies we need for travel."

Vannek was no one's follower, but rather than point this out, he sought explanation. "What will you be doing?"

"Looking for magical assistance." She turned and headed into the dark temple recesses.

"What do you want to do, Lord General?" Muragan asked softly

"We will have to leave, and we will need supplies. We might as well work with her. I don't think we'll be any good at helping her with Dendressi sorcery."

"She assumes she's in charge."

Vannek snorted. "If she's our way out of here, she is. I don't like her tone, but then I suppose she has as little reason to like us as we have her."

Over the next half hour, the two of them searched among the fallen, recovering shoulder packs and wineskins. They then harvested the abundant fruits and some broad plant leaves they discovered to be not only edible, but delicious. Finally, they rounded up all the Altenerai mounts. They took bits from all of them so they could graze, and took saddles from all but the six they led back to the temple.

The moon climbed higher. Vannek munched on one of the supremely delicious golden fruits as he looked over at the nearby statues, idly wondering who they were, and who had built them. On his third bite he heard the click of Varama's bootheels on the flagstones.

The alten spoke to them as she stepped out from the archway to the inner structure.

"Did you find any magic?" Muragan asked.

"Some," Varama answered. "It's hardly sufficient, but we shall have to make do." Her eyes took in the pile of saddlebags Vannek and Muragan had gathered. "There looks to be ample food. You selected a variety, including nuts?"

"We did," Muragan said.

"Did you find enough magic to get us back with the others?" Vannek asked.

"No. It will be more than challenging to form a portal here because the realm is . . . solid."

"I noted that." Muragan nodded and rubbed at his beard, black in the moonlight. "It feels even more substantial than the heart of Darassus. And most of the ambient magic is gone. I'm guessing the Goddess absorbed it."

Varama eyed the mage keenly, as if reevaluating him. "Yes. I will have to attempt opening a portal once we reach the shifts."

"How far away is that?" Vannek asked.

"Assuming that the map was roughly drawn to scale, we're at least one full day's ride from the border."

"And what if you can't open a portal there?" Vannek asked.

"Then we will have to travel the deep shifts. Come. Let's saddle the horses."

Vannek frowned at her back as the alten turned away.

He had little hope for the future, but for one idea. If they could neither link up with their people or get anywhere else, before the world ended he would give himself the satisfaction of killing Varama.

15

The Sorceress in the Night

Knowing N'lahr would only explain further if he felt safe to do so, Rylin didn't press the commander for details, the least of which being how he could state so certainly Varama lived.

And so Rylin mastered his joy, though he could not quite contain his smile.

"Thank you for that," he said.

N'lahr nodded minutely. "The Naor are going to start building cata-pults. I'll look in on that, but you should thoroughly familiarize yourself with the fortress. Understand its defenses." His dark eyes met Rylin's, who understood that, once again, the commander meant more than he said. "I can think of no one better suited for that duty."

"Yes, sir," Rylin said. "What are the Naor planning with the catapults?"

"Anzat suggested they might be used against the Goddess. It's humor-ous on the face of it, but perhaps not utterly stupid. Even a deity might find large rocks hurtling at her distracting, especially if she's already ha-rassed by magical attacks."

Rylin concurred that the idea had some merit.

"Gather your information and report to me when you can," N'lahr finished.

"Yes, sir."

N'lahr brought his hand halfway up to his chest and then halted, as though he'd been struck by some brilliant idea. But he did not speak, nor move further.

"Commander?" Rylin asked.

N'lahr did not respond.

"Sir?"

N'lahr completed the salute as if nothing at all had gone wrong, and as if he himself were unaware of the delay.

Sadly, Rylin returned the gesture. "You had some sort of slowing epi-sode there, Commander."

"Did I?" he asked, then continued, without a hint of pleasure: "Excel-lent. I'm fine for now. You worry about your orders."

Rylin didn't argue. He supposed that the first place he should familiar-ize himself with was this room, so he remained behind when the com-mander departed.

Unsure of how much time he had, Rylin first approached the most ob-vious point of interest, Cerai's office. He looked through the inner world as he drew close, finding magical threads draped about the door. To cur-sory examination they didn't appear overly difficult to unravel, but he was reminded of the trap that had been sprung upon Thelar in the queen's office.

Fortunately, there were alternate ways to gather information. He care-fully sent threads through the wall. Judging from stray spell energies he encountered, Cerai regularly used magic in the space, which hardly sur-prised him. Most intriguing of all was a cylindrical object about the size of a spear haft. Its matrix was so perfectly shaped it had to have been built through magical means. As if to confirm its origin, sorcerous power lingered around it even though it produced none of its own.

No more answers were forthcoming from that examination, so he stepped from the door and prowled about the laboratory and desk. While there were well-ordered parchments with columns of numbers and notations in some of the cabinets, they made little sense. Some were measurements of distance and weight, so perhaps these were notes on fashioning this fortress. Cerai had almost certainly shaped this entire building herself, for the whole seamless structure reeked of her magic. Once again, the level of her power and skill bewildered him. Sooner or later, he knew, they would have to cross her, and he had no illusions about the ease of the coming fight.

For the next several hours, he devoted himself to not just learning the layout of the fortress, but its very makeup. Once he examined the underlying structure, he was pleased N'lahr had acted so cautiously during their earlier discussion, for he found evidence of spellthreads extending into every chamber in every hub of the hexagonal structure, all leading back to Cerai's rooms, as spider silk traced to the center of a web. Most of the threads were inactive, but it was easy to guess that Cerai could innervate them at will and immediately monitor anything taking place within her fortress.

Five of the six wings, he discovered to his horror, were turned over to storing a vast selection of sorcerously frozen creatures from the five realms. Though the astonishing menagerie of predators and prey—mammals, lizards, amphibians, avians, and even insects and plants—fascinated him, it was also a monstrous reminder of Cerai's character and capability, of which he was already abundantly, depressingly, aware.

He wandered nearly wherever he wished, apart from a closed chamber in a first-floor tower. Two guards were posted upon a bench outside it. Given his previous interactions with Cerai's staff, he thought a direct approach would provide the information he needed, and he greeted them politely. "Hail, soldiers of the goddess."

They climbed to their feet and stood straight. "Hail, Alten of the Ring," one of them said.

"What are you guarding?" Rylin asked as if the answer was of no great import.

"The hearthstones of the goddess Cerai," the other answered. Rylin decided against confirming this by looking too far through the inner world. Cerai had mentioned her soldiers were sensitive to magic and might perceive too much prying as hostile. Besides, he thought he sensed the hearthstones.

"Keep them safe," he said, and they promised they would as he moved off.

The upper floors of the administrative wing of Cerai's palace were mostly barracks and empty quarters, some of which were now populated by the gear of squires and Naor soldiers.

Rylin wandered the battlements, eyeing the troops stationed in each location and considering the line of sight in each direction. The spellthreads he detected throughout the building extended to the grounds, and, more sparsely, beyond. The only surprise was to the south, where he spotted Drusa and Lelanc lying in the shade of a hillside grove. He made a mental note to check in with them when he finished scouting.

Once he had familiarized himself with the disposition of the soldiers along the walls, he departed to inspect the courtyard, lovely but unremarkable apart for one feature. At first glance the stables hardly appeared of great interest, large though they were. And then he discovered two of Cerai's servants dragging a hay cart down a ramp in the rear of the building where it abutted the ramparts. At the ramp's base he spied a set of open doors, as well as a pair of soldiers readying to close them. They eyed Rylin suspiciously as he descended.

Beyond them lay a hay-strewn stone corridor not very different from the one serving the stalls above, save for its depth underground and dimensions. In the lantern-lit gloom he saw more pen doors. He also smelled the familiar odors of horse and manure, though there were other less identifiable scents. And then there was the matter of the ceiling, which was much taller than the one above. Why was this chamber so large?

The guards retreated inside the hall and pushed its doors closed behind them. Rylin heard a heavy thud, as of a crossbar being dropped into place.

He considered the best course of action before he put a fist to the door and knocked politely.

"Who seeks entrance?" A muted voice asked through the wood.

"Alten Rylin."

"You are not to enter here," the man told him.

"That's fine. I'm just looking for a number."

There was a brief delay, then a curious query. "What number?"

"I need to know how many mounts we have so I can choose the warriors who're going to ride them." Rylin thought that sounded straightforward enough, but wouldn't necessarily generate the precise information he needed, so he pressed on. "I know how many horses we have up here, and I know how many ko'aye we have, but no one's told me how many of each animal we have down here."

Neither of the men answered for a long moment, and Rylin worried these soldiers might be more capable of reasoning than the others.

A lighter voice replied: "Why are you the one who counts?"

"I'm the best counter," Rylin said.

His reply must have made sense, at least to former kobalin, for it earned him an answer. "There are eight of fire horses, and one air beast. Each fire horse takes two, and the air beast can take a five of riders."

"That's twenty-one," Rylin said, demonstrating his prowess.

"That was quick counting," one of the voices told him.

"That's why they sent me. Enjoy the rest of your day." Rylin tried not to feel too self-satisfied as he started up the ramp. In addition to gaining information, he had fully confirmed one of Cerai's weaknesses. While her soldiers would faithfully execute her orders, they had little understanding about the purpose behind any particular command.

He wondered why Cerai kept what sounded like a more impressive selection of mounts hidden, and supposed she must have toyed with the idea of hosting guests like themselves who wouldn't have approved of the creatures, or who would ask uncomfortable questions about their origins. Or maybe the beasts were simply easier to manage underground.

Apart from one large plow horse, the main level stalls were either empty or occupied by unsettlingly similar black mares. Rylin spent a few moments trying to decide which one acted easiest to work with, discovering they were identically compliant. With some disquiet, he saddled one, fit it with reins and bit from a nearby rack, and led it from the stable.

Before long he had arrived at the spread of oaks where he'd seen the ko'aye. He swung off before his mount came to a complete stop and started up the hill. A lumpy shape in the grass resolved itself into Lelanc, who raised her head on her swanlike, red-brown feathered neck and regarded him through lambent orange eyes. Drusa was nowhere in sight.

He bowed a few steps shy of his friend. She lowered her sharp-beaked head in return.

"I bring you greeting, Lelanc," Rylin said.

"I return greeting, Rylin. You and I ride the winds in strange times."

"Yes. Where's Drusa?"

"She said she wished to see the limits of the land. Do you know that the storm is so bad there is nothing now but night sky past this piece?"

"You mean the void?" Rarely did the storms grow so bad in the shifts there was no land to be found. He had read about such things only in historical accounts.

"I do not know that word," Lelanc said. "But there is no land, only an endless sky."

"That's what we call a 'void,'" Rylin explained, wondering what this information meant for them. Nothing good, he guessed.

"Drusa says that all the lands may fail. That all may perish before we can reach them. She said Kyrkenall spoke to her of such things, before the battle."

"We're worried about those things," Rylin said.

"And Drusa says we have to fight together, those of us here. But how can we fight such a thing as that dark woman who is bigger than all others? Even the greatest of you could not harm her, and she rules the winds."

"We are finding ways to fight. Kyrkenall and Elenai went off to seek a special weapon that can hurt her."

Lelanc let out a soft, eager caw. "I have wished that there was a thing that I could do. A battle I could wage." She eyed Rylin sharply. "I wish to kill Cerai. But she is in the fortress, and you are there with her now."

"I wish we weren't," Rylin said. "I can't stand her," he added. "But I'm afraid we have to work with her to fight the Goddess."

At the flap of large wings he looked up to see Drusa gliding in. Her long neck scar stood out as a pale line through her bright blue feathers.

"The winds shift too much," Lelanc went on. "First the Naor are enemies. Now they are allies. The mind-stealer Cerai betrayed us, yet we must work with her."

"The Naor surrendered to us," Rylin said. "That's different . . ." He saw Lelanc's steady gaze and sighed. "You're right. I'm confused by it, too. Look, everything's falling apart and we all have to work together. There's really nothing more to it than that."

Drusa hit the ground at a run, near the foot of the hill. She was seasoned enough that she had chosen to land opposite the horse, although the beast didn't appear particularly alarmed by her.

Lelanc stared at Rylin, and he wondered if he had made his point with her, or if the gap in understanding was simply too great. He read nothing from her demeanor.

Drusa folded her wings as she climbed the hillside, then stopped and bowed her head formally to Rylin.

"Good morning to you, Alten," she said, her voice rasping. "I have flown to the edge and looked over the darkness. It is a sky that never ends."

"Rylin names it void," Lelanc told her. "He brings word that Kyrkenall and Elenai seek a weapon that will hurt the giant woman thing."

Drusa cawed. "That is good! Have you come to tell us of a weapon we can seek?"

"There's not another I know of. We're still trying to decide what else we can do."

"What do you want of us, Rylin?" Drusa asked shrewdly.

"I came to learn if there was anything you required."

"We desire a battle."

"I was thinking more along the lines of food."

"We hunt among the grasses. We are well, for now. Is there no place we can fly together and seek enemies?"

Rylin felt himself smile. He liked the ko'aye, both for their direct and honest thought processes, and because of their readiness for action. "If I find a place, I'll tell you on the instant."

Drusa lowered her head. "If there is no more fight here, then we will fly the void to fight with our own when comes the enemy to our nests."

Rylin winced inwardly at this pronouncement, but bowed his head in acknowledgment. "I understand. There will be more battles. We're still planning them and we expect the enemy to come here soon."

Drusa let out a trilling warble. "We shall await them," she said.

"These words make for good hearing," Lelanc agreed.

Rylin sat with the ko'aye while he composed a written report for N'lahr, then bade both ko'aye farewell. Once back in the fortress, he stopped off in the quarters he shared with the exalts to freshen up, only to find Tesra standing at the window, overlooking the courtyard.

She turned at his entrance, and then both froze. Nothing lay between them but ten paces of wooden flooring. Bunk beds stood to his right and left, and he debated simply nodding at her and reaching into his pack on the uppermost bunk for his toiletries.

Then he realized this might be one of the few opportunities he'd get to speak to her alone, and so he forced himself to speak. "I'm glad you got out all right," he said.

She cut him off before he could say anything more. "I'm not sure I want to talk to you, Rylin. There's a lot going on."

"There is, but there's a wrong I need to correct." Sensing she was about to object, he spoke quickly: "When I was last with you, I took advantage of our friendship. I wish I had seen another way. And I—"

Tesra cut him off. "Another way. Do you know, it's not so much that you deceived me, it's that you were so pleased with yourself while you were doing it. You liked tricking me."

"That's not true," Rylin said. He didn't tell her he'd been impressed he'd succeeded, because that would muddy his actual regret. "It's troubled me ever since."

"Are you going to tell me now that you were under orders so I shouldn't hold it against you?" She took a step that while toward him he knew was intended to be toward the door.

He could have pointed out that she'd been part of a traitorous enterprise, and that his connection to her had been one of the few avenues to learning more about the Mage Auxiliary's secretive activities. But he chose instead to discuss his own actions. "No. I want to tell you I'm sorry."

She was quiet for a long time, watching him. Finally, she spoke with subdued challenge. "Do you expect me to accept your apology?"

He shook his head. "I've no expectations. I'm merely giving what I think is owed."

Tesra let out a long, slow breath, watching him. "You used me, and that hurt. But then it turns out we not only deserved to be investigated, the exalts deserve to be disbanded and put on trial. Our actions were criminal. So I've been wrestling with that. Among other things."

"You weren't the one who imprisoned N'lahr. You didn't kill Asrahn."

"No. But I conspired with the queen to bring back a Goddess. The sad thing is that even now I feel like I betrayed my queen and my friends, even though I know that they—we—were wrong. I've been trying to figure out how I got so twisted around by it all, and I think I wanted to belong to something greater than me. Something that had a lock on the truth. I fooled myself. But then it turns out I'm easy to fool." She looked bitterly at Rylin. "I had this crazy idea people who said they were my friends wouldn't use me. If I'd known better I would have understood everyone is always using each other."

He'd resigned himself to enduring each of her insults, but this statement pulled him up short. "I don't think that's true."

"You wouldn't."

She thought he was still referring to himself. Rylin decided to clarify. "Over the last few weeks, I've seen tremendous acts of courage from people who expected nothing in return."

"Apart from a few songs and poems in their honor?" Her voice was mockingly sweet.

Though he very much wished to soothe her resentment, he couldn't let that stand. "You're turning a blind eye to the best of us. People who die doing the right thing even when no one's watching, people who hold the line so a few more people have a chance to get away."

His tone must have alerted her to a change in his thoughts, for she sounded sympathetic. "You mean Varama? I—"

He didn't let her finish. "I mean Aradel. I mean Renik. I mean Lasren. I mean Varama." He meant Commander N'lahr, carefully planning a battle he himself might not live to wage. Rylin's emotions threatened to overwhelm him. His voice grew hoarse. "I mean dozens of squires and soldiers from Alantris whose names you'll never know. You think it's about glory and it's not. The honors, the nicknames, the ring—I'd trade any and all of it if I could have gotten one more person alive out of Alantris. Or if I could have saved my friends." He wiped moisture from his face and continued. "Hate me if you like. I know my failings. But I am sorry. You deserve better, and you deserved better from me."

She was quiet for a long time, watching him. "I can see that you've suffered," she said finally. "Maybe you've even changed. It's . . . I don't even know my own mind any more. Which thoughts come from me."

"Synahla could twist people's minds," Rylin said.

"I think she was working her way with me for the last week or so, and I can feel her spell trying to bend me, even now. But blaming her is an easy way out, Rylin. She didn't weave me until long after it was obvious what we were doing was wrong. What I did was my fault. I don't know how I'll ever make up for that."

"What we do next, together, is a lot more important than what happened before."

"I hope you're right," Tesra said quietly.

An awkward silence followed. Rylin knew he'd achieved nearly all he could, but decided to share a final observation. "You're a good person, Tesra. A kind one, and a skilled mage. We're stronger with you on our side, and I'm glad you're here." He grabbed his pack and turned away.

"Rylin."

He stopped. She was a long time finding her way to whatever was troubling her. "I'm glad we talked," she said finally.

"Me too."

She offered the barest trace of a smile. He returned it, then retreated to the washroom before searching for N'lahr. He wasn't able to visit privately with the commander until that evening, when he handed his written report to him, complete with maps. He was certain N'lahr would burn it the moment he'd committed it to memory. Rylin had hoped to learn more about Varama, but there was no way to safely discuss her. N'lahr instead spoke about the arrangements for the funeral ceremony they were holding in the morning.

Rylin was leaving N'lahr's room when he spotted Cerai's chief servant, Sorak, approaching with a lantern. Rylin moved to one side, thinking the man would pass, but Sorak drew to a halt and bowed his head.

"Alten Rylin, I bid you greetings. The goddess Cerai wishes to speak with you, if it is convenient."

The framing of the invitation surprised Rylin, who guessed Cerai rarely, if ever, worried about anyone's convenience. "Do you know what she wants?"

"I do not question her," Sorak answered.

Naturally he wouldn't. What could she want from him? Was it possible she had observed what he'd written for N'lahr? He thought it unlikely, but then he wasn't truly certain about the extent of her abilities. Regardless of what she had heard or seen, she clearly wanted to learn more from him. The trick would be learning something from her while revealing nothing. He couldn't afford to pass up the opportunity. "All right, Sorak, lead me to her."

The man guided him to the ground floor, escorting him into a cozy inner chamber lit by walled sconces, sumptuously furnished with long couches sewn with blue cushions. Cerai stood at a buffet pouring liquid from a decanter into a goblet.

She turned as Sorak announced Rylin, and once again he had to admit to himself just how beautiful she truly was. She'd put no special effort into her appearance and was all the more striking perhaps because of that. Gone was the elaborate hairdo from earlier in the day. Instead, her dark hair was pulled back in a simple ponytail. She had shed her uniform and now wore a loose white blouse, a pair of flared slacks, and matching slippers.

"I have brought the alten, Goddess," Sorak said.

"Thank you. Leave us."

"As you command." Sorak bowed.

He retreated, closing the doors behind him. Cerai gestured at one of the couches. "Join me, Rylin. Do you want some juice?"

"No, thank you."

He wondered if he was wrong to be so cautious of any drink she offered. He followed her to the nearest grouping of couches. She sat in a loose-limbed, confident way, still clutching the goblet stem. "I have wine," she said, "but not a lot. I keep meaning to experiment with making some, but there are so many more important things to worry about."

He sat down across from her. "The juice is excellent," he said. "I'm just not thirsty."

"Thank you for joining me. Did you enjoy your tour of my fortress?" She drank, watching him, and he wondered if she knew everything, or if she was probing to learn more of what he'd seen.

"It's an impressive achievement. I didn't see any marks in the stone, much less mortar. Did you build this all in one go, with hearthstones?"

"The process required multiple adjustments."

"I was surprised you kept the hearthstones on the far side of the complex from your rooms."

"I don't keep all of them there. But yes. Belahn and Leonara kept theirs with them at all times. I think it wiser to make a conscious choice to use my tools, before I get to wondering who is using whom, so I placed the majority of them in a location where I must walk to gain access." She sat the goblet down on an end table. When she faced Rylin once more, she had grown solemn. "We had started out so well, you and I. It should have gone differently, and I hope it still can. I know why you're angry. I meant what I said, you know."

He wondered what she was referring to, but didn't interrupt.

"I really would have taken you with me on the ko'aye if I could have," she continued. "You must understand how important it was to have the keystone. There will be no way to restore the realms without it. You've looked at it now. You know how important it is."

He wasn't sure that he did.

"And knowing that, and knowing that you understand about duty and sacrifice, I hope you can find your way toward letting go of your anger."

So she assumed that he was only upset with her because she hadn't taken him with her when she'd fled Alantris? Her understanding of his motivations was intriguingly flawed. "It's foolish to hold tight to anger," he said.

"Spoken like a seasoned alten. N'lahr told me what you managed in Alantris, Rylin of the Thousand. You were greater than I thought. Potential only waiting for release. I would have liked to have been there to see it."

He feigned he hadn't detected her suggestive wording. "I would have liked that, too," he said.

She smiled in sly self-satisfaction, then grew more serious. "I understand why you respected Varama. She was one of a kind."

"She was."

"Ah, see. You're angry with me still. You're doing your best, but you can't quite conceal it, can you? That actually speaks well of you. I know Varama was incapable of inspiring warmth in others, but you were loyal anyway. A good officer."

"I hope I was." He saw no reason to correct any of her erroneous assumptions.

"I hope you won't hold her death against me. She could have come through, you know. She must have seen someone else running for the portal."

"It might have been the Naor general," Rylin suggested.

"Yes, N'lahr mentioned him. A curious-sounding fellow. But not worth sacrificing her own life for, surely. You know as well as I what a great asset she'd be to us now."

Rylin could only nod.

"Why, look at you. You really were attached to her. That's commendable."

"She was cold," Rylin said, though he knew she only presented as such. "But she was brave, and very smart, and I looked up to her."

"You saw only her best points, and admired her for them. I like that. I hope we can get past all of these misunderstandings." She reached out for her goblet once more, though she did not drink. She rubbed its stem. "I realized late in the day that I'd been high-handed with you. I got to wondering why, and it dawned on me that I was treating you poorly because I was mad at you for being mad at me. As though we were teenagers in the midst of a love spat."

"We're all under a lot of pressure."

"I'm sure that has something to do with it, but the truth is, I had thought you and I had a connection, and I was angry it seemed broken."

Rylin knew that if he seemed too eager to agree, he wouldn't be believed, so he offered a rueful smile and told the truth. "I felt that connection myself."

"I knew you did. It was easy to see you respected me. And me, well, I recognized your potential just as Varama did. She was an odd one, but she could spot excellence. And so does N'lahr. Who did he send away with Kyrkenall? Elenai. Who did he keep close? You."

Once again, she had seen the same events and arrived at a different causal relationship behind them.

She ran a well-manicured finger slowly along the rim of her goblet. "I need people I can depend upon, Rylin." She looked at him through long lashes. "We will stop the Goddess. Even if the realms don't need restoration—and I think that they will—they will certainly need repair. You've noticed how the borders are shrinking. Because of my preparations, once we defeat the Goddess we'll be able to draw on her powers. Almost nothing will be beyond us." Her eyes gleamed with either joy, or madness, or both.

He worked hard to appear curious rather than alarmed. He thought he managed the former. "That sounds like a lot of responsibility."

"It will be. And it will take a certain kind of person to handle it. You see the help I have here. Their loyalty is without question. But they're not independently minded."

"Are you thinking of me?" he asked.

"Almost from the moment I met you," Cerai said. "You made quite an impression, holding off that Naor cavalry all on your own."

"I seem to remember that you arrived just in time to help."

"You see? I'm not all bad." Cerai smiled and was beautiful. "When this is all over, a dedicated force will have to manage the queen's energy, and I'd like you to be one of them." She held up a hand to stay any unvoiced objection. "Don't decide now, and don't talk to me about how you're Altenerai first and can't be anything else. Times will be different. A new and greater order of heroes will be required to rebuild our realms. And there will be benefits, for while we can follow the basic design, we can also shape things after our own desires. Lesser women and men might use that to their advantage."

"Yes," Rylin said, as if this all made perfect sense.

Cerai set down the goblet and rose, gracefully. "Well, I'm giving you a lot to think about."

He stood. "Indeed you have."

"We can talk in more detail about it tomorrow. It's been a long day, and we should both get our rest."

He gave her his best smile as he offered his hand.

She laughed even as she presented her fingers to him. He kissed her knuckles, noting he felt no callouses on her fingertips. Artifice, he was sure, for he'd seen her wielding a sword only a few weeks ago, and one didn't remain that skilled without frequent practice.

"Until tomorrow then, dear Rylin," she said.

"Until tomorrow." He left her then, alone with her luxuries and her lunacy, and climbed up through darkness to seek his dreams.

16

The Visitor in the Sky

In the darkness before dawn, they gathered in the courtyard near a small pyre. Cerai and a dozen of her warriors watched to one side, while Anzat and a few of his Naor stood on the other.

Rylin, the exalts, squires, and aspirants stood in rows facing the fire as N'lahr solemnly welcomed everyone to the ceremony of remembrance. He reminded them that parchment and ink had been placed upon a table to the right, if any of them had not already written a note, and then he bade them to reflect silently upon their favorite memories of the fallen, mentioning each one in turn.

Rylin had drafted a short message to Meria, thanking her for her bravery and dedication and expressing his wish that they could have had more time to know one another. He had meant it to say more, but his thoughts while drafting had been sluggish. He'd written something similar in his note to Vannek, who's passing actually struck him harder. He was incredibly thankful he hadn't had to create a note of farewell to Varama.

As he waited his turn, Cerai, in uniform once more, caught his eye and gave him a subdued smile. Until their talk last night, he would have been concerned he didn't look as shattered as someone who'd lost their mentor and close friend. He now understood Cerai wouldn't be suspicious of his manner, for she lived under the foolish assumption no one would deeply mourn Varama.

Once he had consigned his messages to the flame so that they could be read in the undying realm, Rylin returned to formation, head bowed, his memory shifting through not just the lost of this battle, but those brought down over the course of the struggle. Every one of those needless deaths could be laid at the feet of a ruler focused with single-minded abandon upon her own selfish aims.

When he looked up, a final five squires were queued in front of the pyre. The Naor soldiers watched in curiosity, and for the first time Rylin wondered about their own traditions for the dead.

Once the farewell portion of the ceremony concluded, the commander returned to the front of his troops. He looked over them for a long moment, then drew himself up, preparatory to speech.

But he said nothing, nor did he move. Rylin grew troubled as the moment stretched on. Thelar turned his head to him and arched an eyebrow, as if to spur Rylin to act, but M'vai beat him to it, walking forward to touch N'lahr's arm.

"Commander?" she asked.

N'lahr's eyes were fixed, looking to the left. They did not blink.

"Commander N'lahr?" M'vai persisted. She gripped his arm and shook it.

N'lahr's dark eyes moved, meeting hers. "She's drawing close," he gasped, as though he'd been holding his breath. Then he added more forcefully: "The Goddess. She's almost here."

The squires stirred uncomfortably at this news. Rylin had never known the commander had sorcerous ability, but Cerai called out: "He's right! Soldiers, to your stations! Weavers, with me, to the walls! She's coming from the west!" Cerai hurried off.

A distant horn call rang in the morning air. Someone far away had inexpertly blown an alarm. A slightly less terrible version of the call rang more closely, until the best trumpeter yet sounded his horn from high atop the wall.

Rylin joined M'vai to check on N'lahr.

"I'm fine," the commander said. "Go with the mages. Both of you. Hurry!"

Before very long Rylin stood upon the battlement with M'vai, Thelar, and the aspirants, staring into darkness being burned off by the growing daybreak at their backs.

Cerai's servants hurried out of the stairwell with a wooden table, which they deposited before their ruler. Four others carried perfect cubes of flawless crystal a small degree larger than a helmet. These they placed upon the table. Cerai spared them only a moment's attention. The renegade alten was holding a pasty-white cylindrical object almost the length of a small bow.

Rylin realized it must be what he'd sensed from outside her office.

The dawn brought out the shapes of trees and bushes and even the roofs of the village across the gray sward below them. Rylin sensed Cerai staring into the inner world and resisted the impulse to do so as well. Checking to see if he could spot the approaching Goddess when so many other mages were there to do the same would be a waste of his limited energies. Instead, he stepped to the merlon and looked down, for he'd heard Anzat shouting for his men to "put their backs into it," as well as the rumble of wheels.

Two finished catapults were being pushed forward by a combined force of Naor and squires. Pairs of wooden wheels were attached to a heavy platform at the bottom of each war engine. The launching arms hung slack behind them, and the stones they were meant to fling were carried in a thick wagon being pulled by the plow horse and four of the black riding mares. Rylin didn't see N'lahr. He hoped he was on his way, and not struck with immobility somewhere.

On the battlement, Thelar was in hushed conversation with the exalts and aspirants. Rylin hadn't had time to consult with them about their battle plan, so he stepped up and waited for an opening. "What are our tactics?"

Thelar answered. "The aspirants are going to release the chaos spirits. Cerai and M'vai and I will try to rip energy from the Goddess while she's distracted. You and Tesra will feed us energy from the hearthstones."

Even as he wondered where the stones were, Tesra pointed to a pair of canvas satchels the servants had just set beside Cerai.

"What's that cylinder Cerai's holding?" Rylin asked.

"It's a shaping tool," Cerai answered, though her gaze was fastened still upon the distance. "It helps refine hearthstone energy and was a huge aid in raising the fortress. It might help this fight, though I'm not sure how much."

N'lahr arrived at last with a trio of squires. Cerai's troops scattered along the battlement to either side of the mages, and were armed with spears, slings, and bows. An attack with those would be about as productive as flinging sugar at an armored warrior, but Rylin supposed they couldn't just do nothing.

"Here she comes," Cerai murmured.

The Goddess was a dark figure drifting from the dying night. She floated rigidly, relentlessly, toward the citadel, growing larger by the moment. Rylin estimated she must easily be thirty-five feet tall. As the sun rose in her face, the black of her skin was so intense it glowed against the color-muted landscape coming to life behind her.

Rylin grew aware of a long trail of change in the deity's wake. The landscape had altered as she passed above it so that everything directly beneath her was white as bleached bone.

As the Goddess drew within a few hundred yards, Rylin's attention grew more and more fixed upon her personal characteristics. Her face was exquisite perfection. The black gown and her long hair trailed behind her. Her arms drooped listlessly, and her feet hung slack dozens of feet above the ground.

"I want to speak to her," N'lahr said, and Cerai turned her head in surprise. Rylin thought to hear her object, but she said nothing. The commander moved to the edge of the battlement and raised his voice to the troops ready with the catapults below. "Hold until my command," he shouted.

"Holding!" Elik called back. Anzat gruffly repeated the order.

N'lahr made a speaking trumpet with his hands and called out with his parade voice. "We do not wish to fight you! What do you want?"

The Goddess drifted past the final cottages of Cerai's village and halted, suspended upon the air twenty yards beyond the citadel. A voice came from her direction, though Rylin did not see her mouth move. The answering words were honey smooth and utterly calm. They were loud enough to hear, without sounding as though they had been shouted.

"I am here for what is mine."

Rylin glimpsed a movement to the right; the male aspirant, Veshahd, had lifted both his hands, preparatory to launching a spell. Rylin saw fear in his eyes, wondering if it shone in his own.

N'lahr said: "What will you do once you have it?"

The Goddess' voice lacked emotion when she answered. "I shall wipe clean all that has been wrought, and start anew."

Rylin's heart, already hammering, skipped into double-time with that pronouncement.

N'lahr would not relent. "Can you not create elsewhere, and leave these lands to us? We would care for them, and honor your work."

"This work is flawed, and cannot stand. And your honor is meaningless."

The Goddess didn't so much as shift her head or twitch a finger, but Rylin sensed a change in the air as surely as he would have felt the onrush of a thunderstorm. Magical energies washed over them. Surrounded by such, he could have woven a complex spell without strain.

"She's stealing the hearthstone energy," Cerai cried, and Rylin, even tangentially connected to the inner world, saw she was right. Threads were being ripped from the ground itself and drifted into the hands of the Goddess. "We have to stop her!" Cerai leveled the shaping tool.

Already the power of multiple hearthstones streamed from the satchels and into the base of Cerai's cylinder. Brilliant golden light sprayed from the cylinder's far end and struck the deity in the chest, which began to crystallize and shine with a rainbow's spectrum of colors. At long last the Goddess' face portrayed expression; her eyes widened in profound astonishment. The crystallization spread quickly down her gown, the changed surface resembling hearthstones.

"Attack!" N'lahr cried.

The Goddess raised her right arm toward the battlement.

A mass of rocks hurtled toward the Goddess from one of the catapults. Thelar and M'vai visibly strained with flexed fingers, pulling upon air so rich with energy it shimmered even before Rylin looked deeply into the inner world.

His understanding of the battle changed the moment he did. The Goddess radiated an overwhelming spectrum of colors even as gleaming energies streamed up to her from the land on every side. Thelar and M'vai struggled to tug the closer of those strands away. Cerai, meanwhile, was reshaping the Goddess as the energy of the tool sprayed over her.

The catapult stones slammed into one leg and sent ripples of red energy through the gargantuan limb.

In the next breath, even as Tesra shouted at him to push more power toward Cerai, several things happened at once. The energy from the shaping tool spread through the whole of the Goddess' chest. Three aspirants released a swirling mass of glowing energy from the table cubes—the freed chaos spirits spiraled toward the Goddess, a shining haze that enlarged as they moved. M'vai and N'lahr shouted for everyone to get down. And the deity's hand pointed to Cerai.

Thelar and M'vai threw themselves flat. Rylin hit the sturdy timbers a moment after Tesra. He turned his head as he hit, wondering if he would merely witness the attack, or if he, too, would be swept to nothing like poor Meria.

A strand of the crenellation blew into snow-like fragments ahead of a roaring wind that turned over the table even as all but its legs transformed into white ash. The cubes that had held the spirits dissolved as well; Veshahd clutched the remaining cube to his breast as he rolled away along the right wall. Two of the women had likewise thrown themselves clear, but the third woman was too slow, and Rylin watched in horror as she vanished like so much powder, leaving nothing behind but her borrowed sapphire, which rattled against a merlon. Tesra cried out in despair.

Cerai hurtled backward, a large swath of her skin and clothing flaking away. Her shaping tool twirled up and over the crenellations and into the courtyard.

Rylin felt certain that great black finger would shift along the battlement and the Goddess' power would eliminate them all, but the chaos spirits had coalesced into a single humanlike shape reaching with outstretched arms, and the Goddess' mouth rounded in alarm. She recoiled, raising arms to ward herself, then rotated in midair and soared off at great speed. The chaos spirit, now grown almost to her size, was right on her heels. As both figures dwindled into the distance, the men on the catapults cheered.

Rylin hopped to his feet, frowning in expectation of the horror he would see.

One of the aspirants knelt by the ashes of her friend. The small one, Tavella, helped her male companion rise as he clutched the remaining cube to his chest.

Incredibly, Cerai's flesh and even her clothing was knitting itself together as she climbed to her feet. So advanced was the spell work she didn't even appear conscious of its activity. She walked for the gap blown into the battlement even as muscle and flesh regrew over one cheekbone. By the time she stood at the breach she was almost fully restored.

"She's getting away," N'lahr said, staring into the distance, his delivery detached. His dark eyes were glazed and strange. "Already she's healing the damage, and she could return, but she fears the other, even in his weaker state."

"The other?" M'vai prompted. She walked toward the commander.

But N'lahr didn't answer. He continued his trancelike pronouncements. "She is confused; angry. Her children's experiments dared to use her own power against her. She will heal. She will regain her other energies first. . . ." N'lahr paused, blinking. "She's dimly aware of me. I dare not pry further."

"How can you know what she thinks?" Rylin asked.

"Because of an accident, I'm linked to a hearthstone," N'lahr said. "And that means I'm linked to her."

"What's this 'other'; you mentioned?" Thelar asked. His eyes somberly followed Tesra as she joined the aspirants to look on the remains of their friend.

"I can't be sure," N'lahr answered. "But she thinks of the chaos spirits not as a them, but a single entity, one she knows."

"Interesting," Cerai said. "The shaping tool was better than I'd even dreamed, although it was the chaos spirits that really turned the corner." Only a minute or two earlier her face had been ruined tissue and exposed bone; now her beauty was unmarred. At their stunned regard, she smiled.

"I told you I've built the land up. I'm tied to it in more ways than one. But the Goddess pulled some of the energy out, and when she tore into my realm she weakened its border. I'm going to have to start repairs soon, before it begins to destabilize."

"You put yourself back together," N'lahr said. "Can you do anything for Tivissa?"

Cerai looked over at the group of mourners. "That's beyond even me, I'm afraid. My physical well-being is part of this realm. Hers wasn't. It's too bad she didn't get out of the way."

N'lahr's answering look was stern, but he changed the subject. "Will the weapon we sent Kyrkenall and Elenai after be more powerful than the shaping tool you already possess?"

"I think so. It's supposed to channel chaos energy. If someone else were using the weapon while I used the shaping tool, and we were distracting her with chaos spirits, we'd be sure to beat her." Her gaze shifted speculatively to Rylin. "We have only one trapped chaos spirit left. We'll need more. Many more."

And she apparently meant him to be involved in capturing them, an idea that honestly terrified him. While Rylin tried to come to grips with the necessity of the concept, he stared out at the landscape, noting that the deity's line of departure had varied from the line of her arrival. As a result, two avenues of white stone, straight and even and twenty feet wide, stretched through to the edge of Cerai's lands. The Goddess had wrought those changes without obvious effort, in the realm Cerai had claimed to be reinforced against magical calamity. Astounding. And yet . . . they had hurt the Goddess. With a little more effort, they really might be able to bring her down.

But then there was a good chance they had caught the Goddess off guard, and that when she returned she wouldn't underestimate them.

N'lahr was already contemplating the next moves. "Can we predict how long it will take for the Goddess to search out other hearthstones?"

"It can't take too long," Thelar said. "There weren't that many we didn't find, surely."

"And I have a great many of those," Cerai said. "But there are probably others, in the shifts or deep in the Naor or kobalin holdings. Given that it took her several days to arrive here, and that any undiscovered by us are likely quite remote, we might have several weeks. There's no real way to know for certain. Suppose there's only four or five hidden in the Naor realms? If that's the case, we may have no more than a week."

"How easy are these spirits to catch?" Rylin asked. "Can you really find more in just a few days?"

"I'm not going to find them," Cerai said, her gaze bright and piercing. "You're going to find them. With that ko'aye you're so friendly with. You'll need them to fly out into the void because that's where the chaos spirits roam."

"Why can't you seek them?" N'lahr asked.

Cerai answered without hesitation. "I have to repair the realm. And besides, I don't think the ko'aye want anything to do with me."

On the surface, her explanation made a great deal of sense, but something she'd said only a short while ago had Rylin wondering. Might she be reluctant to leave her realm because away from here she wasn't indestructible?

Cerai pressed on. "Rylin, why don't I explain the magical theory to Thelar. He can go with you. You go convince your ko'aye."

Rylin turned to N'lahr for confirmation, and found him unmoving. "Commander?" he prompted, alarmed.

N'lahr nodded as if with great effort, then looked up at him. "Yes. Go seek the ko'aye. Thelar, we need the spirits. The rest of you—come with me."

The feathered serpents proved just as amenable to the venture as Rylin had anticipated, and within a half hour he was helping them don the equipment they'd left under the tree they claimed. Varama had cunningly designed the saddles so that a ko'aye might pull an emergency release to free them, but they were far easier for someone without claws to secure. Rylin told Drusa and Lelanc to meet him back at the fortress, then rode back on his borrowed horse.

N'lahr was waiting outside the stables, and walked with him into the stall. He then curtly ordered Cerai's stablemen to go and turned to Rylin. "I'm as reluctant to send you away as you are to leave, but these spirits proved a powerful weapon and you have the most field experience."

Rylin supposed that was true. "I know you have other long-term plans. But you probably can't share them."

"I dare not speak them aloud. Trust me that they're well under way."

"If we fight the Goddess here, Cerai will be able to do whatever she wants with the leftover energy."

"I'm aware of the challenge," N'lahr said.

"And what about you?"

"I may not have much time left, but I'm leaving detailed plans after me."

"That's not what I mean."

"I know what you mean. I don't like what's happening to me. But it's not your lookout. We have to stop a goddess."

He didn't say whether he meant the giant deity or the one whose people called her that, and Rylin guessed N'lahr meant both.

"Understood."

"I'm glad. Be alert for communications."

He nodded once to that, though he didn't know what it meant. He expected it would become clear in time.

Finally, the commander offered his hand. "It has been a pleasure serving with you."

To Rylin, those words might as well have been the toll of a funeral bell. The commander had just confirmed that he did not expect to be alive upon Rylin's return. And so when Rylin clasped N'lahr's arm and felt those firm fingers tighten below his elbow he wished he had better words to explain the depth of his appreciation. He spoke with sincerity. "It has been a privilege and honor to serve under you, sir."

The cry of ko'aye rang outside. Neither had wanted to enter the courtyard, and had promised to land beyond the central gate.

N'lahr released his arm. "Get out there and find those chaos spirits."

17

In the Wasteland

The sunset stretched their shadows across the sands and bathed the surrounding sky in ochre and orange.

Elenai rode at Kyrkenall's side through the parched landscape. A mile to her right she glimpsed one of Cerai's soldiers before he passed behind a dune, and knew that a mile beyond him another rode, on out to six miles distant, all in parallel. She had arranged the men to her left in the same fashion, hoping that one on either side might spot the plateau she'd described to them in the midst of the dune sea.

So far no one had seen a thing. Cerai had promised each warrior was sensitive to magical energies, and that she'd told them the kind of thing they sought. Upon arrival, Elenai had supplemented that instruction with information of her own.

While the mountains loomed in the distance, Elenai saw nothing that definitely resembled the peak from her vision.

The heat of the day finally faded, and was but a memory shortly after the sun vanished beyond a distant ridge. Soon she was wrapping a blanket over her shoulders, wishing she had gloves. So far at least the horses seemed untroubled by the conditions.

Again and again she returned to her memory of the vision. She had expected things to work out before this, for all of her previous insights had come true almost immediately.

Kyrkenall raised his wineskin to his lips. "Thirsty?" he asked.

"No."

Kyrkenall knew her well enough to guess what troubled her. "Don't worry," he said. "We'll find it."

"You say that. But what do I do in the mean time? Keep traveling and hope for the best?"

"You're overthinking this. We just search as we would even if we didn't know we're meant to find the thing. It's really all we can do now."

While she appreciated his supportive tone, it didn't ease her worries.

She ordered the soldiers closer so they could see one another by moonlight, and when they reached a region with larger dunes that more regularly blocked line of sight, she ordered them closer yet.

As the hours passed, they used the stars to hold true to a course partly shaped by detours around the mounded sand. She searched intermittently with her magical senses, restoring them with her borrowed hearthstone shard. The artifact made her vaguely uncomfortable, as though she were riding through an open field where she knew archers were hidden. Worried that the shard's use might be sensed by the Goddess herself, she kept to its shallows, lest she be detected and enveloped like a tiny fish consumed by a monster surging from the river depths.

At midnight she called in the troops to share a meal. Cerai's men didn't seem entirely familiar with picketing horses, much less starting fires, so she and Kyrkenall managed, the archer again demonstrating his dexterity by striking a blaze to life in a matter of moments, using half the wood scraps they'd packed.

Without the warmth of a horse beneath her the desert proved even colder, and Elenai sat gratefully beside the fire. The nearby dune might as well have been a mountain of ice, for it radiated great frigid waves.

Kyrkenall chewed placidly on some smoked trout and Elenai envied his calm. Wasn't he worried about Kalandra, or N'lahr, or the others left with Cerai? Maybe he set store in the thought Rialla would appear, and they'd be able to tell her to go back and fix everything, saving the world and erasing much of Elenai's life in the process.

Detesting her self-pity, she returned her attention to Cerai's soldiers, wolfing down their dried rations and crackers. They traded turns beside the little fire, sitting closer in upon one another than humans would have.

"So all of you have found hearthstones before?" she asked.

They looked up at her almost simultaneously. Though not entirely identical, they resembled one another; large, broad men with short dark hair and bright eyes. They were clean-shaven and dressed in white long-sleeved shirts and pants. Each answered with a loud yes that overlapped the replies of his companions.

"How many hearthstones did you have to find before you were rewarded by the goddess?"

They talked over themselves, saying several numbers, until one in their center held up his hands and shouted for silence. "The goddess named me as commander, and I will answer." He checked to see if the others would quiet before facing Elenai. "Those who came needed only one. Later she gave the award for two. And sometimes she gave the reward for those who had helped others find the stones." Somehow Cerai had not only managed to convince these kobalin to be altered voluntarily, but to bring her hearthstones to make it happen.

"Our goddess is Altenerai," the lead soldier said. "Like you. Why are you not gods?"

Kyrkenall grinned. "Maybe we are."

Three of the soldiers stared fixedly at him while others muttered doubtfully among themselves.

The leader grunted. "Do you have powers of making? Where are your followers, and the things you have made?"

"We aren't gods," Elenai said quietly. "Are you sure Cerai is?"

All those sets of eyes widened at nearly the same moment, and each of the men chattered similar things about creation and change and power until the leader once more held up his hand.

"It may be you do not understand, though you have seen," he said. "We came to her as monsters, and she made us wonderful."

"Wonderful," several of the men repeated.

"She came to a waste, and she made it into a place of bounties."

"Bounties," all of the soldiers repeated. Elenai wondered if this was improvisation or a prayer to Cerai that these men had said before.

"She sees farther than all others. She plans better than all others. She leads and guides us and shows us the way."

"The way," the soldiers sighed.

"Looks like they know a goddess when they see one," Kyrkenall said lightly. "And I guess that settles the whole question about my divinity. No one's ever invented a prayer to me."

"I bet there've been plenty of curses, though," Elenai said.

Kyrkenall chuckled.

Elenai wished her own spirits were as bright. She looked over at Cerai's soldiers and feared their loyalty was as absolute as it seemed. And she wondered, again, at the mind of the woman who encouraged others to think her a god.

She reminded the soldiers what they were looking for, and they ably repeated exactly what Cerai had told them. She wasn't sure whether they knew or cared about the reasons for the search. They were simply acting to please their goddess.

While she suspected the horses had been engineered in a similar way by Cerai's magic, even they were reluctant to get moving after the meal. They probably thought they were through for the night. Lyria clearly did, and looked sidelong at Kyrkenall and flicked her ears, as if she couldn't believe he was seriously saddling her again.

They rode off under the bright moon, each of Cerai's men no more than a hundred yards out.

"They remind me of Ortok," she told Kyrkenall wistfully.

"Well, they're kobalin. Sort of."

She couldn't help remembering the last time they'd seen their huge, black-furred friend, when he'd stayed behind to challenge a group of kobalin warriors to buy time for her and Kyrkenall to escape. "Do you think Ortok won the challenge?"

"We can't know what odds he was against." Kyrkenall shifted in his saddle. "I'm rooting for him, but . . . you have to remember, as long as he's alive, he's planning to kill N'lahr."

"I know. But surely we can find a way to stop that."

"That would be nice. But you've probably figured out that some people aren't reasonable, even if you love them. Especially if they're kobalin."

"How can you be so calm?" Her question came explosively, surprising even her. She hadn't realized how frustrated he'd made her.

"There's nothing more I can do, Elenai," he said simply. "There's noth-

ing more you can do until we find this tool, or Rialla finds us. Worrying
about it just makes for misery. It's like riding into battle. At some point
you commit, and do your best. If you overthink every step, then you're
going to end up dead or wishing you were."

"I'm not sure I recognize this new, even-tempered Kyrkenall."

"I'm the same, I swear," he protested. "But cold weather sure makes
you grumpy."

The hours dragged and fatigue pulled at her, just like the chill. Eventually Kyrkenall rode closer. "We're not going to be able to stay in the
wastes. It's time to turn back."

Her eyes widened in surprise and she shook her head, no.

Kyrkenall explained further. "We need to pull back to the desert rim. If
we head to the edge now we ought to make it just as the air's heating up,
some time after nine bells."

"We have to press on. My vision—"

"Right. Your vision probably assumes you're not acting like a crazy
person."

"I've been in deserts before," she insisted.

"You haven't been in *this* desert. This isn't like anything Arappa can
throw at you. There's no way we'll get any rest sleeping in the heat of
midday. We'll just degrade our ability to perform, and the horses will
suffer worse than us. We have to get out, get rest, then search again this
evening."

Elenai let out a long, low breath. He was right, and she dearly wished
he wasn't.

"We'll leave a different direction from the way we came, then come
back in from a different one yet, so we can search more ground." Kyrkenall was trying to make the best of the situation.

"And if the Goddess comes to Cerai's stronghold while we're asleep?"

"This isn't going to be a fast search and I don't think success lies right
beyond the next horizon."

"I'm afraid it won't lie over any horizon," she said softly.

He gave her a wry look. "I know you're drawing on the hearthstone to
keep your own energy levels up, but the rest of us aren't."

"I know. I'd use it more, maybe to shield us from the heat, but every
time I open the thing I'm afraid the Goddess is going to notice. I swear I
can sense her in the stone."

"Fabulous. Something else to worry about."

"Lots of somethings." Elenai signaled to the soldiers, and they turned
their mounts. Kyrkenall took the lead, guiding them northeast.

"This will get us into a decent spot with some grazing and shade, and fresh water."

"Is there any part of the realms you don't know?" she asked.

He was a moment answering, and did so finally with flat affect that effectively brought an end to their conversation. "I got to know everywhere pretty well while I was looking for Kalandra."

They plodded on through the rest of the night. The sun announced its coming with a stunning rose-gold glow on the horizon. Then it climbed to blind them. The heat it brought had soon chased off the night's chill, and Elenai was glad for it.

When they finally reached the smaller dunes, their horses were flagging. Cerai's soldiers slumped with exhaustion. Elenai surreptitiously drew on energy from the stone to keep herself awake.

Low hills loomed a few miles out, scattered with scrubby trees and bushes. Slowly they drew closer, slowly the sun rose, and swiftly its warmth transformed from a comforting hand to a steady assault. Elenai felt its pressure on her skin like a physical force. The heat grew so pronounced it seemed to suck her clean of moisture before sweat even surfaced on her skin.

They closed on the hills at midmorning. By then, even Kyrkenall and Lyria drooped. The archer didn't relax, though. He ordered the soldiers into a column, taking point, and scanned the hills as they took a low rise between them.

The horses scented the water before Elenai did, raising their heads and upping their gait, and it was only then she grew conscious of that reassuring sense of humidity rising.

Kyrkenall looked over his shoulder at her. "There's a lake over beyond that next hill, where the trees are."

Spears rained down from a nearby rise. One struck Kyrkenall in the upper back.

As he slid in his saddle a spear slashed the flank of Elenai's horse. The animal made no sound but leapt forward in surprise as more spears fell among the soldiers.

Elenai brought the mount back under control with astonishing ease—she'd momentarily forgotten it had been altered by Cerai—and turned it to face the attack.

She noted a number of things in the same instant. Thankfully Kyrkenall lived; he was already upright and reaching for his bow. His Altenerai khalat had kept the spear point from biting into his shoulder. A small army of Naor warriors, between forty and fifty, charged down the dusty slope from the right rear flank. Their attack had been aimed primarily at the larger body of Cerai's troops, and had taken a deadly toll. Most of the men and their animals were down. A few soldiers struggled to turn and face their assailants. The leader was pinned with one leg under his dying mount.

Elenai couldn't guess what the Naor were doing here, on the edge of a wasteland in the realms. It didn't matter. She sent a blast commanding the four nearest to sleep. They dropped in their tracks.

In a heartbeat Kyrkenall shot three more. A few of Cerai's troops got to their feet and pulled their weapons, but they were swiftly overwhelmed.

Elenai reached deeply into the shard for more spell energy.

And the hearthstone Goddess felt her. Elenai experienced the spiritual equivalent of placing a hand on a hot stove. She pulled free on the instant, stupefied, and it was sheer chance an axe tossed at her head missed by a handspan.

Kyrkenall yelled to retreat. He pushed Lyria into a gallop and Elenai belatedly kicked her own animal after as the Goddess' awareness spread through the stone.

She shut it down, and knew blazing pain as a spear slammed into her lower left arm. The khalat kept the point from piercing, but the impact numbed her, and lent extra volume to her shout as she galloped in Kyrkenall's wake. He took a low hill some twenty feet off and spun Lyria so he could rain arrows over her head. From the shouts and screams behind she guessed he took a fearful toll.

Elenai joined him and turned her mount, both reins in her right hand. She tucked her left arm protectively against her chest.

More than a dozen Naor were dead or down, and others had fallen back with arrow shafts through arms or standing out from their armor. The unwounded were rifling through the gear of Cerai's fallen soldiers. A few pointed up toward them.

"About forty left," Kyrkenall said.

"What are they doing here? They can't be scouts for some new army, can they?"

"Them? No. These are probably survivors of that ass-kicking we gave them in Arappa. They must be working their way through the wilds to their homelands." He swore. "I was distracted, and I was thinking about getting Lyria to water."

"I wasn't watching, either."

"Well, it was a good ambush. They picked their spot, and let the front rank ride past so they could attack the larger body. And Cerai's people used to be kobalin. They don't know how to fight from horseback."

"How's your shoulder?"

"There'll be a damnable bruise later. What's wrong with your arm?"

"I'm not sure. I don't think it's broken. They got my horse, too." She looked back and saw a bloody gash along his right flank. She returned her attention to the Naor. "Are they going to follow us?"

"Maybe. Let's put some distance between us."

He turned Lyria and guided her over the next rise.

There they found the little lake that had been their goal, surrounded by thick grass cover. They passed numerous booted tracks. Elenai had to fight her horse, one-handed, to keep it from turning, then resisted the urge to use the hearthstone to soothe or close the wound. The animal quivered when pushing forward off the right rear hoof.

After letting their horses drink, Kyrkenall led them up a rocky hill. From there they had a view of the lake, the distant ambush point, and the pass into the desert.

"Bad luck," Kyrkenall said after he had surveyed the land from all directions. He hadn't yet dismounted. Grass grew only sparsely at the height of the hill, and on the gentler slope beyond.

"That's putting it mildly," Elenai said. "Those poor men."

"If we'd come in through a different pass we'd have seen the tracks." He pointed down. "You can see them from here, coming in and out. But not from our direction. Hastigs. They were camping there at the lake, and they must have had someone on that hill there, watching. They would have had plenty of time to spot us and get ready."

Elenai looked down at her arm. It still smarted and she couldn't close her grip without intensifying the pain. "I'm going to have to look at this, and my horse."

"Climb down from there. I'll look you both over."

"What about those Naor?"

Most of the warriors were still sifting through the stolen belongings, although a few were leading the surviving horses around, gauging which were best. Apparently they hadn't noticed they were identical. A lone sentinel monitored them while his fellows bickered.

"What about them?" Kyrkenall asked.

"Do you think there are more?"

"It looks to me like they threw everything they had at us." Kyrkenall steadied her horse as she swung awkwardly down.

The black mare had only a superficial flesh wound, which Kyrkenall smeared salve over. After carefully feeling her arm he declared it wasn't broken, just bruised, then made a proper sling from a spare shirt. The injury felt worse than a bruise to her, but she took his word.

By the time he'd finished tending her, the Naor had moved off, and Elenai saw the dust cloud of their passage northeast. Those few on horseback traveled slowly enough that those afoot could keep pace.

"Now what?" Elenai asked.

He answered carelessly. "We rest. Then at sundown we look for the weapon."

A powerful surge of energy pulsed from the pack on the ground beside her. She started.

"What is it?" Kyrkenall asked. He followed the direction of her gaze.

"Didn't you feel that?" She fumbled one-handed with the strap, then gave up, using both hands and ignoring the shooting pain. In another moment she had the flap up and saw the hearthstone glowing within.

She pulled back.

"I don't understand," Kyrkenall said.

"It's come on by itself." Elenai gulped down her fear.

"How could it do that?"

"Because the Goddess knows where it is. I think she might be coming to find it."

His eyes widened. "Can you shut it down?"

That was easy to suggest. As Elenai studied it through the inner world she grew conscious of a difference in the way its power manifested. It remained radiant and compelling; now, though, looking at it with magical sight was akin to locking eyes with someone across the room and being unable to break away. She deliberately turned her body to disrupt the gaze.

Free at last, she relinquished her view of the magical threads and discovered she was breathing heavily.

"It didn't work, did it?" Kyrkenall asked.

"I can't even get near it. She's looking back at me."

Kyrkenall glanced at the pack. "Do you think she can hear us, too?"

"Probably. I'm going to try something else." This time when she opened her eyes to the magical world she looked to the hearthstone's side. She felt its regard at the corner of her vision and refused to pay it heed. For all her discomfort, there was one benefit to having the object lit so brilliantly at every level: the flaw in its structure that allowed closure was more obvious.

The moment she touched her threads to it she trembled with the entrancing strength of its energies, for the surface was alive with sorcery the way only centers used to be, and she knew she'd quickly be overwhelmed. Fortunately, she had no intention of using its power. She twisted the energy in the flaw, then pulled away from the inner world.

Even that didn't seem enough, though, for she pushed to her feet and took a long step back, staring at the saddlebag, alert for any hint that the stone would reopen on its own.

"That feels like it worked," Kyrkenall said.

She nodded but did not look away.

"You look like you found a snake in your pocket."

She stared at the stone. Long moments passed.

"That's a slow count of thirty," Kyrkenall said. "And it's not coming back on."

Elenai felt her elbow in its blue sling and grunted in pain. "Maybe she got distracted."

"By what?"

"What distracts a goddess? Maybe a large cache of stones. Or maybe . . ." She faced Kyrkenall. "Maybe she knows where the stone is and doesn't need to leave it on to come find it. Either way, there's nothing we can do."

"If she comes, I guess we'd better let her have it. For now, we ought to see if the Naor missed any supplies."

The Naor raiders proved to have been thorough, although they'd missed some dried meat stored in one of the dead men's pouches.

Kyrkenall arranged the bodies in a line, and then Elenai offered up a prayer for them, wondering as she did exactly why she prayed to entities that she'd been told weren't really gods and wouldn't have watched over kobalin in any case. Because, she knew, it was the proper thing to do.

Kyrkenall guided them a half hour north, to a place where the rocky hills overlooked a few miles of scrubland prior to giving way to the desert and the dunes, just visible on the heat-scorched horizon. There, with the wave of a hand, he revealed a wide cave mouth six feet above a steep slope, under an overhang. His sapphire glowed feebly as he shined it within, and Kyrkenall sighed. "I never expected I'd lose the power of my ring."

He rooted through the supplies in their saddlebags, then prepared a simple torch, winding the rest of the torn shirt fabric around a sturdy stick. He dribbled oil on the cloth and quickly lit it. It flared to life and he raised it aloft.

"Expecting to find something dangerous?" Elenai asked.

"There wasn't anything big the last time I was through. But little things can be poisonous."

He started up slope and stepped inside. Elenai saw the flare of his torch diminish as he moved farther in. "All clear," his voice echoed back. He returned shortly, helped her from the horse, then took her saddlebag.

"I can manage."

"You can manage," Kyrkenall said, "but why don't you let me help you this once? Rest your arm. I'll get everything unloaded, picket your horse, and get the saddles and bits off the animals."

"Thanks." Tired as she was, she couldn't help noting, again, Kyrkenall's solicitous manner. It wasn't that he'd never been calm and helpful before, it's just that any such characteristics were usually interspersed with displays of impatience and temper.

Advancing with the torch, she found the cavern wide and long and dry, and also empty, apart from a scattering of rock and dirt near the entrance.

Kyrkenall followed her up, sat down her pack, then laid out her bedroll on a flat spot of cave floor. He even rolled up her spare garments for a pillow.

"Thank you, Kyrkenall."

"You sound puzzled."

"I am. You're in a fine mood."

Kyrkenall chuckled but didn't comment.

Though he helped ease her out of her khalat, she still wrenched her arm. She didn't remove anything else but her boots, and elected to leave off the sling while she rested. Kyrkenall headed back out for the rest of their equipment, and by the time he returned, Elenai was struggling to keep her eyes open.

"Wake me in four hours for my watch," she said.

"Five," Kyrkenall countered.

She thought she objected, but she wasn't sure, because the next thing she knew, she dreamt.

Rialla appeared in a flash of light. Elenai readied to ask for answers, but the ghostly alten announced she had come to sing with Cerai's soldiers about flatulence. Elenai demanded Rialla listen for once, only to receive a fiery lecture on the importance of tooth care.

She wakened to the echoing click of horse hooves on stone and looked up to find a man in a khalat leading a horse into their cave. The depth of the darkness outside surprised her, as well as the whistle of the wind.

"You let me sleep too long," she said groggily, and sat up. Her arm immediately throbbed in pain.

Lyria already waited farther inside the cave. It was Kyrkenall's entrance with her own animal that had wakened her.

"It's only been about six hours," Kyrkenall said.

"You were supposed to wake me after five—wait, why is it so dark?" By her reckoning even six hours would only have been early evening.

"There's a sandstorm coming."

"That's terrible."

"We'll be safe here," Kyrkenall assured her. "And it will probably blow over by night time."

Elenai was no expert on sandstorms, but thought Kyrkenall was un-characteristically optimistic. "Did you get any rest?"

"Lyria was on sentry."

While Lyria was as effective as a well-trained watchdog, Elenai remained unimpressed. "Do you think she would have noticed if the Goddess came over the horizon?"

Kyrkenall returned from the cave rear, where he'd left Elenai's horse. "She noticed when the storm came and alerted me with whinnying. You're worrying too much. We both need rest if we're going to be up all night looking for this weapon."

Elenai pulled on boots with one hand, stomping them into place, and stalked to the cave entrance, peering out at the landscape. Due west she perceived a long line of darkness. The wind moaned, rising and falling like a ghastly chorus of spirits. She looked over her shoulder to Kyrkenall.

Her horse made no movement to the cave rear. Lyria, though, walked calmly to her shoulder to look outside. Kyrkenall stepped forward to rub her nose. "It won't fill up this cave, but I bet there will be quite a sand drift."

"Maybe the storm's clearing up." Elenai pointed to a bright spot grow-ing along the edge of the horizon, right at ground level. Around and above it dark clouds rolled, but in that spot she saw only a soothing white-yellow glow. "What is that?" she asked. "Some kind of counter wind?"

"No," Kyrkenall said, staring fixedly.

In a few moments it became clear that the brightness drifted ahead of the storm. "It's the Goddess." Elenai felt numb as she said it. "She's come for her hearthstone."

"What a run of luck we're having," Kyrkenall said. "For our own sakes, maybe you ought to toss the stone down the slope and hope she doesn't come any farther."

As the bright glow drew ever closer, Elenai detected a jet-black woman in its dead center. "If I give up the hearthstone, it's going to be a lot harder to search for the weapon. And impossible to contact Cerai and get back." There was no other way to reach their forces.

"I wish I had some better ideas," Kyrkenall said. "But I don't have any

Goddess-slaying arrows, and blasting her with hearthstone magic's probably just going to make her feel better. Sometimes you have to retreat."

They'd already retreated from the Naor. Now they'd be retreating from the Goddess.

She had grown obvious in the light, a human shape with flowing hair drifting unmoving three yards above the desert, feet hanging slack, arms loose at her sides. A long straight line of white stretched out behind and beneath her.

"This is going to sound stupid, but we could try talking to her," Elenai suggested.

"I don't think she'll listen, but sure. Just make sure she can get the hearthstone first."

Elenai retrieved the stone and rejoined Kyrkenall. She hated feeling so helpless, and wished there was something more to do than watch the deity's approach. She guessed the Goddess was only a quarter mile away now.

"You want me to toss it?" Kyrkenall asked.

Elenai looked down at her good hand. "No. I'll do it." She moved forward.

Two paces out from the cave the storm howled. Even though the greater mass of the storm lay behind the oncoming deity, grit and dirt already swirled through the air.

The Goddess flew on, beautiful and black, surrounded by a perfect round halo of warm white energy. Her steady, remorseless, effortless glide should have been chilling. Instead Elenai found it a challenge not to stare in awe. Finally, though, she reared back and lobbed the stone, wincing as the motion jerked her injured arm. The stone glittered with emerald light as it arced away.

A few feet from the ground it shot away in a perfect line, glowing with inner fires, flying straight toward the Goddess.

"Damnit." She'd thought the Goddess would have to come at least as near as the bottom of the slope to get the stone. "I was hoping she'd come close enough to talk."

The hearthstone struck the Goddess' chest with a bright flash of light. She continued to float directly toward them.

"Well, you're in luck then," Kyrkenall said. "Because here she comes."

48

The Other Way

Tesra watched the shambling, awkward run of the ko'aye bearing Rylin and Thelar, astonished that such graceful creatures were so clumsy on the ground.

Once in the air they transformed almost immediately from ungainly feathered reptiles to lithe and lovely predators. She admired them as they retreated into a cerulean sky.

The audience who'd gathered to see them off retreated to the fortress, talking among themselves. Tesra, who didn't properly belong to any of the groups, waited to one side for them to precede her. M'vai passed, in close conversation with N'lahr. Neither paid her any notice.

Tesra still couldn't reconcile the loving organization of which she'd thought she'd been a part with the secretive cult that had imprisoned General N'lahr and murdered noble Asrahn. It didn't help that she had grown suspicious of her own emotions, memories, and judgment. She had been angry with Meria and M'vai for betraying that organization. Now she mourned for the kinder of the two sisters and envied the intense survivor for being trusted and valued by those the auxiliary had betrayed.

"Are you wondering what they're talking about?"

Cerai had come up behind her so quietly Tesra flinched in surprise.

The others had disappeared into the gloom of the fortress. Cerai waved away a servant who poked out his handsome head to give her an inquiring look. She continued as though Tesra had answered in the affirmative, sounding and looking composed and cool, if tired. "N'lahr has been infected with order. I'm sure you've noticed. And M'vai's increasingly worried about him. But there's nothing to be done."

Tesra had seen the commander's strange symptoms as well as his peculiar energy matrix, though she struggled to make sense of the description Cerai had provided. She repeated it slowly. "Infected with order?"

Cerai smiled thinly. Because the older woman had visited the queen and the exalts infrequently, Tesra had never known her well, though she had always admired her. Master of her own fate, Cerai would slip into and out of Darassus whenever she pleased and seemed to be the only alten whom both the queen and Synahla completely respected, though in recent months both had grown suspicious of her. Tesra inferred that the Altenerai had the same misgivings about her, for Cerai had apparently been playing her own canny little game for years, preparing for a crisis neither side had fully understood.

"Didn't you notice it happening to the queen?" Cerai asked.

That question pulled Tesra up short. She had never thought of the change in the queen's personality as an infection. "The queen did change," she said. "But I thought that was just because she was growing more powerful. I don't know N'lahr at all, so—"

Cerai didn't wait for her to finish. "You probably weren't examining the queen closely through the inner world, were you?"

"No," Tesra said. One simply didn't do that. Scrutinizing a fellow spell caster was impolite, although not entirely avoidable if you happened to be working spells together. "What happened to N'lahr?"

"Well, several things. I'm sure you knew he was trapped inside a hearth-stone for something close to seven years?"

She'd heard only that he'd been imprisoned. This information astounded her. "How could he fit in a hearthstone?"

"You really didn't know? I thought you were highly placed."

"Not that high, apparently," she said.

"Interesting. Well, N'lahr told me he was trapped within the defensive reaction of a hearthstone. A kind of stasis. It left its mark on him, and the mark is getting stronger. Apparently he was also attacked by the queen during the battle. Did you see that?"

Tesra shook her head, no. Once again she felt woefully underinformed and overmatched.

"Battlefields are chaotic," Cerai allowed. "As to N'lahr, unless some-thing's done he's going to end up looking very much like one of the crea-tures stored in my menagerie. Fairly soon." Cerai didn't sound entirely unmoved by his circumstance, but she was far from distraught.

It was horrifying to contemplate the loss of the savior of Darassus and the five realms. "Have you told him how much danger he's in?"

"I think he knows."

"If something happens to him, what will we do if the Goddess attacks again?"

Cerai's look at her was one of disappointment. "I don't think a sword, even Irion, is much use against the Goddess. N'lahr is nearly useless in the battle to come."

"But that doesn't mean you won't help him, does it?"

Cerai laughed softly. "Isn't it your queen who had him frozen?"

Tesra didn't understand why Cerai seemed to think the situation funny. "I didn't know about that," she said. "She shouldn't have done it."

"She could probably tell you were a sentimentalist. I have a small amount of sentiment left myself. For old time's sake I suppose I should examine him. Maybe you'll help me."

"Of course."

"But that's not what I wanted to speak to you about," Cerai said.

"Oh?" N'lahr's health certainly seemed important to Tesra, but perhaps Alten Cerai was more worried about the Goddess.

"We're in an interesting predicament. While I would certainly like to have the spirits and weapon I dispatched Rylin and Kyrkenall to find, I don't plan to wait around for someone to come save me. A woman has to make her own way and plan ahead. Do you plan ahead, Tesra?"

"I'm not sure what to plan for anymore."

Cerai put a hand to her arm. "Then plan with me. I can use someone of your skills."

Nothing seemed to trouble Cerai, and Tesra envied the alten's self-assurance. While she demonstrated a similar arrogance to the queen and Synahla, Cerai possessed more awareness than either, and a dark irreverence that was oddly appealing. "What do you want to do?"

"First? I've changed my mind. Let's follow your suggestion and go look at my old friend N'lahr." Cerai patted her arm, then headed through the open doorway into the fortress.

They found N'lahr and M'vai in a reception room with a tiled waterway swimming with decorative fish. The two sat in a furniture grouping through which the water flowed. The young redhead had always been the more serious of the two sisters. Recent events appeared to have aged her, for her eyes and mouth lines and furrows in her brow were more pronounced as she studied N'lahr, seated on the couch across from her.

As for the Altenerai commander, his plain, gaunt features revealed little of his inner thoughts.

Cerai stopped near N'lahr. "I know you're getting sicker. Are other symptoms manifesting?"

M'vai watched suspiciously, but N'lahr answered without hesitation.

"I lose track of moments. Observers tell me I freeze up." He lifted his arm. "Sometimes my body responds slowly or gracelessly."

"So nothing I haven't seen from you already," Cerai said. "If you'd like, I can examine you. I have some experience in understanding how living structures are assembled."

"I've heard," N'lahr said.

"Just stand still, then. I'll study you a bit."

M'vai's brow furrowed more deeply.

Cerai spoke to the commander in a quiet, thoughtful way. "I'd say that you're unusually quiet, but that's not really accurate, is it? What I mean to say is that you're silent and yet have something on your mind."

N'lahr held himself still, as though posing for a painter's brush. "There are a lot of things to worry about."

"Indeed there are," Cerai said. "And I know I'm one of them. I'm no fool."

"I never thought you were."

"But I know how your mind works. You're direct. Uncompromising."

"I'd say that's fair."

Cerai's eyes held that slightly glazed, absent quality of someone staring into the inner world.

Deciding it would not be rude to do so, Tesra studied the commander through the inner world herself, finding the structural features typical of a living human body, registering as bright reds and golds. But a silvery latticework existed in parallel to the skeletal structures and energy lines, reminiscent of the matrices within hearthstones. She'd never seen another living object embedded with the like. More troubling was that new threads were growing on the latticework even as she watched.

She looked at Cerai to gauge her reaction, and discovered the mage's body had something strange within it as well. All of Cerai's life threads glowed with excess energy.

Cerai eyed N'lahr, and spoke to him, sounding faintly amused. "I know you don't trust me."

"I don't fully understand some of your actions," N'lahr admitted.

"You wonder why I didn't try to stop the queen."

"More specifically I wonder why you didn't inform the rest of the Altenerai about the queen's plans. Actions could have been taken to save lives."

"I judged we Altenerai wouldn't be effective, and it was better to make alternative preparations. Surely you understand that. A commander has to pick her battles and protect her resources."

"What's my condition?"

"You've no comment?" Cerai asked. "I take it that means you remain uncertain of me."

Though the mage clearly wished to pretend they were engaged in playful banter, N'lahr appeared deadly serious. "Very well, Cerai. Given that the hearthstones twisted our queen and one of the kindest and most skilled of the Altenerai, Belahn, I think you should rightly be concerned they might have altered your own judgment."

"Oh, my judgment has changed," Cerai said. "But go on."

"You excuse actions that would once have been anathema to you. You were willing to assist Alantris only so long as you could access the keystone, which you thought more important than the people of the city you were sworn to protect."

"How can I protect the people if the realms are slated for destruction?" Cerai shook her head. "The hearthstones allow me to see further than others. My judgment *is* different, but it's not deluded. I know what I can achieve. And surely you recognize that if I had not made these preparations, if I had not reached out to save you, you would already be dead."

"I do see that."

"And yet you still distrust me."

"Are you going to tell him his prognosis, or not?" M'vai asked.

Cerai glanced at her with mild annoyance "Your guardian grows impatient, N'lahr. As to her point, you are infected with order, and it's rooting ever more deeply. I think your condition's accelerating."

"How quickly?" N'lahr asked.

"I can't know that unless I look at you again in a few hours."

"And the final result?"

"Probably what you fear. I think you will become a statue. One permanently suspended between life and death."

The commander nodded once, as if she had merely confirmed his suspicion.

Tesra felt as though her heart had dropped away. M'vai pressed hands to the sides of her head as though she couldn't stand to hear much more.

"You've identified the problem," N'lahr said. "Can anything be done?"

"I can attempt to remove these extra threads."

"How dangerous is that?"

"This is hearthstone magic, and interfering with it can provoke a reaction. It varies from stone to stone, and I don't know how my efforts will interact with your body."

"I've experienced and witnessed some of those hearthstone reactions," N'lahr said with grim resolve. "Very well. Look at me again in an hour. If the advancement has accelerated, we may have to risk action."

"Of course. I'm happy to help."

"Thank you. Now if you'll excuse me, there's something I must do."

Cerai gestured for him to exit, then turned to M'vai. "I know you've appointed yourself his caretaker. Why don't you keep an eye on him? There's something I want to show Tesra."

M'vai glumly nodded agreement, and then Tesra followed Cerai to a cozy office on the third floor. It had a secondary door along one wall, across from a bookshelf-lined fireplace. A window looked down upon the courtyard.

Cerai crossed to the desk, the room's central feature, and took a seat in a plush chair. Behind her, just under the window, a shelf unit of mixed cabinet doors and open shelves displayed pieces of turquoise Arappan pottery and five small crystals that were almost certainly memory stones.

Tesra sat on the wooden bench beside the main door and waited to see what Cerai had in mind.

"This morning, Anzat was sitting there. Do you know what he offered me?"

"Did he propose?"

Cerai laughed. "No. He offered me not just his soldiers, but his soldiers in Darassus. As if I wanted to bring through a few hundred more Naor."

"He's trying to turn you against the Altenerai?" Tesra asked.

"He said I couldn't trust them. As if I didn't know that, and as if he thought I would trust him."

Tesra wasn't sure what to say, so she nodded politely.

"He's right about one thing, though. I really don't have anyone I can trust. The Altenerai are too limited to understand what's really underway here. And the Naor jockey for position, as always, so that they may end up on top. It doesn't matter if that top is the very highest spot on a collapsing tower. It's that momentary supremacy that's important to them."

"What are you going to do?"

"What do you think I should do?"

Tesra hadn't expected that question. "Isn't there a way to work with both? Even after we stop the Goddess?"

"How optimistic you are. The Altenerai will try to arrest me for my imagined crimes. That won't go well for them, of course." Cerai set her hands on the table, fingers interlaced. "I don't think you've decided where you stand. Your relationships with both the Altenerai and the exalts are awkward. And allying with the Naor is abhorrent to you. So you're trying to take my measure."

"You're so forthright."

"Why shouldn't I be? We don't have an excess of time. Tell me what you want, and we'll see if I can accommodate it."

"I'm not sure what I want anymore," Tesra said truthfully. "Unless it's to be on the right side the next time I choose one. I've been fooled by all kinds of people I've trusted. I don't want to be tricked again."

Cerai straightened in her chair. "Do you know what will happen when the Goddess is destroyed?"

"I'm not sure." Tesra wondered how this tied into any of her own wants.

"All of that magical energy will be free at once. It has to be channeled or it will have the same effect it did when the death of the Goddess left The Fragments, well, fragmented. It will be worse, because then there were multiple gods fighting to contain those energies."

Tesra was most concerned with Cerai's primary point. "We have no gods to contain the energy," she said.

"You have me, though. I've been preparing for the moment when that power would be released for years, though it happened differently than I predicted. I'd thought I'd be channeling power when the queen opened the hearthstones. Now I'll have to kill a goddess, but the end result will be the same one I've trained for. That power will be mine. It would almost be limitless. And I mean to share some of it."

"Really?" Tesra asked, hoping her concern was hidden by the interest she feigned.

"I plan on enlisting a few trusted allies. People of great integrity imbued with hearthstone energy. That's all the Gods we worshiped really were." Cerai leaned forward again. "Think of all the problems they could put right. Why, they could stop quakes, storms, and pestilence. If a conflict flared up for some reason, a sentinel could quickly bring the people to heel."

Cerai seemed to be missing an obvious drawback. "That level of power could be abused."

"Indeed it could. That's why it can only be granted to the best people."

She was at least as mad as the queen. Tesra hoped her polite smile still served as a mask.

"Surely you see where this was going. You're a spell caster of moderate strength and better-than-usual skill. You're well-trained. You're patient. And I think you've seen just what unchecked power has done, so you'd be reluctant to act thoughtlessly."

Tesra had no problem agreeing with that sentiment, and nodded.

"There are naturally the obvious benefits, but you may not have realized that my sentinels would possess extended longevity. You wouldn't age, Tesra. You would be beautiful forever."

Cerai appeared to have thought that an important point, so Tesra nodded once more.

Cerai rose, tucked the chair back into her table, and opened a cabinet door behind her. From it she removed the shaping tool. "I'll let you try it out so you have a taste of the kind of power you can wield if you join me."

"Where did it come from?" Tesra asked.

The alten hadn't yet relinquished hold of the staff, which, while seemingly carved of stone, was absolutely, perfectly cylindrical. "Our 'gods.' They used it to focus their magical energies when they built the realms. It's been a tremendous aid in building my little oasis here."

At Tesra's awed look, Cerai smiled, and passed over the staff.

Tesra's hands glided over the cool, smooth surface. She was so absorbed with the monumental astonishment of holding something that had shaped the five realms, it was a moment before she could speak. "How does it work?"

"Come with me. I'll show you."

19

Reunions

Maybe she's just going to pass right over us," Elenai said. The Goddess drifted ever nearer. Kyrkenall made a counter speculation. "Maybe she's going to take vengeance."

"You always were an optimist."

Kyrkenall chuckled. He gripped his sword hilt, released it, then placed his hand upon it again. "I'd like it to be said I died with my sword in hand, even if it does seem kind of pointless." He drew Lothrun with a flourish. "Not that there's likely to be anyone who'll find us."

"The sword." Elenai said with growing horror. "There's hearthstone energy in Lothrun. And in your bow. They were all crafted with hearthstone magics."

"You think that's what she's after?" Kyrkenall's brows climbed his forehead in dismay.

The dark goddess loomed gigantically as she advanced, the white road growing beneath her.

"I'm afraid so."

Kyrkenall swore, then looked at his sword, a beautiful blade of blue-black steel tapering to a curve. He then advanced down the slope to lay it reverently on the rocks.

The Goddess had advanced to within a few hundred feet. Elenai could see her eyes now, or where her eyes would have been visible if they were not perfect black orbs. Much, she thought, like Kyrkenall's own. The deity's expression remained utterly blank.

Kyrkenall lifted his famed bow from the holster over his shoulder and even from behind Elenai felt the breath leave him as he lovingly brushed the intricately carved warriors battling on its surface.

He looked almost as broken as a man abandoning his child to oncoming flames when he laid the great bow upon the stones beside the blade. He stood over them both as the Goddess drew closer and closer yet, now only fifty feet off, towering over them. Kyrkenall bowed his head.

"Get back here," Elenai cried, and he hurried to her side. They retreated to the cave mouth as the Goddess halted above the weapons.

She raised two perfect palms at the same moment. Elenai searched her flawless face and grew entranced by her beauty again.

"Don't look at her eyes," Kyrkenall advised, which snapped Elenai from her reverie.

She didn't have to be locked into the inner world to feel the energy drawn up from the weapons. She looked down at the masterfully crafted sword and bow, thinking to see them disintegrate, or return to their original shape—the carvings, perhaps, disappearing from Arzhun so that it was once more a simple horn.

But the forms of the weapons remained the same. It was the magic residing in their cores that vanished.

Still the woman's hands were extended. Elenai gasped in fear as a rush of magical energies passed through her. From behind rose the shrill squealing of a horse in abject terror, and the stomp of hooves. Elenai and Kyrkenall threw themselves clear as Elenai's horse bolted past, sliding down the slope, raising a cloud of dust and scattering rocks. It then banked sharply left and galloped out of sight.

"Damn!" Kyrkenall had already rolled to his feet. "What was that about?"

Elenai winced in pain and forced herself up. "Cerai used hearthstone magics to shape her. The Goddess drew it back."

"You think she has any more surprises?" Kyrkenall asked.

The dark entity lowered her hands and drifted upward.

"Wait," Elenai cried, shouting to be heard above the rising storm.

The deity actually halted, and those huge dark eyes fixed her without emotion.

Elenai called up to her. "If you unmake the world, you will kill all the creatures your children labored to create! All their work will be undone, and you will have nothing left of them!"

The answering voice was calm, sweet, and beautiful, though completely without feeling.

"It is time to put away their dabblings, and start anew."

"You, who longed to be restored, must surely understand we, too, want to live! We want to see the things that we love live on after us."

"You want these things because you were made to want them," the Goddess said. "My children wrought their creations poorly." She floated upward, the cliff face changing to white as she passed in front of it.

"Let us be!" Elenai cried. "Fashion something new! You need not destroy!"

"I shall not leave flawed creations after me," came the answer.

"Please!" Elenai shouted. "We will honor and revere you! Whatever you want . . ."

But the Goddess had drifted up and away and was lost to sight above the height of the hill.

"Maybe you should have started with that last bit," Kyrkenall suggested.

Elenai wiped tears from her eyes, grit from her thumb abrading her cheek.

Kyrkenall advanced to look at his weapons. He hefted his blade first and took a few swipes before sheathing it. Arzhun he held at arms length, inspecting it up and down.

He was so absorbed by his study that for once Elenai was the one who saw something first.

"Kyrkenall."

He looked up.

The passage of the Goddess through the realm appeared to have punched a hole through its composition, like the hull of a boat punctured so water sprayed into its gunnels. Chaos flowed in her wake. The storm

swirled with reds and greens and even a pulsating blue. Chartreuse lightning crackled among the clouds, and from time to time the ground shook.

"Gods," Elenai said softly. "She's rent through the heart of the realm."
She stared at the splendid, terrible storm, then looked to Kyrkenall, still
holding his lovely bow.

"She stripped out every bit of magic," he said, voice barely audible over
the wind's howl. He laughed shortly as he surveyed the clouds, exploding
toward them. "What does it matter? We might be looking at the world's
end!"

"Let's get back inside," she said.

"You think the cave will protect us?"

"It will shield us from the sand and the wind," she said, then added,
irritably, "unless you're ready to give up?" She ducked inside.

She heard Kyrkenall's boot soles scrape over sand and stone behind
her. Lyria had wisely retreated deeper into the cave, and was sniffing Kyrkenall's saddlebags.

The archer came up to his horse, still snuffling at the leather, and firmly
swatted her flank.

Lyria looked at him with a snort.

"Grubbing for treats?" he asked.

The horse moved out of the way.

"She's not a bit ashamed." Kyrkenall undid the pack's straps and felt
around. Lyria looked away as it became obvious no horse-related items
would be produced. The archer pulled out a velvet sack.

Elenai looked down at her ring, and realized it was completely useless.
"Kyrkenall?" she asked. "Does your ring work?"

"No," he said after a moment.

"The Goddess drained them, too. She must have done it when she pulled
magic from my horse."

The failure of the sacred emblem and tool of the corps hit like one
more punch in a sparring match when it was already called.

Dejected, she lowered herself onto the flat, slanted corner of a boulder
and cradled her injured arm.

Kyrkenall set the bag aside and, as the light dimmed further, unwrapped
the three glass plates and locked their copper frames into the base of a cunningly crafted field lantern.

Darkness blotted the sky, and roaring wind blew sand into the cave
maw. Tiny pebbles and sharp grains mounded in the entrance.

Kyrkenall lit the lantern.

"If this is a normal storm, and not the end of the world, will it really be over by nightfall?" Elenai asked.

"Probably. So it won't interfere with our nighttime search. And if it's over sooner, the temperature might be reduced, so we can look during the day."

"With no hearthstone, which means no way to get back."

"I thought you were angry when it sounded like I was giving up."

An immense roll of thunder crashed through the storm's roar. The cave floor shook so violently the flame in the lantern wavered and grit and pebbles rained down.

Lyria snorted in concern. Even Kyrkenall looked alarmed, and scanned the ceiling, as if he expected it to fall in.

The ground rumbled more gently, and Elenai waited breathlessly, wondering what she should do.

"Be a damnable thing if this is how it ended, wouldn't it?" Kyrkenall asked.

"Smashed in a cave, you mean?"

"Right. I always figured I'd go out fighting." There was nothing playful in his tone as his head turned toward her. "There are no happy endings."

"There can be happy endings," Elenai objected.

His lips twitched into a sardonic smile. "Only if you stop the story in the right place. Say, the day when you won the ring, or maybe when we saved Darassus. But that wasn't really the end. Life keeps going until it stops. The death part is never a happy ending, is it?"

"Sometimes," she said. "If it's a mercy."

"If it's a mercy, then the moments leading to death aren't happy, are they?" He shook his head. "All storytellers are liars. If this were a play, we'd survive, and you'd step up to be a noble queen, then marry the bravest, handsomest warrior in the kingdom. Probably Rylin. And Kalandra would be miraculously restored so we could ride off to explore the wilds together."

Elenai didn't think her own happy ending would have much to do with marriage, a subject to which she'd never given much thought, but the mention of Kalandra reminded her just how central she was to Kyrkenall's fondest wishes. For him, there could be no true happiness without her.

Something out there in the dark struck the ground with earth-shattering force. The resulting rain of pebbles was smaller this time, but no more comforting.

"It almost sounds like an angry god is out there with a hammer," Kyrkenall said. He pulled a small glistening bag from one of his belt pouches, then withdrew something from it and held it up near the lantern. A gem of some kind, Elenai saw, then realized it was a fist-sized emerald.

"That's Kalandra's emerald, isn't it?"

"Aye."

"I thought you left it in Darassus."

"I brought her with me. I figured if things didn't work out, I'd go down with her."

Elenai swore.

Kyrkenall shushed her. "'What times are these, when youths abandon sense, and curse and mock the wisdom of the aged?'"

"That's why you've been so calm. You've had her with you the entire time!"

"I suppose you're right."

Elenai paused, struck with a curious thought. "Why couldn't I sense the emerald before this?"

"Near as I can tell, the fabric has an enchantment that blocks sight of magic. I didn't know that when I grabbed it from the queen's chambers. But I noticed later on when I was looking at magical stuff with my ring, and didn't see the emerald unless I took it out of my bag. Apparently even the Goddess couldn't see past it."

"That fabric might have come in handy when the Goddess was seeking my hearthstone shard," she said, then laughed as she saw Kyrkenall's dejected look. "It's all right. It wouldn't have fit." She shook her head, then laughed once more.

"What?" Kyrkenall asked.

"I was just thinking that maybe you're right. If I'm swearing so much even Kyrkenall the Eyeless is chastising me I could stand to cut back."

"It's hardly becoming of a queen," Kyrkenall said with mock gravity.

"Queen? Of what? The cave? Darassus may already be rubble. So might our cave, in a few more moments."

"Maybe it's just a storm."

"Maybe." She extended her right hand. "Why don't you let me see that?"

He was quiet a long moment. "Why?"

"I'm going to take another look."

"I thought it was too dangerous to open."

"Probably."

"And you don't have a hearthstone."

"If this is the world's end, I don't see any reason to hold this off any longer. Maybe I can make your ending a happier one, a final moment with the woman you love."

She opened herself to the inner world.

Kyrkenall still didn't relinquish the stone. "Playing with the wards on this flattened Thelar."

"I've a vague recollection," Elenai said. The energies that shielded the stone looked just as intricate as she remembered. They wrapped the stone tightly, in remarkably consistent bands of gold and green light. Thelar had tried to use the power of a hearthstone shard to break those bands, but the protective spell had almost surely been placed by someone wielding a hearthstone as well. She'd need something more. "If this really is the end of the world, and she really is in there, don't you want to say good-bye?"

"So I lose both of you?" Kyrkenall asked after a moment.

"If it's the world's end, you're losing everything pretty soon already."

He laughed. "These days you're a strange mix of romance and pragmatism." But he passed the stone across at last.

Elenai slowly rotated it in her good hand. So long as she simply studied it through the inner world she thought she was in no danger. But any attempt at linking her threads to those about the stone would blast her at least as thoroughly as Thelar had been.

She glimpsed a spark of energy out of the corner of her eye and looked to the cave maw. Beyond the accumulating pile of sand myriad energy lines raced within the storm.

"I'm going to try something." Elenai stood and moved toward the entrance, passing Lyria on the way. After a few steps, she was walking on a slope of sand, and soon her boots sank into it. She shielded her eyes as grit blasted her face, then set the emerald at the top of the pile. Through narrowed eyelids she watched the energy threads coursing in the storm. She found it hard to breathe in the choking air.

Though her magical endurance had grown over the weeks since her first exposure to hearthstones, it was far from endless, and it began to ebb. She wasn't sure how much longer she could continue to watch.

And then a bright purple slash of energy blossomed outside the cave maw. She seized its edges with her threads and directed it toward the emerald, now half buried by accumulating debris.

Even brief contact with the emerald's threads sent pain lancing through her body, as though she'd been pierced with needles over every inch of her skin. She staggered back. Her knees failed and she was grateful Kyrkenall caught and steadied her.

"How badly are you hurt?"

It took her a moment to answer. She saw only red, as if her eyes were awash with blood. But the pain eased, its memory a dull throb that retreated to her injured elbow, and she saw the warring energies of stone and storm. A snake of red lightning hung through the shifting curtain of sand, its end point drifting across the surface of the emerald, which glowed from deep within. The stone threw off sparks that looped out to attack the red lightning, which flickered but did not relent.

"How bad are you?" Kyrkenall repeated worriedly.

"Better now."

They moved apart when he confirmed she was steady, and then both watched the display of light. "That's pretty clever," Kyrkenall said.

"I thought the energy might wear out the protective spell," Elenai replied.

"And here I thought you were out of ideas."

The lightning disappeared. At the same moment the stone's glow failed. The gloom seemed deeper.

"What do you think?" Kyrkenall asked. He reached back for the lantern, shining behind them.

Before she could answer, a figure flashed into existence directly in front of the sand mound.

Kyrkenall shone the light at the figure, even as a chill touched the back of Elenai's neck.

She had seen Kalandra before, but this was no ghostly image. Before them stood a harried, dark-haired woman of medium height, her oval face bronzed by the sun. Her khalat was soiled and worn, and one high collar was badly frayed. Her dry voice had a peculiar, echoing quality, as though she spoke from within a deep well. "Kyrkenall?"

20

A Final Consultation

Tesra found N'lahr at a second-floor window, looking down onto the courtyard where two lines of squires traded practice thrusts as a curly-haired sixth ranker paced among them offering advice and encouragement.

She knew they couldn't hope to counter anything a goddess could throw, and guessed other reasons for their preparation. The sixth ranker probably needed to keep them busy. And he might also have meant to demonstrate to any onlookers his force was capable.

Tesra had no doubts. A handful of Cerai's troops watched from the side with great interest, and so did a pair of Naor she suspected had been assigned to monitor them.

The rest of the Naor worked on catapults outside the fortress. The aspirants, along with M'vai, had departed with Cerai, who carried the shaping staff.

Tesra had witnessed her repair of the battlement, and even had the chance to use the amazing artifact. Cerai had claimed the tool purified things, but that wasn't quite accurate. With the staff, and a hearthstone, you had only to direct the energy into what you envisioned and it came to pass, and thus the ruined battlement had swiftly been rebuilt, so smoothly that the repair could not be distinguished from the original.

Tesra had initially ridden off with them to strengthen the borders, but M'vai had grown more and more anxious about N'lahr and an exasperated Cerai had finally sent Tesra back to check on him, almost cruelly suggesting M'vai attend to the renovations in her place.

After Tesra had greeted him, N'lahr simply said: "I'm feeling about the same. How do I look?"

Some five hours had passed since Cerai had performed a second examination of him, and Tesra saw that his extra white matrices were intertwined more thoroughly with the gold threads of his life force.

"Bad?" he asked.

Her concern must have shown on her face. "They're getting worse."

"I see." N'lahr looked out at the Naor. "How long do you think I have, Tesra?"

"I'm no healer."

"I don't think that matters. You're a mage. You can tell how quickly the problem is growing."

She hated to think what that might mean, and hated to tell him. "But I don't know how much more your body can endure before you're so badly hurt that you're . . ."

"Fully incapacitated?"

"Yes. And I don't know how much faster it's going to get."

Somehow, he remained calm. "Just tell me how much it's changed in the last hours."

"The change isn't large. But if it continues at this rate I think you may be in danger as early as tomorrow. I wish there was something more I could do, for you, or for all of us." Her hands tightened on the stone windowsill. She glanced over her shoulder at the open door behind them, then to either side, then spoke quietly. "I'm working my way into Cerai's trust."

"That's a dangerous game," he replied softly, without looking at her. "She's very perceptive."

"She thrives on the attention," Tesra said. "It leaves an opening."

He looked at her shrewdly. Tesra had the sense his own estimation of her had risen.

"Nevertheless. Act with care."

Tesra spoke rapidly, but softly. "She means to make herself and a few chosen servants virtual gods. She's structured the energy matrices here to funnel that power so that when she destroys the Goddess her energy will be controlled, just as she needs. Stored, so she can tap it whenever she wants. And she herself may be very hard to take down."

He accepted this information with a single nod.

"You know," she said, astonished. How could he? But then she remembered how she herself had begun to sense the way power flowed in Cerai's realm. Thelar or M'vai might have studied and deduced something odd about it, and told him.

"What are you going to do?" Tesra asked.

"Let's just say that I am preparing to meet these challenges."

Tesra translated that to mean he had some kind of plan, but wasn't willing to share it, probably because he didn't trust her.

And then he offered one of his rare smiles. "It's brave of you," he said. "But I want you to understand that she'll be vicious if crossed. More vicious than you may know."

She looked out at the squires. "I swore I'd start making my own, better choices. And after failing so badly, I owe it to everyone else to take some risks, if there's a chance it will help."

He put a hand to her upper arm. "You give me hope." He turned. "I've something to see to. Thank you." He left her.

Tesra gave him his privacy rather than following his every move, and watched as the sun dropped behind the outer wall. She debated with herself about how deeply to play along with Cerai's aims. Was it even useful to do so, if N'lahr had deduced her plans?

Yes, she decided, because with Cerai's confidence, she'd understand those plans in greater detail.

Alerted by another of the poorly rendered horn calls, Tesra headed quickly to the outer wall, in time to see Cerai ride back with the rest of the mages. Most sagged in their saddles.

They'd worked a final change upon their return: both roads the Goddess had left behind had vanished utterly. Where white stone had stretched away, grass flourished once more.

But what difference could that make, in the long run, if the Goddess had effected those changes in moments without any obvious effort, and correcting it had exhausted every one of these mages?

Tesra took the stairs down to meet them. Cerai was already out of saddle and talking earnestly with N'lahr and two of her soldiers, one of whom held her horse.

As the aspirants swung stiffly out of the saddles, M'vai exhorted them to eat, then to get right to sleep. "Tired spell casters make mistakes," she reminded them.

The two women and one man filed past Tesra with brief nods of greeting, trailing the smell of horse and their own sweat. M'vai stopped before Tesra and pushed slick hair from her forehead. "I just caught a look at N'lahr. He's worse."

"I don't think he's going to be safe much longer. How did the repairs go?"

M'vai's mouth twitched. She looked at Tesra as if doubting her for a moment. "The realm's been strengthened. Aren't you worried about the commander?"

"Of course I am."

M'vai looked over her shoulder toward Cerai and N'lahr, then turned back to Tesra, peering closely at her. "Come with me," she said.

M'vai hurried inside, walking farther from the mess hall, no matter the entrancing aroma of fresh baked bread. It was one of the few foodstuffs Cerai's kitchen staff had really mastered.

Soon they were standing in one of the strange storerooms arranged with thousands of creatures held in magical suspension, this one featuring creatures from Kanesh. M'vai stepped into the shadow of one of the great predators of the plains, the terrible birds known as ax-beaks. Tesra had never seen a living one in Kanesh, but knew the cunning flightless birds were capable of great speed and could outrun horses for brief periods.

M'vai barely gave the monster a second glance. "N'lahr's going to die, soon. And regardless of what you think, you have to know that he's a good leader, and that our people are stronger with him."

"Of course I know that. What did you think—"

M'vai cut her off. "We have to try to save him. He didn't talk to Thelar much about his condition, Goddess knows–" M'vai paused to curse. "Why do I still say 'Goddess'? What I mean to say is, who knows why. Probably because Thelar's mission was more important to N'lahr's plans than his own welfare. But I think I should try to reach out to Thelar, to see if he can help. He's the best theoretician we have left."

"You're talking about a sending? That's incredibly dangerous."

"And you don't think it's dangerous trusting N'lahr's health to Cerai?"

"That's different!"

M'vai sighed so loudly Tesra knew a flutter of anger. "You think she'll help him? She lied to the queen and all of us. For years. She brought us only a few hearthstones at a time, checked in to get any important information, then kept all the others she was collecting for herself. She's a practiced liar."

"I'm not stupid," Tesra said.

"Then you agree? We need to act fast to save him. Thelar is the best magical resource we have."

"I want to help the commander. But I don't think this is smart."

The younger woman scowled. "She's grooming you, you know. Just like Synahla groomed us."

"I know—"

"We were working for traitors. Do you want to work for another?"

Tesra shook her head. "I'm on your side. I swear this is so."

"Then help me." M'vai looked up at the looming ax-beak, poised as though he were ready to rend them. She walked through a careful arrangement of waterfowl, and Tesra reluctantly followed. They knelt together at a back wall, and M'vai removed a hearthstone from a side pouch. Tesra swallowed her surprise. In the dying light, Tesra decided it was likely a white or pale yellow in color.

"Where did you get that?"

"Cerai gave it to me. She wants us all to be attuned to a specific stone." M'vai snorted. "She wants her tools to be as useful as possible to her. Meaning we're the tools."

Tesra said nothing to that.

"I'm going to focus myself with the stone. You anchor to it lightly and help me watch for dangers. Warn me if I'm too deep in or too far away."

"All right. But isn't this going to be more risky if the Goddess is, well, conscious now?"

"Yes," M'vai said testily. "But you just have to focus on drawing power from the upper layers. I did it while we were making repairs."

"You make it sound simple."

"It won't be."

"I'm just—. Be careful. Do you have to argue about everything?"

"Sorry," M'vai said gruffly. She placed her hands on the hearthstone, and Tesra was reminded of a final objection.

"Didn't you just tell the others that a tired mage was one who made mistakes?"

"This can't wait, Tesra. I'm going to show Thelar my memory of what I saw within N'lahr, and get his feedback. If we wait until I'm feeling 'rested' it may be too late."

Tesra kept further reservations to herself, and slipped into the inner world at the same time as her friend. A moment later, both women were connected to the hearthstone. The energy washed over Tesra, who smiled at the familiar rush.

M'vai rooted her threads to the stone and launched her spirit from her seated body. She soared away, leaving a powerful line of energy trailing after.

With her view devoted to the inner world, Tesra took in the nearby environment, seeing evidence of what she already knew, for the perfect statues standing all about her were living beings held in stasis. Their life force still shone, but did not shift.

Something stirred deep within the hearthstone. It glowed fiercely, like a miniature star. It felt as though she had walked out of a dark tunnel to find an entire stadium glaring at her.

"M'vai!" She shouted the name both in the real world and through the ether, reaching with her threads to tug at her friend's line at the same moment she shook the redhead's shoulder.

Thankfully, she witnessed M'vai's sinking into her body, though her threads were still tangled with the stone. "Did you find Thelar?" Tesra asked.

"No," M'vai said, laughing with alarming pleasure. "But I found beauty! She's found more and more and her power grows and she knows the way and she is the truth and the end to all and the way and the road and the light—"

Tesra had dropped her view of the inner world. The hearthstone beside her friend burned with inner fire. "Get out! Shut it down!"

M'vai rocked back against the wall, shaking.

Tesra gulped and reached for the stone, fighting to find her own courage as she struggled to close it.

But doing so was like reaching into a burning oven. "Get your threads clear!" she shouted. Lethargically, M'vai extricated herself, and Tesra worked to untangle her own spirit even as she felt the brilliance and the mastery and the perfection and the beauty—

And then M'vai was free and Tesra shut the stone and sat back, gasping. The stone pulsed still with faint light.

Her friend sank to the floor, her mouth still moving. Tesra bent to hear her.

"So beautiful." M'vai's smile widened, and her face shone in ecstasy.

For a moment longer she remained a whole, healthy young woman, and then she was nothing more than a rain of white ash that fell into the outline of a body.

Tesra had stopped screaming when N'lahr and Cerai found her a few minutes later, but her mouth still hung open in horror.

24

Out upon the Road

Dawn's arrival had been muted, for a storm sprang up. Vannek and his companions headed into it as they neared the border. So far they'd only felt occasional raindrops, but whirls of circling blue-and-white lightning crackled in the ebon skies and to either side of a narrow trail of white sand stretching into the blackness until it was lost to sight in the starry void. They'd followed the same track, left by the passage of the Goddess, across the land to this edge.

While they stood in contemplation of the alarming road, their mounts and baggage animals cropped grass behind them.

A flash of lightning threw a long shadow behind Varama as she stepped apart, and wind whipped the edges of her khalat.

"What's that alten doing now?" Vannek asked.

Muragan answered softly. "Looking through the magic world."

After a night in the ludicrously comfortable grass, Vannek had wakened in pain, both in places he'd known about and others he hadn't noticed the previous day. In addition, he felt weak and flushed. He'd walked for hours without mention of his discomfort and did not mean to begin complaining now, although he hadn't objected to the chance to dismount and rest against a hillside. It, like all land in this strange realm, was rich with fragrant flowers. This particular patch had yellow blooms, edged with white, and smelled faintly of a Dendressi dessert he'd sampled in Alantris.

Muragan sank down beside him. "How's your arm? You look feverish."

"I'm fine, old man."

Muragan chuckled without mirth. "Fever is the sign that your body spirit fights demons of injury. It doesn't mean you're weak, it just means some of your strength is diverted for an inner fight."

"We can't delay for me to rest," Vannek said, "so there's no point in talking about it." He jerked his chin to indicate the woman. "What's she thinking about?"

"I don't think she likes that storm," Muragan said.

Vannek grunted his assent. "She'd be a fool to like it. Tell me this. If we do find the others, what then? Swords won't be any use against the Dendressi demon goddess."

"Sorcerers might. If we get enough of them, together, in one place. Maybe even blood mages."

Vannek looked sidelong at him. "You think other blood mages will help us?"

"What do you think we should do, General?" Muragan asked instead.

He was saved from having to answer when Varama walked back to them.

"I'm going to venture onto the white road," she said. "I won't attempt opening a portal until the storm blows out."

"What if the storm doesn't blow out?" Vannek asked.

"Then I'll attempt it despite the hazards," Varama replied irritably.

Vannek pushed to his feet. "We will go with you."

The alten mounted her animal. Vannek climbed with some difficulty into saddle and followed. Muragan brought up the rear, leading the pack animals.

The storm flashed and boomed all about them as they headed onto the road. On either side nothing but black emptiness shot with lightning stretched on forever. It was as though the white sand was an endless bridge, hung upon invisible arches across the night. What, Vannek thought, would happen if he were to ride from its edge? Would he fall, forever, or would the hungry lightning burn him?

It flashed again and again, sometimes near, sometimes far, but it never struck the road itself.

Once, Vannek looked back, and saw the realm where they'd battled the queen hanging in sunlight and worried their departure was folly. Almost he asked why the woman didn't chance working her magics. And then he thought about Varama's relentless determination throughout the course of the Alantran siege. She certainly had no lack of courage. If the alten thought there was a certain way to open an escape portal, cowardice wasn't holding her back.

As they traveled it grew clear that the road itself projected a kind of dim radiance, for the darkness never completely closed upon them. No matter the storm, and the lack of sun or moon, theirs was a twilight journey.

Eventually Varama called a halt, and they climbed from their saddles. Varama shared out grasses they'd gathered for the horses, and then while the animals ate, the three of them sat for their own repast. Lightning flashed through the darkness, near and far, usually white or yellow, though sometimes it bore a bluish cast.

Varama leaned against her pack and watched the endless storm, and Vannek watched her. From far away he thought he heard the happy laughter of children at play, but there was no possible place from which that sound could have come.

"I didn't know the shifts could extend so far," Muragan said. "Where are we?"

"We are under," Varama said, but didn't explain further. That rudeness was the push Vannek hadn't known he was waiting for.

"I don't understand you," he said. "You always make us fight you for details."

"I have provided what information is necessary, but perhaps I overestimate my audience. What other answers do you require?"

Her reply was another irritant. "You're saying I'm a stupid Naor," Vannek said. "That Muragan is stupid."

Varama pushed away from her pack. Vannek noticed a vein pulsing along her light blue forehead. "I assure you, you aren't the only person frustrated by our circumstance."

"It's not the circumstances I'm frustrated with." Vannek heard Muragan softly suggest dropping the challenge, but ignored him. "I'm just tired of your attitude. You give us one-word answers. You're rude."

"Rude," Varama repeated flatly. "After practicing enslavement and extermination while you occupied Alantris, you concern yourself with conversational reticence you perceive as a personal slight?"

"If you hadn't resisted, your people would not have suffered—"

"Are you saying none would have been raped, tortured for amusement, or worked to disability if only we'd submitted to your theft and wanton destruction?" Varama asked caustically.

"Not so many would have died."

The alten had apparently been holding back, for this time, when she answered, there was fire in her eyes. "No, they'd just have had to live for your whims. No matter how dark, or selfish. Or do you not count the deeds you facilitated? How many did you murder? You killed my squire, but how many more loved and skilled protectors did you personally slay?"

"Your squire," Vannek repeated, wondering which one the woman meant.

"Her name was Sansyra. You fled from her on dragon back."

"That one." Vannek's lips curled. "She killed my . . . She killed my mage."

"You speak of him like he was a possession."

"He was more than that."

"I see."

"You see nothing," Vannek said.

"I think she sees quite a lot," Muragan said. "We fought on opposite sides; hers won. There's no point in this quarreling. Now we have to work together."

"We're not working together," Vannek said. "She's not telling us anything. Why are we still here, on this road? She said she'd try opening a portal if the storm didn't stop. Well, it hasn't stopped, so why hasn't she opened a portal?"

The alten answered in a tightly controlled tone. "You want to know why we're still here? I lack a hearthstone. All I have to open a portal are a few memory crystals, which hold a fraction of the power of the smallest hearthstone shard. And I must employ that power to attempt a procedure for the first time, a magic I barely comprehend. I do not wish to undertake this experiment where the threads I wield could be interrupted at any time by the chaotic energies of the storm that surrounds us and has strengthened rather than waned as we seek a calmer surround."

As if to punctuate the challenge, a blast of blue lightning forked in the sky to the right.

"Liar," Vannek announced triumphantly. "I've seen your hearthstone. You pull it out of your inner pocket, where you keep it in some kind of shining bag."

Varama didn't like having been called out, for her nostrils flared.

Once again the blood mage tried to ease tensions. "I don't think it's a hearthstone shard, Lord General," he said quickly. "It doesn't have nearly as much energy. But I've seen it too. What is it, Alten?"

"It is a shard, but one I cannot use to power a portal. When I investigated the queen's chambers, and those of the exalts, I discovered a number of experiments. Few were successful, but one of them was the pouch in which I keep this shard." She patted her uniform, where Vannek had seen Varama store the thing in an inner pocket. "It effectively blocks magical energies. I keep the shard there not because I'm hiding it, but because I mean to shield its effects, which are detrimental to the commander."

"Commander N'lahr?" Vannek laughed without humor. "He's nowhere near us."

"Proximity doesn't matter. Whenever I open this shard, I am linked with him. I dare not do so for long, because its mere existence appears to be injurious to him."

Vannek wasn't entirely sure he understood the shard's threat to N'lahr, but that was secondary to the rest of Varama's admission. "Wait. So you've been communicating with your general?"

"Yes. I informed him of our condition, and he has informed me of his, and we've made plans."

"You know how my people are?" Vannek's voice lifted in anger. "And you didn't say anything?"

"I didn't wish to alarm you. Your mood is foul enough already."

Rarely had Vannek been so eager to hit someone. He barely held back. "Are they all right, or aren't they? Where are they?"

"They are in a fortress controlled by one of our erstwhile comrades, an alten and mage named Cerai whom I trust far less than you. Your soldiers are following the orders of Anzat, who seems likely to support Cerai's aim for utter domination rather than Commander N'lahr."

"Why didn't you say something?" Vannek climbed to his feet, but Varama was there faster. The general was reminded of something he'd forgotten as the alten's aspect changed. While Varama usually presented as distracted and aloof, in a moment she had transformed from a gangly woman with frizzy hair and an irritated manner into a dangerous combatant.

"I have said all that was necessary." Varama's voice was thin. "You waste your energy, and my own."

Muragan drew to Vannek's side, and came very close to putting a hand on his arm. He seemed to decide at the last moment not to, which was fortunate, because Vannek was fairly sure he would have struck him. The blood mage addressed Varama. "You should have told us you were in touch with Commander N'lahr. I don't think the Lord General would be as upset if you'd done that."

Vannek wasn't entirely sure that was true, but that simple declaration from Muragan apparently hit home, for Varama looked thoughtful.

"You're right," she said at last. "I was reluctant to reveal the commander had a weakness, but given the circumstances, it might have been an injudicious course."

"Thank you," Muragan said. He glanced to Vannek, then continued: "And it must be said that your manner overall hasn't been entirely welcoming."

"Lessons in courtesy from a blood mage," Varama said slowly, as if to herself, as if she could not quite believe it. But before Vannek could muster the insult forming on his lips, the alten replied: "Perhaps I have been brusque. My worries have me preoccupied, but there is no benefit in behaving more impolitely than I intend. I apologize that my manner was discourteous."

"We thank you," Muragan said.

Vannek decided not to reprimand him for speaking for them both. "You said you and Commander N'lahr were working on a plan," he said with icy courtesy. "Would you share the details?"

"There are many moving pieces, but in short, the Goddess has been stopped before. Elenai and Kyrkenall are seeking a weapon once used to successfully oppose her, and Rylin and Thelar are seeking another of proven worth against her. We are to obtain certain tools in Darassus, then join them."

"Do my men in Darassus know what's happened?" Vannek asked.

"No one in Darassus is likely to have learned anything about the battle. Anzat will not have been able to usurp your authority over the soldiers there."

Varama had bluntly gotten right to Vannek's chief concern. Before he could ask more, the alten turned to stare at the horizon as a landscape flickered into existence for the length of several breaths, one where the heights of trees were storm tossed and dark clouds rolled. It vanished.

"Is that good, or bad?" Muragan asked.

"Good," Varama answered. "Natural order may be fighting to reassert itself." When the landscape failed to reappear, the alten frowned. "It does not appear to be winning, yet."

"Would it help to use blood magic to open a portal?" Vannek asked. "We might use one, or several, of the horses."

"An interesting idea," Varama said. "But I don't know how to wield blood magic, and it delivers tiny results for great expenditure. Also, Muragan knows nothing of the complex theory of portal magic, so he himself is poorly suited to attempt what you suggest. Additionally, the thought of murdering these well-trained, loyal Altenerai mounts is abhorrent to me."

"I don't think blood magic could be woven together with what she's doing, anyway," Muragan said. "Perhaps I could be of assistance without the blood. I've studied some Dendressi sorceries."

"Studied and deployed them in battle," Varama said, and at Muragan's surprised look, she added, "I am aware of your reputation and skills, Muragan. You are quite talented. But I barely understand portal theory myself, and it would be dangerous to involve you in its workings. We might as well get moving." With that, Varama walked back to her mount and began to restore its pack.

Muragan eyed Vannek doubtfully.

"You shouldn't have spoken for me," Vannek told him.

"Sometimes you shouldn't speak for yourself. What was your goal? Why were you testing her?"

"My goal was to have her treat us with courtesy."

"You chose a dangerous way to do it," Muragan said, and before Vannek decided how to respond, he'd stepped to his own horse. Almost he asked the man what Dendressi magics he had mastered, but decided silence was the better course.

Soon, Vannek joined them, and then, together, they rode off along the impossible white road, the lightning dancing in company.

22

The Last Resort

N'lahr and Cerai arrived with a lantern, and in its beam the beak of the giant, motionless bird of prey loomed dangerously. Squinting to see beyond the light, Tesra saw a gaggle of squires and Cerai's soldiers crammed into the narrow corridor behind them.

She managed to convey that the powdery dust had once been M'vai.

Tesra backed away from the remains, though she couldn't stop looking at them.

N'lahr ordered the others off and stood frowning, burdened with one too many tragedies. Cerai's eyes narrowed in cold fury as Tesra struggled to explain what had happened to M'vai. "She was worried about the Commander," Tesra said. "She insisted on trying to consult with Thelar."

"And you helped her?" Cerai interrupted. "Why didn't you come see me?"

"She said she was going to do it right away, even if I didn't help. And I didn't want her to be hurt. . . ." Tesra's voice trailed off.

"Well, that didn't work out, did it?" Cerai asked.

She was right, and Tesra felt tears restart their flow.

N'lahr's question snapped her back. "How did she end up like this?"

"She—we—encountered the Goddess. I just brushed against her. But M'vai was in deeper. She talked about beauty and perfection and then crumbled." Tesra sobbed and then forced herself quiet, as though she were once more a squire in line before Asrahn.

"I can sense the Goddess more and more easily," N'lahr said. "Her power's growing."

Cerai and Tesra shifted their attention to him.

"What have you learned from her?" Cerai asked.

"She's mainly concerned with the attack from the chaos spirits. She didn't expect we could consort with them. She thinks of those chaos spirits as fragments of the other."

"You said something about that before. Do you have a better sense about what it is?" Cerai asked.

"A lover. A peer. Something she cherishes and fears and misses and despises all at once."

This made little sense to Tesra, but Cerai's expression cleared, as if some long-standing mystery had been explained. "Do you have any sense about where she is?"

"No. But she intends to build strength before she returns; she seeks the last of the hearthstones." N'lahr shuddered.

"Commander?" Tesra asked.

He stilled, mouth partly open, left arm raised. Not a muscle moved upon him, not even a nostril flare.

"Commander?" Tesra repeated.

"Sounding shrill won't help," Cerai snapped, and touched N'lahr's sleeve. A moment later he blinked, and lowered the arm.

"It's getting worse," Cerai told him bluntly. "We have to address this while we still can."

"I agree," N'lahr replied, with the grim determination he was known for.

She turned to Tesra. "Are you in any kind of shape to assist?"

"Yes."

"I'm not sure I believe you," Cerai said. "I'm not sure I should trust your judgment at all."

"You can trust me," Tesra insisted.

"I suppose I'll have to." Her eyes flicked to the powdered dust that had been a talented young woman. "We'll see to your friend's remains later."

Tesra wiped her eyes and looked purposefully away as they left.

Cerai led them to the second floor, and a rectangular room roughly sectioned into two areas. At one end, near a hearth, a desk was grouped with some chairs and couches. Cerai placed the lantern on the desk. "Do you want to lie down on the couch?"

"Will that make this easier for you?" N'lahr asked.

"I don't believe so."

"Then I'll stand."

"Do you want me to get the shaping tool?" Tesra asked.

"That would be like wielding a sledgehammer to sound a tuning peg. I will do this with my hands." She faced N'lahr. "I don't mean to alarm you but . . . have you given orders to your chosen successor?"

"Yes."

Cerai's mouth twitched into a faint smile. "Of course you have. And you're probably not going to ask me for the likelihood of success."

"You can't predict it. But I know that I will be useless soon if my condition worsens."

Cerai paused, then spoke with quiet candor. "I have always respected you, N'lahr. I want you to know that if this doesn't work, I'll use what I learn to better our future."

N'lahr had no reply to that insensitive bit of comfort.

Cerai adjusted a lock of hair "Ready yourself, Tesra. I'll attempt to do this without a hearthstone, but I may need to draw upon one, and if so I want you monitoring. Do you understand?"

"Yes."

"Good. All right, N'lahr. Let's try this."

Before Tesra had even opened herself to the inner world, Cerai was at work, deftly touching her sorcerous energies to the threads of N'lahr's life force. The white latticework wrapping him like a second skeleton had thickened even since Tesra had last seen it. Cerai gently brushed one edge of it and nothing happened.

"Do you feel any different?" she asked.

"No."

"That may be good." Cerai paused for a moment, then her fingers twitched as she directed her lines of magic to bolster N'lahr's own life force.

The commander breathed deeply. He seemed to stand taller.

The white threads pulsed once, then thickened.

"It's growing faster!" Tesra cried, though she felt stupid afterward. Cerai had already seen that, surely. The older woman pulled back her efforts to increase N'lahr's energy and instead chipped away at the expanding white threads. But for every one that she snipped, three more snaked up in their place. It looked an awful lot like what had happened the moment the dragon attacked the Goddess statue in Darassus. The hearthstone energy inside the commander was responding defensively.

Cerai's brow beaded with sweat and she reached for a hearthstone shard she kept in a belt pouch. She wove its energies into her ongoing battle.

But the white threads had exploded exponentially through the commander. After a moment, Cerai dropped her hands, ceasing the hearthstone access at the same moment.

"N'lahr?" she asked.

The commander neither answered, nor moved. His eyes remained open and unfocused.

"Commander?" Tesra asked softly. She didn't expect a reply.

Cerai let out a slow sigh. "It's no use. He's completely in stasis now. More protected than he was in the stone."

Tesra didn't process what Cerai had revealed for a moment, then failed to conceal her surprise. "You saw him when he was trapped in a hearthstone?"

Though she'd suggested only a few hours earlier she herself hadn't known about N'lahr's imprisonment until he'd told her, Cerai spoke with blithe confidence. "I didn't know originally," she said. "But Belahn and I were brought in after that idiot Denaven couldn't free him. I couldn't see how to do it, either, but I learned an awful lot about holding bodies in stasis. If he were frozen like that this time, I might be able to free him. But this—I just don't see how."

Tesra pretended to accept the explanation. "Why were you trying to strengthen the lines of his energy first?"

"To make him more resilient. I was trying to protect him in case something went wrong."

Had she been? Tesra wondered.

Cerai locked eyes with her, as if judging the strength of Tesra's belief in her. "We shall have to tell the aspirants and squires what's happened. Don't look so glum. We won't need him for the next phase anyway. And if we survive, we can try again. His life force is protected now, thanks to me." Tesra nodded numbly. Cerai was watching her once more. "You should never have let M'vai attempt that nonsense on her own."

"There wasn't time to come and get you."

"Is that the real answer? Or is it that you don't trust me?"

Tesra thought quickly, for she knew her indecision was obvious. "I want to believe you. But like I've said, too many people have tricked me over the years. The queen tricked me. Rylin tricked me. I think M'vai tricked me, too. It's hard for me to really trust anyone."

Cerai, uncaring that one of the greatest heroes of the five realms was for all intents and purposes a statue beside her, folded her arms. "You need to decide where you stand, Tesra. And who your friends really are." She considered N'lahr the way someone might evaluate a potted plant. "I think I'll put him near the couch, over there."

"Right now?"

"No, I'll have the servants do it. You and I should go speak to the squires and aspirants."

Tesra nodded, but her eyes didn't leave the commander. "I'd like a moment alone with him."

"He's not really dead. You don't have to make a formal good-bye."

"But he may not be alive ever again," she said.

"Very well." Cerai frowned. "I'll go talk to them by myself. Find me when you're finished." She turned and left the room via the far door, leaving the lantern behind.

Tesra had never directly served under N'lahr as a squire. She'd grown up south of Harata, far from the regions regularly menaced by Naor. She'd never known anyone during her childhood who had suffered at the hands of the enemy, as he had. Yet she well knew all that he had done to keep similar tragedies from other people of the realms.

That Cerai had known about his earlier imprisonment was just one more secret she'd kept that might have changed history. The alten had explained away her knowledge of it with a clever excuse. Everything she said might be a lie, or come from a twisted perspective, or omit a few details to cast her in the best light.

Had Cerai truly been building up his life energies to help sustain him? Or had she been trying to learn more about altering them in a new way, since his structure was already reinforced by the ordered matrix that had invaded him?

Tesra suspected the latter. Tears streamed down her cheeks as she stared into the immobile face. N'lahr's features were constricted, as if in his final moments he'd felt pain. His right hand had dropped toward the hilt of his magnificent sword. How long, she wondered, before Cerai bequeathed the weapon to herself?

Tesra straightened with resolve. The others had to be warned. She had made so many bad choices that no matter the risk, she owed it to her people. She would have to tell Rylin and Thelar what had happened.

"And maybe, in the end, one of them can save you," she said to the immobile commander. She placed a hand on his shoulder. "I don't know if they'll be able to save me. But that's not important. It sounds like the kind of choice an alten makes, doesn't it? Maybe it's my numbered day."

For no reason she fully understood, she gently kissed his cheek before she left him.

23

Splitting Forces

Rylin had never flown through the shifts before, but that wasn't what made this journey his strangest yet beyond a border.

Once travelers left a realm, they usually encountered a shifting land that resembled what they'd departed, unless they rode well beyond the five realms, or an exceptionally violent storm had passed. Occasionally the void itself might be glimpsed during a storm, but usually reality rebuilt itself over the blank canvas.

This time, there was nothing. When the ko'aye had said only dark skies lay beyond the borders, he hadn't fully imagined what that would look like. The star-shot black stretched to infinity. So alarming was this sight that Rylin dug out a notched coin his father had given him and used it to sense for Erymyr.

After a long, agonizing moment, he found the realm. It served as a reassuring beacon star to orient him. He breathed out a sigh of relief.

"What has happened?" Lelanc asked, turning her feathery neck to glance at him.

"I was just making sure the Goddess hadn't already destroyed everything." Rylin looked over to Thelar, riding dark-feathered Drusa. "I sensed Erymyr."

"What of the other realms?" Thelar asked.

It was a worthy question. Just because Erymyr existed didn't mean the Goddess hadn't destroyed the others. The two spell casters gradually verified the existence of four more realms using bits of clothing and personal equipment that had been crafted there. The ko'aye asked if there was a way to know if their home aerie was intact as well, but neither man could help, for they hadn't been to that land to acquire anything. The Fragments, where many of the ko'aye had relocated, were as intact as ever, which was the only solace Rylin could offer.

After, they lapsed into silence. Rylin kept expecting Thelar to comment upon the joy, or fear, of flight, but he remained quiet. Rylin didn't intrude. They both had a lot to think about.

They flew far and wide, ranging not for realms and fragments, but for the spaces between, where the chaos spirits roamed. And search though they might, they found none.

After many hours of this, the ko'aye informed them they needed a rest, and Rylin, whose legs and back had grown stiff, didn't object. Lelanc told him they'd sensed a fragment far beyond his sight. By mutual agreement they bore toward it.

It proved little more than a quarter mile across either way. But it held a small freshwater lake and a meadow. They landed, and Rylin and Thelar dismounted and removed their gear. The ko'aye snuffled at the dark grasses, striated with lines of turquoise. Apparently they were palatable, for the animals set to.

"I thought you were meat eaters," Rylin said.

Lelanc looked up at him, a long strand of vegetation hanging from one side of her beak. "We eat whatever is best to be eaten."

Rylin and Thelar made do with a waterskin and jerked meat that tasted like someone had put too much salt on a wet boot.

Afterward, the two ko'aye lay down where the humans sat and the four discussed their next steps.

"We know the chaos spirits are drawn to magic," Rylin said. "What if we activate the shard and see if that lures them here?"

"A reasonable idea," Thelar said. "But what if that attracts the Goddess? She's out hunting for hearthstones, and that might get her attention."

"Good point," Rylin said.

"I have thought another thing." Drusa's voice, as ever, was rasping. "Ko'aye can seek spirit things and then chase them to you. It is like a hunting trick."

"That sounds dangerous," Rylin said.

Drusa squawked. "We have no fear. We know what they are, and teach our young to escape them, for many lives of elders. We can outrun them."

"We fly better without you," Lelanc said. "Do not take offense."

"None taken. But are you sure?"

"I am eager to move again," Lelanc said. "This land bores me. The hunting mood is mine."

"It will be easier to capture the chaos spirits if we're on solid ground," Thelar mused. "I was worried about how I'd work the spells and steady the containers while we were flying."

After only a little more debate, the matter was decided. Rylin watched as the ko'aye stepped to the edge of the fragment and threw themselves into the void. They caught a current, spread their wings, and circled away. Rylin had convinced them to wear their saddles, arguing that if the chaos spirits proved too dangerous and all four of them had to flee, there'd be no time to put them back on.

Drusa and Lelanc banked over the top of the lone hill near the center of their fragment. Before long, the starry darkness swallowed them, but he began to pace, lost in worry.

"Asrahn would tell you to rest and save your energy," Thelar said after a time.

Rylin inwardly agreed that the Master of Squires probably would have advised against the pacing, but Thelar saying so was an irritant. Rylin sat down and uncapped his waterskin. Thelar was already seated on a smaller boulder across from him. When Rylin finished drinking he found the exalt watching, as if he had something on his mind and was reluctant to speak.

"If you've something to say, say it," Rylin said. "We've apparently got time."

"I was wondering how your talk with Tesra went."

That caught him off guard. "How did you know about that?"

"M'vai mentioned it."

"Oh."

"I don't mean to pry," Thelar said quickly.

"No, it's fine. We parted friends. I think I said what I needed. I apologized," he added.

"Did she forgive you?"

"I think she's moving in that direction. That's not the important thing, though, is it? I mean, that part's her choice. My part is acknowledging what I did."

Thelar seemed to mull that over, then spoke hesitantly. "Can I ask you something else?"

"Go right ahead."

"How do you . . ." The exalt's words trailed off.

"How do I what?"

He sighed. "One of the things that was always so irritating about you is that you'd just go and do something. You don't think very carefully about it at all, but most of the time it works out for you."

Rylin let out a bark of laughter.

"You think that's funny?"

"Your perspective's funny. I made a fool of myself more times than you know."

"I know about plenty of those times," Thelar said bitterly. Then he blinked. "Sorry."

"It's fine. I trust my instincts. I didn't have any right to, earlier, but now I have experience. And you're doing it yourself. You're impressed I apologized to Tesra? You kept your cool with Cerai from the start. You set aside all your anger and worry about your family, because you knew we needed Cerai's knowledge and tools. Asrahn would have been proud you could do that."

"It may look like I'm setting it aside," Thelar said. "But I worry about them all the time."

Rylin was hardly surprised. "How many are there? You've said your family's in Alantris, but that's all I know."

"My parents. My brother and his wife. My two sisters. Nephews, nieces, three uncles. Cousins, dozens of family friends. . . . Surely some of them made it." He looked down at his feet, lost in his own terrible visions. "I find myself rooting for this one or that one more than another and then hating myself. I'll be delighted if any of them survive." Finally, he forced himself away from dark musings. "Where's your family?"

"Erymyr. Mostly around Lake Dahrial."

"That's right. I remember. Pretty country. I've always liked the water, although I've never had much time with it."

"Maybe when this is all over you could take up sailing."

"You're assuming a lot, aren't you? Including we come through alive? You always were an optimist." He almost sounded light. "I'm not sure I'd have time to learn sailing, even then."

Rylin dismissed his worry with the wave of a hand. "Let's say it all turns out well. What *do* you want?"

"I haven't gotten much further than wishing my family alive."

"Do you settle down? Do you want to join the Altenerai? I'd stand for you."

The exalt's dark eyes met his own, their regard so piercing it felt as though he bored into them. His brows were drawn, and Rylin worried that he suspected mockery.

He affected a casual manner. "I can about guarantee Elenai would back you as well. And Commander N'lahr. We need more sorcerers in the corps. I'd stand M'Vai, too."

"What about Tesra?" Thelar asked.

"That depends on what she does next. You and M'vai have already proved yourselves."

The exalt exhaled slowly. He was silent for a long moment. "I'm honored. Truly. I'm honored. You think they'd have us?"

"Damned right we'd have you."

"What would happen to the exalt auxiliary?"

Rylin hadn't thought that far. "It seems like it was a bad idea to split our forces. If the Altenerai had been getting better magical tutelage the last few years rather than having it mostly focused on the exalts maybe I'd be a better mage."

"An adjunct corps isn't necessarily a bad idea, if it's done right. Don't set it up like a rival group, but an organization where those who have fine magical abilities but can't meet the other martial requirements can train to be useful in combat situations."

There were other venues for magical training in the realms, but there had never been one set aside quite as Thelar suggested.

"That's not a bad idea," Rylin said. "If you join the corps, maybe you can see it happen." He pointed over to packs. "Speaking of sorcery, maybe we should go over how to trap the chaos spirits. The summary version you gave me was fine, but it seems like we have extra time."

Thelar stilled.

His friend's change in affect was so pronounced Rylin immediately took note. "What's wrong?"

Thelar didn't answer, and Rylin recognized by the inward stare and focused breathing he had engaged with the inner world.

Before Rylin did the same, he searched the nearby environment to en-sure its security, and even as he confirmed that, he felt a presence besides their own, one that came with a sense of urgency.

Someone was using a hearthstone to reach out to them. Someone anx-ious. Was this the communication N'lahr had told him to be ready for?

Thelar activated his shard.

An image coalesced out of the darkness, a feminine shape built of mist and moonbeams. Tesra. She brushed long hair from her forehead.

"Thelar," she said, with a sigh of relief. "We haven't long. Listen. Ce-rai made a pretense of helping Commander N'lahr. She was really ex-perimenting on him and now he's trapped in suspension. I think he's still alive."

Rylin started to ask for more detail. "Why is she—"

"Just listen! She's keeping the commander's body in her laboratory. Cerai's been altering her own body so that she's kind of a living hearth-stone. She's also planning to make a god of herself when she destroys the Goddess."

Rylin was aghast about N'lahr. He wasn't entirely surprised by the rest of the information. "Is Elenai back yet?"

"No, there's no word from her or Kyrkenall. Look, I don't think you should come back. If we fight the Goddess here, Cerai will kill her, and then she'll get all of her power. And listen, there's more. Using the hearth-stone attracts the attention of the Goddess. M'vai tried to contact you but she got the Goddess instead and it killed her, through the connection. M'vai's dead. She just . . . disintegrated into powder."

Rylin hadn't known M'vai well, and only while she was under constant duress, so she probably wasn't always driven and humorless. While he had respected her skill and bravery, he was still startled by how hard the news of her death struck him, because he hadn't thought of them as close. The-lar let out a shaking, low-voiced no.

"You've got to be careful using the stones," Tesra continued. "I—"

"There's something in the hearthstone now," Thelar interrupted. "A presence."

He was right; Rylin detected its approach.

Tesra looked quickly behind her. The illusion of her proximity was so profound Rylin peered over her shoulder before understanding whatever worried her was in her physical location, not theirs.

"Cerai's coming," Tesra said. Her hands spun frantically and Rylin guessed she strove to close the hearthstone she used. Then one of her hands lifted to her temple as if she'd been struck by a headache. Her image vanished.

Rylin stared at where she'd been. Thelar shut down their hearthstone. "Tesra's in terrible danger," Rylin said.

"Yes," Thelar agreed. "If that was Cerai, she's going to know, very soon, exactly what Tesra told us."

Rylin nodded slowly. "I'm sorry about M'vai."

"Yes." Thelar didn't add that he was the only one of the loyal exalts left. Of the five, one had died in battle, one had resigned, and two had been slain by the Goddess.

"We can't just sit here," Rylin said. "Waiting. We should try to reach Elenai."

"You heard Tesra. I'm just about certain that was the Goddess down there in the stone. If we use it again, right now, she'll find us."

"Suppose Elenai heads back to Cerai with the weapon? Tesra was right. I think fighting the Goddess in her realm's a terrible idea. We have to warn her and Kyrkenall."

Thelar's habitual frown deepened. "I hear you."

"Let's get on with it then. I know Elenai; I helped train her."

"You may be better suited for the search," Thelar admitted grudgingly. "But if I sense the presence of the Goddess rise very much I'm pulling you back."

Rylin sorted through a belt pouch for the red stone he'd taken from Kanesh as a squire stationed there years before.

"Don't anchor yourself too deeply in the hearthstone," Thelar advised. "Not like last time. If I have to shut it down fast that could get you trapped."

"Understood."

Rylin rubbed the smooth Kaneshi river stone between thumb and forefinger, then stretched his shoulders. He exhaled. "Let's do this."

Thelar bent to the hearthstone and cycled it open.

Rylin threw his threads into it then launched himself up and out, thinking of Kanesh.

Either owing to his intensity, or growing experience, Rylin found himself hurtling forward far faster than when he'd sought Varama. He had a vague impression of stars flying past on either side, and then he appeared in a realm of howling darkness. Where was he? The wind screamed like a living thing.

Rylin willed himself up, seeking perspective, and finally caught a hint of muted light, reddened by a vast storm of sand sweeping over the land-scape. So maybe he had found Kanesh.

If he had arrived in the right place, now he had to find the right person, and so he thought of Elenai's chestnut hair and shining confidence, her steely-eyed determination and certainty. Her hearthstone.

Thelar shook his shoulders violently.

Rylin shot back to his body, and while he blinked in disorientation he saw their shard glowing like a miniature sun.

Thelar shut it down and sat back, breathing heavily.

"What happened?" Rylin asked.

"We definitely had the attention of the Goddess. Did you find Elenai?"

"I found Kanesh, but couldn't sense a hearthstone. Maybe if I'd had more time. There was a huge sandstorm. I hope she and Kyrkenall weren't caught in the open."

Thelar continued to stare at the stone.

"Why are you watching it like that?"

"I've got a bad feeling."

Nothing happened, though. "Should we try again?"

"Let it sit for a while. I know you want to do something. So do I. But right now I feel like we've been lucky and we should wait before we push it."

"So we just sit here on this rock in the middle of nowhere?"

"Asrahn always said it was the waiting before battles that was the hardest. Remember?"

Rylin remembered. And knew.

Thelar kept talking. "He said it was toughest when you were waiting for a scout to get back. That's kind of where we are. We need more infor-mation before we can act. We dare not try much without it." Thelar contin-ued as though he were the direct conduit to all of Asrahn's wisdom. "What he would probably advise us to do is rest."

Almost, Rylin had forgotten how Thelar could sound like a know-it-all. He resisted a strong temptation to point out he had more experience in the field than the person quoting advice. Not only would that be coun-terproductive, it was beneath him. "You're right. Why don't you try first? I'll take watch."

"Very well. Don't let me sleep long."

While the exalt lay with head pillowed in his arms, Rylin sat staring into the void, occasionally rising to pace and ensure the security of their position. He didn't expect anything dangerous to come wafting out of the darkness, but he was still cautious.

There was no sign of the ko'aye. Rylin's mind wandered down dark paths, seeking solutions and finding only their absence. He longed for Varama's counsel and again pondered N'lahr's words. She was alive out there, somewhere, and she and N'lahr had been making plans, probably using more information than he himself knew. They might already have been in touch with Elenai.

He felt certain the commander had anticipated his own eventual capture or debilitation and wondered what he had set in motion to counter it. Most of all he wished that he had been included in the planning, and that there was something more for him to do besides wait.

When he traded places with Thelar he fell quickly to sleep, but his dreams were plagued with worry. Shapely ghosts beckoned toward the void's edge, where Varama's voice called advice he couldn't understand. That voice resolved itself into Thelar, and Rylin felt a nudge against his back.

He came awake not knowing what Thelar was saying, for his attention shifted almost immediately to the moaning wind.

A storm cast up the soil in a stinging cloud that pelted his skin.

"It came up out of nowhere," Thelar said.

Rylin pulled on his boots and grabbed his khalat. Beyond their little island the sky had grown alive with lightning. Thunder rolled. He couldn't imagine how he had slept through any of it.

He worked swiftly to hook his uniform coat closed. "Any sign of Lelanc or Drusa?"

"No. Nothing."

"I hope they found somewhere to roost."

Thelar's reply was interrupted by a loud cracking sound. Both men looked to their right, where an immense boulder on the edge of their fragment splintered and dropped into the void, followed by nearly ten feet of soil. A fault line followed in its wake, zig-zagging toward the center of their fragment, accompanied by alarming rumbles. Even a huge storm shouldn't have been shaking a fragment apart. But then this looked to be no ordinary storm.

"I hope *we* have somewhere safe to roost," Rylin said. "We'd better grab our gear."

He snatched his sword belt, watching their surroundings as he buckled. A blast of blue lightning tore through the sky.

Thelar hefted his saddlebag and pointed to the lone rise beyond the little freshwater lake. "That's the most solid point."

A second and third crack in the firmament crept in from the edge, and then accelerated toward them. As the ground trembled, Rylin grabbed his saddlebag and the two raced toward the center of their sanctuary.

The devastation moved faster. The crack sped on, diverted before them, and widened. Rylin jumped even as the gap lengthened. He conjured wind threads and pushed both of them up and over the gap. He stumbled. Thelar hit and rolled, losing grip of his saddlebag. Rylin dragged him to his feet as the exalt snatched his gear.

They ran toward the little lake and the hill beyond as rocks and sand rose, turning slowly, as though they were being inspected by curious, invisible giants.

The water floated into the air in a shimmering contiguous mass, and the storm winds delivered it directly into their path.

Before he could counter, Rylin was in the midst of the water, and had to swim to move forward, kicking with booted feet. The saddlebag was torn from his hand, and there was no time to lament its passing, for he was fighting to survive. The water obscured his vision, and he couldn't tell if he was actually moving forward, which was all the more frightening because he had little air in his lungs. His head pounded and spots shone before his eyes. His body was desperate to breathe, no matter that doing so would kill him.

He kicked on. His vision spiraled.

Then he dropped free from the water, sodden, landing hard in black mud. He took in a grateful breath. The wind picked up and the water fell away like a wave of rain against his legs. He pushed himself up and spotted Thelar lying two bodylengths behind, within a shallow pool of water. He dashed over to lift him, pounding the exalt's back. Thelar coughed and struggled to get his hands under him.

Rylin saw that only about five feet of solid ground remained to their rear. The water was flowing that direction and plunging over the side, right past Thelar's saddlebag.

Thelar spit up water. The ground behind them crumbled further.

"Up!" Rylin cried.

Thelar was slow to move. Rylin pushed at him and set him stumbling away, then dashed back, sliding in the mud. As he reached for the bag the ground rumbled once more and a huge crescent of land shuddered, dropping away, taking the saddlebag with it.

That meant all the stones for capturing chaos spirits were gone. They'd each carried two. There was no time to worry about them. He sprinted away as the land shook, crumbling into the void behind him. Ahead, Thelar had tripped, and struggled now to push to his feet. Rylin wrenched him up and pulled him forward. After the first few steps Thelar got his balance back. An over-the-shoulder glance showed the destruction following them in a wave.

They arrived finally at the base of the rise and forced their way up. Once on its height, no more than a dozen feet above their little domain, Rylin searched their surroundings. More a plateau than a hill, it was less than fifty feet across, and apart from it they had no more than ten ragged feet of soil in any direction, most of which was slope. The hungry void clawed at the edges.

"I don't think this is going to last much longer," Rylin said. He looked down at his ring. Even with a command to activate, its glow was dim. "And the rings aren't going to help us. You'll have to use your shard."

Thelar coughed and nodded, but he looked so peaked Rylin chose to use the device instead, activating it from within Thelar's belt pouch.

Just as he cycled the stone open it blazed so brightly it was visible even through the leather. Thelar yelped and shut the thing down, shouting about the Goddess looking at them.

Water trailed from the flattened mass of Thelar's dark hair and down his cheek. He was soaked through and looked utterly miserable. "I thought you liked water," Rylin said.

"I don't like drowning."

It was a feeble-enough joke, but Rylin laughed.

"What are we going to do now?" Thelar asked. "We've nothing left to trap the spirits with."

"Or even to fuel a fire." From the corner of his eye, he saw a flash of light. Turning his head to find it, he witnessed a landscape glimmer into and then out of existence. For a moment he thought he had dreamed that red mountain, but it reappeared, then melted away like candle wax.

"I've never seen anything like that before," Rylin said, and as he finished, a second landscape blinked once, twice, then resolved into a purple body of water lying beside a land of red dunes.

"Now you have," Thelar commented dryly.

Rylin watched as the land vanished once more. "Any ideas why this is happening?"

"I'd hazard that there's something fundamentally awry with the foundation of reality," Thelar said.

"That's comforting."

"I'm glad one of us is comforted, because I'm certainly not."

A hilly gray landscape blinked into existence. Red spiked plants sprouted sparsely across its surface. On their right, Rylin saw sprays of diamonds lying on higher hills. Their own plateau appeared to be resting, somewhat off center, upon a low mound.

Rylin was peering over the side when Thelar called to him.

"Rylin. Look up."

Just as it seemed the Shifting Lands had settled into a comprehensible pattern, the sky had split open to reveal a void alive with slowly spiraling golden stars.

Two winged figures flew out from the gap, their feathered heads stretched out ahead of them. Lelanc and Drusa.

While their appearance was reassuring, Rylin spotted shifting lines of white force in pursuit. Something about them suggested grasping eagerness.

"They found the chaos spirits," Rylin said. "And we've nothing to trap them with."

24

Among Friends

Kyrkenall spoke the name of the woman before them with quiet awe. "Kalandra. I don't . . . I . . ." And then he was walking toward her across the floor of the cave.

Elenai recognized the missing alten from an encounter with her image in the shifts weeks ago, though Kalandra had clearly suffered since that other version of her had been sorcerously stored, transformed from athletically slim to truly gaunt. Her eyes had sunken and grown fever-sharp, her cheekbones pronounced. Her dark, shoulder-length hair hung in untidy ringlets.

Kalandra smiled as Kyrkenall stepped toward her, but then, in the moment she raised her own hands to receive his embrace, her expression fell.

A moment later, Kyrkenall's hands swept through Kalandra, and he stumbled through her. She proved no more substantial than smoke. Kalandra's image reached out in an attempt to steady him, then looked down at her hands, thin lips curling in anger.

Kyrkenall whirled, looking to Elenai. "What's happening?" he demanded. "I thought it worked!"

For a brief moment Elenai had been proud she'd achieved the impossible. Now she wished that she'd failed. Before her friend lay another painful confrontation with only a memory of his love, something that mimicked her appearance but could provide little more companionship than a well-painted portrait.

Unlike the previous memory image, this one did not stand static, awaiting conversation. Kalandra studied Elenai before reaching out for Kyrkenall. She emitted a sad sigh as her hand passed through his sleeve. The first memory of Kalandra they'd interacted with hadn't demonstrated half as much initiative.

"You're not real, are you," Kyrkenall said sadly. It was not a question.

But Kalandra answered it. "I've given that a lot of thought, and I don't know." Her voice was oddly flat, as if some of its tonality were absent. "Where are we? And who is this?" She indicated Elenai with a lift of her chin.

"We're in a cave, in Kanesh," Kyrkenall answered. "At the end of the world. And this is Elenai Half Sword, who would have been queen of the five realms."

"Hail, Alten," Kalandra said. "Or should I say Your Majesty?"

"Hail," Elenai replied softly, too impressed with the sophistication of the spell simulating Kalandra to deny that she was queen.

The image of the long-lost alten faced Kyrkenall once more. "What's this about the end of the world? And does this mean you've killed Leonara?"

"She's dead, but we didn't kill her. It's not even important," Kyrkenall answered.

"Leonara opened the hearthstones and the Goddess was called forth," Elenai said. Kalandra's brows lifted in surprise. "The Goddess passed through here to take a shard I was using, and left this storm in her wake. We're not sure if it will ever stop." Elenai wanted to make sure Kyrkenall understood what they were experiencing, though she hesitated to be rude to even an image of Kalandra. So she chose her words with care. "You're a much more sophisticated spell than the first one we met."

Kalandra turned her attention to Kyrkenall. "So Leonara's goddess is loose."

"It appears so," Kyrkenall said woodenly.

"What year is it?"

"You've been missing seven years. Do you know where you really are? I mean, where you are, not this . . . thing?" The archer indicated her with a wave of his hand.

The image laughed without humor. "Kyrkenall, this is as much of me as you're ever going to get. I am here—or at least everything that's left."

"What do you mean?"

"I mean that I transferred myself into this stone." She pointed to the emerald. "Or I made a truly sophisticated copy. I'm not sure which."

"Why would you put yourself into a stone?" Kyrkenall asked in disbelief.

"Because I was dying," Kalandra answered, a bite in her words. "Out in the wastes. Denaven overpowered me and made off with my hearthstones. I had no way to keep going."

"Wait," Kyrkenall said. "Denaven?"

"Him and some of his circle. I managed to drive them off, but I'd been badly hurt."

"That means he knew. All this time. Elenai killed that hastig," Kyrkenall finished with a snarl.

"Good," Kalandra said, with matching venom.

Elenai studied her in growing wonder

"What happened to your body?" Kyrkenall demanded.

Kalandra shook her head slowly even as the wind whipped sand through her image. "It's long since dust. Now come. Tell me what's going on. I've heard nothing but Leonara's rantings for a very long while."

Elenai suggested they move into the cave depths, and scooped up Kalandra's stone before they retreated.

Lyria snuffled and pricked up her ears at Kalandra's image.

Through stages, interrupted by Kalandra's questions, Kyrkenall explained everything that had happened since her disappearance, for they soon learned that while the queen had occasionally spoken with her, Kalandra had little knowledge of events beyond Leonara's office, where her stone had been kept. And so she listened to the story of N'lahr's staged death, the treaty with Mazakan, Asrahn's murder, N'lahr's recovery, and the Naor invasions. Elenai then spoke of Cerai's scheming, and the attack against the queen and the retreat to Cerai's stronghold. Kyrkenall finished at last with information about the weapon they sought. His scrutiny of their weird guest had grown more and more pronounced, as he himself appeared more and more certain that she really was what she said.

"What are you planning to do next?" Kalandra asked. "If the storm plays out, are you going to keep searching for the weapon?"

"I don't know what else we can do," Elenai replied. "I think it was in my vision, but . . . Do you think the weapon even exists?"

"Most likely. As to where it's hidden, you may be on to something."

Kyrkenall cleared his throat. "Cerai can alter bodies. Maybe even make them. She might be able to help you out."

"You're sweet, Kyrkenall, but I wouldn't trust her to make a sandwich, much less a body. And I have virtually no idea how to inhabit one I wasn't born with."

"Will you at least sit?" he asked.

"I discovered some time ago that there's really no point in trying to rest. I'm not really here. So I can't feel any better than when I started this whole . . ." She looked like she was going to say something else, but ended with, "misadventure."

Kyrkenall spoke with grave sincerity. "I looked for you. Almost from the moment you vanished, I looked for you. I love you. I should have told you that. And that record you left, that talked to us—she told me you had always loved me, too."

"I do." Kalandra's expression softened. "I'm sorry, Kyrkenall. But what good is the love of a fading ghost?"

"You seem pretty real to me," he said.

"Do I? Or do you just want me to be real? You were always too good, my charming champion, at seeing what you wanted. It's ironic, really, given how fine your eyesight is."

"No," Kyrkenall insisted, "It's you. I feel it."

"What's the greater tragedy, I wonder?" Kalandra asked. "To be a disembodied genuine, or a deluded counterfeit? A question for the poets, I suppose. We don't have time for it. If any of us survive—assuming I actually count as being alive—we can worry about defining my existence later."

"How did you put yourself in here?" Elenai lifted the emerald.

"If I'd been thinking clearly I wouldn't have. It was a terrible idea. I'm hardly inclined to share the process."

Elenai hadn't planned on emulating her example, and was embarrassed Kalandra had misunderstood her curiosity. "How long can you last in this form?"

"I'm not entirely sure. But I'll know when it grows low."

"Do you have any way to recharge the stone's energy?"

"A hearthstone would be able to do it. Leonara did once herself, after toying with me." Kalandra's lips curled in a dry smile. "Really, if the Goddess is loose, you're worrying about the wrong things."

Elenai was not dissuaded, for there were other matters she remained curious about. "Why was there such a strong ward placed on your stone?"

Kalandra confirmed her suspicion with the answer. "That was so I couldn't get out on my own accord. Once I was in the palace, I discovered I could wander farther and farther from the stone itself. The queen didn't much care for that."

"So what was Leonara doing with you?" Kyrkenall asked.

"I am a gifted conversationalist," Kalandra said with the hint of a smile. "But she wanted only my information."

"And you didn't share any," Kyrkenall said.

"On the contrary, I shared almost everything. But she and Synahla wouldn't listen. All they wanted were bits that supported their preconceived beliefs. They thought they had a lock on reality. If Leonara believed the sky was orange, even pointing to the window to show her it was blue wouldn't convince her. I got tired of trying."

Kyrkenall swore. "How did the queen get ahold of you? Denaven again?"

"Naturally. He didn't come back until he was sure I couldn't hurt him anymore. He put the original ward on the stone, but I broke that one." She smiled with satisfaction.

"Who knew the queen had you?" Elenai asked. She hoped she would not say Thelar, or M'vai and Meria.

"The queen. Synahla. Denaven. Cerai."

"Cerai?" Kyrkenall's voice was thick with anger.

"I used to exchange information with her, when we were both exploring what the hearthstones really were. Cerai found out about the entire origin of our realms from me. Once I was captured I thought she was pretending to ally with the queen and would find a way to set me free."

"She's on no side but her own," Elenai said.

"That became obvious."

"It might be that the hearthstones warped her," Kyrkenall said. "Made her worse than she had to be."

"Or maybe it gave her an excuse to embrace her worst characteristics," Kalandra said. "You were always soft on her."

"I keep telling him he can't trust her," Elenai said.

"A queen who speaks the truth," Kalandra said. "That used to be more commonplace."

"I'm not really queen. Not yet. Maybe not ever." Elenai looked out at the storm. Speculatively she touched her sore arm. It didn't feel any better. "It looks like we have plenty of time before we leave."

"Or maybe just a little before the world ends," Kyrkenall said.

"There's the optimist I know." Kalandra's smile lit briefly in response to one from Kyrkenall. It died a moment later.

Elenai looked from one to the other. "I should go up front and give you some time alone."

"That's kind of you," Kalandra said. "But right now it's probably more important to fill in the gaps so you're prepared for the next act. It sounds like there are a lot of things you don't know."

Kyrkenall granted her permission to speak with a grand arm flourish. "Speak on. We're yours until the storm clears or the cave falls in, whichever comes first."

"Let's start at the top. Long before the days of the grandmothers, before Darassa had walked the circuit of her golden city, even before her birth, She-Who-Creates and He-Who-Alters danced in the great void. You could say that she made and he unmade, but it was more involved than that, because sometimes by unmaking he fashioned something new, and sometimes by making she destroyed what had previously been.

"They had begun with things so tiny they cannot be glimpsed by the sharpest eyes, and for uncounted eons played theme and variation so long that wonders emerged. The stars were wrought and set shining through the heavens, and lands were set to drift beneath them."

"This is all true?" Elenai asked in wonder. "This is what really happened?"

"It's what Kantahl and Darassa were told, and what they recorded on their memory stones. She-Who-Makes and He-Who-Changes delighted in the inspiration they brought the other, and one day they came together and gave birth to something new, their first child."

"Darassa," Elenai suggested.

"No. This was Sova. It fashioned strange and wild things and places as it played, ephemeral regions with impossibly high mountains, deep rifts, titanic waterfalls, and far stranger creations that are sometimes glimpsed in the Shifting Lands. Sova was an accident, an impermanent construct, and when it died unexpectedly, both god and goddess mourned. They preserved its memory by keeping some of its favored locations, then decided to make more children, and design them more deliberately."

Elenai understood then who the extra statue in the queen's paradise realm had represented.

Kalandra continued, her voice backed by the sound of the storm outside. "Even long after the births of those new children, She-Who-Orders mourned her lost first child. Her children grew and their realms changed, and while this pleased He-Who-Disorders, she worried the new children, too, would die. She grew alarmed that their realms overflowed with flowering trees and bushes all very different from one another, all changing and dying. They quarreled; she accused him of deliberately twisting their co-creations to triumph and torture her. And one day she made a weapon, and killed him."

Elenai swallowed. It was no wonder the Goddess had no interest in listening to her. She was ruthless.

"The rest I think you know. When the Goddess told her children they were to stop playing with the realms and build something far more co-herent, they didn't want to abandon their lands, much less the creatures they'd created. Some of them had even taken human lovers. They couldn't appeal to their father, because he'd disappeared, and their mother would tell them nothing of where he'd gone. Shaping tool in hand, Darassa led them to confront their mother in what are now The Fragments. They argued, Syrah and Sartain were killed, and the others used the shaping tool to temporarily make She-Who-Orders nothing *but* order. This briefly made her rigid and statue-like. Before she could reconfigure herself they blew her apart with the chaos weapon."

"Hold on there," Kyrkenall said. "What's the shaping tool?"

"It's about the length of your bow, but straight. Cerai didn't tell you about it? I see from your look she didn't." She shook her head in disgust. "I'm sure she still has it. I helped her figure out how to use it."

Elenai wondered what else the traitorous alten had kept from them.

"What does it do?" Kyrkenall asked.

"It helps build and restructure energies as you'd like, to lend physical-ity to what you imagine. Our gods used it to construct their realms, and they used it against their mother. Once they'd broken her, they scattered her energies through the realms and beyond."

"The hearthstones," Kyrkenall said.

"Yes. And the stones have been stabilizing the realms ever since, although our gods knew that was only a temporary measure. Our gods didn't use the hearthstones for other purposes much, because they were afraid they'd ac-cidentally bring the Goddess back. That's partly why they kept all her pieces so far apart, so they couldn't be drawn together."

"Cerai said the realms aren't permanent. Is that true?"

"It is," Kalandra said. "When the queen started snapping up all the stones and putting them in one place, it accelerated a decline already well underway. They're growing more and more unstable all the time."

"What happened to the Gods in the end?" Kyrkenall asked.

"They faded, as She-Who-Creates worried they would. Eventually they perished like normal men and women."

The roar of the storm had risen and fallen intermittently over the course of their conversation. Over the last little while, though, it had ebbed and never climbed in return. Elenai looked over the sand mounded in the cave mouth to see that the storm had receded. No longer pitch black, the atmosphere was now overcast by charcoal-shaded clouds.

Kyrkenall walked to the entrance to look outside.

Elenai was still sorting through all the information Kalandra had just presented. "The Goddess—She-Who-Creates-and-Orders—was out here searching for stones. Would she be seeking the weapon as well?"

"I suppose it's possible." Kalandra sounded doubtful. "But she's probably trying to gather all her energies. She can't function at full strength until she has all of the stones, all of herself, back."

"Then she would first have gone to Cerai's fortress," Elenai said. "Cerai has the largest supply of hearthstones."

"That would make sense."

"The storm's over," Kyrkenall called to them. He lay on the chest-high pile of sand deposited in the entrance, peering out through the slim opening left them. "The desert's still there, and the road the Goddess laid down. But there are strange things scattered over the landscape, the way there are when there's been a storm in the shifts."

Had she a hearthstone, Elenai could have fashioned a wind to blow the sand out. But she had none, and using her own energies would completely drain her.

She looked back at Lyria, standing with head bowed. She and Kyrkenall could probably fit through the entrance, but to get the horse clear they'd have to dig.

Kyrkenall produced a small spade from his own saddlebag and set to work. Fortunately for him, the slope was fairly pronounced.

Once he'd finally conquered the pile of sand, they stood in the cave mouth and took in the view.

"It's oddly beautiful, isn't it?" Kalandra asked.

Great change had been wrought upon Kanesh. An immense inverted pyramid of rock, hundreds of feet high, stood a half mile out, its middle bisected perfectly with a line of red marble. Closer in, a forest of red basalt columns stood in neat rows, and only a few hundred yards away a strange crimson lake bubbled, sending great clouds of steam into the air.

Stranger even than that was what appeared a jagged tear in the sky itself, through which twinkling stars shown, occasionally obscured by a shifting red and orange kaleidoscopic pattern. A cold wind blew, and Elenai might have imagined it, but she felt as though it was sweeping down from that hole in the sky.

She felt like cursing, and decided against it. Queens, she thought, should curse if they wish, but a leader and role model should better learn to moderate her responses. Besides, her father had once told her she should save swear words for only the most important occasions. She resolved to practice that advice.

She turned to look at the woman beside her. Kyrkenall's lost love existed under her own lighting conditions, and blowing wind didn't disturb her hair, or her frayed khalat. She produced no noise as she appeared to step across the rock, nor was there the sound of a sleeve brushing against her side as she moved, or a breath, or a cough. Kalandra's body did cast a shadow, though it was oddly gray.

Kyrkenall moved aside for Lyria, who poked her head out and regarded the horizon with disinterest. Finally the horse stepped free and started down. To the sound of her hoofbeats on stone, Kyrkenall swept a hand at the bizarre landscape. "If the Goddess creates order, why does chaos follow in her wake?"

"A fine question," Kalandra said. "Maybe chaos rushes in to attack the order she puts in place, like water rushing through a dam break." She seemed to note for the first time the fist-sized emerald Kyrkenall held in one hand.

He looked down at it himself. "I think my instinct was to hand it to you, but . . . you can't carry it, can you?"

"I can't do much of anything, Kyrkenall."

"You can walk at my side," he said. "The world and I both will be better for that."

Elenai's heart fluttered to hear those words. "Why don't I give you two a moment alone. I'll go sort our gear." She returned to the cave without waiting for a reply.

It didn't seem likely her horse had survived, so she transferred the heavier items into one pack, then took the field lantern apart. While she was hampered by her injury, for the sake of the two lovers she still worked more slowly than necessary.

When she emerged at last, she placed the first pack out alone to alert them she was nearly done.

When she returned, the two were still talking earnestly. Kyrkenall kept reaching toward Kalandra, as if to grasp her shoulder, or take her hand, then remembering he couldn't touch her. It was painful to see.

After a final word, both faced her.

"Looks like you have us ready," Kyrkenall said. "Kalandra's going to retreat into the emerald for now to conserve energy."

"Just let me know when you need me," Kalandra said. "Being inside there is the closest I can feel to sleep. Although it's more like meditation." She bowed her head to Elenai with great dignity, then looked to Kyrkenall. "I'll talk to you both later."

She winked out of existence, and the land around them was somehow twice as empty.

Kyrkenall let out a single low oath and looked down at the emerald in one hand. He then turned his attention to the overcast sky. "Looks like mid-afternoon. One nice thing about that storm—it's not going to be hot today. That gives us more time to search. We can take turns riding Lyria."

Elenai nodded agreement. Without her horse, travel was going to be a lot more challenging.

"So," Kyrkenall said with affected breeziness, "what do you think of her?"

Not so long ago, Elenai had been jealous of the absent Kalandra, for N'lahr and Kyrkenall had held her in such high regard it seemed she herself couldn't possibly measure up. And sometimes, when she'd been tempted by Kyrkenall's innate charisma, she'd been jealous of his strong attachment to someone who wasn't there.

"She's not like I thought she'd be," Elenai admitted.

"No?"

"No." She had expected someone insufferably competent. "She's clear-sighted, and grounded." And sad, Elenai thought, but she didn't say that, because Kalandra had ample reason for sorrow.

Elenai contemplated the desert stretching on beyond the lake and pillars. She was already tired, and they had far to go. "Let's get on with it."

"You really think we still have a chance?"

"To locate a small weapon hidden in a vast desert that we don't know how to work? I'm feeling as optimistic as you are. But I'm Altenerai. And so are you."

"Right. We'll meet our numbered day while smiling, and all that."

"Let me know when to smile."

"Oh, I will." His sense of humor seemed muted. Elenai understood that the potential of Kalandra had been more sustaining than a Kalandra who might not be real, or restorable, and her heart ached for them both. United at last, but separate still, perhaps forever.

Kyrkenall lifted the heavier saddlebag onto Lyria, then shouldered the other. Elenai insisted on letting the archer ride first, because she'd had more sleep. They then headed out past the bubbling crimson lake, on a course that would take them beyond the basalt pillars toward the dunes.

Only a half mile later, as Elenai looked back, she saw a trio of broad, squat figures climbing to the top of a hill formed of sheer gleaming bronze, rising beside the hills they themselves had just departed. It hadn't been there before the storm.

A tall, horned figure reached its flat summit and the other two climbed to join him. Her spirits brightened at the sight of them, and she reminded herself not to assume anything as she called Kyrkenall's name. As she pointed, her friend turned Lyria in her tracks. The horned figure pointed at them and the climbers conferred.

"First Naor, now kobalin," Elenai said.

"Aye." The archer had lifted his bow. Normally he did so without consideration. This time, though, he tested the weapon's pull, as though he'd never shot from it. Of course. Without its magical energies, he worried Arzhun would not be as resilient. He met her eyes. "Maybe it's your vision about to come true, but I think we should be careful."

The kobalin at the top turned his back to them and appeared to be waving his hands to someone out of sight.

"Excellent," Elenai said. "There are more of them."

Kyrkenall had knocked a gray fletched arrow, though he didn't lift the black bow into shooting position.

The signaler and the other two descended quickly and came on at a jog. He carried a double-bladed axe. The other two bore sheathed swords. All were scaled in reds and oranges.

"Do any of them look like the one from your vision?"

"No. He was smaller."

"These look like kobalin lords. They're probably after a challenge."

"That's not good," she said.

"It might be. Once I win the challenge, they'll probably hear me out, and then we might have some help looking."

Elenai measured the kobalin, then considered Kyrkenall's cool aplomb. He was considerably smaller than all three. And both his great bow and his sword had been drained of energy. "Let's try talking to them first."

"Anything we say is likely just a preamble to a challenge."

"Maybe I should challenge one," she suggested.

"We need you," Kyrkenall said.

"We need you, too," she retorted.

He smirked. "I don't think I can find the weapon we're searching for. Besides, I've fought a lot more kobalin than you have. Actually, have you ever fought kobalin?"

"No," she admitted.

"There you go, then."

Much as she disliked it, his reasoning was sound. "Maybe you should consult with Kalandra. Do you know how?"

"She said it's like activating one of our rings." He looked at the saddle-bag on Lyria's flank and a moment later Kalandra appeared.

She quickly took in her surroundings. "So some kobalin are on their way to meet us. I thought you might just be missing me."

"I always miss you," Kyrkenall said without the slightest trace of humor.

The kobalin slowed a bowshot out and then walked confidently forward. Like Ortok, they were broad and powerful. The horned one bearing the axe was a head taller than the others, his orange scales less delineated. He alone wore ringmail. Rough kilts clothed the loins of all three, and the other two each carried a shield.

They halted only a short distance out, the armored axe-bearer at the point of their triangle. The red-scaled one on his right had a pronounced snout he lifted to sniff them. The third was more lizard-like, though possessed of wide, thick-lashed brown eyes.

Kyrkenall hopped gracefully down from Lyria.

"You have magics," the leader said, his voice a surprisingly mild alto. "But where is the power of your rings? Are you true Altenerai?"

Kyrkenall spread his arms. "It might be that I'm Kyrkenall the Eyeless." He raised the black bow. "Slayer of Nemrose. And it could be that this is Kalandra Storm Strider, breaker of shield walls and that this is Elenai Half-Sword, slayer of traitors and generals. But maybe we've just killed a few Altenerai and are wandering around in their uniforms."

The orange-snouted one and the lizard-like kobalin exchanged puzzled looks. The leader frowned in thought. "No," he decided, "I think you are Altenerai. I had heard Storm Strider was a magic worker, but not that she was formed of magic. Of Elenai Half-Sword I have not heard. Is she sister to Elenai Oddsbreaker?"

Elenai perked up at this question. There was only one source from which they were likely to have learned her name.

"One person can have two names," Kyrkenall pointed out. "I'm sometimes called Kyrkenall of the Black Bow."

"That sounds more like a title, but I take your meaning. I am Urchok Bone Spitter. The Naor know my name and fear me." He clouted his chest. Probably his armor was of Naor make.

"There are stories we could tell, Urchok," Kalandra said. "It's good to share them with other warriors."

Urchok grunted affirmation.

"But this isn't a time for stories," Kalandra continued. "We're not on a battle quest. We're on a hunt. If you join us, we will share its glory."

The kobalin behind Urchok straightened, and the one with the snout snuffled again.

"That is a fine offer," Urchok said.

A stream of figures descended from either side of the bronze hill behind them. At first Elenai thought they numbered in the dozens, then their count swelled higher and higher.

"But our duties are given us by the great Ortok, Skull Render," Urchok continued. "He has spoken much of you, and I think he would wish to meet with you before we do anything else."

25

———~———

The Secret in the Sand

Elenai made no effort to fight the fierce smile spreading across her face. Ortok lived. That, at least, was good news.

As the kobalin army descended the hillside, Lyria watched them skeptically with her wide brown eyes. A few groups took up sentry positions farther east and west.

None drew closer than ten paces, but as their numbers swelled into the low hundreds this meant the armed host ringed them in a way Elenai had seen popular actors surrounded by admirers, absent fangs and weapons. Bearing mismatched gear, the kobalin stared and talked among themselves. Elenai overheard discussions of Kyrkenall's height, and Kalandra's shimmering magical dweomer, and a few mentions of how slight all the Altenerai seemed; there were also admiring comments upon the blue of their khalats.

Search though she might, Elenai did not see the kobalin from her vision, and worried that she might not remember him well enough to recognize him among so many others.

Finally, a lane opened between the kobalin and a familiar, shaggy black-furred form strode down it to meet them.

Elenai beamed as Ortok lifted both of his massive arms in greeting.

"Ho! Three companions, and the noble Lyria! How good to see you!"

She embraced him, not minding that the pressure of his body against her sling brought a jab of pain. She felt Ortok startle. The crowd murmured in surprise. Still smiling, Elenai stepped back.

Ortok showed fangs in a broad smile of his own.

She decided against telling him she'd been afraid he was dead. She didn't want to suggest she thought him weak. She defaulted to kobalin-style formality. "I am pleased to see you as well."

"Word reaches me that you have a second name now, Oddsbreaker! I would hear of that. And you, Kyrkenall! You have found Kalandra, or she has found you!"

Kalandra bowed her head with dignity. "Hello, Ortok. It has been a long while. You look as though you've risen in glory and gained a mighty host."

"I have earned many worthy stories," Ortok said without sounding boastful. "Have you become pure magic?"

"I suppose I have," Kalandra answered.

Ortok grunted, clearly impressed, although not astounded. But then Elenai knew transformative changes were commonplace among his people. "And how are you, Kyrkenall? You have the pleasure of the Storm Strider's company again."

"I do," Kyrkenall said. Ortok might not have detected the reservation in his reply, but it was clear to Elenai. He avoided answering the kobalin's first inquiry and changed subjects. "I knew you'd win your challenge."

"Your faith was placed well," Ortok said. "Tell me, does N'lahr still live?"

"He lives," Kyrkenall answered, "and his glory grows."

Ortok nodded as though that were expected, and then he thought of something else. "You must tell me if Steadyfoot is also living."

Kyrkenall grinned. "Alive and well. He's in the stables where I got Lyria."

"That is good to hear."

"What are you doing here in Kanesh?" Elenai asked.

Ortok indicated the watching kobalin. "I have my army. I have come to fight Naor. Do you want to fight them with me?"

"We've already fought some here," Elenai said.

"There are many left. We tried to follow your trail, but the place you went was surrounded by mad god storms, so I decided to lead my army to where the Naor live, so I could fight them, and on the way we found many of them wandering here. We have been fighting them ever since."

"It has been a time of battles," Kyrkenall said. "The Naor marched on Darassus. They broke its wall. But with N'lahr to lead us, we broke the Naor, and Elenai faced down their sorcerer king."

"It sounds a great tale!"

"Their king sliced her sword in half," Kyrkenall continued. "But she did not relent! She took his head from his shoulders with her shattered blade!"

Elenai enjoyed the shortened version of the victory, but not nearly so much as Ortok.

"Ho ho!" Ortok's eyes shone, and there were mutters of approval from the nearby kobalin that spread as these details were relayed through their ranks. "That is good," Ortok said. "But we should share such words while we sit and eat." He motioned to herd them forward, but Kalandra interposed herself.

"Those are fine suggestions, and good to hear," she said. "But we hunt something that must be found before we feast. There is glory in its finding. Enough for all here."

"This must be a great something indeed. Tell me of it."

"Our queen called up a powerful goddess, Ortok." Kalandra gestured to the lands around her. "The Goddess transformed this land simply by passing through. She means to destroy everything. The land. The sky. All places, all people, everywhere."

Ortok stroked his furry chin. "Your queen should not have summoned this Goddess."

"You always see right to the heart of the problem," Kyrkenall remarked, without the faintest hint of sarcasm.

"This Goddess will be a most worthy opponent. So we will fight her!"

At Ortok's declaration the nearby kobalin shook their weapons in the air and this gesture rippled outward through their ranks. A roar of approval swelled over them and dropped away.

Kalandra slowly shook her head. "The Altenerai already brought her battle. Yet nothing can harm her but a special weapon, older than the oldest of our elders' elders, and hidden deep within the wastelands of Kanesh."

Elenai couldn't help marveling over Kalandra's mastery of the moment. She clearly knew exactly how to speak with kobalin and win them to her viewpoint.

"And it is a magic weapon?" Ortok asked.

"Yes," Kalandra replied.

"And will it bring victory over this great foe?"

"If the legends hold true, and our fight is clever," Kalandra said.

"We will help you find this thing," Ortok vowed. "And then we will have a battle for the ages." He raised his voice so that he might address those nearest as well as those who surrounded him. "You see? It is truly valuable to be friends with Altenerai, so we can find strange gods and fight them!"

Murmuring among those nearby seemed to indicate Ortok had scored a point in some longstanding kobalin dispute.

"You will have to tell us what we look for." Ortok dropped one massive hand on Kyrkenall's shoulder, completely obscuring it, then turned to speak to his followers.

His deep voice boomed. "Listen well! My Altenerai friends will tell you of a magic weapon! We march now to seek it, and then we shall battle a god. Great will be our glory!"

At this word, the kobalin erupted into cheers.

Kyrkenall leaned closer to Elenai. "And here you were probably thinking we needed some kind of eloquent speech."

Elenai chuckled, and, surprised at the sound, wondered how long it had been since she'd actually laughed. She marveled again at how skillfully Kalandra had tailored her message for her audience. She was the kind of leader the realm needed. No matter her own challenges she remained calm and certain, and spoke from a well of experience. What would it be like having a ghost for a queen? Kalandra would be virtually immortal, so long as energies could be fed into her crystal.

Though she had been growing more and more comfortable with the idea of sitting the throne in Darassus, finding someone better suited for the role didn't trouble Elenai in the least. Before she could consider the idea further, though, she had to join the conversation about the weapon.

She explained to the kobalin that they searched for something hidden in a plateau among the dunes. Kalandra described its likely magical aura. Before long the furred, scaled, and occasionally armored army was trudging with them toward the desert. While the host advanced in staggered lines to right and left, Ortok walked with the Altenerai. Lyria trailed Kyrkenall.

"I would rather have heard you speak of battles around a fire," Ortok said to Kyrkenall, "but I know it will be good telling even as we walk. Speak on, friend."

"Gladly, but I want to hear about your adventures first. How did you win your army?"

The kobalin's eyes lit. "Oh, yes. It was a great contest. I fought Olbaht the White. He was pale, and broad, and had pointed teeth! The fight was long, and much blood was spilled! Twice he struck me, four times I struck him, and felled him finally with a blow to his chest. Then he declared me worthy as he died, and his followers acclaimed me, and I made a fine speech."

Elenai couldn't help noticing that Ortok was still working to describe important details in groups of threes, as he had thought Kyrkenall had been suggesting to him. "What was Olbaht's army doing there in the wastes?" she asked.

Ortok plodded in thoughtful silence. They drew near the long line of immense red columns deposited by the storm. Scalloped indentations rose along each of them at even intervals.

"The seers smelled a change in the air," Ortok said finally, "as sometimes happens, and banded together to seek matters and best challenges. They had heard of the goddess of the wastes, who transformed our folk into Dendressi, and they meant to fight her or swear fealty. But the way to her lands was blocked. I had told N'lahr that I would find an army and fight Naor, so I did. And now I see I chose rightly, because fighting the little groups of Naor led me to you. And I do not want the Goddess to destroy all. It is one thing to stand and face challenges, but if there is no place to stand, how is a warrior to prove himself?"

Elenai had forgotten how much she enjoyed Ortok's reasoning.

The kobalin shifted his attention to Kalandra. "You don't glow as much as the last time I saw you."

"I'm not that memory," Kalandra explained.

Elenai had expected Ortok to ask further, but the explanation seemed to satisfy him. "Where is the rest of you?"

"This is all that's left."

Ortok appeared incapable of perceiving the tragedy of her circumstance. "It is very interesting," he said. "Now that you are here, when we are done killing the Goddess, I hope to see that play with you. Elenai has also invited me, so perhaps we can all go, and see two plays."

Kalandra's smile for the first time betrayed not the slightest hint of sorrow. "Ortok, I hope to see as many plays as you like."

Elenai shared her sentiment. "If I ever become queen," she said, "I'll make certain everyone knows you are welcome to every playhouse in the five realms."

Ortok's gaze swung to her. "Do you mean so?"

"Of course!"

"General of Armies. Friend to Altenerai, Watcher of Plays. And you will be queen? Did you kill the last one?"

"No," Elenai said. "That was . . ." That, she decided, might take too long to explain. "No. The people were grateful when I killed the Naor general."

"You mean the Naor king?"

"He was their leader," Kyrkenall said.

"You should be leader of the Naor, then," Ortok said, "if you killed theirs."

"In a way she is," Kyrkenall said. "The surviving warriors pledged to serve her."

"Ho!" Ortok slapped Elenai on the back the way he did with N'lahr. The blow stung even through her armor, and set her arm throbbing. "You killed the Denaven commander, and the Naor general king. You never bother to kill small warriors."

Elenai thought of the soldiers of Mazakan's honor guard who'd fallen to her, and the Naor warriors she'd faced on the wall. So many had come against her she couldn't really guess their numbers, and their faces were blurs. But mostly she remembered the surprised eyes of that first person she had ever slain, the guard at the north tower from whom she should have demanded surrender.

For the first time, Elenai understood how her lack of experience had influenced that moment. She had been frightened and uncertain. She didn't forgive herself, exactly, but she understood the younger Elenai who had taken that action, pitying her almost as though she were a different person. There was nothing now to be done for the soldier but to remember that attack so that she never again struck without thinking.

But then it occurred to her that maybe she'd already internalized that lesson long ago, in the staying of Kyrkenall's hand against Gyldara. Fine, she thought, but if so, it was a lesson to be overlearned.

Ortok was still musing on a similar topic. "It is a good thing to be confident of your power, so that you wield it only when needed."

"It is," Kalandra agreed.

"N'lahr and I have discussed this," Ortok said. "We think alike, he and I."

Elenai had never heard a better opening, and seized it promptly. "Please tell me you still don't mean to fight him."

Kyrkenall sucked in a breath through his teeth. Elenai felt Kalandra's close scrutiny, wondering why she sensed disapproval. But she kept her attention upon Ortok, who eyed her as though she were mad. "I gave my word!" he said.

"That may be so, but if either of you die, I will be very sad."

Ortok nodded sagely. "Facing him will create a sadness. But sorrow is a part of being alive. I have welcomed much trouble to prove myself worthy to challenge him."

Elenai tried another line of attack. "If you or N'lahr fall, your enemies will rejoice. Is that what you want? Or do you want them to fear you, as you both live?"

"It is good when your enemies fear you. But I gave my word and offered challenge. Now I will see to my people." He strode stiffly off along the right wing of his army.

"That was a bad time to do that," Kyrkenall said. "Can't you push on that later? We may not even have to worry about it if the world's about to end."

"He's planning to fight your best friend to the death," Elenai reminded him. "And it was the right opening."

"N'lahr can handle him," the archer said.

"You don't think I know that?" How thick was he? "Do you want Ortok to die?"

Kyrkenall frowned as though he hadn't considered that side of the issue.

"Your intentions are good, Elenai," Kalandra said. "But right now we need Ortok's help. N'lahr himself would have advised you to remain silent."

She found both of them frustrating, and went quiet, almost as if she played the part of a sullen teenager scolded by both parents. She didn't fully understand their reasoning. All else was out of their control, and this course, at least, she might be able to shape.

Yet it might be that their greater experience with kobalin was a better guide than her instincts, for her prodding seemed to have created a rift. Ortok kept clear of them as they marched into the desert.

Neither Kalandra nor Kyrkenall said anything further about the matter, but Ortok's withdrawal left Elenai feeling hurt.

Eventually Kalandra retreated to her emerald as Kyrkenall and Elenai walked on in silence, trading off riding Lyria. Even under cloud cover the temperature climbed, though it never approached the heat they'd experienced that morning, perhaps because an odd wind blew intermittently cool. They stopped as the sun descended, digging into their rations while the kobalin ate in little groups spread out toward the horizon. Then they resumed their march.

The great dunes had been blown by the storm, but remained obstacles that had to be detoured around. Once the sun sank, the cold chill of the naked stars swept through the desert, such that Elenai shivered even under the blanket she wore like a cloak. From a strange gash in the dark sky a series of suns slowly shifted past, and warmth flowed down from them, though never enough to fully shield them from the frigid night.

Kyrkenall, walking at her side, sometimes sang to himself in a pleasant alto, and sometimes talked to Lyria, but he didn't say much to Elenai.

Finally, in the late hours of the night, the dunes receded around a mesa so low it hadn't been visible until they were almost on top of it. Nor was it particularly large, a rough crescent only a few hundred feet across at its widest point and perhaps a thousand long.

The kobalin on the right flank climbed it first, then Elenai, Kyrkenall, and Ortok joined a handful of the kobalin warriors struggling up a sandy slope to arrive at the mesa's height. Scattered rock littered its top, occasional impediments to an otherwise wide vista over the surrounding dunes. She scanned the hills visible upon the weird horizon, lit now by a bright red sun seen through that jagged opening, and beheld the split mountaintop from her vision. This was the right place.

At the summit, Kyrkenall contacted Kalandra, and the woman's image walked silently with them as their footfalls crunched sand and grit along the hardened surface. Ortok practically bubbled with excitement, and Elenai hoped this meant the earlier awkwardness between them was forgotten.

Elenai reminded the kobalin searchers that the artifact might feel like a lack of magic, and they unflaggingly spread out to search, as they described it, "for a hole where magic wasn't." Before very long, Urchok, the armored one who seemed to be Ortok's chief scout, ran back to report. "There is a feeling where the sands lie in the midst of this flat rock place," he said. "We think the weapon is there, under much sand."

Rounding a large stone Elenai discovered the scout's description essentially accurate. In the midst of the flat mesa lay a sandy area scattered with rounded boulders of roughly equal size. Dozens of the kobalin were already scooping great handfuls of dark sand and piling it to the side. A dry smell reached Elenai's nostrils, reminding her of uncured hide left rotting in the sun.

"There's a strange energy here," Ortok said to Kyrkenall. "How big is the weapon we look for?"

"The length of Arzhun," Kyrkenall answered.

Elenai searched amongst the kobalin for the one from her dreams. But it was difficult to judge much about any of them as they labored in the near darkness. She fought off a shiver, then opened her eyes to the inner world and considered the sand-filled pit. She grew distracted by a glimpse of movement where she hadn't expected any.

She shifted to get a better look. Something was odd about the surrounding rocks. Most were about half the size of a horse. Each was immobile, but they were hollow, and a complex construct squirmed inside every one of them. "These aren't rocks, they're eggs," she said.

"We sensed the boulders had energy," Ortok said. "Would they be good for eating?"

"I'm not sure I'd try that." Elenai peered more intently at the outline within the nearest, and recognized the flattened head, the multiple limbs, and the little wriggle along a jawline that met vertically. Alarm stabbed at her, especially since Ortok had walked to the nearest and readied his sword pommel for a good smack.

"Stop!" Elenai cried, and was relieved that Ortok paused with his weapon raised. "I think these eggs are of the beasts we fought. The ones that send pain when you attack them," she added to clarify.

"Oh." Ortok lowered his weapon. He called to his followers. "Do not break the egg boulders! The Oddsbreaker says that these are the glow crawlers!" He turned to Elenai. "Do you think they are ready to hatch?"

"They look fully grown inside," she said, not knowing how to judge.

Ortok grunted.

"Hey, I've got a question," Kyrkenall said. "Whatever laid these eggs has to be pretty big, given the size of these things. Where is it?"

"That is a good question," Ortok said.

"Did you and your army see any huge tracks?" Kyrkenall asked.

"I saw none. My followers would have told me if they saw something worthy of challenge."

"There won't be any tracks after the storm," Elenai pointed out.

Kyrkenall shot her a warning look. "You're assuming the mother left before the storm." He stepped away, Kalandra walking with him.

"You'd better tell your sentries to watch for a really big glow crawler," Elenai told Ortok.

"I had thought of that."

As Ortok started to lift hands to make a speaking trumpet, she quickly added: "Maybe shouting's not a good idea, if the mother's close."

He turned and looked at her, then grunted assent. He called Urchok to him and quietly relayed orders. As Urchok jogged away, Ortok considered the kobalin laboring in the hole, then faced her. "Can you not magic glow crawlers away, as you did when they chased Kyrkenall and you and me?"

"We're not in the shifts, now," Elenai reminded him. "I can't poke a hole through an actual realm. It's too magically solid."

"We will have to have a plan then, if the bigger one comes."

"The regular-sized ones are bad enough," she said.

"Maybe you will need this weapon for killing it."

If they found it. If she could figure out how to use it. And if using it against the monster didn't feel like she was blasting herself with ancient goddess-destroying energies.

Elenai moved to the edge of the depression as the kobalin labored at what looked an almost insurmountable challenge. Each time they scooped sand, more streamed in from higher upslope and Elenai was reminded of Kalandra's analogy of chaos rushing in when there was a break in order.

We're close, she thought. She just wished she'd known that they'd have to contend with what Ortok called "glow crawlers" in the process. Her visions were certainly useful, but they were hardly flawless.

Gradually, the kobalin made progress. Every now and then the diggers traded out with new workers.

Kyrkenall returned to report he'd found no tracks, adding almost defensively that he hadn't expected to. Kalandra lingered at his shoulder like a ghost, and it occurred to Elenai that she had haunted his mind and heart for years, but only now was her presence visible.

After what must have been several hours, a squat, furry kobalin let out a cry of joy and pulled something free, lifting it high over his flop-eared head as it dripped sand upon him.

"I found it," he cried. "I, Othmar, Finder of God Weapons!"

Other kobalin crowded forward to peer at the thing he brandished but didn't wrestle it from him.

Through their shifting bodies, Elenai drew the impression of a simple cylindrical staff, almost as long as a headless spear haft and a little thicker.

She smiled tiredly as Othmar struggled up through the cascading sand, eschewing aid, then, in the moment from her vision, bounded up and down in excitement. He bowed to Ortok, who'd stepped to her side.

The dark-furred general grumbled deep in his chest. "You are the God-Weapon Finder, Othmar," he said, and a shudder passed through the smaller creature.

"I will take it now," Elenai declared with dignity. "Well done, Othmar."

Othmar blinked at her in surprise. "But I found the weapon," he said. "I shall use it against our enemies!"

"You will forever after be known as Othmar, God-Weapon Finder," Ortok said. "But this weapon is for the enchantress, who does not just see magics, but makes them. She will need it when we fight a goddess."

Othmar clearly wasn't convinced, but when Ortok extended a huge dark palm, he advanced to gently place it in his leader's grasp.

"There," Ortok said, and turned to Elenai. "Half-Sword Oddsbreaker, I present this to you, on behalf of the kobalin of my command, this God-Weapon, found by Othmar God-Weapon Finder."

"Thank you, Ortok," Elenai said. "Thank you, Othmar. I will never forget this." She bowed her head to them both. At that, Othmar brightened, then regarded those around him, turning this way and that, as if to ensure they had seen his glory.

Only then did Elenai take the staff from Ortok.

26

The Wielder of the Staff

The weapon had appeared as if it were carved from marble. It was too light for that, though it felt perfectly smooth in her palm, and lacked the grain of wood.

"Is this the thing you seek?" Ortok asked.

"It looks like stone." Kyrkenall reached out to stroke it with a finger. "It feels like marble," he added.

"It has that strange absence of magic inside, as you told us," Ortok said.

"There's order surrounding chaos magic." Kalandra had been silent for so long her airy voice startled Elenai. "A tiny bit of the chaos is leaking out."

"I see it." Ortok tapped the far end with a blunt finger.

If chaos were dripping it didn't do so in any obvious way. Elenai was about to open her sight to the inner world when she saw a flare of light from beside Kyrkenall. Kalandra's finger glowed as she herself touched the staff.

Kalandra had suggested she had no way to interact with the physical world, and Elenai immediately wondered if the alten were endangering herself by the examination.

The older woman seemed to breathe in—though she made no sound—then closed her eyes and ran her hand all along the far end of the staff.

A moment later the glow about her finger subsided, and she stepped back, her eyes still closed.

"How did you do that?" Elenai asked.

"I tapped energy from my gem."

"You shouldn't do that," Kyrkenall objected with anger. "That's what's keeping you alive."

Elenai had the same sentiments.

Kalandra flashed an easy smile at them both. "Don't worry." She descended into the pit. The kobalin scrambled out of her way with an odd mix of fear and courtesy, for once they were beyond arm's length they bowed their heads to her.

Though curious to see what Kalandra had discovered, Elenai examined the strange staff on her own. The tool proved free of blemish. It didn't retain warmth from where anyone had held it. The end that had excited such interest didn't reveal anything to visual inspection. In the inner world, however, that portion was faintly marred. Tiny threads of warped energy dripped free, slowly lengthening, reminding Elenai of a leaky old pump spigot on the training grounds near the stables. Here something far more interesting was taking place. Elenai was tempted to eye the staff's end directly, but doing so seemed akin to examining an arrowhead point first while someone had the shaft nocked to a bow.

The thread didn't radiate energy in the same way as a hearthstone, nor did it behave in the way even threads of force in the Shifting Lands did, for it twisted as it grew. Finally part of it broke free and dropped to the sand. Instantly the surface changed. Where before there had been a rounded pebble now there were smaller ones with rough sides, as if the original had shattered.

Alarmed, Elenai made sure to shift the end of the staff out of line with anyone nearby. "Keep away from that end of it," she said. "Don't even touch it."

"Elenai's absolutely right." Kalandra's voice emanated from below, less tinnily and remote than usual, and Elenai looked down to see the woman standing in the sand, her hands glowing with golden energy again. "If you look at the connective threads of this mesa I think you'll see ragged ends everywhere. Chaos has been leaking into the environment here for millennia."

"You're using too much energy," Kyrkenall told her.

Kalandra winked out of existence, then appeared beside Kyrkenall a heartbeat later. "I don't suppose I really have to walk," she said, her voice once more sounding as though it was delivered from a well. Her sudden appearance started three nearby kobalin and Elenai herself.

"If you pop around like that you're going to frighten someone," Kyrkenall told her.

Kalandra chuckled.

From somewhere off to their right came the rumble of moving earth. The ground shook. A distant kobalin shouted, but Elenai couldn't make out his warning.

The trembling drew closer. She pivoted to discover its source. An immense glow lizard had scrambled from beneath a nearby dune and was now headed straight for the mesa, trailing a plume of sand.

Easily rivaling the size of one of the Naor dragons, the giant beast must have stretched on for more than hundred feet if its swaying tail was figured in. Its vertically hinged jaws, big around as a temple gate, opened in a roar like a cross between a sandstorm and a furious hawk. It charged on a multitude of clawed legs, now and then vanishing from view, for its colors shifted so that it blended with the sand around it.

Even as Ortok shouted to his followers not to use their weapons, it was upon them, and his warriors struck out defensively. Those who attacked collapsed in rebounded pain. Others fell because they were too slow to evade its clawed feet, and were snapped up by the great jaws. It barely paused, and soon it barreled on for the mesa's slope.

Kyrkenall swore.

"Fall back!" Elenai shouted. "It just wants its eggs!" At least that was what she hoped.

Ortok shouted for his soldiers to retreat, and all of them reached the side of the mesa at about the same time the monster glow lizard climbed the slope to the far edge. It scurried toward its eggs, snuffling at them while a hideous tongue licked in and out of its strange mouth.

Below, Ortok's soldiers regrouped, weapons ready. Ortok, Kyrkenall, and Elenai still watched upon the rim, along with the ghostly Kalandra.

"Maybe we're fine," Kyrkenall said softly.

Elenai didn't think so, and looked down at the weapon in her hands. Probably she was going to have to use it against the monster, and probably the moment the weapon struck the beast the pain would pass to her. Her lips thinned in determination. She might get just one shot, then, before she herself was incapacitated.

Assuming she could figure out how to fire it.

The mother lizard swung toward them, opened its mouth, and flicked out its bumpy black tongue. Its tread shook the ground as it padded toward them.

"Make haste, friends," Ortok called. He started down the mesa's steep slope, and Elenai and Kyrkenall followed, sliding when not running. Kalandra flashed into existence ahead of them.

They stopped at the mesa's foot, and looked back to find the monster standing where they'd just been, moving its head back and forth.

"It smells us," Elenai said quietly.

"I think it's after the weapon," Kalandra said.

Elenai shot her a curious look.

"It must be attracted to it," the other woman insisted. "It built its nest over it."

"Ho," Ortok said. "You may have truth there."

The thing's head cocked as though it were looking down, although it didn't appear to have eyes.

They backed carefully away, Elenai considering the rod she held. Maybe the best way to work it would be to pull on the emerging threads and throw them toward the monster. Staff under her arm, she reached up to undo the sling, then shifted part of the staff's meager weight to her bad hand. Light though it was, the pressure pained her.

The beast roared so loud Elenai's ears rang. And then it raced down the slope at them.

Swearing silently, Elenai leveled the staff at its face, threw threads of intent, and pulled on the chaos at the weapon's tip.

The energy flowed forth like water from a broken nozzle and struck the beast along the right side of its mouth. It shrieked.

Elenai's own cry of pain erupted at the same moment. It felt as though her cheek, bone and muscle both, were being rearranged with a hot scrambling fork.

The beast halted. Elenai, in such agony she could barely focus, had somehow retained hold of the staff, though her grip was weak.

The weapon was yanked from her hands and she looked up in dismay to see Kalandra, hands glowing once more. The beast tore through the sloping sand for them, frighteningly fast and huge.

The creature's snout was only twenty feet off when the energies struck its opening jaw. Either Kalandra was lucky, or she had a much better idea how to manage the weapon, for her first attack reduced half the thing's right jaw to dark ash that wafted away, then shifted to one of its front legs and blew through a leg joint.

The beast tottered, keening. Ortok dragged Elenai back as Kalandra continued her remorseless assault. The rebounding pain link apparently had no effect upon someone without a physical presence.

The mother glow lizard screamed in agony. Its tongue reached almost to Kalandra, who sprayed the chaos energies across its face, transforming the thing's features into dripping haze and flaking bits of bluish fluff, borne upward in the chill air.

The beast collapsed, although a back leg continued to twitch. Elenai felt certain it was dead, but Kalandra kept up the attack until nothing remained of the monster's head but a bit of seared bone, and all the knee joints on its right side were destroyed. She then advanced up the mesa and wielded the weapon against the only egg Elenai could see. She moved out of sight.

Elenai's own pain had faded to a searing throb by then, and she straightened, hands to her jaw. It astounded her that it could hurt so much even though she'd endured no physical damage.

A somber Kalandra returned. She passed off the staff to Elenai, and then her hands ceased their brighter glow. Beside her, Kyrkenall stared bleakly at the emerald that housed her real essence. Elenai opened herself to the inner world and saw Kalandra's energies had faded by more than half. Always sensitive to magics, Kyrkenall had already known.

Only Ortok failed to register the gravity of the moment, and let out a war whoop. "What a glorious weapon!" he cried. "Kalandra, spirit warrior and slayer of monsters!" He turned to his soldiers. "See the friends we have! See what they can do with the god-killing weapon!"

A mighty if ragged cheer spread through the ranks.

Kyrkenall's voice was almost lost in the sound. "You've drained a lot of the energy keeping you alive." His eyes were only for Kalandra.

"I did what I had to do. And I've enough to keep me going for a while. Maybe that's all any of us have, anyway."

Elenai couldn't think of anything else they might have done, and nodded once in profound gratitude to the stalwart veteran.

Kyrkenall started to object, then lowered the emerald and stood stock-still, his expression puzzled. Ortok, who'd turned again to his friends, stared at him, his ears stiffening. His fur bristled.

The black-eyed archer faced them and smiled; not in his usual sly way, or even in his contented, almost self-conscious manner, but with an air of open wonderment, as though their regard was the most astonishing thing he'd ever beheld.

"Something is with him," Ortok warned.

Kyrkenall laughed.

Wearily, Elenai focused her view through the inner world and saw Ortok was absolutely right. Kyrkenall's energies had gone completely awry. While his own structure remained, something shifted and fluctuated within him. It was almost a mirror to what had happened to N'lahr. Where ordered threads had overtaken the commander, chaotic fly-aways had sifted into his best friend.

Kyrkenall pointed at them with his left hand. "Who are you?" he asked. "Are you children of hers?"

"He-Who-Unmakes has him," Kalandra said, voice low with dismay. "The God."

Elenai doubted her hearing. "How? I thought he was dead."

"It wasn't a weapon," Kalandra said, her voice sharpening as she reasoned it out. "It was a prison. She-Who-Makes didn't kill him, she had him trapped in there so she could control his energies. Even our gods got *that* part of the story wrong."

"Give me the answers, little ones," Kyrkenall said petulantly. "Are you her children?"

"We are descended of your children," Kalandra answered, voice surprisingly calm.

"What's happening to him?" Ortok asked.

Kalandra explained. "A god's energies were trapped in the staff. When we used it, some escaped, and now it's in Kyrkenall."

"How do we get it out of him?" Elenai asked.

Kalandra didn't answer, and Kyrkenall continued beaming. He looked up at the stars and laughed. "I know this place, and yet it is new. It delights me." He raised both hands and breathed in and out, then laughed joyously. "I know this man now, and *he* delights me." He reached for his wineskin, popping its top and taking a long swig. He lowered it, smacking his lips. "Oh, the pleasure this brings him, and me!" He took another drink, wiped his mouth with the back of his hand, and then his eyes fixed upon Kalandra. "How he longs for you! Come, kiss me, and then we shall mate!"

Kalandra remained calmly withdrawn. "I can't do that without a physical form. And had I one, I still wouldn't, because it's him I love, not you, and we aren't alone."

Kyrkenall and the God expressed dejection like an actor playing to the back seats. "Don't you love me?"

Once again Kalandra answered easily. "I don't know you."

The archer laughed, his mood springing from consternation to joy in a heartbeat. "But surely you do know me, one called Kalandra! Look how the wind blows, and the sand forms anew with every breath. Look at the beings here, all cast from a similar mold but different. I am that difference! I am the subtle things, and the large things and in the end I am all things. Now I have access to his thoughts and I know he holds you in high regard." Kyrkenall pointed to Ortok and Elenai. "How strange it is to be mortal. Why didn't I try this before? There is so much love! And there are fears, too, for others he loves who are not here. It is like the love one has for one's children. Where are mine?"

"They're long dead," Kalandra answered.

The manic pace of Kyrkenall's words subsided, and his expression fell. "I so enjoyed them, and the things they built, and the changes they made."

Finally Elenai could take no more. "Kyrkenall, are you still there?"

"I am," Kyrkenall answered. He sounded so much like himself Elenai stared. "And I'm fine, I think," he added.

"Is that you, or him?" she asked.

"It's both of us." Kyrkenall spoke once more, and this time, Elenai sensed in his stance, and inflection that it was he, not his inhabitant. "His thoughts are scattered. They're hard to hold in a channel. He wishes to communicate but is being torn apart by feelings about his children." Kyrkenall's voice grew flat, but strangely bright at the same time. "And I see, yes, I see what this one has learned. That my children stopped her because they thought I was dead, not knowing I was the thing they thought a weapon to use against her! And now they are gone. All of them."

"And now we must stop her," Kalandra said. "Or she will destroy all of us, and all the places we live. She told your children she wished to start again. That this had been an experiment but it was time to do things properly."

"He's not sure what he wants to do," Kyrkenall said. "He wants the rest of his energy. Much of it's trapped inside the weapon. But he can sense other pieces of it drifting out there. Some leaked out over the years, and of course some of it was used to blast her apart. Also, he loves her, even now. He thinks he can talk to her."

"What do you think?" Kalandra asked.

"I've tried talking to a woman who's done with my courting before. Oh, I see this surprises him. She's not a woman, he says, but there's some overlap." Kyrkenall pointed at Elenai. "Release the rest of the energies, and I will be whole. Then I will speak to her."

"I don't think we should release any more energy," Elenai said.

"It's mine," Kyrkenall asserted. "It's me. Not yours. Or you."

"We have no other way to stop the Goddess," Elenai said.

Kyrkenall looked blankly at her.

"Why don't you stay with Kyrkenall for a while?" Kalandra suggested to him. "You'll find it diverting."

Kalandra ignored Elenai's stunned look.

"You have no right to keep me from myself," the God declared through her friend, and Elenai thought he was actually quite right. She shook her head no anyway.

Kyrkenall staggered as white-gold mist sped from him and straight on for Elenai. She cried out in surprise. She didn't have time to try anything magical. A force battered her consciousness, dizzying her, working to overcome her hold upon her body.

She fought it, thinking of herself, beside her father, watching her little sister jumping up and down on the stage while her mother laughed. She was still Elenai, with her family, in the place that she remembered all of them best.

Her mind flailed with the tumbling desires and fears and desperation of a being whose own mind was alight with a hundred ideas at once. It was more than an avalanche, it was like a wave that swept up to engulf her, each drop of water a world of ideas and possibilities.

She thought of her mother's smile, her sister's joy, her father's laugh. The ideas billowed uselessly, then fell away, and streamed back to Kyrkenall.

Elenai sagged, gasping.

"I guess he can't endure for long without structure right now," Kyrkenall said. "He's back, but he's weak. Since he's not all here, he's not reasoning as well, and he can't extend himself for very long without growing weak. I guess you're not as good a fit for him as I am."

"It figures he'd choose you," Elenai said.

"Because I'm so charming?" Kyrkenall said with a smile.

"I can't think of anyone standing here who's more emblematic of chaos," Kalandra said lightly.

"The important thing is that we have the weapon," Kyrkenall said. "I think I can handle him until it's time to let him go."

"Are you sure?" Elenai asked. "Because it seemed like you were letting him control you."

"He wasn't doing anything bad," Kyrkenall said. "I don't think he's bad. And I know he doesn't want to stay in me. This is all just temporary."

Ortok rumbled deep in his chest. Elenai had nearly forgotten he was there.

"You Altenerai are never dull, I say you that! We have the weapon. When do we take it to fight the Goddess?"

27

Tunnel to Nowhere

A blurry landscape flashed into existence beyond the white road, then faded before Vannek could fasten upon any details. The winds on either side of them howled. The lightning had yet to cease its flashing.

"I think it's getting worse," Muragan said.

This was so obvious an observation Vannek refrained from comment.

Varama stopped her horse and peered to the void on the left side of the road. Vannek drew up beside her.

Once more the landscape flitted into being, and this time it blurred for a moment, as if seen through drunken eyes, then sprang to life.

Here, in the newborn land, they looked out upon a stretch of ale-colored sands under skies crushed beneath churning storm clouds. A lake so vast no shore could be glimpsed spread out beyond a beach only a few horselengths past the edge of the white road.

Muragan said something Vannek couldn't hear, for the wind was a roaring beast, blowing with such energy his horse sidestepped.

Varama dug into her belt pack.

"What are you doing?" Vannek asked.

Typically, the alten didn't answer.

Muragan moved his horse right up to him, stirrups nearly touching. He held the lead lines to their pack horses with an outstretched arm.

A distinctive white crest appeared on the horizon and the turquoise waters beyond the beach did a curious thing—they quietly pulled away, revealing a wider stretch of smooth gray sands.

The roaring around them intensified and Muragan screamed to be heard: "We've got to go!"

Varama had her hands in the pouch but had stopped her rummage. A spot of hazy air had appeared only a few feet beyond them, no larger than a shield.

"Are you opening a portal?" Vannek demanded.

Varama's mouth moved, but Vannek couldn't hear her.

A dark line of white-topped water sped closer, and the horses danced in worry. Vannek fought to keep his beast still and grabbed one rein of Varama's, as she seemed oblivious to its intent to flee.

Rather than attending to the nearby dangers, Varama bent the fingers of one hand and used them to stir the air. The shield-sized haze parted and a shaking rift opened. The alten gasped in pain and pushed with her hand. The tear widened. Maybe it was tall enough to ride into.

"Go!" Varama shouted, her sharp bark somehow piercing the din.

Vannek needed no urging, for that fast moving line had grown into a wall of liquid finality. He shouted for Muragan to follow, dropped Varama's reins, and kicked his eager mount into motion, ducking his head, and disappearing into a different world. Behind him the frightened pack animals whinnied as they were presumably pulled along by Muragan, but he couldn't tell if Varama joined them. This tunnel differed from the first they'd traveled. It rattled visually with a kaleidoscope of colors, but was eerily quiet after the wave. Vannek struggled for breath in the thin air. Worse, the tunnel's shining sides shook alarmingly. In vain he searched for a point of exit ahead, and saw nothing. Fury threatened to blind him. This blighted magical experiment would be their end. Varama had driven them to their deaths.

28

The Long Way Back

The ko'aye flew on over the mottled red landscape, long white humanoid figures trailing after. The chaos spirits were borne effortlessly by the wind and reached with long white limbs, young women of chalky complexion draped in funeral white, their eyes naught but holes through which hungry emptiness stared.

"I didn't think they'd look like dragons," Thelar said.

"There aren't any dragons," Rylin said in confusion. "Just dead women."

"We're seeing different things," Thelar decided. "What are we going to do? We've nothing to capture them with, whatever they look like."

"I'm more worried about what they're going to do when they get close to us."

"Turn on the shard," Thelar said. "I have an idea."

Rylin would have liked to have known what the idea was, but there wasn't time to ask, so he sent a thread into the stone. It hummed to life so easily it was almost as though it had awaited his coming. Alarmed, he scanned its depths, grateful he didn't sense the Goddess. So far.

As Drusa and Lelanc soared closer, the spirits chasing them slowed their pace.

Someone spoke his name from out of the air on his left. "Rylin."

His senses already tuned to the inner world, he had no trouble recognizing Varama's voice. He turned, starting in surprise at the ghostly image of his friend, suspended above the landscape in an only-partially realized saddle. No horse was visible.

Thelar, meanwhile, pulled energy from the hearthstone and cast it as though he were throwing crumbs to chickens. He shouted for Rylin to help.

"Leave the hearthstone active!" Varama shouted. "I'm opening a portal."

"Rylin!" Thelar cried.

Varama disappeared, leaving Rylin no time to register wonder, worry, or relief, for the nearest of the chaos spirits drifted eerily only a few spearlengths beyond Thelar. Six more of the beings came close behind.

Rylin looped energies deep in the hearthstone and pulled them free, then sent them arcing past the spirits. The closest pale specter and two others diverted toward it, like children chasing a ball. The other four held position farther out, as if indecisive.

The ko'aye passed so close overhead Rylin felt the wind of their wings. He heard the distinctive, raspy war cry of Drusa shouting for him to work the trap, but could spare no time to tell them the traps were gone.

His hair was already on end with so much magical energy in the air, but his skin prickled further with a surge from within the hearthstone. He groaned inwardly. The Goddess, probably come to reduce him to ash. Rylin dragged out as much energy as he could and sent it streaming into the sky—maybe Thelar could escape with the ko'aye in the confusion. At the same moment that the stone's energy grew, as though a monster fish rose from the deeps of a great lake, a wobbly portal shimmered into existence to his right. The Naor general galloped from the narrow slash on a silvery mare. He immediately pulled up on the reins, but Thelar had to throw himself out of the way. The Naor blood mage came close behind, leading several panicking mounts of the Altenerai stables.

All the activity proved of great interest to the chaos spirits. A great white hand stretched out from one phantom to pass through Muragan. He reeled, clutching his chest and dropping his lead lines.

Rylin sent a steam of energy past the chaos spirit's head before she could reach again. The phantom swiveled her whole body to swim through the sky after it.

The riderless animals danced in a tight circle, shying from both the spirits and the ko'aye circling in the sky to the rear. Vannek interposed his restless mare to prevent a crush against the standing humans and his mage, still stricken but maintaining his seat. One horse, a bay, miscalculated its steps and abruptly slid down the steep side of their hill, squealing in fear.

"Pour out more!" Rylin cried, and flung energies for the spirits to consume. Thelar, who'd climbed to one knee, did the same.

At last, a final figure rode through the portal, followed a heartbeat later by what seemed a river's worth of water. Varama turned the animal on the instant and closed the portal even as the waves struck her mount's forelocks and knocked Thelar flat.

Rylin quickly shut down the stone, glancing between the panting figure in the khalat, and the spirits, drifting aimlessly just beyond them. Thelar pushed himself up, shaking out his dripping sleeves.

"They're not going to delay long," Varama said. And it was her, really her. Rylin stared for only a moment, noting how her frizzy hair was awry, and how strained and tired her eyes were. As she set her feet on the ground, he threw his arms about her and pressed her tight. She stiffened, then patted him on the back and gave him a single shoulder clasp.

"I was afraid you were dead," he told her quietly.

"It is good to see you," she said. "But there are things to do."

He stepped apart, then discovered Vannek and the blood mage watching curiously. Drusa glided in close. "Why do you not make to trap them?" she called.

"We lost the traps," Thelar shouted.

"This little shard isn't large enough to fend them off," Varama said. "I'll have to open another portal."

"I thought you said you only had enough energy for one portal, and barely," Vannek said suspiciously. He climbed down from his own horse, which was nervously keeping one eye upon the ko'aye.

"I'll draw more energy from their hearthstone," Varama said.

Rylin raised a hand in greeting to the general, but he had already turned to check on his mage, wobbling in his saddle.

"The Goddess is aware of this hearthstone," Rylin told Varama. "She's already killed M'vai through one, and I sensed an awareness in its depths."

"Then I shall have to work quickly."

Rylin had innumerable questions, but he held off. "Don't take us to Cerai. She's working on her own agenda."

"I'm not surprised." Varama had already opened the stone and drawn upon its threads.

The portal circle that flared into existence this time was more substantial, expanding from a small golden ring into a wide, glittering circle. All seven of the chaos entities snapped to face it, like fish in a bowl turning at the same moment.

"Go," Varama said.

Rylin called to Drusa and Lelanc, gliding in their slow circle to the rear, remembering how little they'd liked the first portal journey. "Come on! We have to move fast!"

"You want us to go through another?" Drusa replied.

"Not to the betrayer again," Lelanc said.

"Darassus!" Varama shouted, voice strained. "Go!"

Vannek motioned for the blood mage, pale and sagging, and he just managed to direct his reluctant horse inside. Vannek, who'd gathered the reins of two of their pack horses, briefly met Rylin's eyes in an acknowledgment, then went after.

"You next," Rylin said to Thelar.

"I'm fine."

"You're wetter."

Thelar chuckled. "I don't know why that's funny," he said, then headed in, guiding the remaining pack animals.

The ko'aye were gabbling at one another. The spirits loomed close, their arms extended. And the hearthstone glowed fiercely, as though it might burst at any moment. The Goddess, Rylin knew, was near.

"We're going to Darassus!" Rylin shouted. "Hurry!"

Drusa called something to Lelanc and then glided down and through, pulling her wings tight at the last moment. Lelanc eyed the portal with trepidation, then her head swung up to take in the chaos spirits. She cawed in alarm and followed her friend, whipping so close to the ground her wings brushed the grass tips. She vanished through the golden circle.

Hearthstone in one hand, Varama pushed at Rylin, and they went through almost together, her horse on her heels.

As they hurried forward Rylin sensed the hearthstone's power ebbing and flowing.

To right and left the walls shook, shimmering first with ebon energy, then with strands of blue and green, as though someone had painted a landscape and then poured water on it so the colors ran.

Varama let out surprised exclamation, for the hearthstone burned brighter than ever.

So distracted was he by it that Rylin nearly missed that they approached the end of their journey. With relief, he ran clear and onto what he quickly saw was the wooden stage of the amphitheater in Darassus. He'd last stood here when he'd stabbed the queen.

Varama came through, pulling on the lead line, though she had eyes only for the glowing shard. The moment the horse was through she turned and lobbed the stone back through the portal, then spiraled the hole closed.

She stared at the place where the opening in reality had been.

Though he was sad to have witnessed the loss of such a valuable tool, Rylin was impressed by Varama's disposal. With luck, that meant the Goddess wouldn't be coming here. The question was why they themselves had. "Did we come here for reinforcements?"

"As well as for tools," Varama answered. "And thanks to the queen, there was already a weak spot that made this place easy to reach."

Rylin turned to take in the shattered ruin of the amphitheater. Lelanc was in the air, circling, Drusa on the stage edge. Thelar, thoroughly wet and bedraggled, squished a foot into one boot as if to emphasize his condition. The two Naor had dismounted to stare back at the cleanup crew, scattered among the stands with mattocks.

"I've many questions," Varama said as she turned to Rylin. "Order your thoughts, and we'll link."

She looked as though she meant to begin immediately, and Rylin held up a hand. "Wait a moment. I've got to get my thoughts together." He couldn't help grinning. "Damn, but it's good to see you."

"Go on and kiss her already," Vannek said softly.

Varama ignored the Naor. "Yes," Varama said. "It pleases me as well. Are you ready?"

He smiled faintly, then counted to five and sorted his recent memories. Finally, he nodded assent.

In a moment she was working her spell, and he thought back through the actions they'd taken since they'd fled through Cerai's portal. How Kyrkenall and Elenai had departed and N'lahr had weakened. He remembered the attack the Goddess launched against Cerai's fortress, and the renegade alten's unleashing of the spirits. He shared Tesra speaking with him about Cerai's betrayal and M'vai's death. Though he strove for discipline, he couldn't fully contain his worries and sorrow over Varama's imagined death, and his fears that N'lahr had been wrong about her survival.

When Varama finally broke away, a smile quirked at the corner of her mouth. "It is good to be so well loved, Rylin. Thank you for that. As for how we survived, the Goddess had little interest in me once I closed the portal. After watching Rialla do it, and holding open Cerai's, I imagined I could accomplish the opening of one, but it took me some time to develop a safe method given our circumstances and the limited power available."

"You seem to have figured it out now," the blood mage said. He sounded both impressed and pained.

Varama faced him, her expression shifting to one of deadly seriousness. "It's said blood mages can contact people across vast distances without a hearthstone. Is that something you can do?"

"It is," Muragan answered with weary curiosity.

He looked as though he meant to say more, but by then the workers were calling to them, asking how they'd gotten there, and if the battle was won. He glanced over at them.

"You are healthy still?" Varama asked.

"I already feel better, thank you."

Varama returned to her main concern. "The land treaders, they serve as sort of sorcerous batteries for your spells. Will you have to kill one for a sending?"

"It may not kill one," Muragan answered. "Why do you ask?"

"Because we have to contact Elenai, and quickly. How well do you have to know a person to send to them?"

Once again Rylin was astonished by the speed with which Varama developed a new idea and implemented it. Behind them, Thelar addressed the workers, explaining that the war still waged without providing expansive details.

"Do you know approximately where she might be?" Muragan asked.

"The wastelands of Kanesh," Varama answered.

"I've never been to the wastelands," Muragan said. "But I've passed through Kanesh. It might be possible."

"I don't need 'might be's." Varama said. "I need you to find a way. The hearthstones have grown too dangerous to use."

Muragan cleared his throat. "Very well. I will find a way."

"Good. It must be your priority. Contact me when you're ready."

Lelanc circled low, asking what she should do, and Rylin called for her to seek food and rest. The squires had set up a rookery for them on the palace grounds after the battle of Darassus, and he presumed it was still there. He raised a hand in farewell as she flapped off. A moment later Drusa followed her.

He turned to Varama. "What are we going to do about the chaos spirits? Should we make more stones and try to capture them once more?"

"I think we shall have what we need without them," Varama said. "And we are short on time in any case."

Thelar formally greeted Varama with a salute and a bow of his head. "We'd been told you were dead, Alten. I'm glad that was wrong."

Rylin felt a pang of guilt for having intentionally kept information to the contrary from him.

The exalt reported the good news he'd learned from the workers: Tretton, Gyldara, and the Darassan troops had returned to Darassus, along with some Kaneshi cavalry.

Varama led them through the rubble on stage and out through a rear ramp. Soon they were on their way toward the city wall. After a brief consultation with Varama, Vannek and Muragan made their farewells and hurried off on their mounts.

"What happened back there after we left the paradise realm?" Rylin asked. Thelar, riding on Varama's other side, listened intently with him as she summarized her encounter with an incurious goddess and her long journey upon the white road with Vannek and Muragan. She then informed them N'lahr had developed a plan that would get them free of Cerai, explaining in brief about the commander's connection to a hearthstone shard.

They neared the main gate to Darassus. The repairs had advanced in the intervening days, for new stones had almost completely replaced those blasted during the Naor attack. More startling was the presence of men who almost certainly were Naor, for few Darassan men wore beards. They were passing stones along to hoists and clambering along the scaffolding as though they belonged there.

"Someone is showing foresight," Varama said. "I wonder who decided to incorporate the Naor into the building crew?"

A horn call sounded from the gate tower, the high clear notes announcing the arrival of Altenerai. The call was taken up deeper in the city, which meant a bugler on duty within the palace had repeated it. Over the last years the queen had dispensed with that formality, and it pleased Rylin to hear it again.

"More foresight," Varama said in approval, then patted her frizzy locks.

"It's pulled to the left," Rylin said.

"Thank you." Varama produced a brush from an inside pocket, unfolded the handle, and set quickly to work with the curling mass of hair. "Better?" she asked.

Rylin nodded approval.

She halted before advancing through the opening gate and eyed them both. "Now we must make haste. For a short time we have Cerai at a disadvantage. We need to act before she knows it. Both our enemies suffer from the same weakness: arrogance. And that shall prove a tremendous advantage." She turned to acknowledge the salute from the gate guards, then led them into the city.

29

What the Future Holds

The dragon was sleek and rippling with muscles beneath its gleaming scales, a tidy nightmare of shadow and fang, small only in comparison to the others Vannek had seen, for it towered over the surrounding tents even when lying on its belly, crunching a bloody cow carcass.

When the other dragons had been eating, they had only responded if something to eat or drink was placed directly in front of them. The rest of the time they merely lay in place until one of the mages commanded them.

This one kept looking over at him and his bodyguard as it chewed, its expression unreadable.

It crunched through a bone so thick it must have been a part of the bovine pelvis. He liked this dragon. It seemed strong. Muragan's two assistants had ably completed the job of healing it, and he hadn't been certain of their abilities.

Only a short while later, he stood before his remaining soldiers, facing him in a half circle. There was no stage, only a chair, which he climbed on to be better seen. Few were here. Some of his people remained within Cerai's fortress, and some were out among the Dendressi. He'd initially been surprised to hear how many volunteered to rebuild the walls they'd dreamed for years of tearing down, but on further reflection it made sense. They were receiving more than food and wine—they had found a purpose through which they could forge fellowships. Men need community.

Those left before him weren't smart enough to recognize the need, or bold enough to seek its fulfillment on their own. He'd have to connect them, despite their vices and prejudices. He'd have to provide both motive and method to move them.

He gathered his thoughts and began to speak. "Twice now our forces and the Dendressi battled the queen and the sorcerous thing she summoned. In the first battle, we struck by surprise and destroyed her followers. I took the queen's head. But her sorcery was mighty and the death goddess she called up flew away, killing the very land she moved over. If the Goddess is allowed to live, she will destroy every realm, from here to the Baneridge Mountains. Nothing will remain. No crops, no beasts, no people. Nothing. Which is why we must ready ourselves for battle."

His soldiers listened in stunned silence. "Most of the men who went with me are still alive, but they're in a fortress with Anzat, and Anzat has allied with a mad Dendressi exile who wants the death god's power for herself. I mean to get them free of her. To be clear," he said, "we face a demon goddess on one hand and a sorceress on the other. You might wonder what ordinary warriors like you and me can do against these creatures. But I think the mages count too much on their sorcery. The right blade, at the right time, can make the difference. I mean us to be that difference. Let the Dendressi fight with their magic. When the time is right, and the opening is there, we will be the sharp blade! We will draw the blood and strike down our foes!"

They stirred at that. He wished he had more to tell them. "Gather provisions. Hone your swords. Sharpen your spearpoints. We must be ready to march at a moment's notice. When the time comes, I will lead the way."

The cheer that greeted that final pronouncement surprised him, and he stood looking out at their glad faces, pretending he understood their acclaim.

Vannek did not let them cheer long. At his signal, they slowly quieted, and then his bodyguard dismissed them. After taking status reports from their leaders, Vannek joined Muragan, who was kneeling in the dirt.

The blood mage had burned away a wide swathe of grass, assisted by the scrawny low-level apprentices. They were the only surviving Naor mages from the battle of Darassus, for they'd been left with the trailing baggage. Muragan wielded a sharpened spear to incise intricate runes, lines, and circles into the black earth.

One of the land treaders munched on a heap of hay nearby. The mound of manure behind the animal was already almost a third the size of the fodder in front.

"Quite a stench," Vannek observed.

Muragan only seemed to notice him then. The blood mage's face was still pale after the attack of the chaos spirit, and Vannek would have asked how he felt, if he hadn't worried about making him look weak in front of the assistants.

"When I told them to bring the beast I should have had them move it farther off," Muragan said. "But we're almost ready now."

Vannek again scanned the two assistants, and once more was underwhelmed by their appearance. But these two, after all, had finished healing that dragon based only on advance instruction from Muragan. "How is this pair doing?"

"They're better than nothing," Muragan said, which Vannek knew to be a compliment.

The apprentices strove to pretend they hadn't heard, but there was no missing the prideful way both raised their heads.

"How likely is this summoning to work?" Vannek asked.

"There is always some risk with such attempts," Muragan admitted.

"How much risk will you be under?" Vannek hadn't meant to reveal his own concern, but the blood mage heard it in his voice anyway and looked up at him. Vannek kept his expression bland.

"I'm taking appropriate precautions. I would like it far, far better if I knew Queen Elenai's precise location, and if she knew I'd be contacting her. But this may work regardless. I'm honestly surprised the Dendressi even considered the idea."

"It's that Varama. I think she's desperate."

"Desperate, or inventive?" Muragan asked.

"Both."

"You look terrible," Muragan said quietly, almost solicitously. "You should rest."

That familiarity set Vannek scowling. Did he think they were friends and equals? That he would trust anything the mage told him without due consideration? He had never yet provided a believable explanation about his almost selfless devotion.

Vannek came very close to reminding the mage of his place. And then he saw just how slowly Muragan climbed to his feet, and that he was so pale even the blue of his eyes seemed lighter, and despite his natural inclinations he felt a contrary impulse and spoke to it with very little fore-thought. "You're pale and sweating," he said brusquely. "Turn things over to your apprentices and rest."

The blood mage frowned, but as he walked toward another batch of lines and lowered his spear, his hand trembled. He swore lightly. "Perhaps you're right, Lord General."

"Come. You can brief me while you recuperate."

After some curt instructions about deepening the lines without length-ening them, Muragan followed Vannek to the general's tent.

Vannek found himself offering the man some of Chargan's wine. Much as he hated to admit it, he'd grown fond of the stuff while drinking with Rylin. He passed it over, then sat on the stool across from the mage. The tent was dim, apart from the sunlight streaming in from the smoke open-ing in the center of the roof.

"Thank you, my liege. This is fine wine."

Vannek nodded his agreement.

"Did you want a briefing?" Muragan asked. "There's not much you don't know."

"What I want is a real answer." He spoke slowly, the way his father had when he was serious, without sounding stern. "You've served me loyally, yet I still don't know why. And don't tell me it's because I'm your liege."

"You have vision, and tenacity." Muragan wiped his brow.

"You could have blended in with the Dendressi long ago. You said so."

"Could I? Maybe. But maybe I'm tired of pretending. I'd come all this way to find Chargan, only to learn when I got here we'd lost again, and Chargan was dead. I thought I would see what you were like before I walked away from it all." He laughed to himself. "I thought I might even mold you, but this pot's already fired. You have greatness in you, Vannek."

It was the first time Muragan had ever called him by name, all the more surprising because of the blood mage's piercing gaze. He continued: "You're the only one of your father's brood with his instincts."

"You knew my father?"

Muragan nodded slowly, gravely. "He was our future. Even Mazakan knew it. Men followed your grandfather out of duty and fear. They followed your father out of devotion. He inspired everyone he met, no matter their tribe. You have some of that same gift. Your brothers were fools not to see it."

"It's because of my woman's shape," Vannek said in disgust.

"More fools us, then. We can learn from the Dendressi, who make space for women to counsel, and to war, and to lead. They do not have to pretend to be men, because they can take whatever path they excel on."

Vannek mulled over the gentlest criticism he'd yet heard of his choice. "My spirit feels like a man's spirit," he said at last.

"If true, then you're as much a man as I. Maybe more. But perhaps that's because you don't know what a woman's spirit feels like when it's not trapped in Naor roles."

"That might be right," Vannek conceded. "I know the only person I've ever desired was a man. If I truly had a man's spirit, I would only like women."

"That's not true," Muragan said with a laugh. "N'lahr's a man, isn't he? Perhaps the best man among all the Dendressi. But he's loved men and women."

Vannek was surprised someone so highly placed had swallowed such nonsense. "Those are just lies grandfather told to make the Dendressi look weak."

"No, those are stories even the Dendressi know. It's not a secret, General. Their only taboos are underage or underpowered mates, and rape. Anything between equal adults who both want it is fine by them. They never say, 'oh, that's a man-loving Altenerai.' Nobody cares."

"Are N'lahr and Kyrkenall lovers?" Vannek asked. "That man is beautiful as any woman."

Muragan laughed with more gusto. "You're too ready to judge by appearances, still! Like someone would do with you. Kyrkenall only wants women. But does that matter, should it matter? Knowing this, don't you still respect him and N'lahr both?"

It was then Vannek finally guessed the truth. "You're a man lover, aren't you?"

He saw the guess had hit home. Muragan eyed him warily.

"By the Three," Vannek said slowly. "Why didn't you go hide among the Dendressi years ago?"

"Because I'm not Dendressi, am I?"

"No. You're Naor. And so am I. That just means more than it did before."

"I would like to think so. Our people would be stronger with more hands and heads allowed to join in the work."

"Yes. Yes, they will." He put his own hand to the mage's shoulder. "Let's get you back to work on that circle."

"I've said too much." Muragan shook his head.

"No," Vannek told him gently. "You've given me the truth and that's a crafting material. Now let's go. We have to win one more battle before we can bring any future to life."

30

The Queen in Blood

Rylin found it sheer joy to drop into the warm water of the Altenerai baths, and almost agony to depart, but he forced himself not to linger. Once he dried off, he found Thelar risen from his own bath and changing into the garments squires had laid out for them, uniform pants and shirts and extra footgear. While they'd permitted their khalats to be cleaned, neither man had turned over their blades, and they wore them as they headed upstairs.

Three figures stood at the duty desk in heated conversation with the squire behind it. The man at the forefront seemed frustrated he could not speak with Alten Varama, or someone, anyone, who could provide information he sought.

Rylin reluctantly accepted he'd have to volunteer himself, then turned at a shout from behind.

"Alten Rylin! Sir!"

Squire Donahla, of the second rank, jogged up to him. The short-haired brunette drew to a stop and presented him with a formal salute.

Rylin and Thelar returned it.

"At ease," Rylin said.

The young woman looked anything but. "I'm glad to see you, sir," she said. "And you, Commander."

"Exalt will do," Thelar said. "N'lahr is our commander."

Donahla's head bobbed nervously, and she tried, failed, then successfully brought her eyes up to meet Rylin's. "You may hear rumors of things I've said. Terrible things. About you. I'm sorry."

Rylin was distracted because he'd heard his name mentioned by the group at the duty desk. "It's fine, Donahla. Squires talk about the higher ranks all the time."

"No, sir, not like this. I said horrible things. And so did Squire Hamar. Neither of us really meant them. And I know we should always say what we mean, but it's like our opinions weren't our own."

"Synahla spoke with them," Thelar said to Rylin.

That partly explained the matter. Rylin smiled reassuringly. "Squire, I don't want you or Hamar to worry. The Exalt Commander used spell work to change a lot of the minds she couldn't fool—it just means you were wiser than she could handle through honorable means. How long did it take for you and Hamar to come around?"

"Honestly, sir, we didn't feel fully right about you until yesterday morning, even after all the amazing things you did at the battle. I'm just so embarrassed. I feel terrible. So does Hamar," she added.

"You're starting to embarrass me," Rylin said. "It'd help if we put it behind us, all right?"

"Thank you, sir."

"Now if you'll excuse us, Exalt Thelar and I are apparently going to provide some answers before we can grab a meal."

"Yes, sir." Donahla snapped off another sharp salute. "Thank you again, sir."

Rylin and Thelar returned the salute and faced the duty desk. The three civilians waited expectantly and the third ranker's eagerness for them to take charge was palpable.

They started forward. "How many more do you think Synahla twisted like that?" Rylin asked Thelar softly.

"I'm not sure. I'd think she would only expend spell energy on the most disruptive."

"Any chance the ones I fought on the stairs were altered by her?"

"It would make deciding their fate a lot simpler."

He might have said more, but their conversation died as they reached the duty desk and the oldest of the three men stepped in front of them. "Alten Rylin," he said, "I'm councilor Brevahn. Do you have a moment?"

"I do. This is Exalt Thelar."

"Exalt," Brevahn said with a courteous nod. The councilor quickly introduced the two behind him as candidates running for open council seats. After they presented themselves, Brevahn spoke on. "Word reached us that a small band of survivors had returned, but we've heard nothing else."

Rylin realized the councilor's agitation arose not just from worry about the troops and the course of the battle, but from the fate of the future queen in whom plans for governance must figure prominently. So he got right to the point. "Elenai was alive, and well, when I last saw her several days ago. We lost some brave warriors, but we partially succeeded and we're readying to take the battle back to our enemies."

"I see. I'm sorry to hear about the losses, but I am glad to learn Elenai's alive. The realms are depending upon her."

"So are we," Rylin said, then decided against explaining exactly what she was doing. Who was to say whether Cerai had informants who might somehow be in contact?

"Can you provide us with no more details?" Brevahn asked.

"We're in the midst of the conflict. I'm afraid other details should wait until it concludes."

Brevahn sighed. "And I anticipate that you won't be able to comment upon when that conclusion might be?"

"I'm afraid not."

Though obviously frustrated, Brevahn bowed his head in acknowledgment. "I understand the need for secrecy. But if Queen Leonara hadn't erred so far in hiding official actions, we wouldn't be in this mess."

"Don't I know it," Rylin said, then indicated Thelar. "We both do. You'll be informed just as soon as the current operations are completed."

"Thank you, Alten. I can be contacted in my council chambers, or at my home. I'm sure the palace messengers will know how to find me."

They made their farewells, and then, finally, Rylin and Thelar headed into the dining hall. Legend had it that Altenerai supped in the queen's banquet hall, but more often they ate in the officers' quarters, with fourth rankers and up, a rectangular room furnished with long tables and benches. Old landscape tapestries from the Allied Realms hung on the stone walls, and high mullioned windows strained bright sunbeams into the space.

Today one of the tables had been decorated with a blue cloth, weighted down with platters of food, pitchers, and goblets.

Gyldara rose at their entrance. Her Altenerai khalat was sparkling clean. With her bright eyes, golden hair, and refined features, she had always been a natural beauty. She came to attention and formally saluted them.

Rylin and Thelar returned the gesture. Rylin's ring no longer lit, as Gyldara's did, and he knew a pang of loss, wondering if his would ever again shine with the sacred light.

"Hail Thelar," Gyldara said. "Hail, Rylin of the Thousand."

Rylin smiled sadly. "Hail, Gyldara Dragonsbane."

"The squires prepared this feast for you heroes of the queen's battle," she said. "Varama went straight to her workshops, though. No one's told me what happened. I was hoping you would."

"It will be our pleasure," Rylin said.

Rylin and Thelar traded out explaining while they ate. Gyldara's lovely face registered shock and horror and worry in equal measures. Although news of N'lahr's condition and Cerai's betrayals firmed her lips, it was the news of the Goddess that shook her most.

Learning that his friend Mehrdok was nearly recovered from his throat wound, Thelar begged off, saying they didn't have very long and he wanted a quick word with him. He departed with a platter of food and a wine bottle.

"You two used to hate each other," Gyldara said once the door had closed behind the exalt. "Now you look sad he's gone."

"I think I'm just sad in general. But he's a good man, and I wish I'd seen it sooner."

She eyed him over the rim of her goblet. "Remember after the ring ceremony, when Asrahn told us we were too eager?"

"I remember."

"I tried not to look eager from then on, but I felt it. I had to prove myself."

"You trained harder than any of us."

"Yes." Gyldara wasn't boasting over a simple matter of fact. None of the Altenerai appointed during Devaven's tenure had spent as much time on the practice field as she. "But that didn't help me when the true tests came. I believed everything Denaven said. I fell for the whole rotten conspiracy. If Elenai hadn't risked her life to spare me, I'd be dead now."

"I believed Denaven, too," Rylin said.

"When we start training squires again, we'll have to do better—somehow keep them from making the same mistakes."

Rylin agreed. "It's there in the oath. Heart and Mind. You can't be too rigid about rules and strictures, but lead only with your heart and you're too easily swayed by passing emotion, too easily manipulated. Varama was right, as usual. I was lazy with my mind."

"We've both been out of balance. We were letting other people do our thinking for us. It's a cautionary example to sharpen all who know of it—and I'll make sure they do."

Rylin raised his goblet. "A toast to a balance. And a toast to you, to be thinking we'll live to train new squires."

She arched one eyebrow as she gently touched the side of her goblet to his own. "You don't think we will?" she asked.

He chuckled. "I hope we will. But who can say? And I worry you have to survive the front line to really understand. It's not like Asrahn didn't drill these lessons repeatedly."

"Maybe veterans needed to tell squires more what it's really like. Maybe the truth would've sunk in."

"And maybe we'd have kept on dreaming of brave deeds and glory."

"We have to do more," she insisted. "I'm sorry. I'm not trying to argue."

"No offense taken. I always liked how stubborn you were. You wanted to make a difference. Now you are."

"So are you! You've saved the lives of so many people. Asrahn would be proud. He once groused to me you needed molding he couldn't provide."

"He was right. He was a wise man. Maybe a wise woman can follow after him." He tipped his goblet at her.

"Me, Master of Squires?" She sounded honestly surprised by an idea that appeared obvious and natural. "Shouldn't that go to a veteran, like Tretton?"

"You're a veteran, now."

"Not like him."

"There's no one better suited. The older Altenerai never wanted Asrahn's duties because they know they lack the connection with students, but you always have a following of squires. And you were the only one in our class who wasn't trying to take advantage of her position. Cargen was Denaven's understudy. Lasren and I were strutting around soaking up the benefits and pretending we weren't upset no one was writing songs about us. K'narr–"

"He was all right," Gyldara said. "I've wondered ever since he died if he was really in on it or if Cargen had just tricked him. Like I was tricked. Maybe if he'd just had someone to show him the lay of things, he might be with us today."

Rylin thought back to the lanky alten and his quiet way with the squires. "He made wrong choices, and sometimes you don't get a second chance."

She eyed him through her lashes as she poured another drink. "Do you know, I think this is the longest conversation I've ever had with you without you trying to get me into bed."

Rylin's mouth fell open and he struggled to find a response.

She laughed. "You thought you were so charming. Here's the funny thing—this is the first time I've ever thought that might be fun."

"Now, when I'm spent and haggard and a little broken?"

"Now, when you're no longer a boy." She laughed again. "By the gods. I've actually made you blush! I wish Lasren could see this." She stilled then, her laughter dying on her lips, the glint fading from her eyes.

He lifted his goblet. "To Lasren."

"To Lasren," she said solemnly, and they drank.

Rylin coaxed her into describing her role in the battle for Alantris, and she wormed from him the account of his own adventures.

Their whole career they had walked parallel paths, overlapping experiences with many of the same people, and in the last weeks they had realized the solitude and weight of the role they'd labored for. Of all others immediately before and after in the ranks, few were left alive, and none of them remained within the corps.

As a callow youth, he'd marveled over her athleticism, her determination, and her physical beauty. Gyldara had never been blind to the effect her appearance had upon others, and had adopted a cool reserve lest any think her friendship something more. She and Rylin had frequently been rivals, first as squires striving always to stand out, then as Altenerai, desperate to prove themselves worthy of the ring they'd been awarded in peacetime.

In hindsight, their past jealousies were laughable. Before him now was no distant comrade, but someone warm and wise and sad, and all the more lovely now that her soul was open to him. He regretted the wasted years when he wasn't the kind of person in whom such trust could be invested.

They were in the midst of conversation when the opening of the door interrupted and a dignified, familiar figure entered. It was Tretton, immaculate in his well-ordered khalat, the white of his beard and mustache standing out starkly against his black skin. He pressed a hand over his chest in salute, lighting his ring at the same moment. Rylin and Gyldara returned the gesture, and once more Rylin looked down at his flickering sapphire.

"Hail, Altenerai," Tretton said, and walked toward their table even as Rylin and Gyldara greeted him in turn.

"Do you want to join us?" Rylin couldn't recall a time when Tretton had shown any interest in doing so, but gestured at the bench across from him.

The older man shook his head. "I just wanted a quick word." His eyes shifted to Gyldara, who started to rise.

"No, stay." Tretton raised a scarred palm. He faced Rylin. "Varama seldom hands out compliments, but when I spoke with her this afternoon she had a number for you. You must truly have impressed her. That's not an easy thing. I doubt she'll ever tell you, herself, so I thought you should know she holds you in high esteem. She says you've grown into a clever, dedicated, and quick-thinking officer."

He'd seen that Varama was fond of him, but the specific words were immensely gratifying. "Thank you for telling me, Tretton." It was strange to address the older man by name. He was so removed from the rest of them it still felt improper to leave off his rank. "She's one of my favorite people."

"As well she should be." The veteran turned his gaze upon them both. "Asrahn worried his recent teaching had been diluted by Denaven, but it seems like he won out. You've both proven yourselves a credit to the corps. There may be hope for the next generation after all."

"All two of us," Gyldara said.

Tretton acknowledged this sentiment with a sharp nod. "The empty chairs at the table, the empty rooms in the hall—those are like piercing blades. Your lot fell faster, but that happens when the unseasoned meet the front line."

"Some of the unseasoned met Kyrkenall," Gyldara said.

"Some of the unseasoned were traitors," Tretton said. "Surely you don't blame him for striking them down."

"No," Gyldara replied. "But I did, because he killed my sister. Then I learned that she, too, was a traitor."

Tretton waggled his finger toward an empty goblet. Rylin filled it and passed it over.

The whitebeard drank, nodded his thanks, and set the vessel on the table edge. "It's easy to lose your way. You have to remember your oath. It's not just a recitation." He smiled thinly. "Ah, you two don't need me to lecture you. You know what you're about."

"I hope we do," Gyldara said.

He nodded and was all business once more. "Varama wants us to ride to the Naor camp. We'll have to use blood magic to contact Elenai." He frowned in distaste. "Much as I hate the idea, I don't have a better one, and I suppose it's necessary."

"How soon does she want us?"

"We're to meet at the stables in a quarter hour." He took another drink, then returned the goblet. "I'll see you there."

With that, and a respectful nod, Tretton departed.

Rylin and Gyldara were silent until the door closed behind him.

"That was remarkable," she confessed. "Did you ever think that old man would treat us like equals?"

"I can't say that I did. Are there any left alive from his day, apart from him?"

"I think Falnas is still living happily ever after in Ekhem."

"Not too many of us live to retire, do they."

"Not lately. I suppose we'd better get to the stables."

"I suppose so." He wanted to tell her that he hoped their conversation would continue soon, then realized, with a surety, that it would.

Before long, they were inside the Naor camp beside one of the giant dray animals and a complex diagram drawn in the dirt. A large canvas wall closed them off from the rest of the forces.

Tretton remained beyond that wall, not wishing to watch a ceremony he looked upon with distaste, and Gyldara, presumably not wanting him to stand alone, remained with him.

Rylin wasn't keen on watching himself, no matter that the blood mage had said the land treaders had been built for this, or that Rylin would gladly have slain all the beasts himself a few days ago if it would have kept the Naor from the walls. Now the injury or death of the smelly beast was distasteful to him.

Perhaps it was distasteful to Varama as well. It was hard to know, for the somber cast to her face might be the result of various facets of their situation.

A curious Thelar paced about the diagrams. Two tired young Naor apprentice mages stood to one side. Muragan examined each line in the dirt, occasionally making a very minute adjustment with aid of his spear-point. Varama walked with him, watching with her habitual intensity.

Vannek joined Rylin. "You're watching their work as though you understand it. I keep forgetting you're a mage. You don't have the manner of one."

"Oh?" Rylin asked.

The general seemed unconscious of the implied prejudice against magic workers. "You remind me of a friend of mine," he continued. "He was one of our mages." Vannek turned his head, though Rylin sensed it wasn't the diagram he studied, but some memory. "There are a lot of stupid things our people do. Instead of shielding those with mage sight, we mock them. We lock them away, and say they're women and worse than women, until and unless they show signs of real power. Someone like you would never have risen to honors unless you were a powerful and well-connected talent."

"I'm not."

"But you have some skill, yes? And it enhances your abilities as a warrior. A wise leader would lift up his mages."

"A wise leader lifts up all his people."

Vannek looked shrewdly at him. "You are more than you seem."

"And you never fail to intrigue me."

The general didn't smile, exactly, but the compliment had obviously pleased him. He looked as if he was about to say more, but Muragan called out then that all was in readiness.

"I can begin," the general said, "if the Altenerai are ready."

"We're ready," Varama affirmed.

Muragan bowed his head to her, then breathed out once, like a diver readying to leap into cold water. He waved to the man on the back of the giant land treader.

The burly Naor drove a pointed spear deep into the large hump along the beast's back.

Rylin winced. The beast itself didn't seem to notice the injury.

The reek of the land treader was joined by the scent of blood, but it was the magic in the air that held Rylin's attention. His arm hairs stood upright under his uniform coat. Muragan closed his eyes, his hands low, one palm to the diagram, the other to the trough into which the blood streamed down from the canvas hose upon the land treader. Astonishingly, the beast stood docile.

Rylin eyed the blood mage, knowing from their previous discussions that he was in the midst of a sending, one to a woman he barely knew, in a part of a realm he'd never visited. "Has Muragan performed a lot of sendings?" Rylin asked Vannek.

"He was one of Grandfather's chief mages, so I'm sure he's done many. I've no worry about him. The problem will be on the other end. Your new queen had better be near some malleable substance. Water, sand, blood. Otherwise Muragan won't be able to appear beside her."

Muragan let out a low groan, twitched a finger, and the ganglier of his two assistants shouted up: "Again!"

Once more the drover plunged the spear into the beast. This time it rumbled, and Tretton remarked outside that the whole affair was distasteful. Rylin agreed. The hose extended down the land treader's back expanded and disgorged a well of blood.

Muragan gritted his teeth. Corded neck muscles stood out.

And then his mouth spread in something that wasn't quite a smile, but more a grimace of triumph.

"I have her," he said. "Ready yourselves."

Rylin watched in horror as streams of slick blood swirled up from the trough, swiftly expanding into the shape of a human woman. His eyes shifted from Thelar, to Varama, and to Vannek, each displaying varying levels of revulsion

"It's just how the spell works," Vannek said, eying him in dark amusement.

In moments the awful figure resembled Elenai.

"Varama?" The bloody mouth moved and Elenai's voice emerged from it, though she sounded as if she spoke while slurping water.

Varama spoke quickly, confirming that Elenai had recovered the weapon. Rylin hadn't realized just how worried Varama must have been about that until he saw her let out a long breath.

Elenai relayed the startling news that she'd been joined by a small kobalin army, but that paled in comparison to their discovery of the lost alten, Kalandra, alive, although Rylin sensed something unsaid about her condition. Varama warned her about Cerai and ordered her to hold her position. After Elenai acknowledged that, she was in mid-sentence about chaos spirits when Muragan had to break contact.

The blood that had shaped the future queen rained into the trough, and Muragan sank to the ground, panting.

Varama looked down at the stinking pool of crimson, not so much horrified as thoughtful.

"Did you say what you needed?" Vannek asked.

"Enough," Varama answered.

"I couldn't hold it any longer," Muragan said wearily. "Not without another sorcerer with more blood on the other end."

"You did well," Varama told him. "It's time for the next step."

"We bring them here," Vannek suggested.

"No," Varama said.

The Naor general's brow furrowed in surprise. "I thought we would all go to Cerai's palace, and kill her."

"While I fully plan to confront Cerai, I don't believe she can be defeated upon her own territory, and I cannot predict what will happen to the Goddess' energy if we fight her there. We will lure the Goddess to the wastelands of Kanesh. N'lahr advised me to pick good ground, and I think that will suit us well. There will be no one in that place at risk but ourselves."

"My people are still with Cerai," Vannek said. "I hope you have some plan that includes freeing them?"

"Indeed," Varama said. "You're not the only one whose forces remain with her."

Vannek didn't look entirely assured, so Varama, uncharacteristically, explained further. "When we rendezvous with Elenai, we will launch a raid against Cerai."

"It sounds as though you're planning to open a lot of portals," Rylin said. "Are you up to that? And do you have the power to do it?"

"I have a shard hidden in my rooms yet. And I am the only one who can open the portals at this point, so there is no question of whether I'm up to it. We've no other option."

He knew her well enough now to be alert to her own subtle signals. "You're worried about using this powerful magic, aren't you?"

"More than I would like," Varama admitted. "Each portal opening weakens my own existence even as it weakens the surrounding reality."

"What do you mean it weakens your existence?"

"It's hard to describe with precision. I haven't had the luxury of study, but I feel . . . stretched out. Weary, disconnected. I suppose the closest comparison is to being dizzy. Whether or not the condition is temporary or has lasting ramifications, I cannot say."

"Alten," Thelar said, "you should have said something sooner."

"He's right," Rylin agreed.

"I appreciate your concern, but we've little choice. I'm less worried about me than I am about our overall chance of success against the Goddess."

"We need you strong enough to fight her," Thelar said.

"Indeed we do. But as Asrahn would often advise, we need to control the ground where we're going to fight. And that means I'll have to open more portals." Her face firmed with resolve. "Enough of this. There's work to do."

31

⎯⎯◆⎯⎯

The Battle Looms

The wastelands were not as Rylin had expected. He'd thought he would step into a barren and blazing heat pit. While the sun hung in the sky above the dunes, it kept company with a weird tear in the heavens through which the night sky peered out and through which bright colors flared at random intervals. A chill wind blew.

The company was strange as well. In addition to the odd mix of squires and Naor—Varama had come through with a force smaller even than that N'lahr had led against the queen—hundreds of kobalin wandered the area in their mismatched arms and armor. The end result resembled an over-decorated scene from an absurdist play set in the deep shifts.

Once introductions had been made, Varama summoned the leaders of the forces to the top of a long, crescent-shaped mesa in the middle of the dunes, and held perhaps the strangest conference in the long annals of the Altenerai. In addition to the Altenerai physically present, including himself, Varama, Gyldara, Tretton, Elenai, and Kyrkenall, there was the spectral Kalandra. Thelar, too, was there, the last of the exalts, and then others who Rylin would never have dreamt would be a part of a formal Altenerai meeting: General Vannek of the Naor, Muragan the blood mage, and Ortok of the kobalin. All of them sat about a low fire but Kalandra, who told them she didn't really have the knack for sitting anymore. She stood beside Kyrkenall, who shifted constantly, in a sharp, birdlike way.

Kalandra explained how she had come to be in her current condition, how the chaos weapon had been found, and, oddest of all, how Kyrke-nall's body was shared jointly by a forgotten god.

"I am only here with him for now," the God in Kyrkenall said brightly. "I will speak to her when she comes."

"He means the Goddess," Kalandra said.

Once everyone had been fully briefed, Varama laid out N'lahr's plan. They were to run a three-pronged raid upon Cerai's fortress, their goals the freeing of their people, the acquisition of the shaping tool, and the obtain-ment of Cerai's hearthstone cache, which would later act as a lure for the Goddess.

It was apparent to Rylin that the discussion phase took far longer than Varama would have liked. Neither Elenai nor Kyrkenall were happy about staying behind, but Varama argued that they couldn't take all of their spell casters, and that Kyrkenall could not be risked, since he housed a deity that might be essential to the battle with the Goddess.

Asrahn had always said that the more intricate the plan, the greater its chances for failure. But then most of the planning of the assault was N'lahr's, so despite the concern voiced by Tretton, Rylin had faith in it, even if he still didn't understand why Varama and Elenai had thought it appropriate the hulking kobalin leader was trusted with the commander's rescue.

While Varama conferenced with Kalandra and Thelar, Rylin stepped apart to look over his equipment. Just as Asrahn had often said, and The-lar had recently repeated, waiting was one of the hardest skills to master. The old alten had impressed upon his charges that you could never be too certain of your equipment. Bored between actions? Check your gear and sharpen your blade.

And so Rylin found a spot in the sand away from the others, and, under the weird sky, took out his whetstone.

He was honing near his sword guard when he heard the swish of foot-steps through the sand. He looked up to find Gyldara before him. He set the weapon aside and pushed to his feet. She glanced back at the greater body of troops, and the shifting kobalin, then met his eyes. "This assault is the moment where we stand or fall. I wish I was going with you. After this it's all up to the mages."

"Maybe. If we're lucky. I wouldn't mind some good luck."

"I hope you have it. I don't want to be the last one left from our little group, so you be careful. Come back."

Rylin saw the depth of emotion in her eyes and wondered if it meant more than she was saying, or if he was just distracted by the pleasure of her company and her knifelike beauty. He'd always understood she preferred the company of women, but she was as private with her trysts as he had been public, and some people were far more fluid in their sexual interests than he.

He smiled, amused at himself. His friend, who happened to be a lovely woman, cared about him. Right now that was all that mattered. "All right then, Alten."

She kissed him on the cheek before stepping away, almost colliding with Thelar as he walked up. They exchanged a brief greeting, and then the exalt glanced curiously at the retreating Gyldara before turning his attention to Rylin.

"I have the distinct impression I've interrupted something."

"Maybe you did," Rylin said. "But I'm not sure either of us will know until I get back."

"That sounds vague. I thought you were a master with women."

"Never with that one. How did the magical conference go?"

"Fascinating. I'd forgotten how brilliant Kalandra was. Varama wanted to make sure we understand portal magics in case something happens to her. I know enough to be dangerous now, but I think Kalandra actually does understand."

"We can't let anything happen to Varama," Rylin said with grim resolve.

"That has to be your lookout."

"I know."

The exalt frowned. "I wish I was going through with you."

"Apart from Varama, we have to keep the best spell casters in reserve. And you and I both know you're better than me."

"I've known that for a long time."

Rylin chuckled more than the joke deserved, and was rewarded with a faint smile.

"Do you think it will work?" Thelar asked. "The whole thing—getting N'lahr and Tesra and the squires and the hearthstones and the tool, luring the Goddess here, blasting her into pieces?"

"Varama thinks it will work."

"Varama thinks it *could* work. If we're smart, and careful, and lucky."

"Then we'd better be all three."

It was at that moment the horn sounded the call to arms. Rylin stood, stretched, and slid his sword into its sheath. "It's time."

32

On Wing of Fire

Varama proved no more genial than ever as she presented Vannek with one of three packs sitting at her feet.

Muragan looked down at them. "What are these?"

"Your way off the dragon, from midair," Varama answered briskly. "I can't guarantee they'll work perfectly, but they're an improvement over certain death. There's one for each of you." She passed one off to Muragan, who eyed it curiously as he hefted it.

"I don't understand," Vannek admitted. "Is this more magic?"

"It's a device that slows your descent, part of an incomplete series of experiments into flight. Pull here, and here, with both hands. Fabric will pop free, and your fall will be slowed. I'd advise you to have a knife ready to cut the straps free the moment you land."

"I always have a knife. Did you use these in Alantris?"

"Those balloons carried no people. As I had none of my normal tools or materials from my workshops in Alantris, I had to improvise an effective system to reach targets without any guidance."

"You improvised your devices in Alantris?" Vannek had a hard time believing that.

"Yes," Varama answered impatiently.

"And this time you had access to your workshops," Muragan said. "I'm starting to feel sorry for Cerai." He flashed a sly grin at Vannek, who fought down an answering laugh.

"Give her no pity," Varama said. "She has an immense amount of raw power at her command. You're going in first, so you'll present the most obvious target for the first part of our attack."

"You actually sound concerned," Vannek said.

Varama responded to the dry humor of Vannek's statement with a crisp assertion. "We need you. If we survive this, we have a chance for lasting peace with your people. But only if someone farsighted like yourself remains in charge. Here." Varama bent and passed over the remaining, smaller shoulder satchel.

Vannek took it only after the briefest hesitation, pushing the top flap aside to reveal four glass vials, stoppered by corks and separated with padded leather. "What are these?"

"Whatever you hit with them should burn nicely. You don't want to drop it on yourself."

"Something else you improvised?" Vannek asked.

"It's an idea I wanted to test in Alantris, but lacked the resources for."

"And you just whipped these up in the few hours we had while in Darassus?"

"I had the ingredients. Until I had spare time to think during our long road trip it had never occurred to me to combine them in these amounts. I'm sure the recipe could be finessed, but it's effective currently."

Once again, Vannek realized the alten was one of the most dangerous of all of those wearing the ring. "I'm lucky you hadn't developed this before, aren't I?"

"If I had developed this before, you would never have taken the city, dragons or no. As to now, are you clear on what you need to do?"

"Yes," Vannek replied. "I'm to cause as much mayhem as possible, and keep clear of those key sections you pointed out. Is that all from you? I always assumed Altenerai led people with stunning speeches."

"I simply tell them the truth. Do Naor need something different?"

"My family usually gave speeches mocking your people and extolling ours."

"I don't do that."

"I'm not surprised."

"Is there anything else?" Varama asked impatiently.

Vannek decided to ask something she had long wondered. "Even the newest Altenerai have famous nicknames. Why don't you?"

The corner of Varama's mouth ticked up in what resembled the start of a smile, then vanished so quickly Vannek wondered if he had imagined it.

"Early attempts to assign me a sobriquet proved disappointing. I discouraged it."

"What were they? Varama the Wise, or Varama the Blue? Something like that?"

"You're extraordinary loquacious today. No. They were worse."

"And no one clever gave you one for inventing things or concocting plans?"

"Or retaking Alantris?" Muragan asked.

"It hasn't come up."

Varama looked as though she had grown uncomfortable, and Vannek was startled he found it endearing. "The most memorable image of you I have is when you stood on the tower, in Alantris, raining fire down on the city. You lifted your ring above your head and lit it. Of course, I thought you were N'lahr at the time."

"As I intended."

"Varama High Ring," Muragan suggested.

Varama fixed him with her piercing gaze.

"That's really not bad," Vannek said. "Maybe Naor should write all Altenerai epithets."

"I'll take that under advisement," Varama said. "Good luck."

"Fight well," Vannek said.

Varama nodded, pivoted, and hurried off.

"All right, Mage," Vannek said. "We have our orders."

"From an Alten, no less." Muragan wrestled into his pack. "Who's actually going out of her way to keep us alive."

Vannek grunted. "Focus on the future, Muragan."

"Here's to it."

They walked for their dragon.

As promised, they emerged in a grove of trees in the gloom of night, under two bright moons, both of which waned just shy of full. Muragan immediately urged the beast forward.

Under his guidance the dragon stretched its wings in the shadow of the trees. It snorted before it lumbered forward. With each footfall it let out another snort and Vannek gritted teeth, certain Cerai's guards would hear. He fixed upon the fortress, visible as a dark blot against the sky a half-mile distant. Lights shown in a handful of its windows, and lanterns blazed every hundred paces along the battlement, rendering the place strangely festive.

Beneath him, the dragon hurried forward, jostling Vannek with every step and every swing of its wings. Abruptly, without any particular warning, they were in the air.

The dragon climbed steeply, circling higher and higher over the trees. The leg straps pressed against Vannek, holding him to the seat, a few feet back from Muragan.

The blood mage looked over the bulky pack he wore on his shoulders, identical to Vannek's. "Are you ready, General?"

"I'm ready. Are you?"

"I am. I've never flown a dragon before. It's exhilarating!"

"Don't forget to put in your ear stops." Vannek pushed small wads of fine cloth into either ear, and Muragan did the same.

He took the dragon up until Cerai's fortress lay hundreds of feet below.

At Vannek's word they swept down toward one of the towers, dropping opposite the moons.

Vannek spotted sentries along the wall and regretted his decision to leave his archers behind. He had expected this attack to require more brute force than pinpoint accuracy, and he had few archers left.

Though the beast was silent, one of the patrolling figures looked up. Vannek saw him halt and stare in amazement, then fumble with a horn. The sentry had it to his lips. He managed a starting blat with the trumpet the same moment the dragon roared. Even while wearing ear stops, Vannek was nearly deafened. He felt the vibration of the attack through his legs.

The battlement gave way, crumbling sideways with the sentinel and the top floor, raining down the front of the fortress.

Muragan let out an exultant cry, then shouted back to him in glee. "That will get their attention!"

A horn call from another tower rang in alert, and another sounded before its echoes died. Muragan banked the animal and Vannek felt it breathe heavily. From experience he knew the beast would need time before it could assault once more. As a result, rather than relying on its attack, when they passed over one of the towers he tossed a vial in front of a door that opened on the battlement.

The toss went long, striking a merlon, but flame blossomed and spread weblike upon surrounding stone.

Vannek, angry with himself, resolved to aim better next time.

Muragan circled up. He meant to keep them out of arrow range while the beast regained its breath.

A yellow light flashed in the courtyard and Vannek craned his neck to observe a portal opening near the stables. Armed figures dashed forth, spreading out. In amongst the Altenerai and the kobalin lords were some of his own. He thought he heard them shouting for Vannek loyalists to come forth, but the words were indistinct through his ear stops. Muragan brought the dragon back again for another sally. The sharp turn set Vannek's stomach lurching.

On this pass the dragon's roar sheared off the front of one tower for nearly three stories. A bank of spearmen raced up to the wall, half-dressed but bearing their weapons, and Vannek tossed a vial at them. It passed just beyond the tip of the dragon's wing, then crashed against the stone walkway only a bodylength from Cerai's lackeys.

One screamed in pain. He glanced back to see flame sprouting, only to be alerted by a call from Muragan.

The mage turned the dragon sharply, for a huge stone had passed them in the air. Someone had launched a catapult.

A rain of arrows whipped in from the left. Vannek heard his name screamed, seeing then that the three archers on the tower's height were Naor, and that the burly one at their height was Anzat himself.

"Bring us back," he shouted up to Muragan.

"I don't think that's wise!"

"That's Anzat! If we bring him down, our people have no leader but me!"

Muragan visibly sighed, but turned the dragon back at the fortress in a tight circle.

Vannek glimpsed warriors trading blows in the courtyard. The portal itself had vanished and only a handful of lanterns pooled ruddy light near doors and walkways.

Anzat shook a spear in the air, shouting. Vannek couldn't quite hear him, but knew exactly what he wanted. The fool was screaming for a personal, face-to-face challenge.

"Blast him," Vannek cried.

Muragan turned the dragon, and Anzat held his hand up to the archers. The idiot actually expected him to land and dismount! It was a delight to see the man's expression fall, to see him turn and run when the dragon's maw opened. Anzat had just reached the door to the battlement when the dragon's roar blew him through it so that the stones showered up and over both sides of the wall. What was left of him and the others fell in bloody chunks mixed with masonry.

Vannek laughed; ahead, Muragan let out a war whoop and brought them around. Even the dragon seemed to be enjoying itself, for it rumbled deep in its chest, like a contented dog after a meal.

"I could get used to this!" Muragan shouted back to him.

A bright blue light lanced out of an upper window and struck the center of the dragon's left wing. The beast roared in pain as flame spread along the limb. It wobbled in its flight and a second flame set Muragan's pack alight with a blinding flash.

The dragon shook. Vannek blinked to clear the glare from his eyes. Muragan's pack rolled with flame. He shouted at the same time the dragon let out a mournful wail.

"Jump!" Vannek ordered harshly.

"Get free!" the blood mage shouted back. The dragon was dropping, its wings outspread even though one of them was afire.

Vannek undid his own straps, then reached toward the mage as the beast dropped lower and lower. He steadied himself against Muragan's low seat back and reached toward the flames that had wrapped his back, patting at them.

Muragan looked back at him through the flame, the white of one eye showing wide. "Get clear!"

He wasn't going to leave his friend behind. One quick slash at the shoulder strap freed the mage. He wrenched him up even as the dragon tilted in the air. They were thrown clear; Vannek pressed Muragan to him, the smouldering bag against his chest. Almost by accident his hand caught the shoulder strap Varama had pointed out to him.

Fabric tore behind him and he thought his drop would end in death, but he heard a whoosh of air. A huge fabric square deployed behind him and he glided, or rather swung madly, toward the battlement.

"It can't carry us both!" Muragan cried.

Vannek feared he was right, for they were falling fast.

Below him, the flaming dragon slammed into the fortress gate. Fire licked eagerly around the shattered wood.

"Let me go!" Muragan shouted.

"We land together, or not at all!" Vannek said through gritted teeth.

It was then he saw the soldiers on the battlement hefting their spears.

33

The Oath of the Ring-Sworn

Moonlight silvered the courtyard grass at the tunnel's end. Rylin stepped through a beat after Varama and took in the hut at the park-like center of the fortress. The walls rumbled under the assault of the dragon he saw swooping above the battlements.

He was ready to move, frustrated by even the brief delay, for it was not Ortok, but Tretton who came through next, pausing only to get his bearings.

Rylin pointed him the right way but wasn't sure the older alten even noticed before sprinting into the darkness.

Varama tended the glowing rift as the rest of their party came through. He saw her mouth compressed, her neck muscles strained. Her hands reached forth, clawlike, as if she held open an immense door eager to slam closed and take her fingertips with it.

Inside the portal, the rest of their band seemed a mile off and then a step later were beside him. Foremost was the dark bulk of Ortok, his footing uncertain after the dizzying passage. Rylin grabbed the kobalin's immense wrist, discovering he couldn't encircle it with his fingers, "Follow me," he said, and darted off.

Somewhere behind him Vannek's dragon roared, and someone screamed, and then came the all-too-familiar sound of collapsing stone. He consoled himself there was no need to fear, for this time the dragon was on their side.

He heard the thud of Ortok's steps to his rear as they neared the western door from the courtyard. When last he'd been here there'd been no locks, nor sorcerous protections, but as he reached for the latch he paused to peer through the inner world. While stray sorcerous filaments could be observed throughout the citadel, the door looked utterly plain, and it opened to his pull. For all its imposing outward appearance, Cerai was too arrogant to believe her building could be breached from the inside, a weakness Varama had anticipated.

A dimmed lantern hung in the hall just beyond the door. Rylin snatched it and turned into the stairwell. As he pounded up the steps he remembered the countless runs Asrahn had sent the squires on, over hills, round and round the grounds, and up and down steps. He and Lasren had complained to each other that the Naor and kobalin were too stupid to make many stairs, and scoffed at spending so much time racing back and forth upon them; Rylin had charitably offered that Asrahn was keeping them fit enough to ensure they'd be first to the top of a wall to defend it. He had never imagined running stairs in an assault followed by a huge kobalin who was not enemy, but ally.

They hit the first landing and had started up the second flight when a light bloomed on an upper level. Heels beat on wood. A squad of Cerai's men hurried down, still buckling their sword belts. All had donned armor, but their shoulder straps weren't secure. Their hair was tousled, their collars uneven.

They looked just as startled to see Rylin as he was them. Rylin's hand fell to his sword, but he didn't draw. "One side," he ordered crisply. And then, seeing their bewildered gaze as they took in Ortok, he added, "He's with me. Get to your posts! We're under attack!"

All four of Cerai's men stepped to one side, curious, but unaggressive. Rylin glanced back as he and Ortok started up the next flight of stairs and saw the soldiers heading down.

"Why did you not fight them?" Ortok asked at his shoulder, his deep voice booming. "We would have broken them."

"We'll waste time if we stop to fight."

"That was clever," the kobalin said after a moment's reflection. "I would have charged into them, and the moments would be spent."

Rylin heard the progress of the soldiers down the rest of the stairs, and the rise in outside noise when they opened the door.

As he and Ortok arrived at the right landing Rylin put a hand to the latch. "Remember—you go for N'lahr, I get the tool."

"I have not forgotten."

Rylin pushed open the door. He'd half expected to confront a stream of enemies, but before him stretched only a stone corridor lit by brass lanterns hung every twenty paces, tiny spots of light in the surrounding gloom. Outside, the walls rattled. A man's cry of anguish rent the night.

"Our dragon," Ortok said at his usual volume, apparently unfamiliar with the need for stealth.

Rylin raised a hand to ward him to silence and started forward, counting doors until he reached the fourth on the left. Watching with inner sight, he saw no threads about the enclosure, but at touch of his hand showed him the door itself was locked or barred.

"Ortok," he said softly. "Get it open."

His ally charged on the instant. His impact rattled the door in its frame. Two strikes later it slammed wide. Ortok stumbled into darkness. Rylin came after, lantern shining.

He'd reached Cerai's laboratory. His light passed over the cases and shelves, then spilled on a figure in a blue khalat standing near the couch against the wall where poor M'vai had once been seated. Ortok exclaimed in surprise and leapt toward it.

Rylin followed, still looking through the inner world. He couldn't help seeing the framework of threads on everything about him. Burning most brightly were living objects, like Ortok, and his own raised arm, in his line of sight holding the lantern with its shifting matrix of fire.

N'lahr's energy wasn't quite rocklike, for it was definitely there. It just didn't shift. He also held four or more times as many structural threads as anyone Rylin had ever seen.

Ortok let out a crooning sound, like a whining pup, and reached gently for the commander's shoulder.

"He's not dead," Rylin said.

Ortok's voice was soft, haunted. "But the flame of his life does not move."

"He was trapped before and revived," Rylin said. "If anyone can save him, Varama can." Then he added, "Be careful carrying him."

"He is my friend," Ortok said simply.

As the hulking kobalin scooped up the commander, Rylin moved for the office door. There was no time for subtlety. He felt for the magical threads about it, sensing that they stretched away from the office itself. While it was possible that they were triggered to the kind of sorcerous protection that had blasted Thelar, Rylin thought it more likely Cerai had tethered the door to herself to alert her if anyone forced their way in.

He took no chances. The floor rumbled as he charged the door with one of the sofa tables. Its corner hit with a rattle and boom. There was no resulting crackle of magic, though Rylin felt threads activate, so he shoved the battering furniture aside, noted with satisfaction the door loose in its frame, and kicked it solidly near the lock. It swung into the wall beyond with a crack.

He flung open the cabinet and grabbed the staff leaning within. As he pulled it clear, certain its radiant magic identified it for what he needed, the closed door in the office's far wall swung open.

Cerai halted in the frame, her sapphire ring lighting her way. Her cool blue eyes narrowed. She was opening her mouth to speak when he launched a blast of wind and knocked her back.

The staff-like shaping tool in hand, he raced back to the laboratory, put a palm to the table, and leapt it. Cerai recovered fast and snapped threads of energy at him. They crackled through the air he'd just left.

Rylin shouted at Ortok to go. The kobalin had been hesitating in the hall doorway with N'lahr in his arms. Rather than diverting around a couch, Rylin vaulted it and dropped. It had been the right call, for Cerai's energies struck the couch and bits of fabric and fragments of wood blasted into the air.

Ortok pounded away.

"Surrender or die, Rylin!" Cerai shouted. He wasn't about to raise his head, so instead he stuffed his hand into the padded satchel Varama had given him and leaned around the side of the couch.

While Cerai had been alert, the movement still caught her off guard. The vial smashed open at her feet.

Fire and oil sprayed in every direction and she leapt back from the flame.

Rylin scrambled for the door. As he reached the threshold pain seared through his shoulder. He stumbled through the doorway and regained his footing.

He saw the bulk of Ortok racing along the hallway ahead, still cradling N'lahr's statue. He ran after. Behind him flame blossomed, casting red light into the hall. His armor was burned and smoking all around his left shoulder, and his arm hung uselessly numb and cold.

Great. No time to worry about that. He shoved the tool under his good arm and fumbled with his pouch for the second and last of his fire vials, whipping it at the lab door he'd left. Cerai appeared in the hall in the moment just before its impact, and much of the contents struck her khalat. She screamed, and Rylin saw her hand rise to her face even as flame licked along her fingers.

He had no love left for her, but dread tore at him as he raced on, the tool once more in hand. Ortok held the door, and Rylin shouted at him to keep moving. He came after. He wondered whether a healer would be able to fix his shoulder, and how long before the limb overwhelmed him with crippling pain.

He risked a glance back before the door closed. Cerai strode purposefully, unhurriedly, after. The flame still roved over her, but energetic threads raced across her blackened features and smoking khalat. Rylin slammed shut the door.

She might very well be impossible to stop. His worry lent him speed. He heard a final shout from her as he and Ortok vanished through the door below.

Cutting across the courtyard was the fastest way to the hearthstone room, where Varama was to open the escape portal. Groups of Naor fought alongside Cerai's soldiers; others fought beside the kobalin. Along one edge, jogging for the doorway, Rylin spotted a mixed band of squires and aspirants. Sword in hand, Elik held the door for his charges to venture into the fortress. He caught sight of Rylin and Ortok as they dashed in his direction and his eyes widened.

Rylin spared a look behind him but didn't see Cerai. He felt relief for only a moment, then reasoned she must be planning something else, which couldn't be good.

The squires and the three aspirants crowded past. "Go!" Elik shouted to them. "Straight on for the hearthstone room. Move!"

They hurried. Probably none had actually seen the inside of the hearth-stone room; probably Elik had made them memorize the citadel layout.

"This is Ortok," Rylin said. That would have to do for an introduction. "Where's Tretton?"

"He went after Tesra."

"She's still alive?"

"I believe so."

Rylin handed the tool to Elik as Ortok loped after the squires. "Get this to Varama. It's even more important than N'lahr, believe it or not."

"What are you doing?"

Rylin had just wanted his sword arm free and was about to say so when a cheer rose from the walls. Rylin saw the dragon dropping, one wing aflame. Figures on its back fell free, one clasped to the other. Immediately a rectangle of fabric sprouted from one of their packs. The two Naor were jerked backward, and descended in something less than a glide but not quite a plummet.

Rylin cursed. He pointed with his good hand. "Get this tool to Varama and get out!"

"But where are you going?" Elik demanded.

He didn't have time to answer. Rylin ran forward as the figures dropped. Five of Cerai's soldiers raced along the battlement toward them with spears. Even if they missed, Vannek was headed for the wrong side of the wall, and was falling too fast besides.

It was a long, long way for one of his own spells, but Rylin saw no other option, and reached with a blast of wind. He used the currents that were already out there and sent them curling back in a spiral that whipped Vannek and Muragan up and over the walls toward him. The spearmen missed their casts as the general and blood mage shot unexpectedly over their heads.

Now the Naor drifted above the courtyard's center. Too fast. Rylin swore that Vannek's eyes met his for a moment even as he shaped the spell from his already breathless body.

Panting, Rylin coaxed the wind further, to set the general and the mage beyond a huge kobalin at war with a band of Cerai's troops. The two cleared them and descended swiftly, eight feet above, now six feet, drifting for the side of the fortress wall. Muragan dropped free.

And then something slammed into Rylin's already damaged shoulder. He didn't feel the bite of a weapon so much as the impact that shook him. He spun and spotted a band of Naor pointing at him. Three were running his direction. They had separated him from the side of the court-yard where he needed to be, so he swerved past a dead man in time to evade another arrow, then jerked open a tower door. Once through, he slammed it shut, pausing to jam his knife through the lock. Then, breathing heavily, he looked to his shoulder to discover an arrow embedded there. Apparently khalats weren't as resistant to damage if they'd been burned.

His first thought was to break off the shaft and pull it free, but it might be barbed. Too winded to curse, he drew his sword. The door rattled in its housing as one of the Naor outside hauled on it. But the lock he'd disabled refused them entrance.

Rylin started into the hallway. He would have preferred to sprint, but he had little energy. As he jerked open the inner door his shoulder woke at last, and Rylin gasped in pain. He leaned against the door jamb as stars splintered across his vision.

Not now, he told himself. Collapse later. He would detour through the building and back to Varama and the portal. It really wasn't that far.

His vision cleared, and he started forward at a jog. For all that it seemed it should require only a little effort, each step felt like ten yards. Every four or five steps felt a mile.

But Rylin pressed on through the weird frozen menagerie of one of the vast storage rooms, all the more unsettling with the glassy open eyes of the animals reflecting the occasional lighted lanterns. He drew closer to shouts of combat and the sound of arms. He rounded a corner and nearly blundered into a pair of Cerai's warriors. They spun at sight of him and raised weapons. He was too tired to bluff, and it might be they'd already been told all Altenerai were enemies. Or learned it.

And so with failing strength he cast himself forward. His was no reckless, laughing charge of Altenerai heroes, but a desperate, brutal attack. If he used finesse it was only years of training pressed into instinct, so that he ducked from a blow and slid his weapon past a parry and drove it home. One man fell and scrabbled at Rylin's legs, to put him off balance.

Rylin stepped clear of the dying guard, threw up his good shoulder to catch a blow, then sliced halfway through the second warrior's neck. Warm blood sprayed partly into his mouth, opened to gasp. He yanked his weapon clear, spat in disgust, and stumbled into a jog that took him into the tower with the hearthstone room. He didn't need his inner sight to feel the power of great energies at work. An intersection loomed ahead and he saw Tretton cross it, a long-haired body slumped over one shoulder. Tesra.

Vannek peered out from the right side of the intersection and saw Rylin, his eyes registering concern. Then they widened in alarm at something heading the general's way from the direction Tretton had come. Vannek pulled back.

Rylin hadn't the strength to look through the inner world, and wondered why he could so easily see the magical threads trailing from Cerai as she stalked past the cross hall and toward the doorway through which Vannek and Tretton had vanished. She didn't even glance at him.

How was her power so obvious? Maybe, half conscious as he was, he was already in touch with the magical world. Or maybe her powers were so overwhelming they were visible to the naked eye. In any case, Rylin's friends would need help.

From somewhere deep inside he conjured the energy for a full run. His injured arm burned in pain from shoulder to fingertips, as though it had been immersed in fire, but he built speed, and as he took the turn into the intersection he rounded into the room with the hearthstones. Cerai was whipping threads of energy at both the shimmering golden portal and Varama, standing at its edge. Vannek, beside her, launched a spear that one of Cerai's threads casually wrapped and tossed away. A wide shelf empty but for a handful of hearthstones attested to Varama's success with that aspect of her mission. Presumably N'lahr, the squires, Muragan, the weapon, and even Tesra had been spirited free. All that was left was to get the three of them out alive.

Rylin felt enormous satisfaction as he closed upon Cerai and saw her spin in surprise. Her khalat still smoked, but her face had already been fully restored. He swung his blade at her legs. She crouched so the khalat took the damage, but his momentum sent her over. He tripped into her and tumbled. His vision went red as he struck the floor, for his arm erupted with agony, the pain so great he almost lost consciousness.

Someone shouted his name, probably Varama, and he forced himself up with his good hand, still somehow clutching his hilt.

Cerai was there. He threw his good arm to block her sword strike and gasped as the point drove through his armored forearm. He groaned in renewed pain, recognizing with some surprise he'd been assaulted with Irion. Cerai glared down the shining blade. She pulled out the sword, and then a knife struck her collar and stood out from her neck.

With her off hand, Cerai tore the weapon free, apparently unharmed even as her own blood sprayed. She turned to face Vannek. The Naor general's arm was still extended. The Naor looked stunned that his lethal blow had achieved so little. Beside him, a shaking Varama fought to hold the shrunken portal. Rylin saw the energies swirling, knew that all he had to do was run, throw himself forward, and reach safety.

Cerai gathered her spellthreads.

As Rylin got his feet under him, he recognized the fatigue in Varama's eyes. For once, emotions were bare upon her face. She was in agony, physically and emotionally. Already she'd held the portal too long. Waiting for him.

He nodded to her. He wanted her to know it was all right, and he saw that she knew what he intended when she shook her head at him, mouthing a single word. "No."

"Get her away!" He shouted to Vannek, then threw himself against Cerai's legs and punched her knee.

The renegade alten dropped, cursing.

Vannek grabbed Varama and dragged her into the portal, the alten shouting in protest.

Rylin pulled the knife from his weapon belt and drove it into Cerai's calf, hoping to catch an artery. She shouted in pain, then flipped around, grabbed his arm as it lifted for another strike. Her hand flickered with eldritch energies.

His injuries had already weakened him, and her strength was heightened. She easily forced back his wounded limb.

"You're done, Rylin!" she cried. "Done!"

He stared up at her, defiant as he felt the portal close.

"I could have made a god of you!" Cerai screamed. She snatched Irion from the floor and leveled it at him.

"I am Altenerai," he said, and died smiling, for he knew his friends had escaped.

34

The One He Liked

Each time Vannek had traveled through the portals had been a nightmare, where stretched landscapes had bubbled past the sides of a tunnel with too little air. Always before there'd been a sense of forward momentum. This time it was like falling from a great height.

Varama cried out in grief, the sound warped by the weird environment. The walls of the portal shook, narrowed. Ahead lay only darkness.

And then they'd passed through some membrane and both struck sand, lying in a heap. The portal shimmered just beyond Varama's outstretched hands.

Vannek looked to either side, saw Thelar, and Elenai, Gyldara, and the ghost alten, Kalandra.

"Close it," Vannek meant to shout, but his voice came out as a wheeze. "Close it!" he repeated more forcefully to the air around him.

"Where's Rylin?" Thelar asked quietly. But not as someone who was curious. More as someone who tried to sound as though the most important thing in the world were unremarkable.

"Close it!" Vannek cried.

Kalandra raised her hands and spiraled the portal closed, even as Varama let out a complaining moan.

He rolled off the alten. Varama still lay on her back, hands stretched toward the vanished opening. He knew that hundreds of kobalin dotted the plains, but he heard nothing more than the gasp of the woman, the wail of the wind, and the thud of his own swiftly beating heart, pulsing in his ears.

And then, again, came Thelar's voice. "What happened to Rylin?"

"He didn't make it." Vannek was pushing himself up when Varama seized his collar. With a madman's strength Varama hurled him to the sand and knelt atop him, eyes blazing, knife to his neck.

Dazed, breath knocked from his lungs, Vannek could only stare up at the alten and gasp. He had thought her without emotion; now bestial fury looked out from those eyes.

Vannek heard the onlookers object, demanding to know what Varama was doing, and why she did it. Elenai shouted for her to calm down.

Varama bent low, eye to eye, her hatred alive and vital.

"I saved you," Vannek said. His hand reached for the knife hilt at his side, but that blade had been cast at Cerai.

"You should have saved him!" Varama screamed.

Vannek shook his head. This, from the wisest of all Altenerai? Varama had to know there'd been no other choice, and that Rylin had given his life for her. They could not have gotten through, much less controlled the portal, while Cerai was launching inexhaustible attacks. But Vannek said nothing. He waited for the death blow.

Varama glared for a long moment, and then the fury left her eyes and she dropped the knife, climbed off, and knelt in the sand with head bowed. At first, Vannek thought she shook from exhaustion. And then she understood that Varama wept.

"What happened?" Elenai asked quietly.

Varama didn't reply.

"Cerai just couldn't be stopped." Vannek sat up. "She brushed off injuries that should have left her dead. There's no way Varama could keep her back and hold the portal at the same time. Rylin yelled at me to get her out. And then he attacked Cerai."

"He might still be alive," Thelar said hopefully.

Vannek thought about the burned, bloody, pale figure that just wouldn't stay down, and felt moisture in his own eyes. "No. She got him, in the end. I don't know how he stayed on his feet. He was burned, bleeding, an arrow in his shoulder, but he just wouldn't stay down. Any warrior would be proud to die so well."

Vannek wiped his tears and pushed to his feet, turning away from the weeping alten. He wondered if he should tell them how Rylin had saved him and Muragan, too. They couldn't possibly have reached the portal if they'd landed on the far side of the wall. Rylin had guided them to safety, probably at the cost of his own life, for if he'd simply raced on, he and Varama could have gotten through the portal together.

It was a debt he would remember, and one he would tell them, when they could better hear it. For now, the Altenerai seemed unsure what they should do. The brooding exalt that had been Rylin's friend stood with head bowed. The golden-haired beauty of an alten covered her face with one hand, tears streaming down her cheeks. Old, dark-skinned Tretton hesitated with his hand poised over Varama's shoulder, but not touching it. The ghost alten drew closer, her expression somber.

Elenai's eyes were red as she came forward, but she did not let grief bow her. "The healers are still tending Muragan," she said.

Vannek had been startled when he'd finally seen how badly Muragan had been burned along the right side of his face. His arm had been blackened, too, and Vannek readied himself for bad news. "Will he live?"

"They have him through the worst of it, and they think he'll pull through."

Vannek grunted at the news, then worked to respond diplomatically. "Thank you. What about N'lahr?"

Elenai looked to the left, and the knot of figures. One was the kobalin, kneeling. Kyrkenall stood near him. "Ortok brought him through." Elenai didn't sound very hopeful.

"Is he alive?"

"I can't tell."

Kalandra called the others to alert, to take their stations, reminding them Cerai might be coming.

"Did my men make it back?" Vannek asked. Only a small portion of his soldiers had gone through, and while he'd seen a few of his people racing with the squires when he and Muragan had been running after, he had no way to count them.

"Some," Elenai answered. "I think we lost two of Ortok's warriors and three of yours, but most made it out. What about your dragon?"

"Cerai killed it, too." Vannek scowled. "And I liked that one."

"Did you see Anzat?"

Vannek smiled fiercely. "For a final time."

The future queen nodded approvingly. Her gaze strayed toward where Thelar and Gyldara stood beside the grieving Varama.

"For what it's worth," Vannek said softly, "he was my favorite."

"Is that Naor for 'I liked him'?" Elenai asked.

Vannek detected a somber joke there, and allowed a faint smile. "Yes. I liked him."

"Me too."

Vannek turned, fumbling for his waterskin. He would have to assess the casualties, speak to those who'd turned from Anzat's leadership, and inform all his troops what might lay ahead. He didn't look forward to any of it. Command, his father had told him, was always lonely, but without Muragan he felt almost as lonely as he had when he'd been flown from Alantris to his brother's camp.

He decided his men could wait and strode up slope to check on his friend.

35

Ortok's Vow

Elenai didn't have time to mourn. While Tretton ordered the troops, she carried Kalandra's stone in one hand so the sorceress could walk back with her to N'lahr, who had been placed near the wounded at the height of the rocky mesa. Thelar visited with the healers Varama had brought through with the Darassan forces, looking over Tesra. Elenai would check in on that situation momentarily.

Ortok and Kyrkenall stood above their friend, oddly similar despite their vast difference in height, build, and appearance, for their expressions were drawn in grief. N'lahr lay on the ground, his face frozen with a slightly pained expression.

Elenai pressed her hands to N'lahr's side. A healer had repaired her bruise and she used both arms normally once more. She sensed that his life force was present, but stilled.

"Anything?" Kyrkenall prompted.

"He's alive," Elenai decided. "But I don't know what to do for him."

"He is dead," Ortok said quietly.

"This tissue isn't dead," Kalandra said. Here in the gloomy daylight, the wind blowing, she looked even stranger than she had in the night, for the wind tugged at the hair and clothing of everyone around her. Her colors were washed out, as though she stood in bright sunlight that wasn't there.

"And that means he's preserved," Kyrkenall said. "That with the right trick you can heal him?"

"I hope so, my darling," Kalandra said. "But this is beyond me. And Varama's spent. Maybe, with time, the two of us can think of something."

"There is nothing," Ortok said without looking up. "I hoped I was wrong, that your magics would save him, Oddsbreaker, as he told you saved him before. But he is not there. My first Altenerai friend is dead, and too his promise to me."

He climbed slowly to his feet, head bowed, and seeing how gravely he was affected Elenai couldn't help but reflect upon her long fear N'lahr would have to kill him.

Kyrkenall's expression had shifted from troubled to bemused, and he searched the faces of those around him. "This Kyrkenall mourns so much for this man," he said. "Yet he did not shape him. The man was not his creation. I do not understand why he doesn't acquire a replacement. There are other men here, with similar size and color."

Ortok scrutinized the little archer. The God in Kyrkenall, meanwhile, waited for an answer.

Elenai gave him one. "None of those other men are N'lahr."

"A friend is not a lucky rock," Ortok's voice was thick with disgust. "When a rock is lost, go to the dreaming river and find another. Friendship is made with memories that cannot be found alone."

"Why is friendship important?" Kyrkenall asked.

Ortok growled. "You are a foolish god. A friend helps your troubles and fights your enemies. A friend tells you when you are foolish, and lightens your burden, and teaches you new things. Maybe they walk a different path sometimes, but when they return and you see them, your whole body feels as though it smiles. We have only one heart, but a true friend is one with whom you would share it, if you could."

Kyrkenall seemed to be mulling that over.

Kalandra spoke gently. "The man you share that body with knew N'lahr since they first walked into the Altenerai arena. He's stricken with grief not just because of the weight of memory, but because of the end of making memories together. He's afraid there will be no more with his friend."

Ortok pushed one palm against the other. "I will find this Cerai, and I will slay her," he vowed. "She owes me the fight N'lahr cannot give."

Elenai looked at the four of them, the morose, ghostly woman, untouched by the wind bannering Kyrkenall's hair. The archer, slack-jawed, struggling to process concepts his shared mind couldn't fully comprehend. Ortok, stern and decisive. And N'lahr, frozen forever in pained surprise.

She didn't want to believe him dead, but she couldn't bear to look at him anymore. And she couldn't really stand to see Kyrkenall like that, either. The two friends, one suspended by order, the other divided by chaos. With a ghost beside them.

Ortok was the only one who made a crazy kind of sense.

Elik, Tretton, and Gyldara approached from her left and stopped to one side.

"Squire Elik is ready with a report," Tretton said.

Much as she worried for N'lahr, they had more pressing concerns. "Go ahead, Elik."

She felt the hair raising approach of Kalandra, who stepped to her right side.

Elik formally passed over a long, staff-like object remarkably similar to the chaos weapon. She inspected its surface before turning her attention to her old friend. The last time she'd seen Elik there'd been a bruise on his cleft chin. That had healed. A stray lock of his curling brown hair draped down across one eyebrow. Superficially he looked little different than he had a few months ago, until she saw how much his eyes themselves had aged.

She thanked him. Her friend then reported that he and the squires were well, and relayed what Varama had told them earlier, about an underground stable where eight mounts described as fire horses were said to be housed, along with a winged beast. Unfortunately, no one had been able to learn more about them or their capabilities. Elik also reported that Cerai seemed to have four hundred and fifty followers in all. Some were more valued than others. Perhaps a dozen Naor remained with her. Almost two dozen had escaped through the portals with them.

"But you saw no other magical tools?" Kalandra asked.

"Something was being used against Vannek's dragon," Elik answered. "But I don't know if it was another magical tool, or a really powerful spell. It set the dragon's wing on fire, and burned the blood mage."

"How long do you think we have to prepare before Cerai comes after us?" Tretton asked. Elenai was surprised to see that he was asking the question of her. But then, with Varama currently incapacitated, perhaps she was the leader by default, owing to her status as almost queen.

"She'll have to learn where we went, and she'll have to plan an attack and gather forces," Elenai said.

"She'll want to move fast," Kalandra said. "She'll surely anticipate what we're planning. And for someone of her skill it may not take long to find us."

"If we've already lured and defeated the Goddess, her coming here won't matter much." Elenai couldn't help her gaze returning to where N'lahr lay, for almost all of this had been his plan.

Kalandra must have understood her sentiment. "I wish he were here, too," she said.

"He's not." Elenai spoke more bluntly than she'd intended. "The first priority is to master this shaping tool. You said you used it once."

"I'm hardly an expert," Kalandra said.

"Make yourself one, fast. Thelar said he saw it used, and you'll want his advice anyway."

"Exalt Tesra wielded it, too," Elik said. "I saw her using it outside the walls."

"Take Kalandra to talk with them both." Elenai passed Kalandra's emerald and the shaping tool to the squire. She looked to the bottom of the slope, where the portal had opened and closed and where everyone who'd survived the assault had come through. Varama lay there still, tended by a single healer and watched by a pair of squires. "I want to know how long it will be before Varama can recover. I really don't want to lure the Goddess here until she has enough strength to help."

"I think that's wise," Kalandra said. "Just remember that we have so many hearthstones the Goddess may turn up on her own before we even turn them on."

"I remember," Elenai said. "I want you to take some of that hearthstone energy yourself."

"That's not important right now," Kalandra said with a shake of her head.

Elenai's lip curled. "We need you. And if you figure out how to manipulate this wand right away, it's high time to figure out how to keep you alive." She shifted her attention to Elik. "Tell Thelar that's a priority."

"Yes, my queen." Elik uttered the words without a trace of discomfort, and it startled Elenai.

"Good," she said. "Go."

They walked away together, the squire and the ghost.

Elenai returned her attention to Tretton and Gyldara, who offered a glum smile. Elenai returned it, then listened as the gray-haired veteran proposed how he would arrange their forces. The mesa was surrounded by a sea of dunes, so he suggested some of the closer ones be swept away with magic, the better to create a killing field. That would entail opening hearthstones, but Elenai supposed they'd be doing that eventually anyway. She told him she'd consider that. "The shaping tool will speed the process," she added.

"We've no way of telling from which direction Cerai or the Goddess will come," Tretton said. He pointed to the sky, where the ko'aye circled. "It will be hard for Cerai to open a portal behind some dune without being spotted. But if she does come through with her forces, we can hold this mesa. We'll keep the hearthstones and the wounded to the center. We'll arrange the kobalin army on the slopes, with Vannek and his Naor high on the left flank, and Gyldara and myself commanding the squires on the right. We can place some spears and other deterrents, but the slopes up to us will be an impediment to start with."

It was a sound plan. "Good," Elenai said. "If Cerai turns up we ought to have spell casters on both flanks as well. I'll assign them posts."

Ortok finally left N'lahr and drew up beside them, waiting respectfully to speak.

"We were just making battle plans, Ortok," Elenai said.

"I wish my warriors in the front rank, so they can make the first blow," he said.

She'd been about to ask him if he found starting in front acceptable, so she merely bowed her head. She might have guessed his wish.

Ortok, though, had more to say. "Elenai Half-Sword Oddsbreaker

Queen, my friend is fallen. I owe him the debt of friendship. N'lahr's absence is like a gap in a wall against our enemies. I mean to stand in that gap."

"Thank you, Ortok."

"I shall join the Altenerai in his place," Ortok declared. "I have given the matter much thought. Is there a ring that will fit me?"

Tretton let out a cry of dismay. Gyldara's mouth fell open, then quickly snapped shut.

Ortok waited for her answer, head lifted proudly.

A kobalin, in the Altenerai? Ortok didn't fully understand what he was asking. After a moment of reflection, Elenai saw how to explain the situation to him. "It's a noble thing you offer. But when you wear the Altenerai ring, you protect our people above all others. Before even your own. I will not ask that of you."

Ortok scratched a shaggy ear. "Yes," he said slowly. "This is true thinking."

"I'm honored to have you at my side," Elenai said. "Down to the end."

Ortok smacked palms together sharply, as if to say the matter were resolved. "It is good to face the end at the side of friends. Perhaps I could wear a different kind of ring, for my people. It would be a friend to your rings."

"That's a fine idea," Elenai said. "When I return to Darassus, we'll make something for you. But you need no ring to show that you're my friend, or that you're a good mentor."

"I am your mentor?" Ortok asked.

Gyldara and Tretton looked even more puzzled by her words than the kobalin.

"You've taught me, just like N'lahr and Kyrkenall. You've shown me wisdom, and clarity, and kindness. You need no ring to show that you are honorable and just. You reveal it with every action."

Ortok grunted. "The regard of a wise woman is at least as good as a ring." He looked away for a moment, then spoke quietly. "My heart pulls me to look at N'lahr once more, but my mind knows that he is dead. I wish to fight Cerai. When will the battle start?"

"We should go arrange the troops, Ortok," Tretton said.

The kobalin considered him. "That is good. I will go with you. We can exchange tales of battle while we wait. It is said you are wily and relentless, but I would hear the details."

Tretton laughed shortly. "We can trade stories." He bowed his head to Elenai. Ortok did the same and the two walked off together.

Gyldara started to follow, then confessed, softly, "Nicely done. I had no idea how you were going to handle that."

"Me, either," Elenai admitted.

"Way to think on your feet." Gyldara jogged to catch up with the others.

Elenai was sorry to see her go. She would have preferred some company. While she'd known Gyldara for years as a superior, she'd forged a friendship with her during the battle of Arappa, and she now seemed one of the few from the old days who remained at ease in her presence. Elik had grown increasingly formal.

Elenai decided to walk the perimeter, eyeing the sloping sides and wondering how N'lahr would have improved upon Tretton's troop placements, which sounded quite solid.

She checked with the healers and learned Tesra had been experimented on by Cerai, and laced with something akin to the order infecting N'lahr. She breathed, but could not be roused. Muragan slept, the blackened skin on his face pink now after extensive spell work. She listened while Thelar, Kalandra, and the aspirants discussed magical theory and manipulated the shaping tool. And she looked in on Varama, lying apart from them all in a sleeping roll, head pillowed on a blanket. The healers said she had strained her magical senses to their utmost and that she needed days of rest. Varama herself claimed she needed just a little time.

Elenai didn't press her. She wanted to tell her how sorry she was about Rylin, but the alten didn't appear to want company, so she let her be.

Lelanc and Drusa occasionally flew down from their vigil above to rest, and during one of Lelanc's descents Elenai sought her out, thinking it would be better for her to hear the bad news from someone she knew.

Lelanc lay near the center of what had once been the depression hiding the chaos weapon. It had since been refilled by the kobalin. The ko'aye barely raised her russet head at Elenai's arrival, but she bobbed it in greeting. "These are ill times, Elenai. One by one my friends die. I am told Cerai killed Rylin. I already had all reasons to hate her."

"I'm sorry," Elenai said. "I didn't know you'd been told."

"A dark wind travels fast. Drusa tells me anger will eat my heart. Right now it is too hot with anger to be consumed."

Elenai sat beside the ko'aye. She looked at the beautiful white feathers along the underside of her neck and wondered when marvels like this had become so commonplace to her she could regard them without comment.

"Do you think about the battle to come?" Lelanc asked.

"It's almost all I can think about," Elenai admitted. "Wondering what comes after is like trying to look over a wall. I'd like to see what's on the other side, but I don't have a ladder."

"A ladder tool is that thing two legs use to climb high," Lelanc said, as if reminding herself.

Elenai looked up at Lelanc's huge brown eyes. "Cerai has to die, but we can't lose ourselves in the process. We've lost too many friends already. If she turns up, don't do anything rash."

"That sounds like something Rylin would tell me. I miss him. He is gone so fast. Like Aradel. I was with neither when they passed." She let out a soft warble. "We did not know each other long, Rylin and I. But our hearts beat as one."

Elenai understood. She thought of how she had come to respect Gyldara, Lasren, Thelar, Meria, and M'vai, and the brave second circler, Derahd, because they had faced terror and triumphed, together. No matter that they barely knew one another, they had forged a deep bond that would only be severed at death.

Three of that number were already gone. "I understand how you feel." Elenai wasn't sure what else to say, but she hoped Lelanc took solace from her company, for it brought her a measure of peace to sit with the beautiful creature.

After a time Lelanc closed her eyes, and Elenai rose and quietly walked away.

The kobalin were arranged now along the slope, and Ortok stood with Tretton beside the carcass of the great glow beast, burned by the kobalin to keep carrion away. Ortok lifted his hands, appearing to mime Kalandra blasting the thing with the chaos weapon.

She turned at the sound of approaching footsteps. Kyrkenall stopped beside her.

"Is it you, or him?" she asked.

"Me. A bit of him." He saluted her with his wineskin and drank deep.

"You're awfully calm about sharing your head with someone else."

"He's not like some evil wizard out to crush my soul and take over my body. He's just waiting for his chance to talk to Savessa."

"Savessa?" Elenai asked.

"Their children named them. She's Savessa, he's Savech. It means maker and unmaker."

"He knows she trapped him, right?"

"Aye, he does."

"I'm surprised he doesn't want vengeance."

"I don't even think he understands the concept. He's confused by death and mourning. It's affected him more deeply than he expected. It's almost like he's eaten mine."

"Is that why you're in such good spirits?"

"It's why I'm not a sobbing wreck."

Below, Ortok and Tretton trudged upslope, deep still in conversation. To the right, Thelar was directing the shaping tool against a nearby dune. Bright energy flowed forth, slowly wearing the sand down.

"So you know what's funny? One of the things that's puzzling him is all my memories from childhood."

Kyrkenall had never, ever spoken of his childhood to her. "What memories?" It was hard even to think of him as a child. She'd heard rumors that his mother had become a squire, but hadn't made it to second rank. The gossip was that she had become a heavy drinker, and had Kyrkenall later in life. He'd lived his first years on the edge of a remote village in Ekhem, and was said to have spent more time in the wilds than in four walls.

He shrugged, abruptly hesitant to explain, then finished his thought. "Let's just say encounters with my peers weren't usually happy. He doesn't understand why the children feared me because of the way I looked. He finds difference and variety loveliest of all."

"Differences can be frightening," she mused, and thought about the alliance of forces with them on the mesa: Kobalin, Naor, Ko'aye, Exalt, and Altenerai. "But they can be a source of strength."

"Aye."

"I'm sorry your childhood was hard," she said.

"It wasn't so bad. I had a couple of great dogs. It was just the people who were terrible. Mostly."

"And here you've spent you life protecting people anyway."

"I guess I have."

He took another drink.

"When you grabbed me to look at N'lahr's sword, could you have guessed it would take us here?" Elenai asked.

"If you'd told me, I'd have laughed. But life has a way of taking weird turns. Maybe it will work out, and we'll save Kalandra and N'lahr. Or maybe Rialla's still alive and we can get her to turn everything back and save us all."

"Right now I'm just hoping we can stop the Goddess. And Cerai. And maybe save the realms one last time."

"I'll drink to that." He lifted the skin again. "I'd offer to share a toast, but I know how much you hate Murian wine."

"I'll take you up on that offer. Just this once."

36

~

The Battle Joins

Vannek, sitting near the mesa edge, swigged from his waterskin. A cool wind chilled his face as he looked up to find the blue ko'aye, Drusa, making another circuit, passing beneath the wound in the sky where the stars bled through. That disturbing aerial scar left from the passage of the demon goddess was the only reason the wastelands weren't blazing in the sun's heat.

A messenger had relayed that the mages were readying to open the hearthstones, and he wished that they'd get on with it. Too much longer and the men would grow restless. Varama hadn't been able to bring many warriors through from Darassus, so his own forces consisted of less than forty, half of those recovered from Cerai's fortress. They sat nearby, looking over their weapons or drawing in the sand or scanning the heavens like himself.

He heard a shrill cry above. Drusa swooped down, calling that many tens of warriors neared.

Vannek frowned and climbed to his feet. Cerai had organized herself quickly.

From his vantage point on the left flank, Vannek looked down on his men, and below them, tiered on the slope, were two ranks of kobalin. While Naor were still inclined to rush for individual opponents, over the last fifteen years discipline had been hammered into many of their units, and the warriors of Vannek's tiny force were among them. While they might long to rush to battle, they'd hold until he gave the order. He had little faith in the kobalin, however, and fully expected them to break ranks and seek solitary combat.

Ortok had told those on the left that Vannek was their officer, news that they'd absorbed without reaction. They'd been less than pleased when Vannek had instructed them to wait for his word before they attacked, but grunted their assent.

The kobalin shifted to peer between two large dunes on the left, beyond the killing field. Most possessed dog, horse, or bat-wing ears, which stood at full attention as they faced toward a gap. Their hands tightened on the hafts of axes, swords, and polearms.

A moment after the kobalin heard it, the faint sound of hoofbeats reached Vannek, and he called to his men to stand ready. "We have to hold. None of them will get to the center through us!"

The bodyguard at his side grunted doubtfully, and Vannek looked to him for explanation. He rarely said anything, although he'd smiled hugely when they'd been reunited and was following him more closely than ever, as if to make up for having been separated from him during the battle. He had not proven to be a skilled horseman.

"I worry that they will not hold, Lord General," the young man said.

"I'll do the worrying. You just keep your blade sharp."

"Yes, Lord General."

The rest of his soldiers stretched arms and loosed their swords. Those few who still had bows planted the shafts in the soil. They tested their weapon grips.

Thelar and a wispy young female squire in an ill-fitting tabard arrived at a jog. "Lord General, this is Aspirant Tavella."

Vannek grunted in greeting and spoke to Thelar. "You think Cerai will throw magic at us?"

"We don't know what she'll do." Thelar slipped on his helmet so that little but his stern eyes, lips, and strong chin showed beneath the metal. He presented a more martial appearance even than Rylin. His assistant, though, only enhanced her childlike appearance as she fixed the chin strap of her own helm. Vannek reminded himself that when it came to mages, outward appearance mattered little.

The first enemies appeared at a notch between two large dunes, four horselike beasts sporting dark iridescent scales and spikelike manes. Two mailed warriors rode along the back of each, the rear-seated man holding a clutch of spears. The helms of a larger host were visible behind them.

Lelanc, now airborne with Drusa, called down that a second large force approached from the right.

"If she's pinning the flanks," Thelar said, "Cerai must plan something for the center."

"True enough," Vannek agreed.

Muragan had explained about the difference between the exalts and the Altenerai, saying further that Thelar was reputed to be a fair swords-man. He had not also said he was a student of military theory.

The lead horse thing let out a loud snort, disgorging dark smoke from its nostrils.

"She'll probably use the winged beast Rylin learned about against the center," Thelar said. "I hope it's not a dragon."

"Hope? Best pray."

"I've no faith in prayers," Thelar said. "Do your Three give you strength or miracles?"

"They deliver victory to the brave and cunning."

"Let that be us, then," Thelar said.

"They come for the fight!" a huge brown-furred kobalin shouted ea-gerly from downslope.

The horses had sprung into motion, churning the sand as they beat for-ward, closely followed by at least a hundred helmed warriors with round shields and axes. They ran in a loose wedge formation, giving vent to a full-throated roar. Vannek heard that mirrored from the right, but spared them no more thought. His job was to hold the left.

Vannek's kobalin shifted and stamped their feet in the sand. When two shook their weapons overhead, others joined in. A handful advanced a few steps, and others moved after and soon both lines of kobalin wavered.

"Hold until my signal!" Vannek shouted. "Hold!" The Altenerai horn call from the central mesa signaled the same order. Kobalin, though, would be unlikely to heed it, no matter that they had apparently been taught the meaning of the sounds.

The kobalin ceased their forward movement. Many scowled back at Vannek.

The horses galloped on, racing ahead of the troops.

"Archers!" Vannek shouted. "Drop those animals!"

A moment later a flight of arrows soared for the enemy.

But the shafts of his seven archers glanced off the shining scales of the mounts. Three stuck out from the armored shoulders of a single spear-man, in back of a rider. A ragged arrow volley followed the first, and while it too failed to stop the horse-things, one of the mounted spearmen was struck and dropped from the saddle.

First blood was apparently too much for the kobalin. One with dark red fur let out a gibbering shout and charged. A second ran after, and then the dam burst and every single kobalin under Vannek's command ran screaming at the enemy, a full minute before he would have released them. He swore, then called again for his men to hold.

There were shouts from the right flank as well.

Two kobalin charged straight for the first of the horse things, axes raised. As they closed into range, a fleshy sack at the back of the horse thing's neck expanded, reminding Vannek of a frog. When the beast opened its scaly mouth far wider than a horse, it didn't make a sound, but a ball of fire immediately emerged to engulf the scaly green kobalin before it. The other threw itself clear, left arm aflame, and rolled in the sand to put out the blaze.

The horses plunged through the kobalin line, burning and kicking as they went, the spearsmen at their rear taking deadly toll.

One stout, red-scaled kobalin, fully alight, crushed the foreleg of the foremost horse. He fell, dying, but the creature dropped and kobalin swarmed over the beast and its riders.

Cerai's infantry ran in from behind, and Vannek ordered his archers to loose their final shafts before the soldiers got too close to the kobalin.

In moments, the flame-breathing lizard horses were charging up the sandy brown slope to the top of the mesa. The kobalin mass stopped the greater number of Cerai's troops, but dozens broke free and ran in the wake of the horses.

That's when Thelar proved his worth. Just as a third ragged volley of arrows rebounded from the armor of the rider in the forefront, and one well-aimed arrow stuck uselessly beside the lizard horse's expanding throat sac, the exalt's fingers worked back and forth as though he manipulated invisible threads. His spell tore the sand from beneath the lead animal and sent it sliding backward. He and his aspirant worked the same trick with the next animal, and sent it head over heels down slope.

The final lizard horse reached the Naor ranks.

The spearsman on its back dropped one of Vannek's soldiers as the beast raced up, and another four felt the kiss of its flame. They screamed as they died.

Vannek led the rush from the left, spear in hand. He'd heard it said Kyrkenall raced to battle with a poem on his lips, but Vannek offered only a bellow of rage. His bodyguard and three of his spearmen shouted with him as they attacked.

The horse-thing reared and its mouth opened. The spearman behind the rider cast and missed Vannek's shoulder by a knife length.

Vannek crashed into the animal's scaled underside, and his men struck a second after him.

One flailing hoof glanced off his mailed shoulder and another hit the warrior to Vannek's left in his helmeted head, dropping him.

But their assault sent the beast over, and it fell sideways, breathing a gout of flame as it struck the ground.

Vannek threw himself flat, hit the sand hard, and slid. His boot felt momentarily hot, and he jerked his feet out of the way, then rolled and scrambled to stand.

Upright once more he discovered Thelar had covered the creature with a blanket of sand. Vannek's loyal bodyguard drove his weapon through the rider's throat.

After that the real battle began in earnest. Cerai's soldiers raced to close with Vannek's troops, fighting with ferocity. Vannek's men held their lines at first, but before long the assault fragmented into the vicious one-on-one conflicts even his own people secretly preferred.

Vannek was at their forefront. He lost all sense of the greater battle, for his attention was rooted only in the now, moving at quarter speed so that each individual moment felt a day's length. This strike Vannek blocked, that arm he hewed, leaving red ruin. That thrust he dodged, another he took on his shield. He swept a leg with his spear, then drove the point down through armor and turned to face another foe.

When his spear lodged too firmly in a chest, he snatched a dead man's sword and carried on the fight. When his shield splintered under a terrific axe blow he grabbed a knife in his off hand and drove it into a screaming enemy face.

He fought his way through the warriors that came and came until he discovered he had somehow survived and all of his opponents were down. When he paused to wipe sweat from his face he accidentally smeared blood from an arm wound he hadn't felt.

Scanning his surroundings, he discovered his bodyguard stood still beside him, and gave an approving nod to the devoted young warrior. The man smiled as though he'd been awarded a land grant. Thelar and the aspirant remained, along with fifteen more of Vannek's men, panting in a ragged line. Others lived, farther down slope. The dead and dying littered the ground on every side like broken grain stalks.

While he'd been fighting for his life, a strange silver beast had appeared in the sky. It resembled a ko'aye, but a second set of wings flapped behind the first upon its elongated back. A helmed woman in an Altenerai khalat rode behind its long neck. That had to be Cerai. Four warriors sat behind her along its sinuous spine. As the beast swooped above the center of the mesa, the enchantress who commanded it directed a burning blue flame at the ground below; someone screamed, but it seemed more a cry of alarm than of pain.

An answering golden beam shot up from the midst of the mesa and struck the beast along its tail. A swath of it fell away as shining flakes and the beast trembled.

Cerai set her beast climbing. The two ko'aye dropped from out of the sun and closed upon the winged thing. Seeing a rider with a bow upon the back of Drusa, Vannek smiled. For long years his people had been the target of the world's greatest archer, and they had both feared and admired him. Being Kyrkenall's ally was strangely thrilling, and he looked forward to seeing the destruction he would wreak.

The ko'aye dodged and weaved away from spears and shafts cast by Cerai's warriors, but the peerless bowman found his marks. Two of the beast's weapons-men slumped with arrows standing from their helmets. Even at a distance, on a moving platform, to a shifting target, Kyrkenall had struck two men dead through tiny gaps in armor.

Lelanc tore another warrior from his seat. While he fell, screaming, both ko'aye dove at Cerai, Kyrkenall firing the while.

An arrow struck her in the throat and a second was engulfed in the wave of blue-white flame rolling out from a shining object she held. Lelanc took the brunt of the attack, and burst into flame. The ko'aye's wings evaporated almost on the instant and her charred, smoking form dropped stonelike toward the desert floor. A loud cry of dismay rose from the throats of many of the watchers, and Vannek wasn't entirely surprised some were his own men, who would gladly have hunted ko'aye only a week before.

Drusa pulled away, one of her own wings smoking. Her neck flared back, her wings spread wide. Kyrkenall, on her back, leaned toward her head, shouting something.

But the ko'aye could not hold its glide, and plummeted. Vannek swore.

Then, only a dozen feet from the ground, Drusa's astonishing speed eased until she drifted slowly down. The ko'aye didn't seem to have anything to do with the action, for she hung limp. Instead, she appeared to be borne gently by invisible hands.

Vannek grew conscious of Thelar, working magic at his side, but he didn't think he had saved Kyrkenall either, for the exalt's hands were still moving after Drusa settled safely. Thelar followed the movements of Cerai, circling back on her monstrous, four-winged ko'aye. His breathing was labored.

"Who saved Kyrkenall and his ko'aye?" Vannek asked the aspirant.

"I think that was Kalandra," the young woman answered, her voice hollow from within her helm. "I don't know how her spell reached so far."

"Why isn't Elenai shooting at Cerai?"

"The weapons don't have that great a range."

"What's he doing?" Vannek asked, looking pointedly at Thelar.

"The threads on the dragon have been torn open," the aspirant said, then paused to take a breath. "Exalt Thelar's pulling on them. The range is too great, though." She spoke to Thelar. "You shouldn't risk—"

Thelar drew heavily down with both hands, like a beast clawing flesh. Above, the dragon simply fell away into wind-borne strands of silver, as though it had been composed of spools of yarn the exalt had unwound. Cerai and her last warrior flailed as they fell.

A cheer went up from the allied troops. The warrior struck ground with a thud. A heartbeat before Cerai did the same, a shimmering violet portal flared into existence beneath her and she vanished through it.

37

———◆———

The Last Farewell

There was nothing she could do for poor Lelanc, but Elenai sent healers running toward Kyrkenall and Drusa. Kalandra strained at the limits permitted by her emerald, peering out from the mesa's edge.

Cerai's monsters lay dead, along with most of her soldiers. Any survivors had retreated, most of the kobalin in pursuit. Only Ortok and a few dozen remained, either tending their wounded or looting Cerai's dead for arms and armor.

Watching from the center, Elenai breathed a sigh of relief as Kyrkenall stirred upon Drusa's back, fumbling with his straps. He then fell sideways, and stumbled, as though drunken.

He climbed stiffly to his feet and Elenai knew on the instant from his sharp, jerky movements, that the chaos entity once more had possession of him.

The ko'aye flapped her wings and shook her neck, as though she were dizzy. She struggled to stand, then decided to lay down. Kyrkenall put a hand to her neck.

In her distraction, Elenai had allowed her chaos staff to stray too close to Kalandra, and quickly turned it aside. She looked to the right where Gyldara, Tretton, and the squires had held the flank. Squires now searched among the fallen and carried the wounded back to the healers, already tending injured soldiers to the left of the hearthstone cache. The stones recovered from Cerai still lay in an unceremonious pile, glittering and beautiful, at the mesa's center.

From afar came the shouts of battle, tinny and indistinct. Somewhere out of sight the kobalin harried Cerai's retreating soldiers.

Varama breathed heavily beside her, the shaping tool in one hand. The two aspirants watched her protectively. They had been extremely fortunate during the attack, for Cerai had gotten off only one spell, and had made the mistake of assaulting Kalandra's image. All that had done was burn the ground beneath her.

"What can Cerai do now?" Elenai asked. "She wouldn't dare assault without another army, and she doesn't have one."

She never found out what Varama was opening her mouth to say, because a glowing violet portal spiraled open in their midst. Elenai stepped wide to face it, leveling her staff, and then a spray of blue lightning crackled forth. One minor bolt hit Varama and drove her to her knees. A larger one struck Elenai directly and blew her off her feet. She slammed backward into the ground, shaken and moaning. Her khalat was smoking and a burnt, acrid stench filled her nostrils.

Cerai emerged, turned a sword blow from an aspirant, and wrenched Varama's shaping tool from her hand. She darted forward and snatched the staff from where it lay beside Elenai, struggling to rise.

Elenai didn't see from where Ortok had come, but he was suddenly in their midst. His axe blow slammed into Cerai's chest. The traitorous alten flew off her feet. Ortok advanced with a howl.

No matter that the Altenerai armor had protected against the axe's edge, it was a mighty blow and should have broken ribs and driven breath from Cerai's body. Yet she rolled the moment she hit the ground, and was up and moving, shaping tool in one hand, chaos weapon under her arm. She raced for the mesa's side. Ortok's next blow would have taken her head if she hadn't moved.

Cerai leapt off the mesa's side.

By the time Ortok had helped her to her feet Elenai understood the sickening truth. Cerai had portaled out with both weapons. She'd taken advantage of their lowered guard and struck surely, as only a veteran could. Elenai was livid with herself for not having anticipated it.

Ortok was vowing vengeance again, but as Elenai struggled from her daze she grew more alarmed at the troubled mention of Kalandra's name by the two aspirants. Varama's brows were furrowed in worry as she knelt beside something on the ground, and Elenai hurried to see what it was.

Kalandra's emerald sat with a fracture in its side stretched up from a black burn mark. A faint pinprick, like an impossibly distant star, burned within.

Elenai's breath caught in her throat and she frantically searched the mesa. There was Kyrkenall, sprinting toward them, but Kalandra herself had vanished.

Ortok had seen the direction of Elenai's gaze. "One of the lightning bolts struck her magic gem," he said.

A grinning Kyrkenall arrived beside them. "That was great pleasure," he said, speaking with the God's voice. "This Kyrkenall delights in the changing of living states. Carnage, he calls it. Hah. Where is his lover? She saved the creature whom he loves, and he wishes to thank her." He searched among their faces, touching his chest. "Ah, how he loves her. It's like a fire. It almost burns out his sorrow. He is very sad the other ko'aye died."

"Kalandra's badly hurt." Elenai looked down again at the emerald, and then to the fist-sized scorch mark burned into her khalat just below her heart. She'd been lucky.

While Kyrkenall's expression shifted from inhuman curiosity to actual human alarm, Veshahd, the male aspirant, arrived with an azure hearthstone shard, which Varama opened on the instant. She poured energy into the damaged emerald.

It was only then that Elenai recovered her full senses, and shouted for the Altenerai to gather and to pull in their lines. Cerai might well return for her hearthstones, too.

Kyrkenall sank to his knees opposite Varama, and it was he, not the God, who spoke. His hands stretched for the gem but he did not touch it.

"My love." His voice shook.

Gyldara and Tretton arrived at a run, along with Elik and a small band of squires. Thelar and Vannek jogged up a few moments later, an aspirant and Vannek's bodyguard with them. Most surprising of all, Muragan himself walked forward, his thick torso clothed in an ill-fitting borrowed shirt. The hair and beard along the right side of his head was singed off, and newly grown skin showed pink and glistening. Vannek grinned and clapped him on the back.

"Cerai attacked," Elenai said. "We need to guard the hearthstones."

Varama ceased her work with the hearthstone, and pushed to her feet, waving off Veshahd's helping hand. She stared down at Kalandra's broken gem. It had not changed.

The pain upon Kyrkenall's face was so pronounced, Elenai turned from him.

When he spoke behind her, though, his voice was level. "She is near."

Elenai whirled, thinking he had meant Kalandra. But seeing Kyrkenall standing and looking up, his face now only faintly touched with grief, she knew it had been the God who spoke. He cocked his head to one side and looked at her. "There is more of me now, since you released my energies to attack the beast of the air. My thoughts come more easily. They are still colored by this one, though."

Elenai spoke swiftly, grasping at this last hope. "Cerai took our weapons. She took the rest of your energies. We have no way to attack the Goddess now."

"I understand."

"Do you understand she will destroy us when she comes? Then she will destroy our world?"

The God in Kyrkenall did not answer. He lifted a hand and the wind rose. The sky darkened.

"What are you doing?" Elenai asked.

"Don't be afraid," the being answered, with the faintest touch of Kyrkenall's own charm. "I call to the rest of me, and I hope to gather before her arrival. Then I shall speak to her. Ah, my love," he said, now with Kyrkenall's voice, and, stricken, looked back to the stone. "She's there. I feel her. But she's weak."

"I will stream more threads to the emerald," Varama said on the instant, and reached for the hearthstone once more.

"Can the God really stop the Goddess?" Elenai asked Kyrkenall.

"He's going to talk to her. Well, not talk really, but interact. He wants to be whole when he meets her. Those chaos spirits out in the shifts? Those are all little bits of him that escaped or dripped away, or were never captured. They've been out there all this time, looking for a way to be a part of a greater whole. They're coming to be a part of him again."

From that jagged tear in the sky, the wind rolled down, carrying with them a vast sweep of giant figures outlined in white. The last time Elenai had seen the chaos spirits they were images of the dead. This time every single one of them was a grinning Kyrkenall.

Those with her must have seen different things. She heard Thelar gasp in horror, and the aspirants cried out. Gyldara let out a soft moan, as of pain.

"We're all seeing different things," Elenai said. "Don't be afraid!" And then she spoke quickly to Kyrkenall. "They're not going to hurt these people, are they?"

"No," the God answered. "They are a part of me. I am fond of this one, and he is fond of you. I will not harm you." Kyrkenall thrust one hand to the sky, fingers splayed.

The figures flowed one in upon the other, their lines blurring and twisting and swirling down, as though Kyrkenall's outstretched hand lay at the bottom of a vast invisible funnel. He took on their energies, smiling brightly, laughing as he did. Finally the spirits were gone. The thing within Kyrkenall had absorbed them.

"Oh, that is glorious and ever so much better!" he cried, and stretched out both hands.

Elenai remembered what Kalandra had said about a mad god of chaos upon the loose. A changeable, shiftable god. How much understanding of humanity would he retain once he left Kyrkenall?

The God's energies drifted free of the archer and left him blinking and uncertain on his feet. Elenai steadied him.

Beside Kyrkenall was a being who was, and wasn't him. One whose eyes weren't black, but burned with distant stars. A being of marble white skin with pearly white hair, garbed in a shining white khalat, who laughed, and smiled. "Oh, what a fine and pleasant shape this is!"

It was then the Goddess drifted down, dark perfection, stories tall. The duplicate Kyrkenall expanded to meet her, growing swiftly in size and levitating into the air.

Thelar cried a warning. "The hearthstones!"

They burned bright, and their energies poured out in concentrated rays, gifting the looming Goddess with their full power. As it streamed into her, she faced the God in midair. Both started at one another, hands outstretched but not quite touching. Their enormous eyes closed.

Kalandra reappeared dimly on Kyrkenall's other side, a ghost through which Varama was visible. Kyrkenall turned to her, smiling in relief.

"You did it!" Elenai grinned at Varama.

"It wasn't me," the alten said. She was on her feet, looking behind them so fixedly that Elenai turned.

The long dead, long-vanished alten Rialla stood there, pale and luminous.

"Rialla," Elenai said quickly, "go back and warn Kyrkenall while you're still alive. Tell him about all of this."

"No, my queen," Rialla said. "I'm sorry I couldn't stop it sooner, and I'm sorry I can't explain, then or now. My time is nearly run, and I saw we had another chance here, if we do better than the first time we tried. There cannot be another." She looked to Varama. "Hold the keystone foremost in your memory. The globe."

That must have made some sense to Varama, who confirmed the instruction with a single nod.

Kyrkenall swore, not in disgust, but with pleasure. Tretton, somewhere behind, laughed genially. And Ortok shouted in joy. "My friend!"

Elenai turned from Rialla. A gaunt, welcome figure hurried toward them from where the hearthstones disintegrated. N'lahr spared only the briefest glance at the giant figures above as he drew to a stop, Gyldara and Tretton on his heels.

Ortok embraced him in his great arms.

Elenai was only momentarily confused about the commander's unexpected revival. Just as the Goddess had pulled energy from Kyrkenall's bow and blade and even Elenai's horse, she had withdrawn it from N'lahr, who'd been lying only fifteen feet or so from the hearthstones.

Ortok stepped away and N'lahr received an embrace from Kyrkenall.

"All of you," Rialla said, "do not interfere with what's about to happen. No matter what you see. I will tell you when to act." She pointed to a high dune less than an eighth of a mile north. "Cerai will attack from there. Ready yourselves. Mages, assist me when the energy falls."

Elenai half expected a portal to open on the dune, but Cerai simply stepped to the top and knelt, a staff in either hand. She aimed one into the sky above.

Bright, warm energies stretched forth in a golden ray. Cerai must have had a better understanding of the shaping tool's energies than they'd managed, for her attack was no narrow beam. It encompassed nearly the whole of the Goddess, transforming her beautiful black surface into shining crystal. She turned her head, reaching with an arm that moved ever slower, and then a blast from the chaos weapon swept down across her body.

Elenai thought the attack would reduce the deity again to hearthstones, but it was raw energies that blew clear from her and swept into the wind. The chaos god spun, his form stretching in an instant toward Cerai, only to have holes torn through his own changing form as the shaping tool's energy laced through him. He lifted hands as if to contemplate the wonder of this new sensation, then his outline wavered and he, too, vanished.

Their energies rolled and sparkled and thundered—and swept toward a violet portal opening in the sky. Cerai, Elenai guessed, funneling the energies to her realm. She had out-planned them all, even Rialla.

But the ghost alten seemed unperturbed, though no less intent. "Now, Commander! Strike her now! Mages, assist me!"

N'lahr shouted for Tretton and Gyldara to guard the queen and for Ortok and Kyrkenall to follow, then sprinted down slope with a borrowed sword. His friends raced after.

Rialla worked the air, hands spiraling in a complex motion. A portal opened upon them and out flowed the energies of the Gods. Pure hearthstone energy, stolen from Cerai. It washed into Elenai with such ferocious pleasure it rendered her mute. Kalandra's form blazed up to full intensity in the onslaught. Varama threw back her head, smiling, and Thelar and Muragan laughed in joy.

"Center yourselves!" Rialla shouted. "Guide the energy to me!"

And this they did. Half blind with power, Elenai diverted the rushing energy toward the smaller woman, who twisted it into hundreds of threads at once and hurtled them skyward, where they curved out and away and off into the horizon. Every mage there was united in their effort—Elenai, Varama, Kalandra, Thelar, even the blood mage and the trio of aspirants— each fighting to capture and divert every particle of energy toward Rialla before it could escape. Elenai smiled the while, but no matter the boundless power at her command, fear wrapped the core of her being, for the mages wavered constantly upon the point of failure. And with that failure might come the end of everything.

The stress was too much for the aspirant Tavella, who sank to the ground. None of them could divert attention to help, and Elenai was glad to see Gyldara pull her clear.

Elenai glimpsed N'lahr and the others drawing close to Cerai as the rogue alten worked frantically to counter Rialla's efforts, but she could spare no more attention.

After a time, the energy had begun to ebb. Muragan had to move away, and a short while after, Elenai realized she, too, was stretched to her limits and stepped apart, doing so with a mix of relief and reluctance, for it was difficult to abandon that tremendous power.

She wavered unsteadily on her feet, blinking dizzily. Gyldara steadied her with a firm grip. Vannek and Elik stood nearby watching the spell work, transfixed with awe by the play of rainbow energies visible even beyond the inner world.

Either less impressed or simply more practical, Tretton knelt by Muragan, who was wearily drinking from a wineskin. Tavella sat watching nearby.

The six other spell casters still labored, and Elenai watched in envy for a moment, then tore her attention away to where Gyldara pointed at the struggling figures on the dune. "They almost have her," she said.

On that height, N'lahr had just missed a savage blow from Irion at Cerai's hand. Ortok swept her from her feet with a great axe blow that surely shattered bone, but she rolled upright with celerity superhuman even by Altenerai standards. Kyrkenall leaned in with a vicious slice, but Cerai slipped past with a savage cut to Kyrkenall's side. Elenai gasped as she saw the spray of blood.

Exhausted though she was, she reached for a spell thread to aid them, but before she'd even fully looked into the inner world, N'lahr thrust. She was too distant to see the how of it, only the result—Irion swirled through the air even as Cerai fell back. The blade seemed to land of its own accord in the Altenerai commander's outstretched hand.

Though still worried for Kyrkenall, Elenai released the spell unborn. Even Cerai couldn't contend with three of the greatest warriors alive, not at the same time. Kyrkenall was on his feet still. Cerai managed to sidestep his attack, but she was too late for N'lahr's slash across her chest. Then Ortok's weapon cleaved through her head, spraying blood, brain, and bone. She dropped at last.

At almost the same moment, the last two aspirants pulled from Rialla's spell. The woman stood blinking. The man sank to one knee. Elik and Gyldara guided them over to where Tavella sat.

Ortok swept Kyrkenall into his massive arms and ran downslope. N'lahr followed after. That didn't bode well. How badly had their friend been injured?

Varama was next to pull back. Though visibly strained, she actually looked less pale and drawn than when she'd begun.

"Where is she sending the energy?" Elenai asked her.

"There was a plan within the keystone for a balanced connection between the realms. In this new configuration they will finally be stable."

"It's a globe, isn't it," Elenai said. "I could feel it forming."

"It's an entire world. A sphere made up not just of our realms, but of all those other lands the Gods had dreamed, as well as vast seas."

Thelar stepped away from the spell. Elenai put her hand to his shoulder, and he looked up at her, eyes still shining. She understood his feelings.

It had been a glorious thing to hold such power, however briefly. The exalt sighed. Only two brightly glowing ghosts were left to spin the energy of the Gods, shooting it out and away toward every horizon.

"I wish we could be a part of it now," Thelar said reverently. "Shaping it at the end."

"We couldn't have endured," Elenai told him. "It would have torn our bodies apart. These two are spirits, and the magic reinforces them even as they work."

"They're finishing," Varama said.

The defensive screen of squires and kobalin parted before Ortok, who arrived bearing Kyrkenall. His black fur was stained with the archer's blood. "There are great magics here," he said. "And part of the God is in him. I feel it. Surely there is a means to heal him?"

Kyrkenall's khalat was sliced open along his left breast. Blood dripped steadily from his mouth. His skin was gray.

N'lahr was only a few paces behind, his brows drawn in worry. Irion's blade was dark with the blood of Cerai, and he passed it off to Elik.

Rialla stepped away from the spell at last. She left Kalandra at what had been the nexus point of the vast energies, her arms lifted to the sky. A thin stream of energy still trailed from the portal toward her; the one Cerai had opened in the sky had vanished only a while ago.

Rialla looked at her friend, whom she had doomed herself and saved a world to preserve. "We have won, Kyrkenall. And the kobalin speaks true. Some of the chaos remains within you. Some of the chaos surrounds us yet. I think you have a choice."

"That's good to hear," Kyrkenall replied weakly. "I'm going to go with not bleeding to death."

"I think I can mend you, for I've learned to mend a world." Rialla's expression softened ever so slightly. "But there is another possibility. You can't truly destroy a concept like the God, or the Goddess. You can only change the expression of their energy. Just as some of the God is within you, some of the energy of the Goddess has sustained Kalandra."

"Yes," Kyrkenall said with surprising strength. "I think I see."

"I don't," Ortok said.

"Neither do I," said Vannek. Elenai hadn't even noticed him come up beside them. Tretton and Gyldara had rejoined their circle as well, watching in awed silence.

"But what about you, old friend?" Kyrkenall asked, his gaze shifting to N'lahr.

"What are you talking about?" N'lahr asked.

"He'll be all right without you." Rialla pushed a hand toward Kyrkenall and did not quite touch him. Blood trailed from his mouth for a moment longer, then halted its flow. His skin darkened.

Kyrkenall's gaze swung alertly to Elenai.

And she understood his unasked question at the same moment she reasoned out what Rialla's vague words hinted at. "I'll be fine," she said. "But what about you?" Her eyes were tearing up.

"I will be with her," Kyrkenall said, and as he did so he swung down from the great kobalin, patting one large arm almost tenderly as he stood.

Kalandra walked forward, reaching out with her hand. Her fingers did not pass through Kyrkenall's own, but grasped them. Not only was she present physically, her eyes were no longer sunken, her cheekbones no longer sharpened by emaciation.

"You are restored!" Ortok cried. "Both of you!"

But Elenai understood as the archer beamed at his lost love and she smiled brightly in return that they were more than themselves.

"Oh, Kyrkenall," Elenai said, her tears flowing freely. She felt his joy, but she feared for him, and she did not want to say good-bye. Not to him. "Do you really want this? You love your terrible wine. You want Kalandra, in spirit and in flesh. You want to ride Lyria to far and distant lands. And you want to laugh with your friend and brother, N'lahr."

Kyrkenall's smile was sad and knowing. He raised Kalandra's hand within his own. "You know the things I dreamt of and I sought. My eyes now look on greater, shining sights. They're leagued like blooms, each opening with thoughts, enticing me with scents and colors bright." He looked just as she best remembered him, beautiful and rakish and charming. He laughed, and she knew it really would be fine.

"It won't be a bad thing to have human faces on these concepts," Kalandra said. "Maybe it will make the universe a little kinder."

"Just promise not to worship us," Kyrkenall said.

The energy she sensed within them was boundless, almost blinding even without looking into the inner world, but she was not afraid.

Rialla, at long last, smiled. Elenai thought she looked dimmer than before.

"Ah, my time is through. I'm sorry for my mistakes. It was hard to work it all out."

"You saved us all," Elenai reassured her, and looked to Kyrkenall for help.

Kyrkenall and Kalandra spoke as one. "And we shall save you. Come with us."

With a wave of Kalandra's hand, their energies caressed Rialla and then she, too, glowed from within. For the first time since Elenai had encountered her, the strain along the smaller woman's high brow eased.

Kyrkenall laughed again, and it was a sound that echoed through the cold dunes. He, and his laughter, and his energy, seemed too small for such a space, no matter its width. He addressed Kalandra, who yet held his hand. "My perspective's already grown so far. It's hard to hold here. But there are a few last things before we leave, don't you think?"

"The wounded," Kalandra said. "We can heal them. And I'll undo Cerai's work upon that poor exalt. N'lahr, old friend, she left a mark on you as well, but I think you'll find it to your benefit."

"Will I? What did she do?"

"Your life threads are resilient. You have long years before you."

"It's payback for the stolen years," Kyrkenall said. "But you don't have to take them. Why don't you come with us? There are wonders to see. We would never be bored."

N'lahr smiled, then shook his head. "No, that's not for me. Is that what you mean to do? See the far places like you always dreamed?"

"That and more," Kyrkenall answered. His grin was infectious.

"We won't remake your world," Kalandra promised. "Much as its imperfections trouble me. It belongs to you. All of you. It's yours to nourish and safeguard." She looked at N'lahr. "What will you do, dear friend? Do you still mean to give up your ring and build a school?"

"I think I do," N'lahr said. "I've spilled blood for the last time."

"Can you bring back Rylin?" Vannek interjected, desire writ plainly, and painfully, upon his face. "And others we've lost?"

Elenai's eyes widened in hope. It hadn't occurred to her that Kalandra and Kyrkenall had that kind of power, and she searched their faces.

"I wish we could," Kalandra answered sadly. "But that's beyond even us."

Vannek bowed his head. Varama hadn't looked hopeful, exactly, but her expression fell, resigned at the news.

Kyrkenall withdrew his great bow from its shoulder holster, extending it toward Elenai. She felt magic stir within it as she touched its surface.

"Take this. See that some future hero bears it in defense of the realms. And Lothrun, too." This he drew in a flourish and passed to N'lahr.

"We will," his old friend assured him.

Elenai lowered the great bow and bowed her head to Rialla. "This victory was your doing. We will never be able to thank you enough. I shall see that all know of your actions."

"It is enough that it worked," Rialla said. "It is enough that I kept my oath."

"Your dedication and skill were phenomenal," Varama said. "You will inspire generations of squires, and the eternal gratitude of the people of the realms."

"Thank you, Alten," Rialla said with a formal nod. Elenai had almost forgotten that by her timeline, Rialla had only been promoted to the ring the night before, and wasn't yet comfortable informally addressing those who'd been superiors.

"Just Varama. You, of all people, can call me by my name."

"What will you do now?" Kalandra asked her.

"I mean to rebuild Alantris," Varama said with resolve. "I had to burn it to save it, which is a dark, humorless joke. I will not rest until I have seen it restored."

"You blame yourself too much," Kalandra said. "You acted to save the people, and they are surely grateful."

"Be kind to yourself," Kyrkenall advised. "And patient. I know patience isn't really your thing, but compassion is, even though you hide it. Spare some for yourself sometimes."

Varama smiled thinly at this advice. "I'll remember that. Is there any chance you'll visit us, sometimes? I'd be curious to hear what it's like, to be a god."

Kalandra laughed gently. "I'm sure you'd have many questions. We shall see." Her eyes settled on another figure. "Tretton, isn't it about time you got out to some of your dreams?"

"Maybe it is," the older man said. Elenai wondered what those were. "Maybe I should turn the ring over to someone else while I've still got some mileage in me." He bowed his head formally to her. "You made me proud, Kalandra. And Kyrkenall, you were always a thorn in my side, but you pained our enemies even more. I was glad to serve with you both. You be careful out there."

Kyrkenall grinned.

Kalandra answered him. "We will. Gyldara, Thelar, Vannek, I enjoyed knowing all of you. Never forget that we won because we worked together. Let that continue."

"I will devote myself to that," Gyldara pledged.

"As will I," Thelar said.

Vannek formally bowed his head.

"What of me?" Ortok asked. "Surely you have words for me."

"Of course I do!" Kalandra said with a smile. "Yours is a brave, bright soul, and we would never have succeeded without you. I hope you will remain a friend of the realms. I can't take you to the theater, but Elenai still can. Seek out Selana's plays. Think of me, especially when you see *The Fool's First Errand* and *Far Falls the Moon*."

"It's the second she always quotes," Kyrkenall said. "And I swear she's just like the queen in *Fool's First Errand*."

"I will remember this," Ortok said.

Finally, Kalandra's gaze shifted to Elenai. "Rule well," she said. "Take counsel from the wise ones here."

"I will."

"And don't forget to laugh now and then," Kyrkenall said. He then turned to Kalandra. "I almost forgot about some people Belahn trapped in Wyndyss. Weeks ago. In another life."

So far as Elenai knew, Kyrkenall had never mentioned the matter to Kalandra, but she answered without hesitation. "We will set them free." She then favored N'lahr with a tender smile. "Be well, old friend. Set your sword aside at last."

"Good-bye, Elenai," Kyrkenall said, and his eyes fell upon N'lahr. "Good-bye, old friend. All of you: live long and well and free of burden." He and Kalandra raised their hands in farewell.

N'lahr addressed them as he and the others returned the gesture. "May your road be long, may your cup of joys be full."

Kyrkenall released Kalandra's fingers, and he and she and Rialla brought their hands to their chests in salute. The sapphire within Kyrkenall's ring lit, and then, at the same time, so did the burned-out sapphire within Elenai's own, brighter than it ever had. So, too, did those on the fingers of each of them.

Elenai and the others returned the salute. She wiped at her eyes, meeting those of her departing friends. She wept even as she smiled, but they, all three of them, were full of life and love.

And then he and Kalandra and Rialla simply vanished, their images fading like the afterimage of a snuffed candle flame. Kyrkenall's ring was left behind, shining for a moment in the sand before it dimmed.

It was very quiet.

N'lahr stared at the spot where all three had stood. Elenai wondered if he'd ask to be caught up, but his first question was simple. "Darassus and the realms?"

"Fine, so far as we know." Elenai wiped at her eyes again.

"I sensed them in the connective threads of the globe Rialla shaped,"

Varama said. "The realms lay securely upon it, along with other lands once planned or dreamed."

N'lahr looked as though he wanted more details and decided against it. He took in the surrounding Altenerai and officers. "And Rylin is dead," he said.

"He died freeing the shaping tool," Thelar explained. He'd accomplished far more than that, but now wasn't the time for a full report.

Ortok walked up to N'lahr, his expression grave. Elenai knew a stab of fear. Why hadn't Kyrkenall and Kalandra foreseen this long dread moment, and done something about it?

"Ortok," she said sternly, "I can't permit you to duel N'lahr. That is my order, as queen."

Ortok grunted and shrugged. "You are not my queen. But a god told him to set aside his sword. How can I fight a man when the Gods have told him to lay his weapon down? Besides, I already slew the one who killed him." Ortok extended his arm to N'lahr. "You offered me friendship. I offer you brotherhood."

"I will take it, gladly," N'lahr said.

They clasped arms then, and Ortok beamed.

Elenai wondered if it were truly that simple for him. But then maybe Ortok, too, had seen N'lahr die too many times, and had reasoned his way out of that final challenge.

"If all these lands have been added, how do we find our way back to them?" Vannek asked.

"I've a sense of where everything lies," Varama answered. "If you're not averse to following my directions again."

Vannek actually smiled at that.

"We will bury our dead," Elenai said, thinking foremost of noble Lelanc. "And we will honor them. Then we'll break into two groups. I'll return with half of you to Darassus. Varama, I wish you to return to Cerai's stronghold. Recover Rylin's body. See if there are other experiments that must be terminated. Take the general and Muragan with you." She faced Vannek. "You want land? It occurs to me Cerai built a fine realm. The land is fertile. There's even a citadel."

"We blew it to pieces!" the blood mage said, laughing.

"Call it partly under construction," Elenai suggested. "Does that sound amenable?"

"It's a good start," Vannek said.

Elik presented a cleaned Irion, hilt first, to N'lahr, who hesitated for a moment before sliding it home into its sheath.

"Do you really mean to step down from the Altenerai?" Elenai asked.

"We've won. Against all odds, I still live. And so, yes. After we see to a few more things."

"It was not about odds," Ortok objected. "It was about the will of the Gods."

"If you won't stay on as the commander of the Altenerai," Elenai said, "I hope you might consider counseling me."

"I would be honored."

"Enough talk," Ortok said. "We have won the greatest victory. It is time now for the remembrances, and the feasting. Let us join together for that, and let us do so on momentous occasions hence forth!"

Elenai bowed her head to him. "Kyrkenall would approve."

Epilogue

Rylin looked down across the little courtyard where a profusion of bright daisies bloomed, and Elenai sadly studied his marble features. Ten years ago he had risked his life to leave Alantris with more than a thousand prisoners, and the city still honored him in countless ways. This, though, was her favorite of all his statues, one of the last works of Melagar, sculpting after intensive mental links with the people who'd known the young alten best.

Other depictions showed him as stalwart and ferocious. Here, though, he looked most as Elenai remembered him in the end; weary but resolved. A slight smile and wrinkle about the eyes suggested his kindness.

In the first weeks and months after Rylin's death, Elenai had often thought about what part he'd have played in the reordering of the corps, and if he would have approved of the way she and Thelar had set up the adjunct sorcerer's corps the former exalt had once proposed to him.

The years since had not been without their trials, but on the whole the realms and their allies flourished, and she couldn't help wondering if the broken state of their lands had been a reflection of the shattered love between God and Goddess, and that the new age of peace and prosperity was connected with the final fates of Kyrkenall and Kalandra, who loved each other deeply. Sometimes, when she was alone in the early hours after dawn, she quietly prayed to them. Not as a supplicant, but as a friend, wondering how they were doing. Someday, she hoped, they might answer.

The double doors to her left opened, bringing with it a chatter of conversation and the bustle of people in motion. Elik closed them behind himself and bowed his head. His Altenerai uniform was immaculate, from collar to boot.

"Your Majesty," he said.

"Alten," she said, affecting a grave nod, as though she were a remote and distant monarch.

He flashed a quick smile. "Derahd asked me to tell you he's taken the children for a walk down to the flower canal again."

Elenai chuckled. Naturally he wouldn't want to turn them over to servants. "Were they getting restless?"

"I'm afraid so."

Elenai smiled at thought of six-year-old Rialla's recent determination to gallop everywhere on an invisible horse. And young Asrahn's determination to imitate his sister's every move.

"The commander thought you should know most of the guests are here now," Elik continued. "But I've a surprise." And with that he opened the doors without her leave, and in walked three familiar figures. N'lahr was at their head, dressed in a plain, well-tailored blue shirt and black pants and boots. Kalandra's words had proven true, for he appeared not to have aged since that day in Kanesh ten years previous. Varama, behind him, was graying at the temples, but otherwise unchanged, apart from her wardrobe. She, too, had resigned from the corps, and today was dressed primarily in green, though her belt was black and a silver necklace hung at her throat.

Lastly came the largest visitor of all, Ortok. His kilt was longer now, and in recent years he'd taken to wearing a matching vest, as well as a broad pendant set with an emerald, her gift to him. Varama had told her she thought it his most cherished possession.

"Ah, Elenai Queen Half-Sword Oddsbreaker!" The kobalin opened his arms wide, and Elenai, smiling in return to the toothy grin, allowed herself to be enfolded in his rough embrace.

Elik quietly withdrew, leaving them to their reunion.

Laughing, Elenai stepped back. "And how are your lands and people?"

"Ah, we find new challenges!" Ortok answered. "We miss the storms, but there are cliffs, and deserts, and many fine things to see. Varama has shown us ways to make our settlements endure, now that the lands do."

"And how is your academy?" Elenai asked N'lahr.

The former commander maintained a small community in the hills outside Alantris, where he offered a home and school for children who'd lost their parents in the war, or suffered other misfortunes.

"Well enough. I'm pleased with the new stewards. I found the idea of the school more exciting than the running of it has proved. It's in the right hands."

"If you're looking for different work, I can always use you in Darassus."

N'lahr bowed his head. "I am at your service."

"And how's your husband?" Elenai asked. "Is he here?"

N'lahr smiled with regret. "That didn't work out. I'm seeing a wonderful woman now. I think you'll like her. She's with the other guests."

"I'll look forward to meeting her." Elenai turned attention to Varama, who'd quietly been contemplating Rylin's statue. "And how is my wandering councilor?"

"Well enough. Vannek wishes to extend you greetings, but did not think his own appearance on the anniversary of the Second Battle of Alantris would be appropriate. He has also given birth to another child, which would have made it inconvenient to travel."

Elenai wondered how Vannek could square his claim on the male gender with giving birth and realized she might never be able to understand. Perhaps she herself was too set in her own conception of gender, or perhaps Vannek just couldn't be comfortable under a different label, having grown up in a society where it seemed impossible to think yourself a woman if you stepped away from your community's idea of natural roles.

Ortok, too, had been looking at Rylin's statue, huge hands at his waist. "I think I like this statue best. The one at Darassus just looks angry. Here he looks determined."

"This one benefited from Varama's input," Elenai said.

"You flatter me," Varama said. "I merely suggested Melagar show a gentler side of him. I had thought he should be smiling. This, I think, is more subtle, and truer."

Varama, head of the recently instituted Council of Scholars, had spent long years traveling the realms, assisting not only in rebuilding, but in enhancing agricultural practices and diplomatic outreach. Her love of invention had never stilled. Some of her balloons now drifted over the city with festive banners, and a few even carried passengers in gondolas. Varama had recently overseen the final construction of an immense clock tower built on the grounds of the old Alantran Council Hall, so tall its faces could be seen from beyond the city wall. Yet no accomplishment ever left her content, for she had half a hundred under way at any time and had admitted once to Elenai she would never live to complete them all.

Occasionally, Elenai saw her smile, though her expression, as she contemplated Rylin's statue, was somber.

Elenai had lost track of the number of statues erected through the realms since the end of the invasion and the defeat of Cerai and the Goddess. She'd made sure that other heroes beyond the obvious had been honored. Naturally, many cities had raised images of Elenai and Rylin and N'lahr and Kyrkenall, as well as Gyldara Dragonsbane, and Thelar, Master of Squires, and all the Altenerai and brave squires who'd distinguished themselves in the wars. But she had decreed that Ortok, too, be depicted, and Drusa and Lelanc, and Kalandra, and M'vai and Meria and even—though not here in Alantris—Vannek and Muragan.

Most important of all, she had ordered Rialla's likeness erected in every capital, insisting further that the alten always stand in the sunlight, surrounded by flowers. Rialla's actions had saved them all, though her role had been the least apparent to the people of the realms.

"Tretton and Enada are here as well," N'lahr said, and Elenai brightened at that. One could never tell if the two retired Altenerai would turn up at special events. They'd been out exploring the new wilds together.

"How's their map coming along?" Elenai asked.

"They say there's no way to finish it in their lifetimes, but they don't seem bothered."

Ortok clapped his hands together. "I look forward to this play we're to see. I hear that it will have music and brave speeches."

"I've heard that, too," Elenai said. "I'm somewhat nervous about it."

"You think it will not be good?" Ortok asked. "Is your sister bad at making plays?"

"No. But it's going to have actors playing us in it," Elenai said.

Ortok tapped his chest. "Me, too?"

Elenai nodded. "You, too."

The kobalin smiled in utter delight. "I'm to be in a play that I am watching! I hope that your sister gave me fine words and great deeds."

"I'm sure she has."

"Those are two of your defining characteristics," N'lahr said.

"Kyrkenall told me everyone has three. Perhaps the third one is hungry."

Elenai laughed. "Well, yes, but you can be more than three things, remember?"

"I remember." He sighed. "Tell me, do any of you miss being Altenerai?"

"No," Varama said. "I feel like this is what I am called to do. In another time, I think this is what I would have done from the start."

Ortok straightened in astonishment. "Surely you miss the battles?"

"No."

"Me, either," N'lahr admitted. "There are many moments I wish I might forget."

Ortok grunted. "And what of you, Elenai?"

"I miss it, sometimes, in some ways. I'll always miss Kyrkenall, even though he was usually a colossal pain. But I don't miss the sleepless nights, and the fear, and the uncertainty. What we have now was worth going through all of that. What about you, Ortok? Do you miss the old days?"

"There are new challenges. I am content. And there are new delights. Like this play. Will we be sitting together?"

"I'm not sure I'll be able to sit through the whole play," Varama said.

"I've been thinking the same thing," N'lahr said.

"Oh no," Elenai cried. "I have to stay to the end, right there in front of all the councilors and Governor Feolia. The least you two can do for your queen is endure it with me."

"I will watch the whole thing," Ortok vowed.

When the doors opened again, it was Commander Gyldara who stepped out. Her bow was far more formal than Elik's, addressed as it was not only to her, but to the revered veterans. "My Queen," she said, "your guests are waiting. And I think if your father goes on for much longer he's going to drive a few of them completely mad."

Elenai laughed. "We can't have that. Come, my friends." She waved the others ahead.

"You are the queen," N'lahr said. And Ortok nodded in agreement.

"We stood as one, and still do," she reminded them. "Walk with me."

And so they moved forward, side by side, into the room beyond.

Acknowledgments

This concluding volume would not have possible without a whole team of people to whom I will be forever grateful. Sarah Bonamino and Sara Beth Haring were wonderful allies for getting the word out. I was delighted to work with the talented Edwin Chapman as my copyeditor for each book of this trilogy and immeasurably pleased by the devoted audio work of Lori Prince. The long-suffering Ian Tregillis once more served as my alpha reader, and then Kelly McCullough, John O'Neill, Chris Willrich, and the Willrich family served as *almost* beta readers. You see, I thought they were getting the beta version of the draft, but their many fine comments made me realize another going-over was absolutely essential. Beth Shope rode in to my rescue at the last minute to point me toward better habits I espouse but had forgotten to practice—and convinced me that one too many characters were dying by book's end.

All through the course of writing this book I benefited from the guidance of Pete Wolverton, Bob Mecoy, and my firstborn, Darian Jones. And then, of course, the counsel of my amazing wife and muse, Shannon Jones, was invaluable from beginning to end. If my allegedly clever characters actually sound and act intelligently, then much of that has to do with my brilliant wife's input and suggestions. She loves these characters as much as I do, and I swear that sometimes she knows them even better. It was she who, long before the first novel was even finished, suggested some of the best parts of this book's ending on a walk one evening. Many, many other portions of this story have had to change, but those suggestions were so fine I retained them to the very end.

Speaking of characters, one of them has a hidden history. Kris Ghosh, M.D., once asked me to give a home to his favorite D&D character from his youth. Kris died far too young, so he never saw these books, much less several mentions of a legendary sorcerer from olden days. I think he would have been delighted that Herahn is regarded as the finest mage in the history of the Altenerai. I can imagine the beaming smile that would have resulted once he saw Herahn mentioned in these books. I wish I could have seen it in person.